CINDER ALLIA

KAREN ULLO

To L. and M., whose princes have not come,
and to K., who found hers.

CHAPTER 1

*S*he should have known. She should have heard the wind shrieking through the hazel boughs above her mother's grave, heavy with new-born sorrow. But the maiden had cried the same tears too long to believe that any part of her heart remained unbroken.

A cloud cast a shadow across the sunny sky, a puff of smoke the shape of a cocoon. Its misty threads tore as if along a seam, pushed open by a pair of silver-bright wings. The glittering creature fluttered toward the maiden, raining tears. She crossed herself and gripped the soft grass upon the grave.

"Allia," the creature breathed, its timbre of birdsong and silver bells dampened by its grief. "Weep with me. Your prince is dead."

"My prince? What prince would ever deign to call himself mine?" She tugged without thinking at the skirt of her rough gray kirtle. She had washed it just that morning in the stream. It clung to her, still stained with ash.

The creature placed its tiny golden hands upon the maiden's eyes. "The one whose body you see lying with the arrow through his breast."

The maiden gasped as images of battlefields assailed her, a

burnished breastplate stained with blood, a dark and handsome face waxing slowly pale. "I flew to stop it," the creature sighed, "but I had never been to war. Allia, I caught the wrong arrow."

"Enough!" She staggered backward into the sunlight, though she knew that without that fallen soldier's smile, even the sunlight would darken.

"Forgive me." Then the creature sang in a language Allia had never heard. The grass and the grave and the hazel boughs returned.

The maiden pleaded, "Let me alone, I beg of you. Perhaps it's true he was my prince, but I was only his subject."

"You should have been more." Then the fairy told the story the way it has been told at every child's cradle-side since fairies first appeared. The maiden recognized with wonder the beginning of the tale; she had long ago succumbed to her stepmother's cruelty. For eight years, the nobleman's daughter had scoured away happiness until her bare soul glistened, as wretchedly clean as the hearth on which she slept. Allia de Camesbry had slowly shriveled into Cinder Allia, silent and forgotten like the dust.

Now her fairy godmother had arrived. But, alas, the prince was dead.

THE BELLS of every church in the capitol tolled in mournful chorus as the body of His Royal Highness, Prince Lennard Matthias Antonius d'Armany, arrived at his ancestral palace. A dozen mounted knights guarded his passage, their helmets clutched to their hearts in salute. The body lay inside a coach with the prince's sigil of a roaring lion flying tall and proud above, brazen in its futility. The Arman people thronged the streets as the procession passed, their eyes wide with grief that denied their fear. The palace, white and weary on its hill, overlooked a lowered drawbridge weeping snow into the melting moat below.

Inside the palace portcullis, eight-year-old Princess Briella held fast to the hand of her governess. Her sharp young face was lined by the tracks of half-dried tears. Next to her, a young man sat on a wooden bench with his face sheltered in his hands, so that only his mop of unruly raven curls greeted the procession. Father Alester Warren, the palace chaplain, clutched his hands together to keep from laying them on the young man's shoulders. He knew that if he did, they both might begin weeping.

King Simon the Unvanquished stood tall and stalwart in the middle of the path. His white hair fluttered happily in the springtime breeze while his dim eyes remained fixed on a past that, to him, was still alive. Yesterday, the king had understood when his chaplain and confessor broke the news that his first-born son was dead. Today, however, madness had brought the king the kind of comfort only madness understands.

"God be with you, good knights. The king thanks you for your leal service." The king's regent, Chancellor Peter Narius, pulled his stocky frame to its full height as the kingdom's hopes rolled into the carriage yard in a casket.

The two leading knights dismounted, one with eyes as dark as the prince's own, the other with a beard as thick and red as the mane of the lion he wore on his chest. They knelt, and the darker knight laid an empty scabbard at the king's feet. "Your Majesty, when we claimed the body, Griffin's Claw was gone. We searched, but it was not found."

The sight of the missing sword stabbed Father Alester as sharply as any steel, and more so because it was fitting. A griffin had no claws without its lion.

"Thank you, Sir Dunstan, Sir Hamran," Chancellor Narius answered. "We all know how you loved him. Think of it no more."

The king himself merely fidgeted with the black ermine edging of his cloak.

Father Alester waved to summon four brown-robed friars across the yard. His own acolyte came with them, a young, bearded man whose broad shoulders would make light work of carrying a prince. "We relieve you of your duty, good sirs," Alester said to the knights. "The friars will prepare him for burial."

The acolyte rolled forward a small cart and then hefted the coffin onto it: a plain wood box that would be discarded before the funeral in favor of something more royal. Yet Alester thought the fallen soldier might have preferred a soldier's grave.

When the palace had swallowed its golden progeny's remains, Father Alester took his leave and returned to his own spare quarters above the palace chapel. He prayed the Divine Office in the quiet of his room. Latin psalms of lamentation gushed from his tongue, free from the restraint he imposed upon his eyes. *My dwelling, like a shepherd's tent, is struck down and borne away from me; you have folded up my life, like a weaver who severs the last thread.* Alester turned and was quietly sick into his privy bucket. He rinsed his mouth with cool water from his bedside jug and then set off into the city.

He walked perhaps a mile through the cobbled streets, hunched under a hooded cloak, his ears attuned to the chatter. A lusty mountain wind threw words about like leaves, all of them the same: *His Highness is dead. The kingdom will fall.* Only a few remembered that there was another prince, and those who did said only, *What will he do, pray the Darrivants away?*

Perhaps Alester had been wrong to train the boy to be a prince and not a saint instead.

The tradesmen's district stank of lye and blood and hot manure. Father Alester had to pick his way through a refuse of fat, flesh, hair, and tannin to reach the locked door of a closet he rented in the rear of a tannery. Inside, it afforded him just enough room to bend and move his elbows—that is, to pull off his coal-black cleric's alb and don a layman's garb. *Forgive me, Lord, and grant me courage.* He prayed that same prayer every time he left the signs of his priesthood in this pantry, knowing it was shame as much as secrecy that made him exchange his clothes.

With his face smudged in coal dust and a battered wool cap shoved onto his thin gray hair, Father Alester peeked through a knothole to make sure the streets were clear before he emerged. He walked another half mile to a tavern dank with smoke, where he nursed a single tankard of weak brown ale for more than an hour before the flower merchant appeared. Father Alester did not miss the momentary flash of fear that passed across the man's grizzled face, but then the merchant smiled and sauntered toward the priest's table.

"You," he said. "I might have known."

"Indeed. No one who strikes a false bargain should be surprised when his customer returns for restitution."

The merchant signaled the barman for a drink and sat down. His tunic always smelled of lilac, but his breath of sour fish. "I told the truth, as far as I knew it. There are no sureties in this game."

"And now the prince is dead."

The merchant indulged in several long sips of ale before he replied. "There were whispers. But they came from a new voice, one I had not heard before and did not trust."

"Whispers that said his position had been compromised?"

The merchant lowered his eyes.

"Who is the voice?"

"Gold where I can see it first."

Alester curled his hands around his tankard until, if it had breathed, it would have strangled. "The terms have changed. Do you see that man in the corner?" They both looked toward a pair of broad shoulders slumped under a head of dark curls. The man's fingers lifted fatty sausages toward a mouth surrounded by an inky beard. Even in this dim light, his purple livery of the palace guards shimmered with gold embroidery, the scales of justice balanced across his barrel chest.

"Answer me," Alester said, "and I will not tell him you have been smuggling provisions to the Darrivants."

The merchant leaned back in his chair and crossed his arms. "If I am jailed, who will you send to do your dirty work?"

"The same person who gave me this." Father Alester tossed a small purse across the table. The merchant opened it, and his face turned the color of curdled cream. "If you do not wish the person who made that to burn," said Alester, "tell me, who is the voice?"

The merchant clutched the purse tight in one hand. "'Tis a woman, and she doubles what you give."

"Her name?"

"I do not know it any more than I know yours... *Father*."

"Father? More's the pity I shall have to see you put to the rack. Which whore was it that I sired you on?"

The merchant drained the last of his ale. "Come back when you have gold instead of threats, and I may be able to answer." He left without paying for his drink.

Alester swirled the dregs in his tankard ten minutes more; then he settled his bill and stepped outside into the dusk. He leaned against the porch rail until the man in palace livery followed him out. "What was in the purse?" his acolyte inquired.

"A love token carved by his Darrivant mistress." Alester smiled, but it reached no further than his pale, thin lips. "Something is troubling you, Tristan. Your knuckles are white."

The acolyte looked toward his hands, gripped like talons around the railing. "Yes, Father. There is something at the palace you must see."

Alester sighed. "Of course."

Back to their separate closets the two men went. They met again, dressed in proper ecclesiastic robes, inside the palace chapel. The stained-glass saints who lined its walls receded into the twilight gray, their colors muffled by mourning.

The acolyte was on his knees before the tabernacle when his master entered. Alester watched a single candle cast its ghostly shadow on the misery of faith.

"Tristan, I am glad you do not let this world's ugliness keep you away from God's beauty."

"Some days, even God's beauty is not enough." Tristan gazed toward the tabernacle with tears in his eyes; then he turned and stood. "Come, Father." He took up the candle and led his master deep underground. Down winding, darkened stairs they descended into the shadows where treasures, enemies, and secrets could be kept. The candle guttered as Tristan pushed his way into the cold stone chamber where Prince Lennard's body lay. It had been washed, dressed with herbs, and clothed in a purple doublet with a lion embroidered on the breast. The friars had tied the prince's raven hair with a ribbon at the base of his neck, just as he had always worn it in life. Strong and proud and handsome still he lay, this boy who never wanted to leave off sword-play to attend his chaplain's lessons about Latin, history, and God. He had learned them quickly, though, on the days when snow or rain chased him inside. Father Alester reached out to touch his student's hand once more.

"Is this all you wanted me to see?"

Tristan lit a torch and set it in a bracket on the wall. "No, Father. I shall have to remove his doublet."

Alester started. "Why?"

Tristan did not answer. With a certainty of hands that did not touch his eyes, the acolyte unfastened silver buttons until the prince's morbid, naked flesh lay bare.

Father Alester leaned in close and knit his wrinkled brow. A clean and simple arrow-hole ought not to be ringed by a fringe of sullen gray—least of all, a fringe seeping slowly outward, as if it could coat the man in darkness and kill him yet again.

"It has grown since I was here," Tristan said.

Father Alester felt his stomach heave, but he held the bile down. "Tristan, go call the prince."

CHAPTER 2

*A*llia hauled her bucket up from the well and drank her fill before she plunged it back inside. An echo splashed against a spring too deep and distant to be tainted by her tears. They flowed without permission, streaking through the cinders that always stained her dove-white cheeks, caking salt and ash into the matted spirals of her golden curls. All night, Allia had lain upon her hard stone bed watching her prince die. What good did it do? What use even to contemplate happiness withered in its bud? Yet the tears would not be staunched as she slung two pails on either end of a pole and carried them like a mule toward home. The brittle grass clutched at her passing feet with barren claws.

"Cinder Allia!" the Lord of Camesbry bellowed as his carriage rattled toward her. Allia set down her load to curtsey and swallowed the urge to scream as the wheels ground to a halt in front of her. Her father wanted to duel, and Allia's wits had never felt so dull.

"Good morrow, my lord," she said as her father's leather soles thudded to the turf. Crouched in her obeisance, she could see nothing above his stockinged, gout-ridden knees, but long years of repetition had burned the image of his disdain upon her eyes.

"Wench, how dare you curtsey like a lady when you ought to snivel like a dog?"

"Forgive me, my lord. Yesterday I was a maggot and the day before, a rat. I can never keep up with your images long enough to snivel properly."

"God willing, I shall soon be rid of your insolence. When you have finished your duties, you will draw yourself a bath and put on the garment your stepmother has prepared."

Allia screwed shut her eyes and tried to take a step backward, but she stumbled. Only one kind of "business" might rid her father of her insolence, and today of all days, Allia could not bear to think what sort of husband he had assigned her.

"Make certain that monstrosity is covered." Lord Camesbry waved at Allia's shoulder where the sleeve of her kirtle had slipped, revealing the dull red X that scarred her just above her heart. "You will conceal the evidence of your repulsiveness, or I will hang you as I should have done eight years ago."

"Yes, my lord. Though some might define 'repulsiveness' as hanging one's own child."

He winced: the only vestige that remained of the man Allia had once known, the sharp intake of air that proved his conscience still had breath. He hefted his stout walking stick and brought it crashing down on her shoulders. "You had best accept what I offer and be grateful. I promise, I will not negotiate for you twice." With that, the man who had once given horsey rides and tickled her until she squealed disappeared inside his gilded coach and sped away.

Allia watched through swollen eyes, tasting blood and dirt, remembering a time when that same carriage had traversed that same road with her inside. She had never beheld the face of the man on the fairy's battlefield while he lived, but she had once beheld the child. Lennard the Lion, the prince who would someday roar with justice to save her from tyranny's ashes. Through eight long, frozen years on her stone hearth, one sunny memory had warmed Allia's dreams with hope.

~

"MOTHER! Mother, look, it's made of diamonds!" Allia pressed her face to the carriage window as if the panoramic beauty might seep into her through the glass.

"Not diamonds, Allia. Quartz. It is a stone that sparkles in the sun."

"A palace made of diamonds," she sighed, ignoring her mother's pragmatism as the glittering castle eclipsed the horizon. All her life— all eleven years of it—Allia had longed to see the world, to soar like the birds toward every nook of hidden charm. Finally, her mother had consented. Never mind that every field of ripe orange pumpkins, every snow-capped mountain spire, was but another stanza in an elegiac journey; a grandfather Allia had met but once lay dying, longing for a final glimpse of his only daughter and his grandchild. Allia spared the old man no thought but a whisper of thanks, that he had set these blessed carriage wheels in motion.

The coach rolled serenely through the city gate, with its elaborate lintels topped by blindfolded Lady Justice holding her scales and sword. Allia and her mother passed unhindered through the bustling city streets, and the palace portcullis opened at the coachman's call. Noble guards in purple livery smiled welcome as they handed the ladies down onto the still-green autumn lawn. Lady Clara blessed the guards with rosy smiles. Her serene elegance had never seemed more beautiful than now, when the joy of reunion bubbled up to drown the sadness that tinged her soft brown eyes. "The palace has not changed since I was here," she said.

Allia bent her neck up toward the glittering white turrets. Of course it had not changed; the work of angels, or magicians, never could.

The young girl's heart fluttered happily while she held her mother's hand. A lady-in-waiting ushered them through majestic halls into a parlor filled with lace and lemon-yellow rugs. Inside, the queen herself sat on a green damask settee, half-hidden behind an exuberance of white orchids. Her olive cheeks creased into a dimpled smile.

"Clara!" Queen Eleanor raised her ponderous body, great with child, and opened her arms. Allia's mother curtsied before she advanced into the hug. "Oh, Clara," said the queen as she kissed her dear friend's face, "you have been away far too long. And this must be your Allia." The girl blushed to the roots of her golden hair as Queen Eleanor took both her hands. "You are as beautiful as your mother told me—and that is saying something."

Allia mumbled, "Thank you, Your Majesty," and curtsied in reply.

They took refreshment on the balcony, the fall air spiced with drying leaves and latent snow. Lady Clara and her oldest friend traded catch-me-ups while Allia watched a horseman who taught jousting to young boys on the grounds. She watched their armor glitter in the sun and dreamed that she could join them.

She turned toward a sound of knocking and had to blink six times before she realized the figure on the threshold was not part of her daydream. A mailed knight stepped onto the balcony, his costume complete but for the burnished helmet lolling from one hand. From atop the gleaming armor shone the face of a mere boy, fourteen perhaps, but tall enough to be a man. A boy with flashing ebony eyes and raven curls attempting to escape from the ribbon at his neck that could not quite keep them bound.

"You sent for me, Mother?"

"Lennard, good! Do you remember my old friend, Lady Camesbry?"

Lady Clara rose and dropped her obeisance, tugging Allia's hand to remind her to do the same. "It is so good to see you again, Your Royal Highness. May I present my daughter, Lady Allia."

Allia's breath caught in her chest as the prince cocked a jaunty smile. "Of course, Lady Camesbry, it has been far too long. Welcome, Lady Allia."

"Lennard," said his mother, "I hoped you would not be too busy to show Lady Allia our home."

"With pleasure." The prince offered the girl his arm. Allia took it, and her gaze fell on the jewel-encrusted hilt protruding from his scabbard.

As soon as the door to the queen's apartments shut behind them,

Prince Lennard turned to face his charge. "My mother has it in mind that I should show you a lot of stuffy portraits and gilded frescoes. Is that what you want to see?"

The glint in his eye made her dizzy, but Allia managed to answer, "No."

"Good. What, then?"

"Well, to begin… Your Highness, may I see your sword?"

He smiled with almost paternal pride as he drew the blade. The steel gleamed more brightly than the diamond hilt in the sunlit hall. "I call her Griffin's Claw."

Allia dared to trace a finger across its shining beauty. "Lagunde steel," she said, and the prince's eyes widened with respect. "My father has one, but not as fine as this. This wouldn't be one of Master Rellan's?"

"It is. You know his work?"

"Only by reputation. I've never seen one before. Why do you call her Griffin's Claw?"

"Because people call me the Lion, but I'd rather be able to fly." He winked, and a thrill quivered down Allia's spine.

"May I hold it?"

Prince Lennard offered her the glittering hilt. Her fingers closed with reverence. "No, like this." He adjusted her grip. "Has your father not taught you how to fight?"

"I have asked, but he says it is not proper."

"But you are his heir!" Prince Lennard furrowed his brow. He took his sword, sheathed it, and turned on his heel. "Come on."

"Where are we going?"

"To begin your lessons."

They went out to the training grounds, where the jousting was just coming to an end. The prince led her into a stone armory filled with swords, shields, lances, and halberds that hung as portraits of well-oiled victory. He found an old crate full of wooden swords and tossed one to Allia. Carefully, she arranged her hands around the hilt.

"A quick study. Good. Now *en garde.*"

Not for her life could she have matched him, but she tried. Allia thrust and danced and weaved while, patient as a nursemaid, the prince taught her. "Set your feet a little farther apart—there—now bend your knees. No, not too much, just enough so you can move. Good. Now parry..." With her pale cheeks set ablaze, she lunged. Prince Lennard twisted away from the blow and caught the flat of his wooden sword against her head. She cried out as she fell.

"A thousand pardons, my lady." He dropped to his knees beside her and removed his gauntlets before he gently brushed back her curls. "You're bleeding. I will call the ladies-in-waiting."

"No." Allia steadied herself against his arm and rose. She picked up her fallen weapon. "Let's go again."

Prince Lennard worked his jaw around words that never came. He took up his own sword. Half an hour or more, the two children dueled, until the prince called an end. "You've done well for your first day." He graced her again with his smile. "Please tell your father that I'd like you to continue."

"I will, Your Highness. Thank you. I am not sure I have ever had quite that much fun."

"It wasn't just sport, Lady Allia. The kingdom needs strength in Camesbry."

She swallowed and gave a silent nod.

"It was fun, though," he relented.

Hot and dusty and dripping sweat, with her hair still caked in blood, Allia followed him to the kitchens for a wash and a draught of cold water. Then, arm-in-arm, they wandered through the endless marble halls. The stuffy portraits and gilded frescoes came alive while the prince narrated the history of his kingdom, written with such grandeur in ochre, indigo, and gold.

"I know this one," Allia said as they came to a tapestry of cavalry laying waste to an army of foot soldiers. "This is my father, here, and yours. The Battle of Carridgeway."

"Yes." He took her hand in his. "Someday, it may be us in these murals, Lady Allia."

Before she could reply, a sight like none she had ever beheld arrested her shining eyes. She watched in mute amazement as a boy with raven curls, very near her own age, crossed through an intersecting hall. He sat, pushing himself forward on a chair fixed with wheels. A priest followed him, tall and lanky, with cat-like blue eyes that landed on Allia's. She dropped a hint of a curtsey. The priest nodded and walked on.

"Who was that?" she whispered.

Prince Lennard's warm fingers tightened around her own. "Father Alester, the royal chaplain."

"But who is that boy on the chair?"

The prince gritted his teeth while lines too deep for a boy of fourteen creased his brow. "My orphan cousin, Timothy d'Immerville, whom my parents agreed to foster... or so I am supposed to say." He met Allia's gaze. "Lady Allia, can I trust you with a secret?"

"Of course, Your Highness."

"You must not tell anyone, ever. Not your parents, nor anyone. Not until I take the throne."

"I am your loyal servant, Your Highness."

"I know." Prince Lennard squeezed her fingers once more. "You have been told I have a brother who was sent to a monastery as a gift to God."

Allia nodded.

"It is a lie. That boy is my brother Raphael. My parents keep him hidden under a false name because he cannot use his legs, but it will not be that way when I am king. When I rule in Armany, my brother will be a prince—and, Lady Allia, if you wish to hold your father's office, then you shall."

The Lion's words were bright as fire. Allia stood on her toes and kissed his cheek, stunned by her own daring.

Prince Lennard blushed and bowed his head. "Come, my lady. Your mother will be wanting you." All the way back to the queen's balcony, he did not let go of her hand.

CHAPTER 3

*J*et-black liquid oozed from the mouth of an iron pitcher, filling twenty tiny vials laid in perfect, ordered rows. The corners of Lady Vivienne de Camesbry's lips twitched with satisfaction at every captured drop. Twenty tiny vials of shadow; soon her alchemy would transform them into twenty large purses of gold. Her buyer was scheduled to arrive in two days' time, which now turned out to be the day of the prince's funeral: a perfect excuse to let someone else leave a signature on the bill of sale. Slowly, carefully, Vivienne stoppered her vials with wax; then she rang for the maid.

Allia was slow to answer her stepmother's summons. "You rang, my lady?"

"Cinder Allia, fetch my daughter to me."

"Yes, my lady." But the girl did not move.

"Have I been unclear?"

"Not at all. I only wondered if you might tell me whom my father plans that I should marry."

"You shall know your father's plans when he is ready to reveal them. Now go."

"Yes, my lady." Allia did not curtsey, but dragged her feet as she walked away.

The clear white skin of Lady Vivienne's brow furrowed as she packed her vials into a crate lined with soft wool. So Allia knew she was to be married, as if the plan had not already been sufficiently addled. The whole affair was supposed to have been concluded in one day so the girl would not have time to ponder *why*. Lady Vivienne could not be certain whether her stepdaughter knew her rights. *Cinder Allia, are you aware that you are your father's only legal heir until and unless you are married?* Even asking the question would guarantee its affirmative answer. But the fact remained that until Allia became her husband's legal ward, she stood to inherit the entire province of Camesbry, and only the king could take it from her. Convenient as the funeral might be, news of the prince's death had been most untimely in its arrival. The wedding would have been a fact by now if Lord Camesbry had not been detained by the royal messenger.

Lady Vivienne sealed the crate of vials, took up a clean parchment, and composed a brief but flowery invitation to Allia's betrothed. Would he do them the honor of accompanying the family to the capitol to share in the kingdom's sorrow? Lady Vivienne could have done without the cloying stench of George Couper's perfumed cannabis in her coach, but she could not give him time to change his mind.

Vivienne had spent two years searching for a suitor willing to buy Allia for her title. It did not help that Lord Camesbry could never be bothered to attend to the problem himself. Vivienne's husband was a genius at warfare, although in recent years his gout had kept him confined to a command tent. But Lord Camesbry lacked any interest or talent for domestic affairs. He had left his wife to attend to the matter of his daughter's marriage, but as a mere stepmother, Vivienne was often rebuffed in her efforts. "Let my lord come speak to me himself," a gentleman would say, but Lord Camesbry was seldom at home, and when he was, he seldom found an hour free from the business of administering the king's justice.

Vivienne's difficulty had been compounded by the need to find a husband gentle enough to entice Allia to leave. Lady Camesbry was no stranger to methods of coercion, but neither did she wish to wager her future on her stepdaughter's willingness to speak her wedding vows. Most days, the girl complied with orders readily enough, though it had required no small number of beatings and missed meals to bring that circumstance about. Still, there was a fire that smoldered in Allia's brown eyes: not defiance precisely, but hope. That hope baffled Vivienne and kept her awake at nights. The girl had nothing to hope for unless she knew her rights as her father's heir, so her stepmother had gone to great lengths to find a suitor whom Allia might accept. The jeweler was an idiot, but a kind one, rich and docile. Lady Vivienne could not afford to let such a catch slip from her hook.

She summoned a messenger and sent her invitation to Couper. Then she put another log onto the fire that brewed her livelihood and began packing away other vials. Yellow, for hair that shone like sunlight; ivory, for skin pale as milk; violet, for eyes that bewitched; rose, for lips that seduced. Lord Camesbry had married Vivienne for the gold her concoctions earned, and neither of them pretended otherwise. Beauty was illusory, love a farce, as a woman who sold both in vials knew well. Money, however, never went out of fashion.

With her packing complete, Lady Vivienne extracted one vial of ivory and one of rose. If Allia knew she was to be married, then the girl must be prepared as a proper noble bride.

"You sent for me, Mother?" Lilliane arrived in her petticoats with a black gown draped over each arm. Lovely as a swan but as decisive as a headless hen, Lilliane almost never arrived in her mother's boudoir fully clothed. "Which do you think more proper for a prince's funeral: to be dreary with grief or to be jeweled and stunning?"

"Somewhere in the middle," her mother advised. "Lilliane, it is a ripe opportunity, but you must not be seen flirting in the midst of the kingdom's woe."

"Of course not. But young men have been known to offer solace to a beautiful woman in tears."

"Be careful what solace you accept. There is not enough gold in all of Armany to buy a title for a girl of sullied virtue."

"Mother! Banish such thoughts from your mind and tell me which gown I should wear." Lilliane held up two dresses, both midnight black.

"Lilliane, do you really have to ask?"

"Well, of course the silk is much finer."

"Let me see it." Lady Vivienne took the gown and, with one quick flick of her wrist, threw it onto the fire. Her daughter gasped as it curled to bright, glowing ash.

"Mother! That was Darrivant silk!"

"And who do you suppose the prince was fighting in that war?"

Lilliane's jaw flapped, searching for words.

"*Think*, child, before you act, or you shall learn to wish you had. Now, go ring for the cinder maid. I must instruct her about the sale of the vials."

PRINCE RAPHAEL D'ARMANY watched through fog and bloodshot eyes as coils of black crepe snaked their way around the palace chapel. A kingdom full of mourners had come to view the body of their beloved prince. Slowly, the coils turned, tightening the morbid grip of hopelessness around the heir apparent's heir. Raphael lowered his spyglass and clutched the rail of the steeple balcony. Caged behind thick iron bars, he sat on the damp stone landing with his useless legs folded under him, his rigid palms slick with fear. He could not even find room inside his soul for the grief he longed to feel, the emptiness where his idolized older brother had lived. The Lennard who had carried him up countless flights of stairs, read to him when he was young, and talked with him as he grew, the Lennard who never saw a cripple but a brother and a prince: Raphael had no time to mourn that Lennard now. Only the Lion mattered, the crown prince who carried the royal standard into battle, the Lion who had been bred to rule, who spoke and every man in his hearing gratefully obeyed. Lennard would have been crowned when the war was over; for the last two years, their father could hardly be trusted to know his own name, and the lords had clamored against the Chancellor-Regent's weak-kneed reign. They stopped short of insurrection only because they knew the man for whom they waited, a man whose rule would be worth waiting for. They loved him and they feared him—but for his reclusive brother, whom they believed to be just an ailing cousin, they knew nothing but contempt. What else had he ever given them to know?

Enough. Raphael could not think how to win their loyalty now. He had not slept since he laid eyes on his brother's spectral wound. Even as reason groped for an explanation of its origin, imagination bombarded him with armies full of demons firing arrows from hell. He could not lay plans to rule a kingdom with such folly usurping his sight. He would go to his chamber and drink a draught of sleeping herbs. If the Fates were kind, he would never awake.

Raphael looked to his human carriage to command a ride, but Tristan had leaned his strong shoulders against the parapet and now sat snoring softly. The acolyte was dressed in a simple tunic and breeches he often wore to play the part of Raphael's valet. Fine droplets of mist glossed the tufts of his inky beard while he slept. With a sigh, the prince wiped the lens of his glass and returned to his spying.

A footstep sounded on the balcony, and a firm hand pressed Raphael's shoulder. He slumped under its touch. "I cannot do this, Father. I will abdicate to Briella."

"And leave Chancellor Narius to fight the war? You know as well as I, within the year, she would have no throne to ascend."

"My cousin Collin is a great warrior."

"He also rips the wings off insects for pleasure and keeps his chamber maid for a mistress. Is that the legacy your brother would want you to leave?"

"And do you suppose *this* is?" Raphael lifted his useless legs with his hands; then he let them flop like puppets back onto the balcony.

Father Alester squeezed his protégé's shoulder. "You must reveal your true name at the funeral. If you do not, you may as well send the Darrivants your terms of surrender."

"Why should I not surrender? Our men are changing sides in the midst of every battle. Perhaps where we are blind, they see a path to peace."

"The Darrivants will never bring peace, and fear will never bring victory."

The prince sank his head into his hands. "Wake Tristan. I must sleep before I fall off this balcony."

"I only praise God you cannot jump." Father Alester gave the prince a ghost of a smile. Then he walked to shake his sleeping apprentice.

Tristan's strong arms curled under Raphael's knees to haul the prince's body down the stairs. Raphael had never scaled a staircase any other way, but today, the shame of it—to feel his feet flopping as limply as a sleeping baby's against the other man's strong chest—bit him to the core. Lennard had written to him from the battlefield about a blond barbarian army inked with spidery tattoos, wielding tar-black ironwood bows. What were the odds that such men would surrender to a prince so helpless that he must be carried?

"Put me in my chair, please," he said when they reached the landing. "I will wheel it to my chamber myself."

They had nearly reached the prince's room when the king drifted slowly toward them down the hall. Raphael and Tristan exchanged a puzzled glance. King Simon was rarely seen in the palace these days, usually confined to his quarters under the care of his nurse. The prince stopped and called out, "Your Majesty?"

"Ah, Raphael! Good!" The king sauntered forward, smiling, while heat rose in Raphael's cheeks. There was no telling by what name his father might greet him these days, but more than once the monarch had nearly undone his own scheme by addressing his son as "Raphael" in public. The prince's disguise remained intact only because no one had taken his lunatic father at his word.

Raphael darted his eyes about the hall, but it was empty. He took the king's hand and said, "Yes, Father."

King Simon ruffled his son's curls. "You've always been a good boy, Raphael. You will ride out and avenge him."

"Yes, Father. I shall ride out under his sigil..."

"Ride out!" The king's lip curled into a sudden snarl. "Yes, ride out to battle in a chair and be trampled by your own cavalry. My son! Oh, God, my son..."

"A thousand pardons, Your Lordship," the king's nurse panted as she rounded a corner at a jog. "He wandered off while I was in the privy."

"Of course. I shall leave him to you." As quickly as he could maneuver around his weeping father, Raphael sped to his own room. The tapestry above his desk fluttered in his wake. He spared a glance at the blind saint woven into the ancient fabric; then he turned away and swatted at his eyes until they dried.

"I'm sorry, Your Highness," Tristan said.

"No, he is right. I cannot..."

"Your Highness, you have to. There is no one else." Tristan moved to draw the curtains as the evening fell. Then he began to light the candles from the fire in the grate.

"How is it," Raphael muttered, "that we sit in a palace full of hale, whole men, yet only the cripple is fit to reign?"

Tristan knelt to bring himself face to face with his liege. "With all respect, Your Highness, only the cripple is a prince."

Raphael looked up into Tristan's eyes—bright, brown, thoughtful eyes that shot fresh pangs of sorrow through Raphael's broken heart because they reminded him of Lennard's.

"A prince is more than his blood. He is a symbol of strength, stability, power."

"And wisdom, Your Highness. No one studies as well as you."

"If the lords ever loved Lennard for his wisdom, it was only because he spoke it while wielding a sword."

"Any yokel can wield a sword. Not one of them knows the law, or the history of the kingdom, or the ways of God's justice."

"You flatter me, to think I do."

Tristan looked toward the flickering candles. "I doubt that any man is ever truly prepared to meet his destiny. But we all have to meet it, nonetheless."

Raphael stared at Tristan's proud profile, formidable but kind, and he could not help but wish it were his own. If only he could wear such a figure, the kingdom might stand a chance.

The prince shuddered as an idea blazed through the chill of his fear. "Tristan... what if you could help me?"

"I am your servant, Your Highness."

"You are good at playing characters other than yourself."

The acolyte's face fell slack with understanding. "Your Highness... No..."

"When the lords see this broken body, this son whom the king could not be bothered to claim as his own, there will be civil war. And while they are squabbling amongst themselves, trying to ascend my father's throne, the Darrivants will burn Armany to ashes. But if the lords saw *you*..."

"Your Highness, it is treason. To deceive the Chancellor-Regent, even the king himself..."

"It was the king who chose to hide me. You will only be helping to carry out what he ordained."

"And what of my own life? My studies with Father Alester, my calling to serve God?"

Prince Raphael closed his eyes, as if mere eyelids could block the course of time. "Priestly robes will not spare you if the Darrivants take the palace."

"I am a ferryman's son. I cannot rule a kingdom."

"Nor shall you. I will guide you. Every word you speak will be mine. I am not half the prince my brother was, but as you say, I am all we have." Raphael reached out and took the acolyte's hand. "I need legs, Tristan. Without them, you and I both know, the kingdom is doomed."

Tristan's great brown eyes reflected the fear in Raphael's own. "What happens when the war is won?"

"I will release you and let come what may." Raphael prayed there would be an arrow to end his suffering before that day came.

Tristan's broad shoulders sagged. "If my legs can save Armany from the Darrivants, then you shall have them."

A wave of pure relief swept over Raphael, so strong that he was glad he was already sitting down so that he did not fall. He smiled. "Go fetch me a pen and parchment, Your Highness. You have a speech to learn."

CHAPTER 4

$\mathcal{A}$llia stood at the window of her stepmother's boudoir gazing out at the vista of jagged gray. The mountain snow receded every moment in the brisk spring thaw. Allia hoped the visible evidence of warmth might somehow touch the glacier growing in her soul. She had not stood at this window, taking in this view, since the room had belonged to her own mother, but no one need ever know she had stolen this fond glance. Camesbry Castle had been deserted except for a few token guards. The family had gone to the prince's funeral in the capitol, and the servants had been granted a holiday in which to mourn. Only Allia remained, charged with the duties of family and servant alike.

She stared out toward the battlements, those talused walls built for warfare that defined her very world. A home filled with arrow slits and murder holes did not inspire smiles, but it was the only home she knew. Had the time come to move on? She held up her ivory and rose-colored vials, the only gift Lady Vivienne had ever bestowed. Allia need only dab them on her face and lips to win the heart of a husband she would certainly despise. But even if she could not love the man she married, perhaps she could love their children. Perhaps she could become a doting mother in a decent home instead of being battered daily like a quintain. Perhaps the treasure inside these vials was not beauty but that evanescent magic, hope.

Hope's sweet melody trilled dissonant as Allia heard a church bell's distant toll. Every person of noble blood in the entire kingdom was sitting inside the cathedral now, grieving for their fallen prince; all but the widow he never married. Here she stood, a maiden still, already poised to take new vows.

Allia threw her vials through the open glass and watched them shatter on the flagstones. "Here is a vow for you, Father. I will not pretend. If your suitor will not buy a cinder maid, then you will not sell my hand."

"That's quite a speech to make to the birds."

She turned on her heel so fast, she had to catch her balance on the casement. There, in the doorway of Lady Vivienne's private chamber, stood a young man in a plain brown tunic with a sword slung at his waist. His every pore was caked in the dust of mountain roads, but his rakish smile beamed bright through the tufts of his chestnut beard.

"Who...?"

"I ought to ask you the same. Lady Camesbry always meets me here herself."

"Meets... *here?* In her boudoir?"

"Ah, well, no, not *here*. That would be far too austere for my taste." He traced his finger across the coverlet of the four-post mahogany bed. "But for you, *here* seems exactly the place I'd like to be."

Allia's spine arched taut. "Hold your tongue, sir. You do not know to whom you speak."

"I assume I am addressing the Lady Allia de Camesbry. Or did I mistake you for some other enslaved daughter in this house?"

He drew toward her with every word. With her back to the window, Allia could do nothing but grit her teeth and hold her ground. "I am Lady Allia, and if you know that, then I hope you also know the penalty in this kingdom for despoiling an unwilling maid."

He unsheathed his sword and offered her the hilt. "Carry it out, if I should harm you."

Allia stared at the glittering handle.

"Take it, or I shall find it hard to believe you are *unwilling*."

With two hands, she pulled the weapon into her grasp: a military sword, the steel glinting with the same sheen her father's officers carried. Allia held it steady at the level of the intruder's heart. "How did you get in? I have been watching the hills from this window. I did not see you approach."

He took a single step away from the sword and raised both hands in surrender. "I rode from the south, and the guards let me in."

"I assume you are the buyer for my lady's elixirs. I believe it is time we conclude our business so that you can be on your way."

He laughed: a rolling, boisterous laugh. The laugh of a man without a care in the world, or else a man who had forgotten how to care. "By all means, let us transact."

She followed him down the winding stone stairs, her strong arms never allowing the sword to waver. The stranger trod calmly through the empty house, seemingly familiar with its every twist and turn. Lady Vivienne had been selling elixirs for many years, yet Allia could hardly believe the client could be so intimate with her home. "Has she left them in the kitchens, as usual?" he called over his shoulder.

Allia mumbled, "Yes."

He inspected the contents of every box and then carried each one separately to the yard. There, he loaded them into his horse-drawn cart, layering each between blankets and tufts of hay. Allia watched his every movement, surprised that a man so brash could be so careful. He was older, too, than she had first supposed, perhaps twenty-nine or thirty. His dusty, sunburnt skin spoke of a life spent out of doors, yet his speech betrayed his education. She watched his brow furrow over every detail of his packing, and Allia could not decide what sort of man he might be.

When at last he finished, the man turned and, like a painter, brushed on his smile. "Now you'll be wanting payment, I presume."

She could not help but smile back. "That is how we strike a bargain in these parts."

He reached under the seat of his cart, opened the lid of a strong metal box with a key, and laid before her an enormous bag of gold, more money than Allia had ever seen together at one time. "There you are, though you shall have to lower my sword if you intend to count it."

"It appears sufficient."

"It is. And this, for the vials you broke on the stones." He pulled a coin from his pocket and held it toward her.

"You do not owe me for those."

"No, but when my lady sees your skin is not infused with cream and your lips are not radiant with seduction, she will demand her coin. I presume you are not as well paid for the services you render as am I."

She raised the sword. "Why should you help me?"

He shook his head. "It is as I feared. They have treated you so ill, you cannot fathom kindness."

"It would not be kindness. She would only rage at my betrayal and demand the source of my income."

He returned the coin to his coat. "So she would. And it is a dark world where one cannot perform an act of charity without causing good people to suffer, as you know all too well."

The small hairs on Allia's limbs stood straight. "I do not know what you mean."

He took off his hat. "Lady Allia, you do not remember me, but my father was the steward in your grandfather's house at Demont. I was there the day your mother died. I saw you fall through the ice. I saw the little girl being drowned in her own love."

Allia's eyes welled with uncertain tears. Who was this man, so calm and grave, who could speak of her life's devastation with authority?

He fell to his knees. "My lady, I have come to this house twice a year for six years to purchase your stepmother's wares. I have seen the unspeakable ways they torment you, and I have ached to show you the same kindness you once showed that little boy. I can only think it must be fate that I find you here alone. Marry me, Lady Allia, and I will save you from your ashes."

Her heart raced with queer, uneven beats, pounding against the part of her soul where the fairy's revelations would forever resound.

She wanted to crush herself inside this stranger's enigmatic arms, to believe that such improbable beauty could be real. But Allia had watched the arrows of darkness fly, and even powers beyond this world could not stop them.

"It is not fate." The sword slumped in her grasp. "The man I was fated to marry is dead."

The peddler studied her moist eyes. "My God. The prince?"

Allia felt herself nod. What release, that a fellow human should finally know her grief!

He stood and bowed before her. "Then we all share your misfortune. The kingdom has been denied its greatest queen."

Her knees grew suddenly weak. Somehow, in her despair, that title had never entered Allia's mind. "Perhaps it is for the best. I have never ruled anything but a broom."

"And the heart of a simple peddler you never knew." He drew toward her with a hunger in his eyes.

She cast her gaze to the cobbles. "I do not know anything about you."

"Of course you do. I travel the world peddling your stepmother's potions to any lady who wishes her hair to be brighter, her eyes more alluring, her life to seem not so gray. You see the bag of gold I pay for these wares; every six months, I make another one like that for myself. I may not be a prince, but I am not a pauper."

"Nor are you a gentleman." She raised the sword so that it brushed the ankle of his breeches.

"As to that, I can only say, look what gentlemen have done to you." Without thinking, Allia tensed her shoulders, where she carried the bruises from her father's walking stick. The peddler stepped around the sword point, inching nearer. "One word, Lady Allia, and this life of gloom is over. Your father and your stepmother will think you flew away with the robins. You will never need to let them cross your sight again."

She gazed up at his tawny eyes, so ardent, so inscrutable, the kind of eyes that hid a man no one could ever truly know. "Tell me your name," she whispered as his hand took hers.

"What does it matter? If my name is John instead of Henry, will it sway your choice?"

"There are names I remember from Demont. Some of them would matter."

"Ah, yes. If I tell you my name is not Rabigny, that I am no relation to the governess, will that suffice?"

Allia shivered as the name stirred dark pools of memory, lighting candles in the corners of her mind she dared not see. "It is not enough. Only men with secrets are careful of their names."

He wrapped his arm around her waist and whispered in her ear. "I have many secrets, Lady Allia. Some of them so beautiful, they rival even you."

The touch of him, the forbidden warmth, buckled Allia's trembling knees. "Please, you don't understand. He planted a tree…" How could she tell him about the golden blossoms on the grave? How could she show him the man her father used to be, the man Allia still prayed he could become? "I cannot leave. Not like this. Please, you have to go."

He stepped away, and Allia saw him brush a surreptitious tear. "As you say, my lady. But first, the bill of sale." He pulled a roll of parchment from his pocket. "Shall we go inside?"

She led him to the library, where pen and ink were kept, and he wrote with a clear hand the number of the vials. He included the two she had broken, adding their cost to the weight of the gold. "Tell her I insisted, that I have buyers already promised." She nodded her mute thanks. "Now your signature, my lady."

Allia duly signed. Beneath her name, the peddler scrawled, *Proxy for Lady Vivienne de Camesbry*. "You may thank me for that someday," he said as his smile returned.

"Will you not sign?"

"So that you may learn my name? No, let one be enough. But remember, Lady Allia, in six months, I shall return. I will not care if you are married to some brash lout of your father's choosing. If you are ready to escape, your chariot will arrive."

Allia watched, wide-eyed, as he departed with a courtier's bow.

Not until his strong frame had left her sight did she realize she was still carrying his sword. She ran after him to the carriage yard.

"Wait!"

He turned, and even those inscrutable eyes could not hide his clear, pure hope.

"Your sword," she stammered.

Hope fled to the anonymity of arrogance, but too late. "You keep it," the peddler answered, pulling a dagger from his belt. "I shall be safe enough without it. I only hope you can say the same."

With that, the peddler climbed into his cart and drove away. Allia stood and watched until the mountain vastness swallowed him. The peddler never once looked back.

CHAPTER 5

The Cathedral of Our Lady of Sorrows had been under construction for nigh on eighty years, its vaulting arches mounting steadily toward the heavens, yet still the southern end lay open to every whim of the flightiest breeze. The spring wind wafted into the stained-glass walls, carrying the fragrance of flowers from the merchants' stalls outside. Lady Vivienne sniffed with disdain. She had never understood the practice of laying cut flowers on a grave—as if killing other living things could somehow brighten the fact of mortality.

Rustling silk and intense perfume intruded on her reverie. "Vivienne, have you heard? Sabrine is five months along, and Lord Morisse has been at war for six." Lady Abbleway always seemed to jiggle when she grinned.

Vivienne managed the thinnest of smiles. No grief was ever dark enough to still these noblewomen's wagging tongues. "As I recall, her babes have all come 'late.'"

"Yes, but Sir Woodsbren has been fighting, too, this time. She's found a new ale for that thirst."

"Sir Anbry," Vivienne confirmed. "He captained her guard at court last year."

Lady Abbleway passed the name in whispers down the aisles, titil-lating the wasted flesh that passed for ladies in this kingdom. Vivi-enne cringed to see her daughter crowing over elegant pin-tucks in the growing mother's gown, as much a testament to pretty nothing-ness as all the rest. Their kingdom stood on the verge of ruin, their prince about to be buried, and these women cared for nothing more than rumors of some cuckolded lord.

A gnarled claw crusted with gemstones darted out to pinch Vivi-enne's wrist. "They are coming," the Dowager Lady Morisse hissed. "My son may already be dead."

"Where?"

"Arcroft, Miccan, the road to Pellain. Their numbers are swollen with deserters. Our own men are burning our villages."

Those villages lay but fifty miles from Camesbry. Vivienne squeezed the old woman's hand. "No fear, my lady. The new prince will surely save us."

"I will count the kingdom blessed if he can speak the words of surrender."

So the crone was lucid, after all. Vivienne gave her a reassuring smile. "I will tell my husband to send reinforcements," she said; then she slinked outside to examine a cart of fresh lavender. "What news?" she whispered as she passed the flower merchant a handful of gold.

His breath smelled of sour fish. "They'll fortify for the siege at Pellain. But..." He rubbed two stubby fingers together. With teeth clenched tight, Vivienne passed another pair of coins. "The Darrivants will ford the river and go through Anniton."

"Anniton?" Vivienne had grown up in that town. She would have liked to see it burn and good riddance, were it not the kingdom's most valuable port, paying taxes to her own husband.

"Aye," the merchant answered, "and there's more." He handed her the flowers and then waited. She sighed and passed him another coin. He leaned in close. "The king's agent wants you. I can arrange a meeting."

The singing of monks wafted through the streets, and before Vivienne could reply, an indecorous hand touched her shoulder. "My lady, we had best take our seats."

"Thank you, Mr. Couper." Vivienne swallowed the indignity of being summoned by a common jeweler and flashed him a smile.

"'Tis a pity Lady Allia's headache kept her confined," Couper said wistfully, dandling a sprig of lilac. "She would have been a worthier object for such bright blossoms than a grave."

Vivienne watched the merchant roll his eyes and, by an act of iron will, restrained herself from doing the same. She gave the merchant a nod to accept his proposal. Then she allowed Couper to take her arm. Together, they retrieved Lilliane from the knot of gossiping harpies and took their seats in the fourth pew. Lord Camesbry shortly join them.

"What have you learned, my lord?" Vivienne whispered.

"The Darrivants are advancing toward Pellain."

"I heard rumors of deserters."

He waved her to silence as the chants of the funeral procession entered the cathedral. A familiar cough soon accompanied the song: Lilliane choking on the incense. The girl was hopeless around the stuff, hacking like a consumptive every time she appeared at Mass. Vivienne passed her a handkerchief.

The line of tonsured monks issuing into the church seemed to stretch for miles. Vivienne allowed her eyes to wander through the congregation, half-searching for a proper husband for her daughter. As soon as Allia was duly wed, Lord Camesbry would name Vivienne his heir, and then Lilliane Delaine, the wool merchant's daughter, would become one of the most desirable maids in all the kingdom. However, being wed to some great lord of Armany would do the girl no good if the Darrivants won the war; in fact, she might soon find her head neatly severed from that pretty swan-like neck. Everywhere Vivienne looked, she observed defeat: lords with hollow, sleepless eyes, ladies whose best black gowns had begun to fray with use. Most telling of all, the lack of soldiers. A handful of knights in freshly-oiled armor kept an honorary guard, but Prince Lennard's company had not come. Only an army on the brink of collapse could not spare a hundred men to bury its greatest leader.

Lilliane would have to wait. Surely, the lords of Darrivane had sired their share of handsome sons.

At last, the train of monks gave way to the Cardinal and his retinue of royals. A cloud of smoky Latin engulfed the casket carved with seraphim, borne along its path to heaven by six strong men in cloth-of-gold. Vivienne recognized three of them, the prince's cousins from Tembria, all of whom were now one death closer to the throne. At the rear marched two knights, one dark and one with a ginger beard, who bore the prince's lion on their breasts. But one pall-bearer towered above the rest, a young man with clean-shaved cheeks and broad, determined shoulders. Equal measures of sorrow and fear tugged at his rugged face.

A ripple of astonished mutters vied to drown the chants. Here he was, Prince Raphael, risen from the cloister as if from the dead.

King Simon followed vaguely behind the casket, holding close to the arm of his daughter, Briella. The pall-bearers placed the casket on a pedestal near the altar. Prince Raphael joined his father and sister in the front pew. He sat like a stalwart dam between two swollen rivers. He threw himself single-mindedly into the Mass, reciting every Latin response in time with the monks, and Vivienne wondered if he were truly pious. She would have preferred a ruler grounded in the here-and-now, but zealots, at least, could be manipulated by appeals to their charity.

She settled into an afternoon of fusty boredom, thinking gratefully of the small squares of parchment she always kept sewn into her petti-coat. If the Darrivants should arrive at Camesbry before the week was out, those parchments would do more to protect her than prayers.

Incense mingled with flowers set half the room to snuffling while, for an hour or more, the monks droned on. But at long last, the Latin ended, and the Cardinal surveyed his flock with eyes that judged their every sneeze on God's behalf. Into the soupy fog of the kingdom's apprehension, the Cardinal introduced, "His Royal Highness, the Crown Prince Raphael Ignatius Bartholomew d'Armany."

~

TRISTAN COULD NOT FEEL his legs as they carried him toward the altar. All bodily sensation seemed concentrated in his shaved cheeks, a disguise of nakedness that made him shiver. Garbed in indigo brocade from Prince Lennard's own wardrobe, with a cloth-of-gold cape on his shoulders and a diamond-crusted scabbard slung around his waist, Tristan did not fear to be mistaken for Father Alester's meek apprentice. Rather, the anxious prickling in his whiskerless skin foretold of triumph.

Father Alester sat at the Cardinal's right hand, his fiery glare burning away any hope Tristan might still have held for his own future. Alester had fumed when he learned of the prince's plot, and Tristan knew he would never again wear an acolyte's robes under the royal chaplain's tutelage. He would be lucky if the priest at his own parish in Carnish-on-Levold allowed him to complete his studies there. Yet there were eyes upon him now that scorched him even more than Alester's. Princess Briella's glare vowed retribution as she fixed her black eyes on the imposter. Her departed brother deserved better than this farce, and so did she. But Tristan pictured the fate of his own young sister if the Darrivants should march through her village, and he climbed the great marble steps before him. At least, if he must sacrifice himself, it was fitting that it should be on God's altar. He looked up toward the true prince seated in the gallery. Prince Raphael gazed down with a white-knuckled grip on the railing. With his teeth clenched, he nodded.

"My brothers." Tristan's voice crackled like dry leaves. He coughed and tried again. "My brothers. My sisters. We are here today, all of us, the children of this great kingdom, brothers and sisters birthed from the same womb of the same dream. That dream, you well know, was justice. Two centuries ago, our ancestors gave their lives to throw off the oppression of the Marignac Kings, barbarians who despoiled every maid on her wedding night and taxed the kingdom to starvation. Our ancestors—yours and mine—liberated us from their tyranny. They built a kingdom where laborers plow the fields with confidence that they will eat what they produce, and that their lords will enforce the rule of law." The congregation murmured assent. "Those ancient dreamers entrusted to my family the future they had bought with their blood. Two hundred years, this kingdom has prospered under my family's reign. Yet now an enemy greater than any we have ever faced stands at our borders with swords and catapults and arrows. The prince we all counted as our savior lies dead before our eyes. The battle lines are falling back, encroaching on our homes, and a man none of you has ever seen before stands on the altar of his brother's requiem begging that you be steady, that you follow, that you persevere."

Prince Raphael had told Tristan to walk to the casket and touch it, but he forbore. He was mightier here, away from death's shadow. "Already, I have heard you whisper among yourselves, 'His parents gave him to the Church, and in the Church he should remain.' I have heard you whisper that I wield a Bible more forcefully than a sword." Steel hissed against leather as he drew the blade from his scabbard, holding it as he used to do on the river when pirates threatened his father's ferry. But that sword had not refracted the sun like this one, bathing his shoulders in rainbowed light.

Tristan pulled himself to his full height. "I am not a general," he said, "but I assure you that I am a prince. I am the son of a great man and a great dream. Justice is my birthright, as it is yours, my brothers. Not for nothing have I spent my life in prayer. I know that where Justice marches, God cannot be absent. Kneel to Him, the King of Kings. Kneel to Him, and then together, we cannot fail."

His voice resounded from the marbles columns, clear as the salute of horns across a battlefield, and Tristan wanted nothing more than to heed his own words, to fall at the feet of the God he loved and cry forgiveness for his lies—lies that cut his heart so deeply because, from Prince Raphael's lips, they would have been true.

Tristan scanned the awestruck crowd. A silent instant stretched tight with the fear of failure and the terror of success. Then a young knight pierced the calm. "My prince! My loyalty, my sword, my life, I swear them all to you." The man fell prostrate at the foot of the altar.

Tristan cleared his throat once more. "God will bless you richly, sir. Arise."

"I am yours, my prince." Another knight.

"And I." The Lord of Falm. "For Justice and for Armany!"

"For Justice and for Armany!" The cry went up, the swords were raised, the knees were bent in multitudes. Tristan stared above their bowed brave heads, sweating through his doublet. All around him, eager faces beamed with hope and faith. Was there no one at this funeral left to cry but him?

He heard a cough—a sob, perhaps—and turned his head. The woman was dabbing a handkerchief at her face, but she felt his gaze and raised her eyes. They sparkled like onyx despite the puffiness of tears, as wide and dewy as a new spring fawn's. She brushed an ebony curl away from her face and smiled straight into his soul.

In that moment, Tristan Ferryman knew that he would never become a priest.

CHAPTER 6

The hazel boughs dripped with tendrils of golden flowers, unobscured by any nascent veil of summer leaves. Allia caressed her cheek against a catkin, inhaling its balmy fragrance. She spread her straw pallet over the soft grass of her mother's grave; then she sat down in the sun's waning rays to eat her dinner of cold water and brown bread. With her family in the capitol, she could have stolen wine and cheese or a salted flank of lamb from the cellar and feasted until her belly could hold no more. She could have indulged in a night upon a feather mattress, huddled under woolen blankets with a fire blazing in the grate, there to remain long after the cocks had crowed. She could have given her body the rest it deserved, but then her mind would have awakened as confused as when she fell asleep. A vigil of sacrifice posed no hardship if it could bring her peace.

She rubbed her hand across a few fragments of fine white stone, the last earthly remnants of her mother's image. When Lord Camesbry first laid his beloved wife to rest on this hill, he had commissioned a sculptor to memorialize her in marble. For nine months, the artist had slaved, while fickle memory distorted Lady Clara's delicate features and naught but a bare plot of soil marked her vanished soul. But finally the work was completed to the mourning lord's satisfaction and the statue placed as reverence to his departed love. It stood but three short months before the rains of winter seeped into invisible imperfections, where they froze and cracked the marble from inside. So Allia had watched the ice claim her mother once again.

The statue lay where it had crumbled. Lord Camesbry had proposed to Vivienne Delaine as soon as the snows were thawed. With the promise of a warm body to occupy his bed, he needed no more ladies made of stone. Allia was glad. Cold ridges of white could never capture the laughing roses on her mother's cheeks, but still, her tiny broken heart had yearned to mark the memory of love.

On his wedding day, in a fit of goodwill, Lord Camesbry offered little Allia any gift she might choose. She answered, "Please, Papa, pluck a sprig from the tree in the garden where Mama used to pray and plant it on her grave."

Thunderclouds stormed across his smile. "How dare a little murderess beg favors for the slain? To the cellar with you, you imp from hell, and do not show your face again until the wedding feast is done!"

Allia had wept that night away with only the rats for company. But in the morning, her father had planted the tree all the same.

It stood now, in full bloom, a golden lighthouse shining through the fog of Allia's broken world. "Guide me, Mother," she prayed in the twilight chill as she pulled her cloak tight and set her head on the straw. Wind whispered sweet assurance through the boughs. The nesting doves cooed lullabies until the daylight faded and the would-be princess slept.

She dreamed about the man she should have loved.

She watched the fairy's tale unfold, the ball with all its swishing silk, a thousand candles that defied the night, a violin just out of tune. She felt the melting in her soul as she turned and met the prince's eyes. He glided as if her presence had unfurled some hidden sail. They danced, two feathers in a giddy breeze, afraid to speak lest the spell of wild symmetry dissolve. Then midnight struck—her slipper slipped— she ran half-shod into the night. Sharp wings as black as solitude thrashed against her path. She writhed, she turned, she cried aloud, while the straight and narrow way twined around her limbs.

The peddler cut her bonds away, bearing on the point of his sword her fallen little shoe. His fingers brushed her ankle as he slid it over her toes. "It fits." He kissed her shin, her knee, while she whispered, "Yes." But the shoes turned poison-green and slithered around their love until the fangs of Eden's serpents found their flesh. A man without a face stretched out his hand and pulled her free. "Faithfulness," he promised as he laced his fingers through hers.

For Allia, it was enough.

She awoke in the chill of the day's first light and stroked her hand against the hazel tree. "Thank you. I will be faithful, too." She packed up her straw, took a draught from her jug, and swallowed her lingering tears. With her shoulders squared, she marched downhill to face a fateful dawn. Allia's family would return from the capitol today with her faceless fiancé in tow. He would find his radiant bride waiting.

THE SPARK of flint on flint jolted Lilliane from reverie. Lady Vivienne watched her jump and hit the side of the carriage as it rattled homeward. George Couper touched the flint to the small clay bowl clutched between his knees, and herbaceous smoke wafted through the coach. Vivienne could identify every tiny dried leaf in that pot, lavender and sage and rose petals, but most of it was cannabis. She smiled indulgently and opened the casement.

"The smoke will calm you, my lady," Couper said, already beginning to grin like a simpleton. "Are your nerves not rattled after such a dramatic affair? To be frank, I thought when Prince Lennard died, we would all be speaking Darrivant this time next year. But his brother seems quite capable."

"Capable!" exclaimed Lilliane. "He is twice the prince his brother ever was. He shall rout the Darrivants in one battle."

Vivienne closed her eyes to keep from rolling them. "He cuts a charming figure, Lilliane, but you must remember he was brought up among monks. If he has an ounce of sense, he will never see battle."

"All the better. There will be no stray arrows to steal him from us."

Vivienne watched her daughter's eyes sparkle with dreams. Vivienne had not missed the look that passed between Lilliane and the prince, a look as old as man and just as fickle, but an undeniable opportunity. A prince reared in a monastery might burn a good deal hotter than most, and, were the kingdom at peace, Vivienne would already have set about arranging introductions. However, with the Darrivants storming toward Camesbry, there could be no less secure position for Lilliane than to become an Arman princess.

Vivienne laid her hand over the parchments sewn into her petticoats. Whoever won the war, she and Lilliane would be well provided for. It was not yet time to choose a victor.

The jeweler's cloying smoke clawed at Vivienne's consciousness with tipsy talons. She turned her face toward the open window, filled her lungs with fresh air, and looked across the coach to be certain Couper's eyes were closed. They were. She took a vial from her pocket and dripped a careful drop into the burning herbs. The white smoke turned to gray, and though the floral fragrance persisted, the talons of intoxication slipped their hold.

A mile or so later, Couper roused himself and smiled. "My hands are trembling," he said as he extinguished the clay bowl with a wad of saliva. "My hands never tremble. A jeweler does not win royal commissions with trembling hands. But then, it is not every day a man goes to meet his wife."

"I assure you, she will set more to trembling than just your hands. Few men are lucky enough to wed the very portrait of Clara de Camesbry."

"I remember her mother. I am a connoisseur of beauty, my lady, and I have never forgotten the blush on that majestic face."

"Her daughter's is twice as lovely." Though it pained Vivienne to admit it, it was true. Allia did not need the potions her stepmother had given her in order to bewitch any man with eyes. All she needed was a bath and a half-decent set of clothes. If the cinders had ever accomplished their work of making the girl docile and ugly, Vivienne would have liberated Allia from them long ago. A puppet heiress was more useful than an insolent cinder maid. But that problem would be solved today, and if Allia's beauty made her saleable, so much the better.

"I must say, my lady, your husband has been most generous in accepting my suit. He is a great man, to look past my lack of noble birth and see that his heirs will receive so many other benefits."

Vivienne could not suppress a gasp. She could not fault the man for using his fortune to ascend the ladder of class and culture; she herself had done the same. But had he really spoken the word *heirs*?

"I am certain my husband will be happy to see his grandchildren well-supplied with a useful trade."

"Of course I will teach them the jeweler's craft, if they are inclined to learn. But the eldest, at least, will need to spend most of his time with his grandfather."

Lilliane laughed. "Lord Camesbry will surely be too fat by then to train a squire."

Couper puffed up like a sail. Vivienne shot her daughter a look that even Lilliane could not construe to mean anything other than, *Hold your tongue*. "Forgive my daughter, Mr. Couper. She has never learned to think before she speaks. It may be true your son will need another knight to teach him warfare, but for statecraft, he shall find no better guide than Eric de Camesbry." She glared at Lilliane again, to staunch the protest rising to her daughter's lips. Was it possible her husband had actually promised this commoner's children his lordship? Lord Camesbry had remained in the capitol to advise Prince Raphael about the war, so his opinion on the matter could not be asked. Nor would it be a good idea to argue the point before the wedding vows were said. If there had been a misunderstanding, Couper might well renege, and then Allia would remain the only possible heir. Vivienne would have to find a better solution than a cacophony of words.

She reached across the coach and gently squeezed Couper's trembling hand. "Your children will have a lord's nobility and a commoner's good sense. We will toast this happy day for Camesbry just as soon as you and Lady Allia are duly wed."

Couper squeezed her hand in return. "You are all graciousness, my lady. I shall be honored to raise my glass to your hospitality."

Vivienne smiled. There would be good wine tonight—floods of it. Barrelfuls for everyone in the castle. And at the bottom of George Couper's cup would be the herbs that ensured he would never father another child as long as he might live.

CHAPTER 7

The fly would not stop buzzing. Prince Raphael swatted it away a dozen times, but the beast continued to return, drawn to the bowl of barley stew on the table before its victim. The royal dining room was packed with guests, but the fare in front of them was not meant to be a feast. Prince Lennard had been quite clear about such matters before he left. "If I die, then bury me, but I want none of the feasting we had for mother. If I die, it means we are losing. Put our resources into the war." Lennard had never spoken a single word that Chancellor Narius did not hasten to obey. The royal tomb had received the prince's body, and that was that. Supper must be served, but it was only supper.

Prince Raphael brought a spoon to his lips and forced his reluctant throat to swallow. The solid beech wood table in front of him could seat sixteen at a pinch, but it was no more elaborate than something a master carpenter might build for his own use. Only a mighty portrait of Simon the Unvanquished marked the room as part of a palace rather than some wealthy merchant's home. It needed nothing more, for, on an ordinary day, only the king, his daughter, and his pretend-foster son ever took their repasts here. This evening's overflow assembly was a matter of practical necessity; most of the nobility who had traveled in for the funeral needed lodging for the night.

Raphael's wheeled chair stood at the very foot of the table, yards away from Tristan, who sat at the king's right hand with a look of solemn determination frozen onto his face. Raphael ached to hear what the imposter might be saying in close quarters with Lord Falm, but the chatter droned too loudly for Tristan's words to filter through. Only Briella's cold glare penetrated the gap. Last night, when he informed his sister of the false brother she must embrace, she had wielded a vocabulary overgrown with thorns. *Cripple. Weakling. Coward.* Briella could not understand that the kingdom needed Tristan precisely because her words were true.

"You're awfully quiet down there, Immerville."

Raphael looked up at his cousin, Lord Collin de Tembria. He and Lennard had been the same age, though Collin, with his iron-thick beard, tree-trunk arms, and prematurely balding pate, appeared much older. The three teeth missing from his self-satisfied smile did not help the matter.

Raphael grumbled, "Am I not permitted to be quiet on the day my foster brother is buried?"

With a fist like the ball of a mace, Lord Tembria caught the fly buzzing next to Raphael's ear. He slowly tore each wing from the creature's body and dropped the still-squirming insect to the floor. Raphael's face contorted with disgust. "Death is an opportunity," said Lord Tembria. "I am only third in line for the throne now, and you're... what? Sixteenth?"

Raphael smashed the barley grains in his bowl with his spoon. "I do not think either of us need worry about the succession. His Royal Highness appears hale enough."

"And quite the orator, too. 'Kneel to Him, the King of Kings...' It's the sort of thing one expects from a monk, I suppose, but I'm surprised the lords swallowed it so easily."

"Why? Do you suppose they are all perfect heathens, like you?"

"No, but I thought they were soldiers. His Highness held that sword well enough, but we all know he couldn't really use it."

Raphael wanted to dare him to prove it with a challenge, but Collin was rash enough to accept and swordsman enough to send poor Tristan to an early grave. "From everything I have observed, living in the palace my entire life, most of what makes a king a good king is that he rules his people justly."

Collin slapped his cousin roughly on the back, shoving Raphael's nose precariously close to his stew. "That's because you've been *in the palace*. If you ever get out past these walls, just see how far that 'justice' takes you."

Raphael was spared the necessity of a reply as the serving girl came to lay out the next course of quail and cranberries. The girl was plump and apple-cheeked, and therefore more interesting to Lord Tembria than his crippled cousin. She slapped away the lord's wandering hand, but she did it with a smile.

For half a second, Raphael could not help but envy his cousin that smile. Then his stomach turned, his sense of decency recoiled, and he quietly pushed his chair back from the table. It seemed to creak more loudly than usual as he wheeled it to his own room.

The prince's boudoir had been built for solitude. The oaken bed he had slept in since childhood would have hardly held a man whose legs needed room to stretch. The small wardrobe that housed his clothes had never grown alongside him. Where the other members of the royal family had cozy sitting areas near the fires in their chambers, Raphael had a giant slab of a table covered with books and maps and vials of bubbling experiment that kept his waking hours occupied. He had never bothered to adorn the walls with any decoration except the tapestry. Raphael hated that tapestry. Faded, graying, punctuated by the meals of moths, a woven St. Lucy stood surrounded by a halo of dim candles with her gouged-out eyes held before her on a tray. Raphael suffered the tapestry to remain only because it kept the winter drafts from creeping into his bones and because it had been a gift from Lennard.

Lucis, the blind patroness of sight; his brother's perverse idea of poetry. Lennard had brought the tapestry back from his first military campaign five years ago, from a ruined church where his army made its base. "I have brought a woman for you, Brother, to warm your lonely nights," he declared as he unrolled the monstrosity.

Raphael was then fourteen and curled his lip with pubescent disdain. "Aye, a mangled virgin martyr ought to keep me warm, indeed."

Lennard laughed and drove a nail to hang it on the wall. "Someday, I shall find you one less holy and less dead, you have my word. But since you only use the room to study, I thought perhaps it could stand a bit more light."

"It's grotesque. I shall tear it down the moment you leave."

"Then I shall hang it out of your reach. Lucy will be a friend to you, once you've grown used to the hollow sockets in her head."

"Because only a fellow cripple could befriend the likes of me?"

The Lion turned on him with danger in his eyes. "No. Because only a blind woman with the power of God at her disposal will ever teach you how to see."

Raphael knew the vision his brother had sought to impart. Too well, he remembered the panoply of learned physicians brought to seek a cure for his worthless legs. Some blamed a tragic alignment of stars at the moment of birth or conception; some sought to blame a demon, and many strove to drive it out. Too well, Raphael remembered a boy who spat in the face of exorcism and shot toy arrows into maps of the stars. Lennard the Incorrigible, Mother always called him, the boy whose antics had planted the seed of doubt—the only seed that kept Raphael from being tortured for the doctors' ignorance until Father Alester finally saved him from the morbid medical parade. Thirteen long years ago, the newly-appointed royal chaplain had created the wheeled chair on the same day he diagnosed the young prince. "The ligaments are missing," he declared after he examined the child's legs. "They must have failed to develop when he was in the womb. There are no demons at work here, Your Majesties, only nature."

"You see," Lennard added, his leonine eyes bright with triumph.

Raphael had repaid his brother's loyalty by sending a novice acolyte to conduct the business of state in borrowed royal titles. Yet

Lennard had never realized that, if the physicians could not look past Raphael's infirmity to see a human being, then men like Collin de Tembria would never be able to look at the same boy and see a prince.

Raphael turned his dripping eyes away from the moth-eaten face of holiness. He gazed at the candelabra guttering on his desk, wetted his fingers with his tears, and snuffed out the very brightest of its flames. "Brother, without you, we are all just sightless cripples." He sat with his sorrow until a knock sounded at his door. "Enter," he called, and wiped his eyes on his sleeve.

Father Alester came in. "His Royal Highness requests your presence." His voice loomed as dark as the circles under his eyes.

Raphael sighed. "He was brilliant today."

"Aye. If I had known what use you would make of him, I would not have trained him half as well."

"If I had made that speech, do you suppose the lords would have been so quick to bend their knees?"

"No, but once they went down, they would have stayed bent. This deception will come out someday, and then the war will be among your own vassals."

"I know." Raphael hung his head. "I only hope to give Briella time to come of age. When the plot is revealed, I will renounce my claim."

Father Alester's forehead creased. "Your brother would weep to hear such speeches."

"No, he would rage. But my brother is dead." Once more, Raphael's gaze fell on St. Lucy. *She will be a friend to you, once you've grown used to the hollow sockets in her head.* Lennard had never understood that only a hollow life needed a tapestry for a friend.

Raphael pushed his chair forward. "Come, Father. We have a prince to train."

CHAPTER 8

*B*ucket after steaming, rose petal-sprinkled bucket sloughed the grime from Allia's skin until gray water swirled in the tub like molten lead. She eyed the scoured-pink scar on her breast and watched her fingers shrivel in the wet: the deformity of cleanliness.

"It's a sin you're still white under those ashes," Beth the ladies' maid observed as she poured yet one more fragrant pail. The Camesbry servants formed two camps where the master's daughter was concerned: those whose eyes swelled with pity and those whose noses turned up in contempt. Beth often found her nose so vertical, it collected rain.

Allia shivered despite the steam. "I suppose the cinders must keep off the sun."

"Seems like God might come up with a punishment worse than sunburn for what you done. He must piss his breeches, to think he made you beautiful." Beth surveyed the sinews of Allia's naked form and rolled her pious eyes. "Lord save us. That jeweler's going to drool all over himself to put a viper into his bed."

"Jeweler? Beth, do you know him?"

Her lips curled into a sneer. "I do."

"Please, tell me…"

Beth offered her a towel and a silent, vengeful smile.

"At least his name," Allia pleaded. "As a woman, surely you can understand…"

"As a woman, I can spit on your 'understanding.'" Beth pursed her lips and did just that. "I will go fetch the talcum while you dry."

Allia bit back a curse. Though she told herself the hazel tree could not steer her wrong, still her heart shuddered. Whoever this "jeweler" might be, her father and Lady Vivienne had chosen him. A jeweler could offer them no power, no prestige; either the marriage had been arranged on strictly monetary terms, or else some personal attribute had impressed two people hell-bent on Allia's destruction. She would rather be sold like a heifer than shunted off into some deeper circle of hell, but she also knew her family did not want for wealth. How, then, was it possible that a man of her parents' choosing could rescue her?

But he would. The hazel tree had promised it.

As she endured the ritual of dressing, Allia rued the anger that had broken her stepmother's vials. She yearned to slather paint across every tiny flaw, to glaze herself like porcelain and shimmer before her betrothed. She ached to harness beauty and smile with the power of true love, but a smile like that came once a lifetime. Allia had squandered hers on a story.

By the time her stepmother's carriage and its escort drove into view, Allia found herself primped and powdered, adorned in a gown of pale yellow damask that had once been her mother's. The puckered bodice was now passé, yet the garment carried Lady Clara's elegance within its very seams. Beth gave Allia an appraising glare followed by a haughty sniff—a good sign, surely. Allia felt the buoyant freshness of every soft blonde curl, and she almost dared believe the impossible had come true: a cinder maid could be beautiful. A cinder maid could be loved.

Men-at-arms stormed the walls with raucous laughter as the caravan arrived. Allia sat in the receiving hall, watching the household guard encircle her like a pack of salivating wolves.

"Look, Alfred, there was a lady under those ashes."

"A lady? I only see a whore." Alfred traced his thick, blunt fingers down her sleeve. "What's he paying for you, precious? Might be I can better the offer."

Allia stiffened. "With what, the gold the devil gave you for your soul?"

The first guardsman laughed, but the one called Alfred clenched her wrist. "It's you the devil loves, my lady. No one here is fooled."

"Unhand her." Lady Vivienne's quiet venom touched the air. "Be glad I left her fiancé outside these doors, or I should be required to have you both flogged. Now get out before I do it, anyway."

With a last leer at their prey, the scoundrels skulked away while Lady Vivienne advanced. Her dark eyes absorbed every facet of Allia's transformation. "I see you have elected not to use my gifts."

"Your peddler insisted I add them to his purchase. He had buyers already promised."

"Hmm." Her stepmother took Allia's chin between two fingers, slowly turning her head. A quick hand slapped Allia's cheek. She cried out while Lady Vivienne whispered, "For the rouge. Now the other one."

Allia bit her lip against the pain and presented her face. This time, when her stepmother's hand connected, she uttered not a sound.

"Good girl," Vivienne crooned. "I know you have been dreading this day. Let me lay your fears to rest. The man on the other side of this door is not a monster. His name is George Couper, a widower and a father of three. His former wife died in childbirth, along with the fourth child. He is a jeweler of some renown, and all these knights wanting to encrust their swords with gemstones before they ride to war have made him so wealthy, he fancies himself in want of a title. He is willing to part with a nice portion of his earnings to secure your hand. You think me cruel, Allia, but certainly we have lived together long enough, you can believe me capable of kindness if it brings in gold. I have made you a good match, far better than you deserve. The rest is up to you."

Allia trembled. She had not thought the man would be a father, that she herself would become "Stepmother." Her heart suddenly ached to embrace those three poor, motherless souls. Yes, the hazel tree had steered her true. Together, perhaps they could heal.

"Where is my father? He should be here to bless the match."

"Prince Raphael is holding council with the lords. You shall have to get your blessings from the priest. We will go to church as soon as you have both given your consent."

"So you acknowledge that I have a choice?"

"We all have choices. No one but you can speak your vows." With that, Lady Vivienne opened the door. "Mr. Couper, may I present my stepdaughter, Lady Allia de Camesbry."

He walked with timid but eager steps, approaching his betrothed as if she were a rare exotic bird that might be startled by the noise. He did not look like a man who could reach into an adder's den and with one hand deliver a beguiled maid. His stagnant eyes seemed somehow vague—not quite simple, but they lacked an acumen Allia could not name. The lack had not permeated his aesthetic vision, however. The cut of his tunic, the length of his breeches, the pale powder-blue of his elegant cravat all evinced a talent for good taste.

Allia smiled with all the cozy welcome her racing heart would allow. "Mr. Couper, it is my honor to meet you at last."

He bowed to her, long and low. "My lady, I have dreamt of your beauty, but I find my imagination has fallen short of its duty. I hardly dare raise my eyes lest you disappear."

His flattery rankled against some long-dormant nerve, but Allia only curtseyed. "Rise, good sir, for I shall not disappear. From this day until eternity, I am yours." She saw her stepmother's bewilderment, but it was the jeweler's confusion she sought to allay as he stood to his full height once more. "My father has chosen you for me, and I have faith in his judgment of brides. He had the good sense to marry my mother, after all."

"And my lady," Couper added with a nod toward Lady Vivienne. "Indeed, his taste cannot be questioned."

Allia closed her eyes and pictured the faceless man who had saved her from the serpents. "My lady tells me you are a jeweler. Is it a family trade?"

"Aye, I cut gems as I was cutting teeth, or perhaps before. Queen Eleanor was buried in a brooch of my design."

Allia could not keep her lips from twitching. "A true testament to your craft. I am sure the worms delight in its beauty."

He laughed, an awkward, throaty guffaw that made Vivienne raise a hand to hide her rolling eyes. Allia wanted to do the same, but valiantly, she clenched her fists and marched the conversation on.

"I am told you have three children, sir. I beg you would tell me their names."

The corners of his fawning lips stretched into a smile. "They are eager to meet you, my lady. Charlotte is the eldest, a girl of fourteen, more an age to be your sister than your child. She is a quiet, lonely soul. It will be good for her to have another woman in the house again. Frederick and Stefan are the boys, eight and six, as rough-and-tumble as boys ever are. Frederick ought to inherit the business when he comes of age, but I should not be surprised if he goes for a soldier instead. It is Stefan who has the jeweler's eye. He sits with me often at my workbench. I shall send him out to apprentice in a few years' time, so he can learn the other masters' styles as well as mine."

Paternal fondness poured like balm over Allia's ears. No, this man was not her prince, strong and perfect, rich in love. He was not an intellectual pillar, nor yet a good judge of character, but his heart could beat with constancy, just as the dream had foretold. Allia reached out her hands. "I shall love them just as if they were my own."

"And they, you, my lady. You are everything we four have dared to hope and more." With tears in his eyes, he raised her fingers to his lips —and stopped. He rubbed his thumbs across her skin, slowly tightening his grip. "What treachery is this?" he seethed, and tiny drops of spittle clung to Allia's fine sleeves.

"Please, sir, I beg you, be gentle..."

He threw her hands away and spun on his heel. "My lady, I demand you keep our bargain! Bring me Lady Allia, or Prince Raphael shall hear of your deceit."

Lady Vivienne glided forward, pale but resolute. "I pray you explain, Mr. Couper. I assure you, my lord has no other daughter than this."

"Her hands," he cried, and grabbed Allia's fingers once more to thrust them into her stepmother's face. "This is some kitchen maid, some dairy girl. You think to dupe me out of my fortune for an imposter. I will not stand for it! Give me what is mine, or I shall ride for the capitol this very day and report this deception to the crown."

Lady Vivienne stood dangerously still. "Mr. Couper, this is the true Allia de Camesbry. You said you had seen her mother. Look into her face and tell me if anyone but Lady Clara could have given it to her."

For a moment, the jeweler froze. He swallowed and turned to Allia again.

"Please." Allia's whisper shook on her tongue. "I am Lady Allia. My hands only tell the story of my pain."

Sympathy touched Couper's anger as he met her eye. He studied every curve of her plaintive face. "You are beautiful," he murmured, turning her chin so that the light caught her cheeks. Then he shook his head again. "You are prettily cut, ma'amselle, but glass can never be a diamond."

Allia stood dumbfounded, but Lady Vivienne spoke, her voice like a razor against a whetstone. "Mr. Couper, if the lady is not to your taste, you may depart and our bargain shall be void. But beware whom you accuse of falsehood inside Lord Camesbry's walls."

"I am not the one who has broken our agreement, my lady. The prince shall know of this, rest assured." Couper took his leave, his cloak fluttering behind him like a curtain drawing closed.

Allia collapsed into her chair. As if to prove the world had gone mad, Lady Vivienne caressed her stepdaughter's hair. "My child, I have wronged you. You played your part better than I had ever dared to hope, and I have wasted your affections."

Shock dried Allia's eyes as she raised them. "My lady, I have no words."

"Nor would any suffice. But do not fear, child. I shall choose more carefully next time."

"Please, if my father is in need of an heir, let him speak to his nephews. I have no heart to marry."

Vivienne's hands tightened around Allia's shoulders. "You are distraught. Let us set these matters aside until we are both calmer."

"Yes, my lady."

"Good girl." With an affectionate pat, her stepmother sauntered out, shutting Allia away inside the great oak doors.

CHAPTER 9

*T*he throne room of the kings of Armany was built like a cathedral, shaped like a cross with the throne placed at the intersection of two aisles, where a church would have had its altar. Prince Raphael looked down on it from the second-floor gallery, glad that it was Chancellor Narius being sacrificed today and not he himself.

The prince often came to court to observe, both when his father had been ruling and after Narius assumed the regency. He watched from the gallery for reasons of simple convenience: his living quarters were on the second floor of the palace, and he could wheel himself to the gallery, whereas descending to the ground floor required someone to carry him. The gallery did not always afford an adequate vantage from which to observe the proceedings; the tapestries and carpets in the throne room seemed to swallow sound, and although Raphael brought his spyglass to magnify the faces, it could not help him hear. Yet the prince preferred the anonymity of the upper floor, where no one distracted him with ugly looks or questions about his identity. In fact, he had not attended court from the ground floor since the day two years ago when one supplicant mistook him for a court jester and demanded that he juggle. Raphael still had not forgotten the sting of the guardsmen's laughter.

But there were some days when Raphael would have given both his arms to have good legs, to be able to descend those taunting stairs and bestow a miracle upon some soul whom justice alone could never serve. He had barely seen the guards open the doors to admit the day's first supplicant—a woman, unwashed, her garments torn, dragging the body of a man behind her—when he realized that today was going to be one of those days.

"Madam Elissa Baker," the page announced, "of Waymond, in Morisse."

Raphael cringed. There had been word only two days ago that Waymond had fallen to the Darrivant advance.

"Lord Chancellor!" the woman cried, "this was my son!" She dragged the body along the plush purple carpet until it rested at Chancellor Narius's feet. Even from this distance, Raphael could see that the dead man wore the red livery of Morisse.

Narius shifted uneasily on the purple cushion of the golden throne. "The crown extends its sympathies to you, madam. However, it is not necessary to bring your son's body all this way to claim his wages."

Raphael cringed again with embarrassment.

"His wages!" the mother shrieked. "You keep your filthy money, my lord! This was my son Paul, who swore his very life to Lord Morisse's service and never broke an oath in all his years. And do you know who killed him?"

"Was he not killed in battle, madam?"

"Aye, in battle with me! When the Darrivants—or what we thought was Darrivants—marched in, those of us as could hold a blade tried to put up a defense, to give the old folks and the little ones time to get away. But the closer they came, the more we saw it wasn't Darrivants, or at least not all. They were our men. And *they knew us*, my lord. They were weeping while they burned their own homes and speared their own fathers. When Paul came—" She choked on the flood of words. "If he had come at me, I would have died, but I could not let him kill his little brother."

A fidgety silence engulfed the sound of the woman's tears. The guards, pages, scribes, and Chancellor all stood fuddled by decorum. Would it have killed them, Raphael thought, to give the poor woman an arm to lean on while she cried?

"Madam..." Chancellor Narius began, but the woman interrupted.

"There is more, my lord. You had to see this with your own eyes." She reached down and lifted the leg of the breeches from the body.

A communal gasp escaped the room. Raphael leaned toward the railing, feeling his stomach pitch as he lifted his spyglass. He had to wait until several guardsmen moved aside before he could get a clear view, but he had already guessed what the body would reveal: an arrow wound on the man's left calf more horrifying than Lennard's. This one had healed over, but it was stained with darkness that discolored the entire leg.

The prince closed his eyes, suddenly glad that his brother had not survived the arrow that pierced him.

"Madam, what do you know of this?" The Chancellor began his inquiry, but Raphael could bear no more. He wheeled himself out of the gallery, huffing as he pushed himself at top speed down the hall. Browbeating a grieving mother would yield no information, not when every battlefield commander had already been questioned. No one could account for the desertions by any means but demonic magic, a theory given credence by the gray-rimmed wounds found too often among the dead. This body of an actual deserter bearing such a mark confirmed it. Whatever the Darrivants were using, it lay beyond any Arman's comprehension. How could a human army fight against the devil?

Raphael stopped his wheels abruptly, nearly causing a collision with a passing footman. The Lord Chancellor had questioned every commander currently in the field. Father Alester had probed every possible informant. But there was one man here, inside these palace walls, whose opinion no one had asked about the wounds. If any man alive could outwit the devil in pitched battle, surely it was Simon the Unvanquished.

The prince set his hands to his wheels and reversed his course. The axle groaned as he rolled to dredge the depths of madness.

The hallway to the king's chamber seemed to have grown longer since the last time Raphael wheeled himself this way. He did not come as often now as he once had. No one did, except the nurse assigned to tend His Majesty in his decline. There had been a time when King Simon often snubbed the throne room for the comfort of his solar, choosing to meet with lords and ambassadors on cushioned couches with the aid of a valet whose wine flask never ran dry. Now, the wine was mulled with opium, the couches peopled by memories. Raphael hung his head as he let the heavy door knocker fall.

"Your Lordship!" the nurse greeted him with a start. "What brings you here?" Raphael's cumbersome wheels just barely made it through the door. His knuckles had grown callused years ago from pushing himself across such thresholds, though not as callused as his palms, made smooth and hard as horns by the chafing of his wheels.

"How is His Majesty today?" The antechamber, with its open window and gold curtains, gilded the prince's dark errand into a sunlit dream.

"Not as bad as some days, not as good as others. He asks for you sometimes."

"For me?"

"Yes. He'll say, 'Send for my boy,' and then he seems to be searching for your name. He seldom finds it, so he'll say, 'You know, the one in the chair.'"

"Then why do you not send for me?"

The nurse blushed to the roots of her auburn hair. "Because whoever I send for, by the time they arrive, he has forgotten that he wanted them."

Raphael reached out and squeezed the woman's hand. "It is a work of God's mercy you do here, madam. It is not often enough that we say thank you."

"You are kind to say so, Your Lordship."

"Take a rest, madam. I shall see to His Majesty for a while."

She squeezed his hands in return. "His Majesty is blessed to a have such a foster son, especially now..." Her sentence trailed. "I shall return in half an hour."

Raphael watched her go, reflecting that he owed the respect she showed him to his father. He had lived his life shrouded in falsehood, and no power on earth could silence the snide glares that followed him everywhere he wheeled, yet no one could say he had been denied a prince's life. Baron Immerville studied with the royal tutor, ate at the royal table, commanded obedience from the royal staff. The life of a king's foster child could not be called hard. Indeed, the life of a king's son was far harder, weighted as it was with expectation. Still, Raphael could not suppress the choler that rose in his cheeks every time he laid eyes on his father. "For your own sake," the king had said so many times when the chains of secrecy chafed against his young son's heart, but only the man who spoke it believed that lie. The king's own honor had benefitted from the deception, but the only protection it afforded his son were the calluses it left on his soul, as thick as the ones his hands.

Raphael pushed himself into the parlor where his father sat enthralled by the mysteries of his own mind. "Good morning, Your Majesty."

The king started. "Ah, yes! It's you..." He trailed off, searching for a name. Raphael hesitated, not knowing which one to give.

"'Tis a lovely morning, is it not?" The king waved toward the windows. "I was just thinking of taking a stroll with my wife. Is she occupied, do you know?"

Raphael smiled sadly. "I believe she is."

"Perhaps tomorrow, then. Time was, I used to spend these pretty days out training with a lance, but that was folly. Sunshine like this should be for love, not war."

Raphael was glad none of the lords was present to hear such a remark. "You are right, Your Majesty. But it happens there is a war going on. I came to ask your opinion of it."

The king's eyes skidded through slippery memories, searching for purchase. "Who are we fighting?"

"The Darrivants. They have launched an invasion."

"So the spiders are spinning their webs here at last."

Raphael watched his father's hand grip the armrest of his sofa and remembered the bygone days when it had gripped a sword. There would have been no cobwebs in the kingdom but for the ones in His Majesty's mind.

"The spiders are doing more than spinning, Your Majesty. They are stealing our soldiers. In all your battles, did you encounter anything that made men change sides?"

"We stole three hundred Fremmans at Bandenbry. That's Baron Questis, you know, I traded him the barony for the men."

"Yes, I remember. This is different. There are wounds, Your Majesty, arrow wounds that spread some sort of black through the men's skin, even after they are dead. It may be some kind of poison."

The monarch furrowed his white brows, pondering the problem in true earnest. "There was…"

Raphael leaned forward. "Yes?"

King Simon held out his hand as if to catch the memory, but then he blinked and let it fall. He shook his head and turned to face the window. "There was a king in Armany once."

Raphael ran his fingers through his hair in frustration, but forced his voice to remain calm. "How would you fight such a weapon, Sire? If you were commanding the troops?"

"What weapon?"

"Poison that makes men change their allegiance."

King Simon waved a dismissive hand. "Poison is a coward's weapon. 'Tis a lovely morning, is it not?"

Raphael grimaced. "Aye. Better suited for love than war."

"Better suited for love!" The king laughed aloud. "Who is the lucky girl that inspires such a thought?"

Unaccountably, Raphael thought of St. Lucy with her dismembered eyes. "No one, Your Majesty." He reached out and took his father's hand. "Sire, is there anyone among your generals you trust above the rest? Someone you might send behind the Darrivant lines to find out what they are doing to their arrows?"

"My son," His Majesty answered.

"Your Majesty, your son is dead."

"Then who are you?"

"Your Majesty..."

"Lennard," the king said, staring straight at Raphael, "I am an old man now. It is your kingdom. You must rule it."

King Simon's great, dark eyes brimmed with the confidence Raphael had seen in them so many times before, the confidence he had yearned for all his life that had always been—and even now, still was—reserved for Lennard alone. He closed his eyes to shut out the mirage. When he opened them, his father was staring fixedly out the window.

"'Tis such a lovely morning. I was just thinking of taking a stroll with my wife. Is she occupied, do you know?"

Raphael sighed. "I believe so, Your Majesty."

"Ah, well. Tomorrow, perhaps."

They chatted about the weather until the nurse returned.

CHAPTER 10

*H*ooves like heartbeats pattered the packed earth, the moon a crescent candle in the night. Lady Vivienne pulled her cloak tight against a chill, alert to every fluttering shadow. The sweating flanks of her black stallion carried her toward the capitol, back down the same road her carriage had traveled just yesterday afternoon. The horse's even canter could not keep pace with the galloping frenzy of her mind.

Allia had proved more docile than Vivienne had imagined possible, and still her efforts to see the girl married had come to naught. Vivienne's only consolation was the memory of Prince Raphael's fevered eyes riveted upon her daughter. To have Lilliane become the future queen would more than atone for the loss of her inheritance of Camesbry. The word *opportunity* would not leave Vivienne in peace, but to seize it meant she must, once and for all, wager her future on the fate of Armany.

She made her way through sleeping villages, where huts of wattle-and-daub respired the moist night while half-timbered extravagance exhaled wisps of smoke. Armany was changing slowly, year by year, as fire or hail or sheer prodigality pulled down thatched roofs to replace them with slate. New churches, new shops, new taverns, new brothels, popped up like mushrooms after a rain. The kingdom was prospering, but the Darrivants would burn it all as they advanced. However, in her heart of hearts, that was precisely the future Vivienne dreamed of.

Vivienne had traveled to the Darrivant capitol in the days when she and her first husband used to live in a merchant caravan, peddling wool. No wattle-and-daub ever dirtied the horizon there; Darrivane's poorest slums had been built of quarried stone. The people of Armany called their enemies "The Spiders," but it was only the soldiers who wore those vermin on their skin. The nobility were often marked with glowing suns and radiant stars. The trading classes had begun to spurn tattoos in favor of jewels and costly garments that could be changed to flaunt their wealth—and the tradesmen of Darrivane had plenty of wealth to flaunt. Vivienne had seen them dance at balls that lasted three days on end, arriving in gemstone carriages pulled by horses with gold-plaited manes. She had scraped together enough pennies to buy one glass of their famed rosewine. Her tongue had reveled in the notes of honey, myrrh, and jasmine, the delicate nectar of prosperity.

Since that hallowed day, not an hour had passed when Vivienne did not dream of a life among the Darrivants. But what that life would truly be like for a woman of her heritage, she could never discover until her homeland lay withering in ashes. The safer course would be to help Prince Raphael achieve his triumph, to give up the dream of living like a queen so that her daughter could become one. She had almost resolved to do it, but first the prince would need to prove himself worthy of her aid.

The whistle of a nightingale shivered through the night, and Vivienne drew her reins. She peered into a forest glade and whistled in return. "Ho, traveler," came a harsh voice as a rider emerged from the trees. "Can you point the way to North? The clouds have masked the stars."

"Put the mountains ahead and the wind behind," she replied—the signal she had arranged with the king's agent. She nudged her stallion into the woods until they had no company but the owls.

A deep brown hood concealed the rider's face from every ray of the waning spring moon. "Here is the offer," he grumbled, and tossed her a purse filled with gold.

Vivienne paused to count the coins before she tossed them back. "It is generous, but I have a different payment in mind."

"Name your price."

"A man has wronged me."

"I shall have him jailed."

"Jailed men can still tell lies."

The hood sat silent, no sound of breath escaping through its folds. "Madam, you are misinformed. I do not broker lives."

"Nor even the lives of your citizens? The siege will not come to Pellain."

A cloud of bats churned through the branches, and the rider's gray mare shied. He muttered curses under his breath as he brought her back to hand.

"This siege will not be the last, even if you turn it," Vivienne said as the frantic whinnies faded. "Chancellor Narius does not have the courage to do what is necessary to win the war. Show me that you do, and I will tell you how."

The rider sat in silence; then he bowed. "Good evening, madam." He turned his horse's head.

Vivienne let him ride a few paces before she said, "I know why your soldiers are deserting."

The rider froze, his horse turning to stone beneath him.

A smile spread across Lady Vivienne's lips. She nudged her stallion forward. "Yes, my lord, I can save your army. But it will cost you this first bargain—and then Prince Raphael's hand."

"That is not mine to barter with."

"Then take the proposal to him. Tell him I offer the maid he spied at the funeral. He will know the one."

"If he refuses?"

"Then he can take his chances on the battlefield. That is my price." She did not wait for an answer, but turned her stallion's tail. "The siege comes to Anniton," she called over her shoulder, "in exchange for the head of George Couper."

CHAPTER 11

*A*llia's bare toes curled around mildewed slime as she slid her body inside the mouth of the stone well. Its builders had installed small iron rungs along the side, a ladder to give them egress after they dug. However, those builders had been dead a hundred years. The very first rung collapsed under Allia's weight. The stone mouth scraped her jaw as she clung to it for life. Yet the ladder had held three days before when she climbed down to hide the peddler's sword. Surely, it could bear her to retrieve it. With a deep breath, she set her foot on the second rung.

It creaked but did not give way. The moment of truth: to reach the third, she had to let go of the rim. "God, forgive my sins," she said and stepped.

Down, down, ever darker, she descended, knowing every breath of mold and gloom might be her last. She had lashed the sword to the ladder far below the sun's last rays, deeper still beyond the pale reach of the moon. But at last, her groping feet thudded against the hilt. She gained her balance and untied it. Then she kissed the cold, damp steel. In a world of fraying dreams, this, at least, was real: the deadly edge of cowardice and the warmth of dauntless breath upon her skin. She cinched the sword to her waist and began the slow, miry climb.

She had been a fool to let the peddler leave. A man who offered kindness, who knew her past and judged her for her love, not her mistakes: how could she have ever let him drive away? Curse the dream with its shoes and its serpents. The peddler was a human being, not some chimera of the night. She would not endure six months of servitude praying for his return; she would saddle a steed and go find him. But a traveling salesman might be anywhere, and war was burning through the land. She could not go unarmed, nor could she wander aimlessly, hoping to stumble on a clue. She had to go where he had been before, to a place where someone could tell his name. All these long, bitter years later, Allia must return to the scene of her crime.

"Demont," she whispered—and the snap of an iron rung plunged her into sorrow once again.

"ALLIA, THERE YOU ARE!" Johan Rabigny found the eleven-year-old beauty in the armory, play-fighting against air. She smiled and made a lunge in his direction. He pretend-parried with his fist.

"Grab a sword," she invited. Since her lesson with Prince Lennard, the budding warrior had not faltered in her resolve to learn. Despite her mother's shock and the queen's embarrassment when she returned to them covered in sweat with her temple oozing blood, the prince had given his orders, and Allia meant to obey. When she and her mother arrived in Demont, Lady Clara had disappeared into the service of her dying father, so Allia had used her freedom to find a sparring partner.

Johan Rabigny, the twelve-year-old son of Demont's governess, had been happy to oblige. Through the last chilled weeks of autumn, the two children had crossed blades, sidled up the trunks of trees, run foot races on rocky slopes, and lounged in thickets drinking pilfered golden wine. At last, however, snowstorms had blustered in to keep them well confined. Now the crystal winter shimmered on the grounds, a siren's banquet singing for the children to come feast.

"Not today," Johan answered. "I've got something better than swords." He tossed his friend a pair of flattened bones attached to straps.

Allia had seen such skates before. The Camesbry men-at-arms often made a sport of gliding on frozen lakes, propelling themselves with poles. The result of this endeavor tended to be a windfall for the old lady in the village who crafted crutches and slings.

"You're crazy. We'll be killed."

"Only if your mother finds out. Did she ride down to Peter's Tower like she said?"

"Yes."

"Then come on!"

Together, they flew across the firmament of white. "Have you used these before?" Allia wondered as she sat on a log near the frozen pond, pondering the straps.

"Yes. Here, just tie them on like this."

She gamely attached the skates to the bottoms of her shoes and took the laurel branch Johan offered as a pole. Together, they tested the ice; then they pushed off into a wild slide. They landed on their bottoms, poles and limbs and skates a-tangle, laughing until their sides ached with joy.

"You've never done this before," Allia accused through merry tears.

"Have so... once."

"How far did you get?"

"About like this."

"Come on, let's go again."

Five, ten, fifteen attempts, and at last the two wobbly ducklings began to glide. But Johan could not be satisfied with success.

"I bet I can skate without the pole."

"How?"

"I'll climb up that blackthorn tree and jump down, so I'll hit the ice sliding."

Allia shivered with delicious brazenness. "You'll break your legs," she dared.

Johan unlaced his skates, slung them over his shoulder, and scurried up the tree. As he sat perched on a branch, re-tying the bones, Allia spied a horse approaching.

"Johan..."

"Here I go! One, two..."

"Johan!"

"Three!"

He landed with a sickening crack and screamed a ghoulish howl. Allia screwed shut her eyes, imagining blood and shattered bones, but when she opened them, the mortal truth sucked the breath from her spirit. Johan's legs had pierced the pond. In icy agony, he stood wedged, submerged up to his thighs.

Somewhere in the corner of her vision, Allia saw the horse leap to full gallop. She ripped her own skates from her shoes, grabbed the pole, and scaled the tree. She thrust the pole toward Johan's hands and screamed, "Grab on!"

He did—and pulled her down.

The vise of burning cold crushed her in its iron jaws. The jagged edges of the ice ripped the skin across her heart. Somewhere inside oblivion, Johan thrashed and flailed. Allia kicked upward, but woolen skirts ensnared her legs and dragged her down again. Blue stars danced before her pounding eyes. She thought of home, of Mama's tears, of Papa so strong and kind. *I love you*, she wanted to cry out, but she swallowed the wet death instead.

Then a buoyant embrace lifted her into a rush of air. She saw one glimpse of soft brown eyes. She heard one word: *"Live,"* her mother's firm command, before life forever disappeared.

Allia and Johan breathed again while Lady Clara drowned.

MOTHER, Allia prayed as she clawed through liquid darkness at the bottom of the well, *you should have let me die.*

A sacrifice of awesome love had purchased eight years of misery, a legacy of regret. Allia kicked up toward the air, her lighter skirts and longer legs sending her toward a hope they could not reach eight years ago. She found her grip on the ladder's lowest rung. With her first breath, she screamed toward the taunting canopy of sky. It was no use to climb; the ladder's steps were set at wide intervals, and her arms could never bridge the impasse of the broken rung. What did it matter? No one would grieve to see her die. The bloated poison of her rotting corpse would cause more inconvenience than the absence of her soul.

Her fingers burned to loose their grasp.

"Holy Jesus! My lady, hold on."

A rider loomed against the starry sky: the castle watchman on patrol. Allia wept to see him unharness his mount, untie the circle of the reins, and lower one end as far as it would reach—far enough to pass the broken rung. "My lady, you have to climb. Then grab it and tie it around you."

"No. I will only pull you in."

He slipped his own belt through his saddle. "Not unless you pull the horse in, too. Climb, my lady. Please."

She looked up through the tunnel, and moonlight fell upon his eyes. Air caught inside her heaving chest. Allia knew this man. Yesterday, he had offered to make her a whore.

"You! You will pull me out and rape me where I land."

"I swear by God and all the saints, I will not harm you. Now, for Christ's sake, take the reins."

She stared into the night, the shadow of her savior blotting out the stars, and Allia trembled with a cold such as she had never known. Not even in the ice of Demont Pond had she sunk so deep in fear as now, caught between a watery grave and a life more suffocating still. In the darkest hour of morning, she could not read the watchman's face, only a world sketched in charcoal against a canvas washed in clouds.

Behind his head came a flutter of silver-bright wings. "Live," the voice of birdsong cried.

Her heart like Vulcan's hammer beat against her cross-shaped scar as hand over callused, tortured hand, she pulled herself upward toward the dawn. A leaden knot of dread coiled tight within her gut, but the ancient iron held, and hazel-scented light blurred her pain to dreams as she cinched the leather reins tight around her chest. The watchman groaned as he hauled her from the tomb. Allia did not feel her pale skin scrape across the walls. She did not hear the clatter of her sword bouncing with her as she rose, nor taste the smear of blood that dripped from her bruised scalp onto her tongue. She knew only the peace of the enchantment and the hopeless memory that told her it must fail.

Pain and life and wonder all returned as she tumbled forth onto the blessed, solid ground. "My lady," panted the watchman as he freed his belt from the saddle, "what the devil were you doing down that well?"

Her eyes darted through the lightening air, craving confirmation, but no wings, no light—no soft brown eyes—remained.

"My lady?"

"I was saving myself," she sighed as she pulled the sword from its cords at her waist.

The watchman's voice hardened as he drew his own steel. "There will be no murder on my watch, my lady."

"Murder! That is the only word anyone knows about me here. Allia, the little demon girl who lured her mother into the ice. Oh, God! Do you think a moment has ever gone by when I would not have traded my life for hers?"

She wept while the watchman hovered over her, his blade still drawn. "What use do you have for a weapon?" he grumbled when at last her tears had dried.

"I was planning a journey and thought it best not to go tramping through a war-torn country unarmed."

"Do you even know how to use that thing?"

"I had a lesson once." Her fingers gripped the hilt.

The guardsman stood and studied her—dripping, heaving, destitute, with a blade clutched in worn hands. His eyes softened with pity. "Just one?"

"Yes, just one."

"That won't be enough." He raised her to her feet. "Come on."

CHAPTER 12

"*A*nniton," Prince Raphael repeated for what seemed the hundredth time. Tristan and Father Alester looked at each other and kept their silence, waiting for the prince to expound on that thought.

Raphael took a deep breath, but the intoxicating flowers of Princess Briella's solarium did nothing to clear his head. Cultivating exotic blooms had been their mother's passion while she lived, and now her daughter had begun to acquire the talent. Like an indoor Eden, the chamber burst with life: lilies, orchids, roses, and wilder buds the prince could not name, imported from lands far to the east. This room was one of the few places where Raphael had ever seen his sister smile, and it tortured him to oust her from her flowers. But the solarium stood next to the council chamber. He had no choice but to commandeer the blossoms in the interest of the crown.

"Anniton," the prince muttered again, shaking his dark curls. "How will they ford the river?"

"The mill dam is nearly complete," Father Alester answered. "If they know that, they need only cross below."

"And we need only open the floodgates," Tristan added.

"They will not attempt to ford the river unless they are certain of success, floodgates or no," Raphael said. "The Darrivants do not make such mistakes. Are you certain of the information, Father? Have you used this informant before?"

"She is new to me, but she has designs on greater things than a handful of gold. She may be misinformed, but she is not lying."

"We cannot lose Anniton," the prince declared, "even if it costs us Pellain. That is your position, Tristan."

"Yes, Your Highness."

"Chancellor Narius will not agree. You must persuade the lords. Narius will not oppose them if they are united."

"I understand."

Raphael sighed. "All right. Go on." He watched the imposter depart, his heart heavy with the ambivalence the sight of Tristan always provoked. Raphael could not have asked for a better stand-in. With only a week of practice, Tristan now carried himself with a princely air even Lennard would have been hard-pressed to match, yet he did not question the real prince's orders. He improvised, to be sure, sometimes deviating from the scripts that Raphael spent his long, sleepless nights composing, but only in verbiage. In substance, Tristan held fast to the opinions of his liege, no matter how the kingdom's most powerful men might challenge or grumble.

It astonished Raphael to see how effective his own words could be with a man like Tristan to speak them. All his life, he had been used to scoffs and summary dismissals, no matter how long he studied or how well he phrased his judgments. He knew that men like Collin de Tembria could never allow a cripple to best them, even with words, but still it had seemed there must be something feeble in his mind for his thoughts to be so universally ignored. Yet in Tristan's mouth, Raphael's thoughts became power. With Tristan as a shield, Raphael could almost dare to cast himself in the role of a king.

"Are you going to listen in on the fun?" Father Alester moved the pots of white jasmine that blocked two small brass tubes protruding from the wall the solarium shared with the council chamber. Gently, he removed the bulbs of wax that prevented sound from passing through the tubes when he and Raphael were not present to listen.

The chaplain pressed one tube to his ear, and the prince wheeled himself forward to listen through the other. They heard the scrape of fifteen chairs as the royal council—all the lords and barons not commanding troops at the front—rose to greet the man they thought to be their prince.

"Be seated." Tristan's booming voice always carried through the tubes. "You have all received my information that the attack will come to Anniton. I put the question to you: how shall we defend it?"

"We won't, because it's nonsense," Chancellor Narius bellowed toward the great brass horn transmitting sound to the solarium. Father Alester had set the horn into a mural of an army on the march, right into the trumpeter's hands. He then covered it with a thin layer of gauze painted to match the original.

"Your Highness, you do not even know the name of the informant," Narius continued. "Why would they risk fording the river when Pellain is so accessible? It is a feint."

"You may be right, Lord Chancellor, but think of the consequence if you are wrong. If we lose Anniton, we lose our trade. How do you propose we should outfit an army without the ability to import steel?"

Narius scoffed. "Every foundry in the kingdom is stockpiled to the rafters. We should suffer more from the loss of imported cannabis than steel."

"So you propose we sacrifice the port?"

"I propose we listen to the commanders in the field, not some fishwife Your Highness's royal mole pays to tell him tales." The Chancellor-Regent knew well the identity of the "royal mole," and had often voiced his disapproval that a man of the cloth should be engaged in the business of deceit. But he had never ordered him to desist.

"Remind me, Lord Chancellor," Tristan replied, "how many times has the royal mole's information proven wrong?"

"Often enough that your brother is dead."

"Indeed. That was the third time in a decade, I have been made to understand. Are you willing to gamble the port on those odds?"

"I am willing to gamble the port on a lifetime's experience leading cavalry campaigns. For the Darrivants to assault Anniton would be like a bandit attacking a company of soldiers while there was an unarmed merchant meandering down the same road. It is a feint to draw our strength back from Pellain."

"With all due respect to your experience, Lord Chancellor, it was my father who led those campaigns. As I recall, you held the front at Carridgeway while my father risked cutting off his whole division to take the enemy in the rear. You slept soundly at your campfire while my father disguised himself to capture the traitor Lord Barrent in his bed. My father is still the king. Now, tell me, all of you who served with him so faithfully for so long, with this information before him, what would he do?"

In the solarium, Raphael and Alester leaned more closely into their tubes, trying to comprehend the chorus of disagreement that echoed through the room. But they did not have to strain to hear the gravelly voice that quelled all others.

"He would hold them both."

Silence greeted Lord Eric de Camesbry as if sound were his to command. He let it linger, drawing every ear under the spell of his authority. "I was with the king on both of those occasions," he finally went on. "It's true he took the dangerous missions for himself, but he never left any position undefended. Your Highness seems not to realize that without Narius charging from the front, the rear assault at Carridgeway would have been suicide, or that if there had been no one sleeping at the campfires, Lord Barrent would surely have noticed that our men were not where they were supposed to be."

Mutters of assent rumbled around the room.

"We will fortify Pellain because it is necessary and because that is what the enemy expects," Lord Camesbry decreed. "We will keep the floodgates closed, just as if we did not expect an attack, and we will fortify Anniton the way His Majesty would have done."

From the solarium, Raphael listened with dropped jaw as Lord Camesbry outlined a plan almost as ingenious as the device that allowed him to hear it. The old veteran proposed strategies of simple brilliance to employ the townspeople of Anniton in their own defense. No hands were too delicate or unskilled to enlist.

Indeed, to hear Lord Camesbry speak, the kingdom itself was an army waiting for command. With a small deployment of elite forces, he explained with mesmerizing surety how to turn a siege into a rout. At last, the council rang out a unanimous, "Hear, hear!" A humbled Raphael would have added his own voice had he been positioned to join in.

A second scrape of chairs announced the meeting had adjourned, and Raphael turned to Father Alester. "You have put me in your debt as usual, Father. If the information about Anniton proves true, then you have saved the kingdom. Even if it proves false, you have shown us the true character of the men on the council."

Father Alester set his jaw into an unforgiving line. "Lord Camesbry is a man of great vision, but I would still advise you to keep him at arm's length."

Raphael started. "Why?"

"Have you heard about his daughter?"

"Only that he has one."

"Eight years ago, he blamed her for the murder of his first wife. He has kept her enslaved as a cinder maid ever since."

A shudder ran down the prince's spine. "Was the girl ever tried?"

"No. I do not think he could bear either to see her hanged or to see her acquitted. The case should have come before your father, of course, but it all happened around the time your own mother passed away. His Majesty was in no mood to hear such tales of his great friend, or hers. Your mother and Lady Camesbry were thick as thieves."

"But eight years..."

"I brought the information to Chancellor Narius when he first assumed the regency, but that discussion we just heard should have taught you that he will not touch Lord Camesbry."

"And my brother?" The word *enslaved* turned Raphael's vision red. Surely, the Lion could not have borne such an outrage.

Father Alester brushed his thumb across the scarlet petals of a geranium. "There were strategies to plan. Your brother needed Lord Camesbry."

Raphael's dark brows drew taut. "I have always trusted you to speak what must be spoken."

"And I have always tried to teach you to trust no one but God." Father Alester stood and stuffed his fists deep into the pockets of his alb just as the chapel bells chimed three o'clock. "You will excuse me. I must pray the hour."

Father Alester shuffled away toward the chapel. He was not always faithful to the hours of the Divine Office, but since his meeting with the woman in the woods, he had not missed an opportunity to pray. The chapel nearly blinded him at mid-afternoon, its stained-glass saints ablaze with sun. Alester lit a row of candles and fell to his knees, imploring God with all his being that the siege would come to Pellain. If the woman's information proved false, then Alester need never pay her. Better still, he could arrest her and watch and her hang for her atrocities. Alester had sent out a search for the man she named as her price: the hapless jeweler, George Couper. Palace guards had found him in a roadside inn, feverish and bleeding slowly into his pillow. Did he know who had harmed him? Couper nodded yes. Was it a man? No. A woman, then. Did he know her name? Yes. But George Couper could neither write nor read, and his tongue had been neatly sliced out of his head.

CHAPTER 13

The siege of Anniton came on a Tuesday as the first light tinged the city's bustling bay. The Darrivants found the river unguarded and floated a lethal wilderness of catapults and towers across. Inside the silent city walls, marksmen masked by crenellations nocked their potent, feathered shafts. On that fateful Tuesday, every fishwife's breakfast kettle bubbled with boiling oil. Every tyke and urchin collected rocks from the shallows, and every man with a cart hauled them toward the walls. Every horse stood saddled, every maiden bestowed a kiss, every mother placed a helm upon her able-bodied son.

By the afternoon, every troubadour was writing songs.

While the citizens doled out hell, an elite company of cavalry captained by their lord himself, the gouty old codger of Camesbry, emerged from hidden forest wilds to pin the enemy inside the river. At a signal from the trumpeter, the floodgates loosed their fury. Forward, the enemy were slaughtered; falling back, they drowned. Fiery arrows set flame to the siege towers. The city opened its gates to release a second wave of makeshift cavalry who wielded pitchforks, scythes, and fishing spears. They chased the meager Darrivant survivors across highways of their dead, deep into the mountains, where they disappeared at last.

The victorious city sang its own praises long into the night, until every cask of wine and ale ran dry. Lord Eric de Camesbry scrawled messages of triumph from his post at the finest tavern's finest table. He sealed his parchments twice: once with his own coat of arms—a kestrel in flight—and again with the lion the late Prince Lennard had worn on his left hand. "The day is ours," he wrote to his old companion-in-arms, the king, praying the monarch might have one of his "good" moments long enough to comprehend. "Anniton will stand."

ALLIA CLUTCHED tight the blanket that held all her worldly possessions as she waited on the grave's soft grass, anticipating the dawn. The blanket itself was stolen, though it held but little: a table knife, her cloak, a bit of food—and most importantly, the emerald necklace her mother had been wearing on the day she drowned. Everyone believed the jewels lost at the bottom of Demont Pond; only Allia knew that Lady Clara had removed them before she dove in. For eight years, Allia had kept the necklace hidden beneath a loose stone in the hearth. Always, she had known the day would come when she must sell it, the only object in her care worth more than a handful of coppers. Still, it felt like betrayal. Once the last memento of her mother was gone, where could she ever turn for solace?

To the peddler, she answered. To the man whose warmth and love would keep her safe from the demons of memory. The peddler was her future, the necklace merely her past. She pushed away the thoughts that stabbed her conscience—the agony of knowing Lady Clara could never have approved her marriage to a common salesman, much less to a rake who dealt in mysteries. Still, her mother would have wanted more for her than a cold stone hearth and a broom.

"Mama, help me. Please." Allia traced her hand through a clump of fallen petals, the hazel tree's annual carpet of yellow decay. In years past, she had mourned to see the flowers fall, but now she knew not what to feel. The traitorous blooms had sent deceit, but even so, in her hour of need, the fairy had come. The fairy who had first appeared beside this very tree; the fairy who, with her mother's words, had saved her life. The fairy who called itself her godmother.

The sound of galloping hooves pulled Allia from contemplation. She dropped her blanket and drew her sword not a moment too soon, deflecting the blow that sliced at her from above. The rider grunted and came about. This time, she was prepared. As the wood of his practice blade hacked down, the steel of her own pried it from his hands. "Hrmph," her teacher snorted: the closest thing to a compliment Alfred ever paid. "Well, you're quicker than you used to be. Hopefully, quick enough."

Allia's eyes grew moist as he dismounted and handed her the reins. "Alfred, this is your own horse."

"Did you think I would steal one of your father's? Better to lose my horse than my hands."

Allia nodded as her teacher fidgeted with the edge of his mail tunic. Most days, his very presence made her skin creep. His slashing sword often caught a hem and yanked aside some snatch of her kirtle, but his eyes like wildfire devoured the garment whole. Still, there were also moments such as this when compassion like a lance broke through his lecherous armor. For three weeks, the uncouth watchman had risked flogging and dismissal to train Allia to save her own life, building on the slim foundation Prince Lennard had once laid. If indeed she lived long enough to find her peddler, it would only be another mark in the mounting column of debts she owed this man.

"Alfred, it is unlikely, but if ever I do inherit Camesbry…"

"Nay, my lady, I didn't do this for a reward."

"Then why…?"

"Because you're not a murderer."

She met his coarse brown eyes, and honesty stripped away the remnants of her fear. "I will come back." She kissed his cheek and watched his blush rise with the sun.

"Throw in a few more of those, and that'll be reward enough."

She smiled as she slung herself into his saddle. "Thank you, Alfred." Then she galloped away.

Fields of new spring oats pushed their stalks up toward the sun, waving in the breeze one last adieu. Further on, she saw the vegetables, peas and lentils and legumes, their flowers a promise of plenty, should war and weather not intervene. So much of life was promise, so little ever fulfilled. Allia recalled the young girl who had once journeyed down this road. The sun had seemed much brighter then, even in autumn's waning rays, the world a tapestry woven of wonder. As she slowed her horse and watched a starling pluck a beetle from the soil, Allia knew that the young girl had never really changed. Even now, she rode headlong into the snares of hope, knowing that the serpents of her nightmare might well prove her only truth. Even if she found her peddler, his words of love and solace might soon echo with despair. Still, what use was it to breathe at all unless some faint dream breathed, too?

The fields gave way to villages, the villages to more fields, a green and granite patchwork of civilization. The road grew more crowded as the day wore on, a parade of fleeting loathful glares. A woman in a servant's kirtle astride a war horse with a sword slung at her side could hardly pass without soliciting some derisive remark. At a crossroads, a sour-faced woman driving a cart snapped her whip and hissed, "Thief!" as Allia passed.

The zip of leather caught Allia's courser in the flank. The horse reared and bolted with the speed of dead men fleeing hell. The reins slipped through Allia's grasp. She gripped the saddle with her knees, her fingers woven through the mane. Allia had been riding since she was three years old, but since her mother's death, she had only been in the saddle for an errand now and then. It had not been enough. A mile down the road toward Anniton—full south when she meant to go west—the animal ground to a halt, and Allia tumbled to the earth.

"Ho, look, it's raining girls!" Laughter shook the midday air. Allia's head seemed bound to split in two, but still she rose. With tender arms, she drew her sword. Her eyes found two bawdy peasants, drunk half out of their minds, keeping wobbly seats on their mounts and brandishing blood-stained blades. "She's armed! It's a Darrivant! Hyah!" One spurred his horse and thrust a blow down toward her head. Allia parried with the flat of her steel and knocked her attacker from his seat. He sighed, surveyed the sky, and curled up sleeping on the grass.

Allia's courser, sensing battle, pranced up to her side. Before the second peasant—even drunker than the first—could find his wits, she mounted. "Halt, knave! I see the blood on your blades. In the name of the Lord of Camesbry, I will run you both through for murder unless you can explain."

He chuckled as he licked his lips. "It was the Lord of Camesbry who put the blood on these blades. He crushed the Darrivants, and we along his side. He would not deny us the spoils of victory."

She leveled her sword. "He would if it were one of his household you chose to spoil." She could not bring herself to say "daughter." She could not bear to hear the drunken laughter redouble at the word. "Tell me the battle you speak of. Where was it fought?"

"At Anniton, just yesterday. I killed a score of them myself. Now come, be a good wench, and let a soldier have his prize."

"If you are truly a soldier, come take it." She kicked her courser to speed. The peasant swayed as she closed and fell before she could strike. With the pair of conquerors down, she turned to find again the western road.

All afternoon, Allia's aching head pounded against the peasants' news. The Darrivants at Anniton? Her father dashing the advance with a band of rustics under his command? Allia remembered the gallant general of her youth, the father who came home to blaring trumpets after every victorious campaign, who lifted her onto his saddle and tousled her hair as he rode. But that man had long since given way to grief and fat and swollen limbs, his legs too painful now, most days, to lift him onto a horse. She had not seen him wear his armor in half a decade; she had not known he owned a suit that fit him still. Could the drunkards be so daft they had mistaken their own lord? Or had the phoenix of her childhood risen from its ashes to fly again?

The chill of evening gave no answer as it drew its dusky drapes. Allia rounded a corner and gasped, looking down for the second time in all her life at the palace rich with charm, the quartz like star-struck diamond gleaming in the sun's red rays. The stately queen who bade her welcome had been gone these many years; the jaunty armored prince would clutch her hand in his no more. But the beauty still screamed of life and joy, and someone she remembered still remained. The little mangled boy with raven locks and wheel-borne chair, the boy she had only glimpsed, whom his brother had burned to acknowledge; Allia had kept the secret and never spoken of him to a soul. Had it been that little boy who sent her father off to war? If Prince Raphael could command the lords in wartime from a chair, then he was twice the lion his brother could ever have been.

"God be with you, sweet prince," she murmured as she nudged her snorting courser down the slope: the damsel knight of the cripple's kingdom blessing sunsets from on high.

She entered the capitol through the massive wooden gates just before the city watchmen hauled them closed. The oaken panels boomed as they swung shut between the marble pillars topped by Lady Justice. Candles flickered in windows packed together wall-to-wall. The jagged line of roofs seemed to form another ridge within the endless chain of mountains. In truth, the city was as flat as any in Armany, held fast within its borders not only by its walls but by the limits of the cylindrical valley where it lay. It was a city that could not sprawl, so instead, it climbed. Story upon story had been stacked as recklessly as children's blocks, but where engineering lacked, enthusiasm overflowed. The higher any building rose, the more it sagged under the weight of balconies, fountains, flower boxes, and ornate iron rails. The sheer faith of it brought a smile despite Allia's fatigue. If these metropolitan dreamers toppled to their doom, at least they would topple in style.

She found a convent with a travelers' lodge far more secure than any inn, where she threw her exhausted bones down upon the communal straw. She prayed for sleep to claim her, but the hospitable nuns had scented the straw with hazel. The fairy, like a magnet, drew her mind. Its first appearance had shocked her so, she had not pondered much the reason why it came. It had wanted to save the kingdom, she thought, and the prince's lowly bride had merely been part of a future now rendered obsolete. But the prince was as dead as ever, and still the fairy had returned. At the moment when she should have drowned, it had come—and now the father of her youth was riding once again. Had he, too, been touched by magic? The fairy had never spoken its name. Might that be because it was called Clara?

Allia tossed on the prickly straw and pulled her thin cloak tight. As taunting as the idea was, her mother had worn no silver wings, nor sung in languages untold. Her mother had cast no enchanted light, nor shed enchanted tears. Most of all, Lady Clara would never have "caught" Prince Lennard's arrow; she would have thrown herself in front of it and let the point pierce her own breast. Only as she lay sprawled, gargling life's last breath, would she have ordered him to live.

Too long had her daughter ignored that command. Let the fairy play what part it would. The tale, for good or ill, was Allia's now to tell.

She rose at dawn and found a merchant to trade her emeralds for gold. She clothed herself in decent garments, bought a scabbard for her sword, and dug her heels into her horse's sides until the mountain pass to Demont loomed at last into her view. Yet even with her mind set firmly on its course, her backbone straight upon her huffy steed, one question lingered still. One question pricked at her resolve, mocking the breath of her faint dream.

On that frozen, vanished day, if Mama had not come, would the watching peddler have jumped in?

CHAPTER 14

A cacophony of victory took the capitol by storm as the heroes of Anniton marched in ceremony through the grateful streets. Trumpets and church bells vied to drown the laughter of a thousand throats while a dozen drums kept time. The noise of raucous joy tolled straight through the palace walls into Tristan's chamber.

The false prince sat on a green damask settee that had once been the queen's, poring over the welcome speech Prince Raphael had composed. Like everything that came from Raphael's pen, it sang of a mind keenly whetted against history and philosophy, science and all things sacred. And, like everything that came from Raphael's pen, it was naïve. "The blood that hallows our riven land and heals the wounds of trespass..." Tristan could never have composed any words so lovely, but that did not change the fact that they were nonsense. Tristan Ferryman had killed more than one marauder on the banks of the Levold River. The wounds of trespass were never hallowed by blood; they were only made deeper.

He rolled up the parchment and laid it in his desk alongside all the others. He took one long moment to stare at nothing—or rather, to stare into his memory at the dewy onyx eyes he had not ceased to see since the funeral. Then he sighed and scaled the stairs to the battlements to watch the conquerors approach.

Princess Briella and the mad king already stood stationed on the parapet above the palace portcullis. Unfortunately, the king did not seem so very mad today. As soon as Tristan's broad shoulders peeked above the landing, the king scowled, nudged his daughter, and pointed.

Briella loosed a heavy sigh. "Father, 'tis Raphael. Your son." She shot Tristan a look of venom strong enough to poison any soul.

He gripped the railing as he took his place beside her. "Thank you, Your Highness."

She turned away to stare at the crowd. "The war is over. If my brother does not end this stupidity, I will end it for him."

Tristan laid his hand over hers. "Your Highness, when the truth is known, no one will be happier than I."

Slowly, so that the onlooking crowd would not notice, Briella extracted her hand. She pulled herself to every inch of her eight-year-old height and seethed, "If you ever touch me again, I will give you to the headsman."

Tristan's naked cheeks stung as if they had been slapped.

The trumpets blared a fanfare while Lord Camesbry and his men made their way to the palace gates at last. "Hail, Your Majesty!" cried the hero as the throngs of citizens parted to let him pass. "Victory is ours! Long live the king!"

"Long live the king!" echoed back from the crowds, and Tristan cleared his throat to begin the speech he had been ordered to recite.

Beside him, the king leaned out from the battlements, his white hair whipping like a flag. "Hail, Lord Camesbry!" he called with a strength his throat had not mustered in many long years. He waved a salute with his crown, so that it seemed King Simon the Unvanquished had returned from behind the veil of his fog. Briella lifted her eyes with a joy that melted Tristan's heart, the first sign he had ever glimpsed that goodness might still blossom in that tender soul.

King Simon cried with all his might, "The traitor Lord Barrent is dead!"

Briella's shoulders drooped as if the spring that watered her spirit had suddenly run dry. Tristan ached to squeeze her shoulder, to let her weep into his arms, but he heeded her words and stayed his hand.

Lord Camesbry bowed atop his steed. "Yes, Your Majesty, Lord Barrent is still dead, and a thousand Darrivants besides."

Simon the Unvanquished seem to freeze just where he stood, his crown still doffed, his hair still fluttering. Tristan stepped forward to fill the void. "Welcome, Lord Camesbry. The crown acknowledges its debt to you and your good men." He took a breath filled with Prince Raphael's florid words and let it out again. Let the prince rage if it suited him; Tristan could not bear to preach callow righteousness here, with the broken heart of childhood looking on. He forced his lips to smile and called out, "You have all supplied the celebration. Let us now supply the feast!"

Shouts rang out, a fanfare blared, and the victorious army swaggered its way inside the palace walls. Swarms of grooms descended toward the horses while serving maids escorted men to the banquet. There would be at least half an hour of bustle and fuss before the first course was served. With a bow to the princess, Tristan set off toward Prince Raphael's chamber.

Prince Raphael sat poring over some mammoth Latin tome, his room forever dim despite the dozen candles that lined his desk. "Why did you not come up, Your Highness?" Tristan asked.

"Because I do not much care for my new valet. It is not pleasant, being carried by a man who wears a perpetual smirk, though at least he never stumbles. How was my speech received?"

"I did not give it. Your father chose to speak instead."

Prince Raphael turned pale. "And...?"

"And it could have been worse. Lord Camesbry smoothed it over." Tristan clasped his hands behind his back. "Your Highness, the war is won."

Raphael turned away to stare at his appalling tapestry. "One battle does not win a war. This is only a reprieve."

"Nevertheless... Your Highness, it is not possible for me to resume my studies with Father Alester. Even if he agreed to continue, I could not live in the palace anymore under my own name."

The prince hung his head. "I know."

"In which case... Your Highness, perhaps I am too bold, but I should like to be a baron when this ends." The girl with the eyes like a new spring fawn's—the noble girl, for only the nobility had been present at Prince Lennard's funeral—could not wed a mere ferryman's son.

A long moment passed in silence with the prince's face still turned. When he spoke, the words seemed old, as if they had grown mossy in his mind. "I should rather make you king."

Tristan's knees grew weak. "Your Highness..."

"But if I tried to have you crowned, my sister would blurt the truth to anyone who would listen. I will have to settle for making you her regent."

"Your Highness...?"

"Ten years. We will crown her on her eighteenth birthday. And then 'Prince Raphael' can return to the monastery where he was raised, to give himself to the Church as his parents intended."

Tristan's brow broke into a cold sweat. A few months ago, he might have welcomed a monastic life, but now it felt like a death sentence. The maiden's eyes wept inside his mind.

"Your Highness, are you abdicating?"

"There is no reason to make the announcement yet, but yes. I have no choice. I cannot crown you; neither can I let myself be crowned. Briella is the only answer, but she is eight years old. Give me ten years, Tristan, I beg you."

"Your Highness..."

"I know your heart is set on receiving Holy Orders. But you came here first to serve the crown." Raphael wheeled himself forward. "Chancellor Narius was never more than a puppet for Lennard, and the entire kingdom knows it. I *must* reign until Briella comes of age. But I cannot do it without you."

Bands of iron wrapped themselves around Tristan's lungs, his breath coming in shallow, uncertain gasps. How could he say no? He,

Tristan Ferryman, could help save the kingdom, the monarchy, the entire Arman way of life, from turmoil and destruction. All it would cost him was ten years of loyal service, all the while living in a palace, as a prince. Yet the maiden's eyes bored resolutely into his weary, lonesome soul.

"Your Highness, I do not wish to be a monk."

"Well, we have ten years to find a way around that problem." Raphael took Tristan's hand and shook it firmly. "Your service to the crown will never be properly recorded, but you will forever have my gratitude. Someday, perhaps, even my sister's gratitude. You are a good man, Tristan." Raphael let go of his hand. "That is perhaps the last time anyone will ever call you by that name. Go down to the feast, Your Royal Highness." In his chair, Prince Raphael bowed.

"As you say... Your Lordship." Tristan took half a step backward, wondering if the prince would be offended by the address that accorded with his alias as Baron Immerville. But Prince Raphael gave a thin smile.

"Good evening, then. Please ask the servers to send me a tray."

"Will you not come down?"

"No. So many soldiers will only remind me of the one who is not there." Prince Raphael turned back toward his book, and Tristan saw him wipe a tear. Every fiber of Tristan's being wanted to protest, to scream that he could not bear the intrigue another minute, that another life awaited him and His Highness had no right to steal it. But Tristan watched a wet splotch stain the Latin page, and he went quietly away.

Ten years. Would the maiden be willing to wait for him that long? Would he be able to resist her for an entire decade?

Reeling on legs that felt made of sand, Tristan stumbled toward the hall where the banquet had been laid. The wide, airy chamber was built of the same sparkling white quartz as the palace's exterior, with ceilings several stories high and a pair of staircases like wings that lifted awestruck eyes toward an upper gallery. The gallery's polished railings had been woven with green and silver ribbons, the ancestral colors of the House of Camesbry. Both Lord Camesbry's kestrel and the king's crest bearing the scales of justice hung down past the gallery floor, as majestic and unyielding as the heavens themselves.

Down the eastern staircase Tristan staggered, seeing no one but the maiden he longed to call his own. He jostled past the jolly knights, barely managing a nod to acknowledge Lord Camesbry among them. He listed into his own chair at the king's side and found a wine glass already filled. He downed it at one gulp: choice wine from Morisse, the sweetest and strongest in the kingdom. Quickly, he called for another. As soon as it arrived, he downed that, too.

Chancellor Narius raised a bushy gray eyebrow. "Thirsty this evening, Your Highness?"

"Aye," Tristan answered, and called for more.

The room was a carnival: laughing soldiers, flowing wine, musicians who plucked and scraped and blew. A trio of dancers, twirling sylphs with tambourines, snaked and twined their way through the raucous mob of men. Servers laid out platters heaped with roasts, soups, pies, fowl, and potatoes. Scents of rosemary and garlic set Tristan's mouth to watering despite the blur of duty, desire, and wine that dammed his brain. He tucked in to the feast, chewing the prince's words with every mouthful. *"You can go off and be ordained, just as you have always wanted..."*

How deeply Tristan had wanted Holy Orders surprised no one more than himself. Since childhood, he had held priests in great respect, men whom he admired for their education and service, but he had never thought of becoming one. He did not love the ferryman's life, where so much depended on his body and so little on his mind; but he was good at it, and his father's ferry was the only way to cross the Levold River for twenty miles in either direction. The income was not grand, but it was stable. Tristan had been content to ply his oar and thank God for his blessings.

Then the pirates had come. The Levold made a rich hunting ground for thieves, its mighty currents clogged with merchants bringing their wares to export in Anniton, many leagues downstream. Tristan's father had cut back the hours of the ferry's operation, careful to have it safely docked before sundown. The family lived only a stone's throw from the dock and kept a fire burning nightly, but still the bandits had come. Tristan and his father had guarded the family at sword-point while they watched a dozen scoundrels armed with blades and torches untie their livelihood and row it off into the night.

The king's forces had responded to the residents' outcries, setting patrols along both shores. In their midst came an astonishing figure, a lanky, gray-haired man who dressed as an officer but seemed to have no company to command. He spent his days questioning the residents, learning anything and everything he could about the pirates' movements, what they looked like, was their speech accented, what did they wear? He insisted on meeting every witness separately, refusing to allow husbands and wives, or fathers and sons, to be questioned together. Tristan's family each took their turns, lined up like sheep outside the man's makeshift headquarters in the Oar and Lantern Inn.

But Tristan would not answer any questions. "I do not trust you," he told the man plainly.

"I am here on behalf of the king."

"So you say, but you are not an officer."

"My insignia is plain enough." He gestured to the scales embroidered on his surcoat. "Do you not think the other officers would object, if I had no right to wear it?"

Tristan narrowed his eyes. "You have a secretary at your command, but no soldiers. You take no part in the patrols. The sword at your waist is good steel, but there is no wear on the hilt. You are not an officer. You only ask questions, and I do not answer the questions of men I do not trust."

Thus had Tristan unmasked Father Alester and earned his way into a life beyond his imagination. He had personally accompanied the king's men when they ferreted out the pirates' den, and—when the killing was done—reclaimed his father's vessel. He rowed it home, but that was the last time Tristan Ferryman had ever lifted an oar.

At first, his acolyte's robes had been only a disguise. Few people knew about the palace chaplain's covert intrigues; only the king, Prince Raphael, Chancellor Narius, and a few of the most prominent lords knew the source of the palace's intelligence. Alester could not openly train an apprentice spy. But as the months wore on, Tristan had found the disguise more appealing than the trade he had pledged to learn. The ritual of prayers and Masses, hours spent in patient teaching or behind a curtain, hearing confessions, cleansing souls... Tristan understood the necessity of intrigue, but it could not compare to the necessity of God. He had begged Father Alester to accept him as a true acolyte, and Father Alester had warily agreed.

Two years had passed, and prayer had become Tristan's only respite from deceit. Even within the palace, Father Alester required that his apprentice maintain numerous facades, now acting as a footman, now a soldier, now a kitchen hand, until even his own proper acolyte's robes began to feel foreign. Gladly would Tristan have traded his palatial apartment for a hermit's cave, given every penny of his wages to escape the net of lies that snared him to the throne. Even before Prince Raphael cast him in the role of a prince, Tristan had considered appealing to the Cardinal for permission to continue his priestly studies in quieter circumstances. But Tristan was not certain the Cardinal knew about Father Alester's peripheral activities, and he did not wish to undo his master's schemes. He only wanted to spend his life in God's service—until he glimpsed the maiden with the onyx eyes.

Tristan surveyed the banquet hall, desperately willing his maiden to appear, but there were no women at the feast except the servers, the dancers, the princess, and her governess. Tristan downed his fourth cup of wine and signaled for more. Part of him wanted to hate the girl who had stolen his heart and his dreams, but he knew he never could. She had infected him, but he did not want to be cured. Better to die in her arms than live without their embrace. Better to be spurned by those blessed lips than to be loved by all others.

Yet such thoughts were insanity. He had never even met the girl, never heard her angelic voice caress his ears, never spoken her honeyed name. Why should he sacrifice his priesthood for her? Worse, how could he even consider endangering the future of the kingdom for a pair of pretty eyes? Yet it did not feel like insanity to ask that, in exchange for his service, he be given a minor title, a small plot of land where he could while away a quiet life at a fireside ringed by children, counseled and consoled by the woman he loved.

The only question was, did she love him?

The room began to pitch at unnatural angles as Tristan finished his fifth glass of wine, but he was not the only one who had swigged more than his share. The drunken laughter in the hall quite drowned the music now. The soldiers had begun to place wagers on who could throw a knife into the mouth of the suckling pig, or who could coax the dancers into parting with their clothes. Vaguely, Tristan noticed Father Alester speaking in whispers with Lord Camesbry, his black alb standing out like a sore thumb in this room of dusty tunics and dented armor. Father Alester's brow creased more deeply into the stormy scowl that had worn out its welcome there of late. But just as Tristan tried to summon him to ask what had passed, a knight pounced upon a table with his glass held high, and Father Alester slipped away.

"Your Majesty, a toast!" cried the brazen man. "To the citizens of Anniton! And to the strapping little maid who gave me this." With practiced showmanship, he drew from a pouch a piece of crumpled, bright blue cloth. With one flick of the wrist, he unfurled the scarf to its full length. A masterfully embroidered unicorn brought a chorus of bawdy laughter bubbling from every ale-plied throat. "Gentlemen, only a virgin can catch a unicorn, but victory can catch the virgin!"

Tristan tried to add his guffaw to all the rest, but it only made thoughts of his own unreachable maiden stab more keenly at his heart. If only he could speak to her, learn her thoughts, discover her wishes. If only he could explain...

The knight was hailed and toasted, carried on his fellows' shoulders, and granted a dance among the girls with tambourines. Soon other men began to cut in, the rhythmic patterns ever shifting as the girls sought to give each would-be partner equal share. The stamping, sweaty crowd cavorted like a jolly dragon, each of its three bedazzled heads capering to take the lead. One sylph bent her elbows as if to nock a bow, and the arrow of an idea struck Tristan square between the eyes. A reckless, wine-filled courage sent him leaping up to his chair as he tapped his crystal goblet with a spoon. *I am a prince,* he thought. *Who will stop me?*

Silence fell, and in the sudden sobriety of quiet, Tristan's stomach seemed to fall out through his shoes. The upturned faces all around him shone with expectation—even the mild, stupefied face of the king and the embattled eyes of Princess Briella. *She will try to have me hanged for this,* but it would be worth it, to meet the girl who was his destiny.

"Gentlemen, our friend has hit the nail and struck it home!" Tristan waved grandly toward the knight who now wore his unicorn like a cape, billowing behind his shoulders. "If victory can catch a maid, why do we bachelors squander it here amongst ourselves? I declare that, two weeks hence, we shall have a royal ball. A night of dance and revelry, and, by my own decree, every maiden in the kingdom must find the means to attend. If it is unicorns we're after, we shall drive in the whole herd!"

"Huzzah!" and "Hip, hooray!" deafened Tristan's ears as whacks of congratulation rained upon his back. The king stood up and kissed the false son upon his brow. The band struck up a lively jig, and soon the ribboned dragon was swaying to the tune. Tristan heard nothing but the buzz of panic in his ears. The part of his reason wine had not washed saw the princess's fury and knew her brother's would burn just as black. But the maiden's eyes inside him smiled. He would find her, and that was all that mattered.

CHAPTER 15

The puffing courser slowed its pace as the wild landscape rose. Allia had forgotten the breathlessness of Demont's steep approach, where air itself evaporated and her hands could touch the clouds. Lady Clara's ancestral home sat nestled somewhere between earth and sky, a provincial stronghold fortified not by walls and soldiers, but by the mountainous grace of God's own creation. Two outposts and their gates guarded the ascent so that the white limestone keep could sprawl across the heights, unencumbered by the walls of war. Allia trembled as she drew to the first outpost, pondering what name she ought to tell the guard.

"What business here, ma'amselle?" A round-faced soldier stepped out to greet her.

"A love affair," she answered, attempting a coy smile. Perhaps if this man knew the peddler, she need not face the scene of her demise. "A man proposed me marriage but forgot to leave his name. He says he came from Demont, so here I am."

"I'll take the credit if you'll have me," laughed the guard, "and you can call me any name you please."

"That's Sam." An older, graver figure stepped out of the gatehouse. "But you'd do better to marry a turnip than the likes of him. What manner of man was your'n? Seems a bleeding shame he wouldn've told you his name."

"Yes," Allia answered, "so thought I. He says he is the steward's son."

Sam shook with laughter. "Hate to disappoint you, miss, but the steward's son is six years old. You've a while yet to wait if you're keen to marry him."

Allia's heart sank to her heels. Had the peddler merely been a rogue keen to abduct a nobleman's daughter? Yet he had known her history. He had watched her mother drown. It could not all have been a lie.

She met the eyes of the older guard, whose brow was furrowed in a frown. "The current steward, aye," he said, "but there was old Charles Regis before him. He's got four sons, all grown."

"Might one of them be a peddler with a chestnut beard? Brown eyes, perhaps of your height, Sam, somewhere around thirty years old?"

Sudden storm clouds blew across the older soldier's eyes. Even Sam's bright smile grew overcast with alarm. "You'll want none of that one, Miss," the old one fairly growled. "'Tis no wonder he dared not speak his name."

"Why?" Beads of icy sweat condensed on her face.

"He's got a price on his head," Sam answered. "Ma'amselle, you would be better off with me, and Garred is not wrong about the turnip."

"What did he do?"

"'Twas witchcraft," Garred declared. "But 'tis worth more than one of your pretty smiles to make me say more'n that."

Allia shivered, remembering the warmth of the peddler's arms around her waist, the way the whisper of his breath raised the hairs inside her ear. *I have many secrets, Lady Allia. Some of them so beautiful, they rival even you.* Every year, her father heard cases of witchcraft, peasants blaming the death of a chicken or a child on the talismans of some jealous neighbor. Lord Camesbry often fined the complainants for wasting his time. But some cases were harder to dismiss: the woman who ate naught but worms while she was pregnant and gave birth to a hermaphrodite child, or the boy who was rendered completely mute after his twin brother drowned. Magic—at least in the form of fairies—was very real, and Allia did not know the limits of its power. A man who could surrender his sword and still wander a war-torn kingdom without fear might have darker defenses at his command.

"How long has he been an outlaw?" Allia found her voice to ask the question most easily answered.

"A year or so," Sam said. "Long enough, 'tis a constant thorn in Lady Demont's side."

A year, Lady Vivienne had been colluding with a wanted man. Allia's stepmother always knew things she had no right to know, and a price on an outlaw's head was meant to be made public. The peddler could not have kept such a secret from her for so long. Why had Lady Camesbry never turned him over to justice, nor sought another buyer for her wares?

"Where did you meet him, Miss?" the old guard asked. "Lady Demont may want to send out a patrol."

"In Anniton," she said, not knowing why she lied. "Some weeks ago. He was selling potions to make the women look fairer."

"And he had the gall to approach *you?*" Sam's swagger now returned. "For that alone, ma'amselle, you ought to discount him as a fool."

"Will you really not tell me what he has done? Nor at least his name?"

Sam opened his mouth, but Garred held up a hand. "Nay, Miss, we've had our say." His eyes narrowed as her courser stamped; it seemed the guard was beginning to wonder how an unescorted girl in a plain linen dress came to acquire such a horse. "And now, Miss, I think it's time you told *your* name."

"Allia." A new voice spoke before she could. All eyes turned toward the gatehouse door, where a third soldier had emerged. His green-eyed, stubbled face wore the expression of a man who has just seen a ghost. "Her name is Allia de Camesbry. Kneel, you knaves. You are in the presence of a lady."

The guards cast each other wary looks while the soldier followed his own instruction. Allia's breath caught in her chest while her gaze seared to the young man's figure as he knelt and bowed his head. Even at the ends of the earth, she would have known that impish frame. Eight years had made him handsome, broad and stalwart at his post, but time could not erase the stain of guilt upon his brow. Allia's lip curled as she hissed his name.

"Johan Rabigny."

THE SHEET of frozen water seemed to stretch for miles. Dripping, numb, so cold her body burned, Allia pried her deadened hand from the boy's convulsing fingers and crawled toward land until her limbs would go no more. She collapsed and watched the bubbles rise that marked her mother's doom. She had no energy to comprehend a tragedy or give thanks for her own breath. Her fingers closed on a strand of glittering green rocks, jewels of envy biting frigid flesh as she watched Johan's mother arrive. The governess flew to cradle her son without a glance at the other anguished child.

It was a stranger who lifted Allia's chattering body from the ice, who stripped her frozen clothing and submerged her in a hot bath. A stranger massaged her bluish limbs until the color at last returned. A stranger applied a foul-smelling paste, bandaged the cut across her heart, wrapped her in furs and blankets, and left her by the fire to cry. Allia never could recall the face that sorrow had obscured, the woman who performed the last kind gestures she would know for eight long years. But she never forgot the caterwaul that echoed through the keep as the governess coddled her frostbitten son.

Alone, Allia watched the flames of her hearth fire dance until it seemed that Mama's eyes stared out, weeping dirty embers. All the while, infection oozed into her wound. Somewhere in the haze of dusk, the nightmare of reality trembled into fiery dream. Days smoldered on like eons, nights like lightning flash, fever molding time like white-hot iron. Allia thrashed on her mattress while doctors dripped her blood into thirsty bowls. Spoons of putrid tonic pried her cracking lips apart; fetid compresses weighed against her head. She had died; her broken heart had shunned the beating of its shame, and now she had descended to the furthest pit of hell. "Forgive me," she moaned, again and again, "Forgive me. I'm sorry. Come back!"

Then the jury in her sickroom on the morning she awoke. Dawn had never seemed so dim, waking such fatigue. With skin as sallow as her world, Allia raised her eyes to see the faces at her side. Papa was here—sweet Papa! She lifted limp arms for his embrace. He came toward her, his scent of horse and leather bringing balm, but as he sat down on her bed, his arms stayed stiffly at his sides. "Allia," he spoke, "did you do this, child? Was it you?"

She should have asked. She should have seen the way the governess leaned to catch her words, a wolf salivating for its kill. She should have looked up at the household guard with their jaws set in lines of grim reproach, so subtly different from pure grief. But a half-dead child with her heart sunk in the tomb rarely stops to look at life before she leaps into its arms.

"Yes, Papa. Mama came in after me."

"I told you!" shrieked the governess. "You thought it would be a good game, to pretend to drown! Brought those poles out there to chip the ice so you could make a hole before you screamed. It only serves you right that you fell through!"

"Enough!" Lord Camesbry cried, rising as a dragon rudely wakened from its cave. "One more word, and I shall see you flogged."

Allia quivered, begging God to let her wake, to let this be one more nightmare inside her fevered hell. But Papa met her eyes, and that anger was no dream.

"Papa, no..."

He struck her cheek with strong, good hands that should have wiped away her tears. "Papa," he gasped as if the word had slapped him, too. "You are no daughter to me! You killed..." He stumbled to his knees and bawled into his hands. "Away with you all!" He waved toward the room. "Get out! And take her, too."

Arms as strong as prison bars took her from the bed, but the face of her sobbing Papa chilled her more than fear. She slumped into the guard's cold grasp, a log to be tossed onto death's fire.

Only then did she see Johan hidden in his mother's skirts.

His eyes met hers, the green inside them blistered by his tears, his face as white as she had seen it last, out on the ice. He skulked behind the fabric hanging from his mother's waist, folding himself into the safety that could not mask his disgrace. Allia pleaded, "Tell them, Johan. Please."

Johan turned his face away and uttered not a word.

HE BOWED BEFORE HER NOW, in the dust outside Demont's gates, his eyes again cast down. Allia tasted anger fermenting on her tongue. The courser whinnied a brassy cry as she unsheathed her steel. "Stand up," she commanded the kneeling soldier who had once been her friend. "Draw your blade and face me, coward, if you dare."

CHAPTER 16

*P*rince Raphael watched Tristan retreat from his chamber with his broad back slumped by the demand that he spend ten years mired in deception. The moment the door swung closed, Raphael wept into his hands. All the tears he had refused himself these last many weeks gushed forth, tears of rage and loathing and relief. It was done. The weight of the kingdom was settled firmly on Tristan's capable shoulders, and he, the crown prince, could hide forever in his chamber, sheltered by his alias, companioned by his scrolls. Cowardice had won.

Raphael despised himself for commandeering Tristan's future to saddle him with the burden of a kingdom, but it was not only Tristan's life he had sacrificed. His own might as well be done. For ten years, he would do his best to keep the kingdom running and to tame his sister. Somehow, he would have to coax from her stony heart the warmth and wisdom of the mother she had never known. He would also need to provide her with a husband worthy to sire a king. When that was done—or when the attempt had failed—he might as well join Tristan in the monastery. There would be nothing left for him here.

Still, it was better this way. The battle at Anniton would not be the last, but the tide of the war had turned. It was past time to return to the business of governing the kingdom. Between the war and the king's madness, a great many everyday affairs had been overlooked in recent years. There were squabbles to be settled, accounts to be set in order, criminals to be caught. By using Tristan as his proxy, Raphael had not only given himself an effective mouthpiece; he had also given himself the ability to be in two places at once. Tristan could hold court while he himself pored over tax ledgers and answered correspondence. Tristan could play host to foreign dignitaries while he drew up trade agreements in his study. These were the parts of kingship Raphael had studied, the parts he had always been prepared to execute in Lennard's name. "Tend to the dull bits for me, Brother, and I will spare you the trouble of being kind to all these sycophants at court." Raphael would play the role he had always been meant to play, only now there would be another man in Lennard's shoes—a man just as tall, just as handsome, just as awe-inspiring.

A man who could never be Lennard.

And so, Prince Raphael wept.

A knock sounded at his chamber door: the tray he had asked for, no doubt, but he was not hungry anymore. "Leave it outside," he called.

A key clicked in the lock, and Father Alester stepped in, carrying a platter heaped with every kind of savory morsel. "You need to eat," he said, before he noticed his student's wet eyes. "Has something happened?"

Raphael hastened to dry his face on his sleeves. "Nothing new. Grief never wanes as quickly as we would wish." He took a sip of wine from the glass on the tray. "I have ordered Tristan to continue in his role."

Father Alester furrowed his balding brow. "Until...?"

"I told you I only hoped to keep the throne safe for my sister. I will act as her regent through Tristan, and when she is eighteen, she will be crowned."

"So that is why my acolyte is downstairs, drinking himself half blind." The chaplain shook his head. "Perhaps it's best. If you have so little respect for your brother's memory, then I do not wish to call you my king."

Raphael gripped both arms of his chair, but took the barb without reply.

Alester ate a sausage from the platter. "Your Lordship, it is my duty to inform you that, in the very midst of victory, four Arman soldiers still deserted from our ranks. I had the news from Sir Berridge, and Lord Camesbry confirmed it."

Prince Raphael's face grew pale. "The devil take them."

"Yes, the devil has been reaping quite a harvest of late. However, my new informant tells me she knows why."

Through narrowed eyes, Raphael watched Father Alester take another bite of sausage. "She offered to tell you why our soldiers are deserting, and you have not already made the bargain? How deeply did you dent the treasury to purchase the news of Anniton?"

"I admit, by more than I was authorized to spend." Even now, George Couper sat jailed above the palace chapel, a breathing memento of how the chaplain had sunk himself into a cesspool where he fished for lies.

"How costly will the cause of these desertions be?"

Father Alester closed his eyes. "She demands Prince Raphael's hand." Alester waited while his student's jaw dropped with understanding. "I do not think it is for herself. Perhaps a daughter or a niece. She said it was 'the maid he spied at the funeral.' Do you recall our beloved prince behaving oddly at all since that day?"

"No... or, rather..." *Your Highness, I should like to be a baron when this ends... Your Highness, I do not wish to be a monk...* "My God. He's in love."

"He wears it on his doublet like a crest. It would not matter, of course, except that apparently he has fallen prey to this Gorgon informant."

"We cannot make this girl queen when the intended groom will never be king."

"And yet, we cannot continue losing soldiers to a vanquished foe."

Duty drove the argument from Father Alester's lips: duty, the harsh and beautiful master who kept the hounds of chaos chained. Twelve years had passed since the day one of Lord Barrent's men confessed to a plot of treason under sacramental seal and Alester persuaded him as penance to bring his claims before the king. Slowly, the chaplain had spun his web: serving maids, sellswords, peddlers, seneschals, whores —all could spill their gossip for an absolution. Or a fee. Every day, the faithful shepherd cringed as he cultivated deception among his sheep, but his perfidy had helped to apprehend murderers, smoke out bandits, and nip rebellion in the bud. Was it not a shepherd's duty to protect his flock from wolves?

Silence hung between two men whose lives were shells of righteousness that hid the rotted flesh of fraud.

"Father, can this woman really save our army?"

"I do not know. But we will never find out unless we try."

An angry knocking shuddered against the chamber door. "Not now," called the prince, but the door flung wide. Princess Briella stood framed in the entryway, her black eyes lit by rage. Her governess panted up behind her.

"What is it, Sister? Your timing is poor."

"And your fake prince is worse. He just told everyone we're going to have a ball for every maiden in the kingdom."

Prince Raphael sat stunned, blinking as if his eyes could correct his hearing. "He... what?"

"He jumped up on a table and said there would be a ball two weeks from today, and every maiden in the kingdom has to come. If you do not give him to the headsman, I will."

Raphael looked up at the governess, who nodded affirmation.

"Briella." He pushed his chair forward and took her trembling hand. "We do not behead people for wanting to throw balls."

She ripped her hand from his. "He thinks he can give orders like a real prince! If you don't stop him, then... I'll tell the Chancellor! I'll get Father to say that *I* will be queen..."

"Peace, Sister." Raphael reached up to wipe her angry tears, but she batted away his hands and ran to wrap herself inside the comfort of her governess's skirts.

"Briella," her brother whispered, "you are not the only one who watches Tristan in those clothes and feels iron pincers squeezing at your heart."

She bared her teeth in a sneer. "He fits them better than you would."

"Indeed." Raphael put out his hands, but she would not take them. He sighed. "Thank you for telling me what happened. I will take care of it. And now, I think it is past time you were in bed."

She was silent a moment, seeming to ponder her retort. At last, she dropped a curtsey slight enough to be a slight. "Good night, cripple." She stormed out with steps like a clatter of hail. The governess curtsied and followed.

Prince Raphael wilted in his chair. "There is never a moment's peace."

Father Alester stepped out from the shadow of St. Lucy's tapestry, where he had stood since the princess arrived. He slipped out the door and then returned a few moments later. "Your sister's report is true, Your Highness. They are toasting him and singing bawdy songs about unicorns."

"Unicorns? Merciful God. Tell the steward never to give him more than one glass of wine! How do we even begin to undo this, with so many witnesses…?"

"The steward is not likely to accept my order—or yours—above the wishes of the crown prince."

Raphael clenched his fists. He took his own wine glass from the tray and hurled it against the wall. The crystal tinkled, bell-like, as it shattered.

"Are you quite finished now, Your Highness?"

Raphael slumped against the back of his chair. "All right. You have an idea. Let's hear it."

Father Alester sat down on the prince's bed. "It will be costly. A ball for every maiden in the kingdom… we may be eating boiled potatoes the rest of the year. But I do believe it will work."

Raphael wiped his sweaty, scraggled curls out of his eyes. "Speak plainly, Father. I am too weary for your mysteries."

"We cannot undo this without considerable embarrassment to the crown, so why not go forward? Tristan may be drunk, but I would still wager his real motive is to find this woman who enchanted him, which is exactly what our informant desires. We will tell her it is a ruse to be sure that she and the prince are both speaking about the same girl. We get her to come here, into the palace, so we can receive the information as soon as the girl's identity is confirmed. We let Tristan and his lady have their dance, the woman tells us about the deserters... and then we throw her into the dungeon, where she belongs."

Raphael drummed his fingers on the arm of his chair. "It is a very elaborate ruse. You do not think she will suspect?"

Alester shrugged. "I'll tell her the truth—that the prince concocted the idea while he was drunk, and now we must make the best of it."

"I do not like it."

"Would you prefer to call the council together tomorrow, explain to them why a ferryman's son played host to the heroes of Anniton, and tell them that you, the true prince, are now revoking his order for the ball? I shall, of course, be there to support you if that is your choice."

Raphael gritted his teeth. "What happens to Tristan? I cannot allow such insubordination."

"Your Highness, when a puppet snaps from its strings because the puppeteer stretched them too tightly, which of them is to blame?"

Raphael looked around for something else to throw, but did not find it.

"The safest thing to do with Tristan, assuming his girl is not in league with this informant, is to let them depart the palace and be wed quietly. You can, of course, still abdicate to the girl who wants to behead a man for being reckless in his cups."

"That is enough for one night, Father. You may go."

Alester stood and put his hand on Raphael's shoulder. "I do not mean to taunt you, Your Highness. But we have a duty." He was silent, but Raphael gave no reply. "There is one more thing."

The prince let out an exasperated, "Yes?"

"This girl of Tristan's: if she was at the funeral, then she is a noble-woman. It is likely our informant may also be highborn. Are you prepared to jail the wife or sister of one of your lords?"

Raphael raised his head, his whole face twisted with rage. "Our soldiers are dying, good men are deserting their posts, and this Gorgon barters with their lives like so many coppers? I am prepared to see her burn in hell."

Father Alester bowed his head. "So be it, then." He patted his protégé's shoulder and went out into the night. The raucous merriment of the feast still echoed through the halls, but he passed it by without a glance and walked toward the chapel. Alester had not told Raphael there was another step to securing the bargain. It was better to leave the prince's young soul unstained. Would that he could do himself the same favor.

He unlocked the chapel, wishing that there were another route to his own chamber. The windows' stained glass saints stood gray and lifeless in their frames, with neither sun nor candle to color their virtue. Behind the altar, the crucifix loomed, the monstrous, broken Christ with arms outstretched to embrace the shadows. Alester wanted to fall at its feet and weep for forgiveness, but surely a God who had died to save his beloved children from death—surely, that God would understand. God could not love the swathes of blood the Darrivants were carving through the kingdom. God must know the enemy was armed with powers of darkness, strange magic that stole good men's free will and seeped like nightfall around dead men's wounds. God must understand that unless Alester learned how to combat such demonic weapons, the Darrivants would march across the capitol and behead the boy whom he had raised from the confinement of his bed, the boy who shrank from power yet still glowed with its light. If the woman in the woods had demanded Alester's own life, he would have paid it to save his beloved child, the prince who had no one but his chaplain to love him. But Alester's own life was not the price she had demanded.

"Bring him into paradise, Lord," he prayed, "and judge my motives, not my crimes."

With hollow heart, he went to sprinkle hemlock on George Couper's morning porridge.

118

CHAPTER 17

"*D*raw, blackguard!" Allia flung herself down from her horse. Johan still bowed to her, never flinching. "Stand and face me, gutless worm!" Blood pounded against her skull as she raised her sword.

"I would give you that satisfaction if I could, my lady, but I am a squire, and in a few months' time, I shall be a knight. I cannot lift a sword against a woman and still be worthy of my vows."

"*Worthy?*" She spat in his face. "You will never be worthy of anything but a grave." With all her strength, she sliced the blade toward his shoulders, but Johan rolled aside.

His fellow guards unsheathed their steel. "We are not knights, my lady," the older one growled. "There's no code of chivalry to stop us. Lay the weapon down."

"Stay out of this, Garred," Johan barked as at last he stood. He turned toward Allia, hands raised in surrender. "My lady..."

"'My lady?' Do you think ladies often travel alone, desperate to marry nameless peddlers? I have not been 'my lady' since the day you let your mother peg me with your crime."

His hand went to the hilt of his sword. "I should have spoken," he admitted, though his voice sizzled with anger, "but it ill becomes you to speak discourtesies of the dead."

"Is that hellcat virago dead? Good riddance. Or did you expect me to pity you for losing your mother when it is your fault I lost mine?"

She took a vicious swing at Johan's head, but this time he drew his blade. The deadly clash of parried steel echoed across the mountains. Stroke after berserk stroke, Allia hacked while Johan danced defense. His height and skills proved more than her match, but still she advanced, her burning arms and heaving lungs no deterrent to her rage. She found a footing where the land sloped up, pounding at him from the high ground until Johan cried, "For God's sake, Allia, I do not want to hurt you!"

She met his eye. With blade pointed down, she raised the hilt above her head and plunged her sword toward his heart.

He lurched out of its path just as a gust of wind tangled Allia's skirts. She stumbled on the rocks. The point of her sword wedged tight into the ground, and momentum dragged her hands down across the razored edge. Blood and screams poured forth while Johan's arms encircled her, lifting her just as once, so long ago, her mother's arms had lifted them both.

"Shh," he whispered, tearing away his tunic to bind her bleeding hands. "Hold still. Let me staunch the wounds."

She watched the swooning darkness circle and knew no cloth in all the world could be equal to that task.

~

"Johan, you cannot keep her here. She is Lady Demont's great-niece."

"A great-niece she has never met. If the two of you keep your traps shut, no one need know."

"And you suppose Sir Lawron will grant you knighthood when he thinks you are keeping a doxy?"

"I shall tell Sir Lawron the truth. He knows whom I intend to serve."

Allia's eyes fluttered open inside the watchtower barracks, a circular stone room littered with smelly, ancient straw. Sunlight peeked uncertainly through slits meant for arrows. Yet from somewhere, the soldiers had found a feather mattress on which to lay their... prisoner? Was that what she now was? Allia reached one bandaged hand toward her side, but the sword was nowhere to be found. Just as well; the lacerated flesh on her palm could not have raised it in salute, much less in battle. She groaned aloud as misery coursed in eddies through her arms, throbbing all the way into the scar across her heart.

"My lady." Johan came and knelt by her side, offering a cup. "Wine and juniper seeds for the pain."

She met his eyes that once had winked with merriment, but then had turned away to deny her in their fear. She could hardly read them now, round and cold like mossy stones, so hard yet still so green with life. He had removed his ruined tunic, which he had torn to bind her hands. He now wore one of mail, the nip of icy metal leaving rings of red against his bare, white flesh. Was it propriety or penance that attired him so? Allia could not know as Johan held the sweet, warm liquid to her lips.

He set the cup aside and took her hand to examine it. "As I supposed, it has bled through. Sam, go fetch clean linen."

"Should I bring the doctor?"

Johan sniffed the wound. "No. There is no infection. We will not alert anyone to her presence unless it is necessary."

"Aye, so the linen is to bind my own broken heart, if they ask." Sam smirked and descended a ladder poking up through a hole in the floor. With a start, Allia realized it was the only point of access to the room. Johan must have carried her up that way. The thought of her unconscious body slung across his back made her shoulders shake.

"Are you chilled?" Johan laid a hand to her forehead, and Allia recoiled. With a blush, he took it away. "A thousand apologies, my lady. I only wanted to be sure you have no fever."

"Johan, calling me 'my lady' will not make it true."

"And denying it will not make it false." He held her gaze, his jaw clenched tight, though Allia could not say whether he was angry or fighting tears.

"There's a rider approaching," Garred announced from his place by the window. "I'll go down."

Johan's comrade descended the ladder, leaving him alone with Allia. She looked upon the craven scoundrel who had stolen her every happy dream. "Do you mean to have me hanged for trying to kill you?"

"My lady, you are the one who gave me my life. It would be poor chivalry to repay you by taking yours."

"Do not speak to me of chivalry. If ever you had any honor, you gave it away long ago."

"Aye, but every sin can be forgiven when the penance has been done."

She looked at his bowed head, the shirt of icy mail, and the scabbard that hung empty at his side. "If it is atonement you seek, then, for the sake of the life my mother gave you, tell me—do you know the peddler, whom your comrades say is wanted for witchcraft?"

Johan raised a glare full of loathing. "My lady, I do not know how you came to want to marry that man, but I will tell you the truth so that you put such a notion out of your head. His name is Solomon Regis. He was one of our troop here in Demont's guards, the best swordsman in the province. That was while I was still a child, around the time you were here. One day, for no reason anyone could fathom, he resigned his commission and began peddling potions to make women beautiful. Made a nice living at it, too, from all accounts. Then, about a year ago, he came back with a new elixir. A love potion, and he told people to pour a few drops into the wine of the one they wanted. The problem was, it worked."

Allia's mind flew backward to the crate of small black vials, so much more carefully packed, so much more dearly paid for than the rest. Lady Vivienne had been brewing love. Allia could not help but cringe.

"You can imagine the results," Johan went on. "A man has a

hankering for someone else's wife, he gives her a drop of elixir. Some toothless servant girl sets her cap for a handsome knight, she gives him a drop of elixir. There were duels and murders and we've had more than one year's fair share of bastard births. The worst of it was, the people who drank it couldn't speak for a week or more, and their fingers and toes turned black. Lady Demont had to confiscate every drop of the stuff and threaten death to anyone who used it. If you fancy yourself in love with Solomon, you're like as not under the same spell."

"I drank nothing while he was with me." Yet it had felt very much like enchantment, the way his voice tingled across her ears.

"My lady, tell me you do not still wish to marry him."

"You don't understand. He is the only person who is kind to me. My father keeps me as a cinder maid, and when I tried to leave, to let myself marry the man my parents chose, he rejected me because my hands are so callused, he did not believe I could be a noblewoman." She looked down at her bloodstained bandages. "I fear they shall look a good deal worse after this."

"My lady, I am to blame for all this sorrow. Since the day I first entered Sir Lawron's service and saw that I could indeed become a knight, I have had no other object than to seek you out and serve the girl who saved me."

"I did not save you. My mother did."

"But you climbed up that tree and let me pull you down."

Allia shivered. "Yes."

"All these years, I have believed I would become just one more polished sword in your cortege. Now I see that instead, I shall have to become your champion. My lady, give me two months more to complete my training, and then I swear, I shall spend the rest of my days righting all my wrongs."

"A knight in the service of a cinder maid. Johan, you're as much a fool today as you were when we first met."

"Says the woman in love with an outlaw who just sliced open her own hands."

She met his impish eyes and felt an old, familiar smile pulling against pain. "And what bread do you propose we eat, and what roof to put above our heads?"

"You are the heir of Camesbry, are you not? I shall convince Lady Demont to keep you here until your father passes, if I must."

Allia shook her head. "I am sure my father has long since arranged for my stepmother to inherit."

"How could he? It is yours by law, as long as you don't go off and marry that dastard peddler."

"What do you mean?"

"Allia, do you really not know? When you marry, you become your husband's ward, but until then, your father must provide for you. Since you have no brothers, that means you must be his heir."

With eyes like harvest moons, she breathed, "How can you be certain?"

"Because that is how Lady Demont came to inherit here. She is your grandfather's sister. I suppose, when he died, Demont should have been left to you, but Lady Helene put forth the right of being her own father's heir because she had never married, and the king accepted it. Allia, here I thought you loved this awful Solomon enough to sacrifice your inheritance, but you did not even know! Praise God you did not find him!" Johan laughed so that the rings of his chain mail tinkled with his mirth.

Allia sat on her mattress, insights rolling out like carpets before her. She saw now why Lady Vivienne had been so eager to see her married; eager enough to choose a husband who might even have been kind. She saw the reason for such brutality as she had endured, crushing her underfoot with labor and disdain, ensuring that the servants and the soldiers could never find cause to love her. It had all been designed to one purpose: to keep Allia from coming to rule. As her stomach turned with new hatred, it jolted, too, with the nauseous thought that keeping her inheritance meant keeping her maidenhood, as well. She pictured Prince Lennard's vacant stare and told herself it was better now not to love at all; but the peddler's warm hands still seemed to brush against her eager skin.

"Johan, who is the heir of Demont now?"

"Your third cousin Olivier may try to make some claim, but under the law... it must be you."

"Of course." This, then, was the reason she had been destined to become a princess. Camesbry and Demont did not share a border, but the only land between them was the capitol and the farmlands that supported it: lands ruled solely by the king. Prince Lennard would have allowed Allia to inherit despite her marriage and thereby consolidated royal power into a nearly-impregnable center that included both the kingdom's richest port and its most defensible stronghold. Eventually, he would have given the lordships to his sons, an even greater fortification of kingly authority. Perhaps he would have loved Allia, too; but perhaps the taint of politics could not leave even fairy tales unstained.

"My lady," Johan interrupted the train of her thoughts, "will you accept my humble fealty as your sworn defender?"

Allia's lips froze in place, but the creak of footsteps on the ladder saved her from an answer. Garred's unsmiling face rose into their view.

"What news?" Johan asked.

"A messenger from the palace." The awkward twist of the old guard's lips left no doubt that was not the whole tale.

Allia demanded, "Have the Darrivants attacked again? Was it about my father?"

"No, Lady Allia, but 'tis a message that pertains to you. 'Twould seem Prince Raphael is throwing a ball, and every maiden in the kingdom is ordered to attend."

Icy, phantom fingers traced a path down Allia's spine.

Johan brought his hands together in a triumphant clap. "You see, my lady, God is good! You can show the prince how badly your father has treated you and ask him to affirm your rights!"

She felt her heart dripping slowly toward her heels. Johan prattled on about doors flung open, but Allia's eyes fluttered in search of the fairy.

"Johan, stop. Believe me when I tell you, this ball is nothing more than a den of intrigue. I will not go."

Garred cleared his throat. "Begging pardon, Lady Allia, but the word was not 'invited.' It was 'ordered.'"

"And do you really think a kingdom besieged by foreign invaders has the resources to compile a census of maidens so as to enforce that order?"

"No," Johan answered, "but I suspect a census of noble maidens already exists. Your absence will not go unnoticed."

"What of it? Will they truly hunt me down to make me dance with a prince who has no legs?"

Johan and Garred exchanged a look of black confusion. "My lady," Johan whispered, "what do you mean, no legs?"

"I mean, he was born without the use of his legs. He gets about in a chair fixed with wheels. Surely now that he is ruling, the rumor must have spread?"

"Where did you get this information?" Garred grumbled.

"From his brother."

The two guards met each other's eyes, each frown mirroring the other. "My lady," Johan murmured, "we were part of the company that escorted Lady Demont to Prince Lennard's funeral. We saw Prince Raphael with our own eyes. He stood taller and stronger than either of us."

Allia narrowed her gaze in turn. "You are certain?"

"The Cardinal introduced him to the whole assembly: His Royal Highness, Raphael Ignatius Bartholomew d'Armany."

"Then he is cured." It seemed the folk of Faerie had been busy plying their trade in this realm. She knew she ought to be happy for the little, broken boy. She would have been happy, if only the news had not been accompanied by the order to attend his ball. Human beings were not interchangeable; legs or no legs, exchanging princes could not make her dreams come true. Perhaps the fairies had written the tale to unite Camesbry and Demont under the crown, but for Allia, only the love story mattered.

"I am glad the prince has found his legs, but I will not go to that ball. Whatever sorcery might be afoot, I will not be its pawn."

CHAPTER 18

*L*ady Vivienne sat at her work table, toiling over parchment instead of potions. For weeks, she had practiced to replicate her stepdaughter's awkward hand, the signature of a girl who had written nothing else since she was eleven. Solomon had been clever to insert that little phrase, "Proxy for Lady Vivienne de Camesbry," on the bill of sale, but if he had known enough to write it, he must also have known Vivienne would forge another copy. He was taunting her, but let him have his game. They would see who was still laughing when the dust of war finally settled.

The forgery gave Vivienne the opportunity to correct another oversight, as well: the true bill accounted for all of her wares, licit and illicit both. It was simpler to make a new one that mentioned only the black vials. With a flourish, she drew her quill through the final stroke of Allia's name and left the ink to dry while she began her toilette.

Lord Camesbry had sent word to expect him home this evening, and his wife had decided to greet him in a gown of lace and seed pearls that fell perilously from her shoulders, revealing a décolletage smoothed by her own concoctions. The subtle sensuality of that bare skin might be the only thing standing between her and the kind of beating her husband often served his daughter when he was displeased. Vivienne had known her share of thrashings long ago, from other hands. She planned to let such bygones remain bygones no matter where the cinder maid had fled.

A blare of trumpets drifted through the window, and Lilliane's sunny smile peeked around her mother's door. "Mother, make haste! My stepfather is nearly arrived."

"I am ready." She stood and tossed the original bill of sale onto the fire.

Lilliane pursed her ruby lips. "Whose happiness are you burning this time?" Twice in the last several weeks, Lilliane had attempted to write to Prince Raphael to inform him of her identity. Twice, her mother had intercepted the messages and promptly watched them burn.

"Your stepsister's, if you must know. Lilliane, roll up that parchment on the table, please, and put it away."

Lilliane took up the forgery, and a smile spread across her lips. "You have outdone yourself, Mother."

"Thank you. Now, go on, roll it up and lock it away."

Vivienne had always been careful how much knowledge of her business she entrusted to her daughter. On the one hand, it was necessary to teach the girl how to duel against the vicious world and win; on the other, Lilliane was neither the brightest nor the most discreet of persons. Lilliane knew that Vivienne had continued to brew her love potion after it was outlawed, selling it illegally for a king's ransom. Lilliane accepted without question the utility of gold. She remembered the months of near-starvation that had followed her father's death. But treason was another matter. Vivienne was not certain, but she thought Lilliane might have imbibed enough Arman allegiance from her stepfather to balk at providing aid to foreign invaders.

"It will serve Cinder Allia right, to be blamed for those potions," crowed Lilliane as she put the parchment away. "Only a fool would sign a bill of sale for wares that were not her own. Though, of course, it will be better for all of us if the matter is never discovered."

Vivienne only smiled in reply while another blare of trumpets announced Lord Camesbry's arrival. Vivienne and Lilliane made their way to the entrance hall, where all the household had turned out to cheer their triumphant lord's return; all the household but one.

"Mother, you did well to choose those pearls. You look as fetching as a bride."

"That is the point—to remind him that's what I am."

Lilliane gave a snort. "Why, do you suppose the king's madness is catching?"

"There is a difference between a man who sees his *wife* and a man who sees his *bride*. One is a polished army marching off to glory; the other is a battlefield sprayed with blood. You had best learn the difference."

"Perhaps you had best learn not to think about marriage as a war." Lilliane curled one dark ringlet around her finger. "I am glad my husband is not a soldier. I shall be able to keep him with me and not dream about swords and arrows."

"Lilliane, you are counting chickens that have not hatched."

Lilliane arched her swan-like neck. "He is throwing the ball just to find me, you know. Why else would he order every maiden in the kingdom to attend?"

Vivienne sighed. Her daughter was right, of course. The king's agent had confirmed as much. Still, Vivienne did not care for the arrangement, to be required to turn over her secrets within the palace walls. She preferred to conduct business in the open, with escape routes and even witnesses. She had only agreed because she held a card the agent did not expect: her name.

"You shall certainly have your chance to find out," she replied to Lilliane as the stout oak doors of Camesbry Castle groaned open.

Lord Camesbry entered without his walking stick to support him, a few of his excess pounds sloughed away by his return to the field. He wore his kestrel crest over his breastplate and pauldrons, a sight that teased his lady's mind, imposing the image of the warrior she had married over the frame of a dumpy old man.

Vivienne dropped a deep obeisance. "Welcome home, my lord.

Word of your triumph precedes you, yet the sight of you safely returned gives me more joy than any victory."

Eric de Camesbry's blue eyes seemed to swallow her. Without a word, he took her in his arms and pressed his lips against hers. The troop behind him whistled while Vivienne fought off a wave of giddy yearning. Not that there was reason to fight—she had every intention of providing a true hero's welcome—but first she must find the words to break the news.

The lord raised his wife to her feet and traced his thumb across her lips. "You are younger than when I left you. I do not care what you say about herbs and minerals. There is magic in those vials you brew."

"And in your kiss, my lord." She dropped dewy eyelids toward the tiles. "Greet the servants, and let us retire."

"Yes."

He clasped his wife's hand tight and then turned to Lilliane. "Welcome home, my lord," she chirped, and her stepfather pecked her cheeks. She bore it with her usual stilted grace. The two had long ago settled into a cautious cordiality.

Lord Camesbry turned to the assembled servants, allowing the women to kiss his hands, soaking up their admiration. At last he reached the end of the receiving line and grumbled, "Where is Cinder Allia?"

Lady Vivienne stood on tiptoe to whisper in his ear. "You do remember, you sent me home to have her married?"

He smiled. "Of course. Come, let the servants tend to the soldiers."

Vivienne trembled as she followed him upstairs. She had no one but herself to blame for her stepdaughter's disappearance. She had anticipated Allia's flight, but she had told herself the girl would not leave because she had nowhere to go. Even now, she could not imagine what plans Allia had laid. Allia was neither inclined to envision growing rich with the gold between her legs nor naïve enough to think a broom and scrub brush could ever make her fortune. No local boys had gone missing of late, so it was unlikely Allia had run off to be married. Vivienne was missing something. It was not a feeling she relished, though she had to credit Allia with a hand well played. She hoped the girl had found whatever she set out to find, as long as it was not the truth.

At the top of the stairs, Lord Camesbry turned right, pulling Vivienne toward her boudoir. He preferred to take his pleasure there, rather than in his own chamber. He said the four-post mahogany bed was more comfortable than his own bare mattress, but the truth was that when Clara had been mistress here, she had almost always slept beside him in his room. Vivienne might have envied the rapture Lady Clara must have found in his arms had she not lived through the loss of a communion just as strong.

Her husband closed the chamber door and pressed his body against hers. "Vivienne," he whispered, rough hands squeezing at her breasts through their veil of lace and pearls.

"My lord, there is something I must tell you."

"After," he answered, his lips suckling at her ear.

"It's Cinder Allia, my lord. The jeweler would not have her."

He stopped, but did not push himself away. Vivienne detested the tremor that ran down her spine as her husband's hands tightened around her. "Then where is my daughter?"

"She is… gone, my lord. She stole a horse and rode away before anyone else was awake."

He drew backward at last, cursing under his breath. "How long ago?"

"Nine days. I sent three men to search. She was seen riding toward the capitol, but if she is still there, they have not been able to discover her."

"Did she steal anything?"

"Only the horse and an old wool blanket."

He kicked the bedframe so that the solid mahogany splintered. "Damn that bloody jeweler! Why would he not have her?"

"When he saw her hands, he declared you were trying to deceive him into marrying a servant."

Lord Camesbry kicked the bed again, this time sending the whole structure tumbling to the floor. "The little pig is not even fit to marry a commoner!"

"Indeed. But no commoner is fit to levy such charges against his lord."

He turned with danger in his eyes, though Vivienne saw him wipe away a tear. "Summon him. We shall see if he is man enough to make such claims in open court."

"I should like to very much, my lord, but I had word two days ago that he was found dead at his own door." The king's agent had returned with not the head but the entire body. Vivienne had left it at Couper's doorstep. Let his orphaned brats deal with the burial.

"Dead?" The word seemed to pull the air from the room. "Aye, 'tis always death that mocks our justice."

"I would say justice merely arrived before you could, my lord. The word is that he was poisoned."

Lord Camesbry sank into a chair. "A coward's weapon." He sighed and pulled the bell to summon the servants. After a moment, the ladies' maid appeared.

"You rang, my lady?"

"No, 'twas I," Lord Camesbry grumbled. "Fetch my captain. It seems I cannot leave Camesbry for even a month without its falling to ruin."

"Yes, my lord." The maid curtsied and went out. Vivienne crept behind her husband, gently lifting off his pauldrons to rub his massive shoulders. She had made little headway against the tension when his captain of the guards came in.

"You sent for me, my lord?"

"Yes. I have had word there was a murder in the village, a man named George Couper. Send Sir Bicken to investigate. Tell him also to deliver the man's children to any relatives they may have, and if they have none, bring them here and let the governess tend to them."

"I can go myself, my lord."

"No." He stood and put a hand on the man's shoulder. "My daughter is missing, Robert. Bring as many men as you need. Chase her to the ends of the earth, if you must."

"And when I find her?"

"If she is living, bring her home. If she is not..." Vivienne watched

132

her husband's fist clench as if around a sword. "Then leave her body on unhallowed ground where the crows can peck her flesh."

The captain turned pale, but bowed in silence and went out. Vivienne, too, hastened toward the door. Couper was not the first man she had sent to face his God, but no tally of deaths would ever steel her against the glimpse of her own she had seen under an angry soldier's fists. "If you have lost the inclination, my lord, I shall leave you. You need only send for me if you desire."

Lord Camesbry grunted in reply. Vivienne skulked away, her body drenched with cold sweat and relief.

CHAPTER 19

"*H*old still, my lady. This may sting." Allia sucked a breath through her teeth as Sam pulled the wrapping from her wound, tearing the linen away from the glue of coagulated blood. He clucked his tongue, sniffed, and then applied a salve of herbs. Allia hated to admit it, but she preferred when Johan tended her wounds. Sam had all the finesse of a drunken ogre. But Johan was accompanying his master, Sir Lawron, on an errand today, so Sam would have to do.

"It should be closing faster than this," he said. "If it's not better by tomorrow, I'm bringing the doctor, and I don't care if you and Johan both run me through with your swords. These need to be stitched."

"Thank you, Sam," she managed to squeak through knives of renewed pain. He was right. A week should have been plenty of time for a scab to form, yet every time they changed the dressing, the wounds bled anew. Stitches were effective, as Allia had witnessed when surgeons tended her father's soldiers, but even those stout-hearted men had squealed like stuck pigs when the needle entered their flesh.

"Don't worry," Sam said, reading her fears. "Garred's wife brews the strongest rotgut in Armany. You won't feel anything but the headache the next morning."

"That is, if it does not actually rot my gut. I have no stomach for strong drink."

"All the better. Drunkards are so used to it, they still feel the pain."

She gave a wan smile, grateful for Sam's unfailing cheer. It would have been a dull confinement indeed with only fervid Johan and dour Garred for company. "Sam, have you any family? I never hear you speak of them."

"Not much to say. Parents are long gone, no brothers and sisters, no woman gullible enough to have me."

"Have you actually asked anyone?"

"Asked you, didn't I?" He tied off the end of her bandage and grinned. "After you've had a few swigs of rotgut, maybe I'll try my luck again."

"So this is the kind of courtesy my guards show my great-niece."

Allia and Sam both leaped to their feet as a tuft of silver hair rose above the ladder, followed by a mulish face. Lady Demont wore a strand of round obsidian beads, the only accent that offset her dress of plain gray linen, yet the upright carriage of her spine marked her as a woman accustomed to being obeyed. Her aging body clambered into the barracks without a hint of toil, followed by two men with swords.

"My lady," Sam bowed low, "I cry your forgiveness for my jest. Permit me to introduce Lady Allia de Camesbry."

"Your jests will be your undoing, Sam, but lucky for you, I have bigger concerns." She strode toward Allia, who had fallen into a deep curtsey. "Lady Allia at last. I expected you would come one of these days, though not that you would tarry in the guard post for a week with such rapscallions. What has happened to your hands?"

"An injury of my own making, Great-Aunt. It seems I am not as skilled a swordswoman as I would like to be."

"And why did the heiress of Camesbry have call to use a sword within my borders?"

"There was a debt I wanted to repay," Allia mumbled toward the carpet of straw. "But I failed, and I am glad of it."

"Hmm." Sharp eyes like polished sapphires surveyed Allia's every feature. "Was that debt the only reason you came to Demont?"

"No. I came in search of someone dear to me, but I have found out he is not here."

"And this is all you came for? You had heard no rumors that I was ill, perhaps?"

"No, my lady. You certainly do not look ill, though if you require care, I shall be glad to give it, to the extent my hands allow."

Lady Demont laughed. "Her tongue is honeyed like her mother's, but poisoned like her stepmother's, I would guess. Lady Allia, if you came here seeking an inheritance, I will offer nothing less than your just due. When last you left this province, charges had been leveled against you, yet no trial was ever held."

Allia glanced toward the two swordsmen and felt her skin grow suddenly cold. "A trial long past its time, my lady. If you want to know the truth about my mother's death, you need only ask for testimony from Johan Rabigny."

"It's true," Sam butted in. "Johan told me. Lady Allia bears no blame."

"I heard the testimony of his mother ere she passed. This is not the tale she told."

"Respectfully, Great-Aunt, that is because Madam Rabigny was the foulest liar I ever encountered. No doubt she feared what might befall her son, were the truth to be known."

"So she did," came a voice from below. "Although she came to believe her own story, after a while." A somber Johan rose into the chamber. He placed himself firmly between Lady Demont and the accused. "My lady, my mother lost four babes in their cradles. I think she would have thrown Our Lord Himself into a pit of hungry lions on that day if it saved her only living son. Still, that cannot pardon her lies, nor the coward who did not refute them."

Lady Demont scowled. "What lies might those be, Mr. Rabigny?"

"It was I who suggested to Lady Allia that we go skating on the pond that day. I jumped down from a tree and first broke through the ice. Lady Allia fell in trying to save me."

Lady Demont's whole body stiffened. "Why have you never spoken of this?"

"Because I always hoped the matter could be resolved without the need to defame my mother. It pains me to speak ill of a woman whose only malice was born in loving me too well. But when Sir Lawron informed me that you intended to try Lady Allia, I rode against his orders with all the speed my horse could muster. I have forfeited my knighthood to be here, if indeed I have not forfeited my life."

"Orders?" Lady Demont narrowed her eyes. "Mr. Rabigny, it was your master who informed me Lady Allia was here. He insisted upon her trial. Why should he...?"

Johan sighed. "My lady, I confessed these crimes to Sir Lawron five years ago, when he first took me to squire. It seems he has grown too fond of me to wish to see me hanged."

"So you have another patron conspiring to save your head. Can you convince me it is a worthy motive?"

"I will lay no claim to such false charity, my lady. I may never become a knight, but I can live like one and own the truth." He sank to one knee. "The fault of Lady Camesbry's death is mine, and now humbly I await your sentence."

Lady Demont pondered the man in silence and then turned to her great-niece. "Is this the debt you sought to settle with your sword?"

"It is. But despite my fury, he has shown me only kindness. My lady, we have both paid for our childish lark in spades, and it does my mother no justice to steal away a life she died to save."

Another moment passed while Lady Demont's shrewd blue eyes considered both the ashen-faced woman and the kneeling man. At last she took a step toward Allia. "It does my heart good to extend you my apologies, Allia. All these years, I have rued the thought of putting Clara's child to the sword."

Allia dipped a mute curtsey as Lady Demont turned and said, "Sam, give me your sword."

White as ice, Sam laid the hilt in Lady Demont's iron grasp. Allia sank against the wall as her great-aunt raised the blade above Johan's bowed head. Johan never flinched.

Gently, Lady Demont lowered the sword against his shoulder. "As for you, Johan Rabigny, while I rule in Demont, neither life nor knighthood can be forfeited by an act of chivalry. What title would you have?"

Johan raised his eyes, tears glistening. "Sir Winters," he answered, "because it was in the ice that this knight was born."

"Then in the name of God, St. Michael, and St. George, I dub thee Sir Johan Winters, forever sworn to their service. Rise." He stood. Lady Demont kissed his cheeks, but Johan had eyes only for Allia. He unsheathed his own steel and laid it bare at her feet.

"My lady, will you accept my humble fealty as your sworn defender?"

Allia steadied herself against the stone and whispered, "Yes."

"Well, then, Allia," said her great-aunt, "I leave you in good care. I have stood in this rank tower long enough—and so, I daresay, have you. If you can contrive to climb down with those gashes on your hands, I hope you will join me for dinner. It seems I will have my work cut out, teaching a girl from Camesbry to become the next Lady Demont."

CHAPTER 20

*P*rince Raphael awoke to a clatter and cursing. He opened one eye, wishing it did not see quite so much sunlight pouring through the window so that he might find an excuse to return to sleep. He listened to whoever was making a ruckus in the hallway, but he did not wonder what the commotion might be. The entire palace was one loud tableau of chaos as the staff prepared it for the ball, scrubbing, dusting, cooking, and receiving shipments of supplies at all hours of the night and day. Raphael groaned as he came to terms with the morning and pulled the bell to summon his new valet.

Since Tristan could no longer be seen to carry a minor nobleman about the palace, Raphael had replaced him with a gruff, red-bearded carter who possessed no obvious virtues except the strength to haul a full-grown man about at will. He arrived still smelling of last night's ale.

"You rang, Your Lordship?"

"Yes. Help me dress and bring me to the cemetery."

"Aye. Right cheerful place to spend a morning."

Raphael did not dignify that with a reply. He only hoped that among the dead, he could escape the clamor of this insidious ball.

Duly, the valet stuffed his master's body into breeches, picked him up, and headed for the stairs. The marble tiles of the hallway glistened, cleaner than they had been on the day they were first laid. Paintings and tapestries glowed, every speck of dust removed by an army of maids with brushes.

The valet stopped at the top of the staircase, where two of the countless maids sat with buckets, scouring away. "Well, Your Lordship, if I slip on that wet, we'll both be in trouble. Looks like you're staying upstairs."

Raphael cursed under his breath. "Fine. Just go put me in my chair."

The valet retraced his steps. "Damned fool idea, a ball for every maiden in the kingdom. I'll wager only the ugly ones even make it in."

"The ugly ones are citizens as much as the rest." Raphael had, at least, invented a better pretense for this madness than Tristan's "herd of unicorns." It was to be The People's Victory Ball, a celebration of the heroes from Anniton and a reminder to all of Armany that its subjects were also citizens, the lifeblood of their country. "Charles, you're dismissed," he said once he was settled in his chair. "If I must be confined to this floor, I can get about well enough on my own."

"As you say, Your Lordship." The man never bothered to bow before he took his leave.

With a sigh, Raphael returned to his room to claim a certain scroll and then wheeled himself toward Tristan's chamber. He had been dreading this errand, and therefore he had intended to put it off until the evening, but now it seemed he might as well go and have it done.

Tristan had been surly and out of sorts since the night he decreed the ball, especially after he was informed of the subplot Father Alester had scripted to smoke out the informant at the dance. Raphael could not bring himself to pity the hapless lover who spent his days writhing in uncertainty, but neither could he ignore his stand-in's sufferings. He had to bring Tristan back to hand, or else they would both be useless.

Tristan was still dressing when he answered Raphael's knock. He let him in and bolted the door behind.

"What have you come to demand of me today, Your Highness?" Tristan said as he slid his arms roughly into his doublet. "Shall I cut off my legs so they can be sewn in place of yours?"

Raphael bit his tongue against a sharp reply. "I have come to say that you may have the maiden."

"'Have' her? What does that mean?"

"I mean that while you serve as my surrogate, she may live here, in the palace—discreetly, of course. We will make her lady-in-waiting to my sister."

Tristan scowled. "The fact that I have resigned my desire to be a priest does not mean I have resigned my desire to be a Christian."

"Wed her, then. Only it must not be made public. We cannot have the kingdom celebrating the birth of a prince who is no such thing."

"No, only subject to the reign of one." Tristan finished his buttons and sat down on his settee. "What would you do if I left today? If I simply got on a horse and rode away?"

Raphael stiffened. It was the question that plagued him every hour of every day, the thought that kept him sleepless every night as he lay on his bed in St. Lucy's shadow. "Will you?"

Tristan stared at him for a long moment before he sighed. "Not today."

"But after you have found her?"

"I do not know. I do not even know if she loves me, or why she is mixed up with Father Alester's horrible informant."

"Or whether she would be willing to marry a ferryman."

Tristan winced.

Raphael took the scroll from his pocket, sealed in wax with the royal crest. "The deed to your lands, Baron Carnish."

Tristan started. "Baron *Carnish?*"

"Yes. I am giving you your home. The village itself and all the farmland on that side of the river for a radius of ten leagues. You will be vassal to Lord Falm." Raphael nodded toward the parchment. "It is signed by Simon the Unvanquished, witnessed by Chancellor Peter Narius and His Lordship, Timothy d'Immerville."

Tristan reached out toward the scroll, but stopped before he took it. "Which means…"

"Which means, if it is ever revealed that Timothy d'Immerville does not exist, that document will be rendered invalid."

"How did you get the chancellor to agree?"

"I told him of the service you had extended in the matter of the pirates, and that you had been secretly in Father Alester's employ ever since—though not, of course, the nature of your work. It may have been stretching the truth to say you led us to the informant who gave the news of Anniton, but not by much, since you will lead us to her at the ball." Raphael extended the document again. "You will need someone to administrate the territory until your tenure here has expired. Your father, perhaps. Chancellor Narius knows you will not be claiming it openly, so that you can continue giving aid to the throne."

Tristan took the scroll, but he did not break the seal. "When the ten years are over and I go to claim this outwardly, what are you planning to tell the kingdom?"

"What we always planned to tell them: that Prince Raphael retired to the monastery where he was raised. There is no such place, so it is not as if I will have monks knocking on the door to demand your whereabouts. And you will grow out your beard again, clothe yourself differently, do whatever you must in order not to be recognized. You are good at that, you know."

"I may tell my wife?"

"Of course."

"And her parents?"

"That depends who they are. Your maiden is coming here to be lady-in-waiting to a princess. It is an acceptable position for a noble-woman, regardless."

"Until she bears a child."

"We will take that as it comes. I swear to you, Tristan, I do not wish you ill. I will let you go when my sister is crowned, and I will see to it that you and your family are provided for, both then and in the mean-time. If Briella proves to be a quick study, perhaps we can crown her in nine years, or even eight." Raphael raised his head, and his eyes were hard as iron. "This is my kingdom. Whatever I must do to save it, I will do."

Tristan traced his finger across the royal seal. "That is the first time I have ever heard you say that."

"Say what?"

"'My kingdom.' It has always been *the* kingdom before."

Raphael could feel his cheeks color, but he did not lower his gaze. "Then I shall say it again. This is my kingdom." Words seemed to well up from inside him, half-formed thoughts that had lived in cages suddenly sprung free. "I have spent my life walled up in this palace, with names like Abbleway and Falm and Tembria echoing in my ears, places that are as unreachable for me as Elysium or Eden or the moon. Yet their land is my flesh and their rivers are my blood. Every man and woman in their borders is my responsibility. That is why I cannot release you—and it is also why I will ensure the safety and, to the extent it is within my power, the happiness of your future wife and children. You are citizens of Armany. That is the only claim you require."

Tristan stared off toward the wall, lost deep in thought. At last, he broke the seal on the scroll and unrolled it on the settee. In silence, he pored over the florid script. "This is already in effect."

"And it will remain so regardless of what answer your lady gives you. Now, once and for all, I ask: will you be my body, so that I can be the justice Armany requires?"

Slowly, Tristan fell to one knee. "I will, Your Highness."

Raphael laid his right hand on Tristan's bowed head. "May God bless you for it, and give us both the strength to endure." He took his hand away from Tristan's head and clasped his hand. But in his heart, where the cage doors had been flung open, Raphael knew the handshake still sealed his abdication. To save his kingdom, he had given it away.

CHAPTER 21

The descent down the tower ladder proved more than Allia's wounded hands could bear. Blood dripped like rain through her bandages by the time her feet touched the ground. "I fear I shall have to take you up on those stitches, Sam," she muttered as the two men clambered down beside her. Sam had to catch her as she nearly fainted.

Johan turned pale. "My lady, I have seen stitches heal, but I have also seen them kill. Why take the risk?"

"Because she can't go through life with constantly bleeding hands." Sam settled Allia gently on the ground. "You escort her to the keep, Sir Winters. The common soldier is going to go save the damsel with some good old common sense." He turned on his heel and marched away. A moment later, they saw him ride off.

Allia leaned her head against the stone wall, letting its cool touch revive her. For several minutes, she sat breathing deeply, until she felt well enough to stand. "Are you strong enough to ride, or shall I bring you on my courser?" Johan asked as they walked slowly toward the stables.

"Thank you, but I will ride."

Johan fussed over her, settling her on the back of an old, quiet pack horse, the steadiest and gentlest in the stable. The knight and his lady remained silent all through the perilous, rocky climb. The horses chose every step with care while the reins bit into Allia's bandaged palms. Twice, she nearly called a halt as the pain threatened to steal her consciousness, but both times she bit her tongue and willed her mind not to waver.

The sun was past its zenith when they reached St. Peter's Tower, the gate through which no evil could enter Demont's sprawling keep. It loomed far larger than the guard post where Allia had been housed, with yard-thick granite walls that comprised Demont's last and best defense. In the four centuries since Peter's Tower had been built, not a single enemy soldier had ever climbed past. Allia and Johan rested there and changed her bandages again. She had to turn away to keep from vomiting at the sight of her own sinews.

From Peter's Tower to the keep, the mountain slowly leveled, broadening at last into a shelf a half-mile square. If not for the sheer drop to doom that formed its border, Demont's keep would have been cozy, dotted with trees and springtime grass watered by a gurgling stream that fed into the pond. So different it seemed now, that little pool bubbling with life, utterly forgetful of its morbid past. In silence, Allia and Johan passed. Neither met the other's gaze.

They reached the welcome of the greathouse, where Lady Demont had left servants with instructions to tend her great-niece and her guard. The chamber maid motioned Allia to follow, and Johan gently touched his lady's elbow. "I shall never be further than your call, Lady Allia. Not today, nor in any day to come."

She kissed his cheek, though her lips were more rigid than she meant them to be.

Allia followed the maid upstairs and endured a bath. The heat of the water revived her, but all the while hellish hammers still pounded at her hands. "Hasn't Sam arrived with the doctor?" She winced as the maid drew silken sleeves over her bandages. The maid went out to fetch news, but returned with nothing to report.

Allia returned downstairs and slumped into a chair at her great-aunt's right hand while supper was laid before them. The limestone hall seemed smaller than when last Allia had dined here, perhaps because she herself had grown. Bracketed torches lit the walls, where they illuminated gilded panels painted with angels plucking lyres. The seraphim seemed determined to reprise the joyful chorus of her youth; but a great-aunt was not a mother, and a sworn champion could never replace her father.

"You're hardly touching that lamb," Lady Demont observed with a frown.

"My apologies, Great-Aunt. The meat is fine, but it is a trial to hold the knife."

"Tell me, was it Prince Lennard who taught you to wield a sword so ill?"

Allia's jaw fell slack. "How... who told you...?"

"All in its proper time. But first, who was it that you were seeking in Demont, risking life and limb to find?"

Allia looked at her plate and said nothing.

"I need an answer, Allia. There are some secrets I cannot allow my heir to keep."

"You must believe that I did not know what you know of him. I only learned it from Sir Winters."

"Speak his name, child."

"Solomon Regis." She dared not raise her gaze. "He asked me to marry him."

For a long moment, Lady Demont said nothing, but Allia could hear the anger in her great-aunt's labored breathing. At last, Lady Demont leaned back and said, "Did you not know that if you marry, you lose the right to inherit both Camesbry and Demont?"

"I did not, until Sir Winters told me. Please, you must believe me, I am not such a fool as all of this must make me seem. I was purposely kept in the dark about my rights and desperate to go anywhere that I could be loved."

Her great-aunt reached to take Allia's hand, but, remembering the bandage, stopped. "You have found it, child. Your mother was as dear to me as if she were my own. From this day forward, Demont is your home."

"Thank you."

"But you have raised the very subject I wanted to broach: that of marriage. Even if you were willing to give up your lands for a husband and home, the one thing I cannot do for you is arrange a match. While your father is living, that right is his alone, unless the king himself should intervene."

"I understand." She sighed. "I suppose I am resigned."

"Then you have less imagination than a great lady should. Allia, delicacy is not my strength, so I shall be blunt. This was found among your mother's possessions after she died. You can see by the date, it had come only the day before." Lady Demont reached inside a small purse she kept tied at her waist, then laid a scroll on the table.

Dearest Clara,

What a joy it was to see you here! We must take care never to be parted so long again. I do hope you have arrived safely in Demont, and that you found your father's condition improved. Your Allia is as lovely as you described, and Lennard was quite impressed with her. I overheard him telling my foster son, Timothy, that he preferred a woman who could wield a sword to one who could wield a needle. He is a bit odd in his reasoning, but I do think he chose a worthy object for his affection.

So, what do you think, dear friend? We shall have to plant the seeds slowly in my husband's mind and pray there are no foreign alliances that need shoring when the children come of age. But I have always known you would have made a better queen than I, if you had not been so in love with Eric, and every strength I see in you, your daughter has been blessed to carry on. Shall we plot to make a match?

Write soon, dearest, for I shall be confined for the birth ere the week is out. Perhaps this time, I shall be blessed with a daughter as lovely as yours!

With my love,

Her Royal Majesty,

Eleanor d'Armany

Allia leaned back and closed her eyes, trying to shut out the tempest of her thoughts, but Lady Demont was in no mood for silence. "He's gone, of course, but it does not change the fact that Queen Eleanor wished to name you as her successor. One assumes she would not mind if you were to wed her younger son instead. At any rate, if you want a husband, he is the only one I can offer. I have no doubt that, if the king read his late wife's last behest, he could find wits enough to bless the match."

"You assume many things, Great-Aunt. Even if the king's madness could be broken by this scroll, and even if I wanted to marry Prince Raphael, you still assume that *he* would want to marry *me*."

"As to that, I can only say, if you want him, go get him. You are bidden to attend his ball. You shall have the opportunity."

There it was: the vortex drawing her down into the fairy's tale. Demont seemed resolved to compensate for every love Allia had ever lost, but she could not feel grateful. "I shall go because His Highness commands it, but I hope you will not be disappointed if I return unengaged."

"A week ago, you were prepared to marry an outlaw peddler, and now the heir to the throne is not to your taste?"

"Please, if I must remain forever a maid, then I am sure you yourself can testify, I shall nevertheless survive."

"Yes, but, Allia, do not be so rash. You are like your mother. You were made to become a great lady through your love for a great man."

"I know. But that great man is dead."

Before her great-aunt could reply, Johan knocked and entered. "Pardon the intrusion, my lady. Sam has arrived with a surgeon for Lady Allia's hands."

Allia stood too quickly. Her head spun, and she had to sink back into her chair.

"Bring the surgeon here, Sir Winters," Lady Demont called, "but Sam was right about the liquor. That needle doesn't touch her 'til she's good and wholly drunk."

CHAPTER 22

*T*ristan stood on the palace parapet, watching in the gray light of dawn as the city teemed with people like ants from a trodden hill. Tonight, the ball would dangle a prince like a carrot before the kingdom. Maidens had poured into the capitol until every house became an inn and the City Watchmen ceased to issue overnight passes. For a week now, only vehicles of commerce had been permitted to enter the city, and those had been bidden to depart ere nightfall. Every town within half a day's ride likewise overflowed. Tristan held the spyglass to his eye and watched a knot of girls stop to gaze in wonder at the palace walls. Between the four hopeful, homespun friends, they could have collected but one full set of teeth.

Tristan's stomach heaved as he turned to the palace steward at his side. "I should have added an adjective to the invitation. 'Beautiful,' maybe, or at least, 'fair.'"

"And how many do you think would have been willing to own themselves plain?"

"Issue a decree that every maiden must be washed and her garments likewise. Tell the guards to deny entry to any with lice or open sores."

"A wise decision, Your Highness. Have you given any more thought to how we are going to fit them all in?"

Tristan ground his teeth. Prince Raphael had entrusted the logistics of the ball to the man who first suggested it—a penance for his thoughtlessness. Tristan would have rather eaten locusts in the desert. "The nobility may remain as long as they wish, but every hour, let the commoners be cycled through. And let a daub of paint be put on their hands to show which ones have already taken their turns."

"Very good. And what about the escorts? Are we admitting only maidens, or their fathers and brothers, too?"

Tristan thought of his own sweet sister back in their riverfront cottage. She was still too young for this nonsense, thank God, but he knew his father would never send her into a den of strangers alone. "Every family may send one chaperone, but sisters may have only one between them, however numerous they may be."

"Very good, Your Highness." The steward departed with a haughty smile. The man clearly saw the folly of this enterprise and took perverse delight in it. At least someone would be well entertained. Tristan trembled to think that tonight, he would finally meet the woman he loved, hold her in his arms while they danced, smell the perfume of her lush dark hair. Years, it seemed, he had dreamed about this day, though in truth it had been but a season. Yet the brightness of the dream could not alleviate the dark of dread festering in his heart. It defied credulity that a tale as twisted as his could end in happiness.

Tristan could not shake the voice inside his conscience that said the girl must be complicit in the informant's schemes. In his heart, he did not believe any girl with such tenderness in her eyes could be involved in such nefarious dealings; but in his mind, he did not believe that a bargain to marry this woman to a prince could be struck without her knowledge. Even if she were innocent, the likelihood that she would agree to marry him under Prince Raphael's terms was slim, indeed. Every day, Tristan chided himself for pledging his life to this infamous charade, but he had done it because he knew it would not matter. The girl he loved was in love with a prince, and that was something Tristan Ferryman could never be.

He swiped the back of his hand across his eyes and turned to descend from the parapet, only to find Princess Briella climbing to meet him. The hostility in her black eyes was cloaked, for once, by worry. "Come," she said. "The Darrivants have attacked."

~

THE KESTREL WOVEN on the standard-bearer's green and silver flag fluttered gaily in the light of dawn as the Camesbry soldiers assembled outside the castle's talused walls. Like a fall of dew, they shone with the day's glad promise, yet the lord at their head wore a brooding frown and grumbled at all who approached him. No leads had been uncovered in the death of George Couper, nor had the captain sent to fetch Allia returned. Yet Lady Vivienne suspected that her husband had another motive to be dreary. It had been at a royal ball where Eric de Camesbry first glimpsed the fetching Clara of Demont.

Vivienne approached her husband where he stood, holding his destrier's reins. "Your men will cut fine figures on the dance floor. His Highness does them great honor, to gather the whole kingdom to spread their renown."

"His Highness was merely drunk and happened to speak more than he meant. Next campaign, every one of my men will leave a pregnant wife behind. What good will that be for morale?"

"They will be more driven to hold the Darrivants at bay, just like the men we are leaving here." Indeed, not every soldier who had been promised a herd of unicorns was returning to the palace to claim them. The wives of those already married had insisted their husbands remain behind to defend Camesbry.

"It's a load of lovey nonsense," Lord Camesbry growled, and his squire hoisted him clumsily into the saddle.

The men, in turn, began to mount, and Vivienne walked off toward her carriage, where Lilliane was already ensconced. The girl's cheeks had turned a shade of such deep rose the last few days, Vivienne at first feared she had a fever; but no, she had only been pilfering cosmetics from her mother's newest stores. She certainly looked like a princess, from her creamy yellow traveling dress to her high-piled ebony curls. She had shown more discretion than usual, choosing a slender gold chain with an amethyst pendant as her only decoration: a subtle, unmistakable hint of royal purple. Lilliane would change dresses before the ball, but Vivienne meant to see that she kept the same style.

She kissed her daughter's cheek. "You will do us all proud today, Lilliane."

Lilliane's eyes glittered. "He loves me. I know."

Vivienne patted her daughter's hand. "I hope so, child." Now was not the time to teach how much more than love it required for a woman to bear the burdens of a man, much less a king.

The coachman whipped the horses, and the coach rumbled into motion at the head of the procession. Vivienne lay back, weary with her long preparations and more nervous than she could admit to Lilliane about the coming evening. In a blue purse tied to her skirts, she carried the forged bill of sale and a single black vial. Lilliane might be right that Prince Raphael loved her, but he would not wed her until the dowry was paid.

The caravan had made but a few miles' progress when a sound of hooves galloping faster than the rest led Lord Camesbry to call a halt. Vivienne descended from the carriage and stood with her husband while they awaited the messenger. The horseman arrived, nearly breathless, in the torn and tattered livery of Morisse.

"My lord," he cried, "we are besieged. The Darrivants have come to Pellain. Lord Morisse is dead. His son Alexandre sent me here to beg your aid."

Lord Camesbry cursed and spat into the dust. "We are ordered to the capitol! Is the garrison still stationed at Pellain?"

"It is, my lord, but they caught us unawares. Without you, we may hold a few days at best, but we have little hope of victory."

"How are you provisioned?"

"We have sent to Anniton for supplies, but we fear to find the town deserted for the ball."

"As well you may." Lord Camesbry gripped his sword and bared his teeth.

A pair of knights rode up behind him. "My lord, we will turn around. Give us half a day to provision ourselves, and we can arrive at Pellain tomorrow."

"And leave the prince with a palace full of maidens expecting to dance, but no men to partner them. 'Twould serve the little monk right."

"That 'little monk' is your liege lord," Lilliane declared, marching over with both fists balled. "You laid your sword before him. He has not changed his orders."

Lord Camesbry's knuckles connected with her cheek, and Lilliane fell sprawling with a cut under her left eye. Vivienne tasted bile rising in her throat as she lifted her incensed daughter from the ground. She whispered, "Hush. He shall have his due for this, but not now."

Lilliane hid her bleeding face against her mother's breast, and Vivienne stroked her daughter's fallen curls.

"What say you, my lord?" the knight asked again.

"You," Lord Camesbry ordered him, "bring five men to Anniton. Confiscate whatever you cannot buy, leave letters of credit in my name, and then make all haste to Pellain. You," to the second knight, "return home. Of the hundred men we left there, take fifty to the garrison. Tell Alexandre Morisse our full force will arrive in three days. And you," he called to a man behind him, "Take a message ahead to the palace. Tell His Highness we are still coming."

The knights looked at each other, each one paler than the last. "My lord...?" one ventured. "Surely the ball can be postponed?"

"It could, with my blessings," Lord Camesbry muttered, "but every maiden in the kingdom is bidden to attend—including my daughter. It will need more than Darrivants to keep me away."

Dawn found Prince Raphael on the balcony of his chamber, gazing northward into the mountains. From this vantage, the city disappeared, leaving only the oblique wilderness of its border. The north-ward road wound away toward the distant province of Lagunde, a region rich with mines but populated by queer folk. They were Arman by allegiance, but they spoke their own guttural language and kept their own ancient ways. Raphael watched a few horses wend their way through the treacherous pass and wondered if even the Lagunders had sent their daughters to court the prince.

Try as he might to evade them, thoughts of courtship enveloped Raphael on this dawn. Every maiden wanted a husband, every soldier wanted a wife, and only he, the prince, dared not think of departing the ball in the arms of domestic bliss. The only woman who had ever smiled at him was his mother. Girls his own age always wrinkled their noses or widened their eyes, expressions proper to beholding a freak. After a lifetime of such treatment, Raphael's heart had grown as callused as his hands. Yet he had not always believed he would die without knowing love; not until death claimed his brother.

He watched the distant horses pick their way through the rocks and dreamed for a moment that one of them carried Lennard. Without his brother, Raphael might never have known that love could grant a vision piercing beyond fault, a friendship deeper than cour-tesy. He had always dreamed that the Lion would bring him a bride from the wars just as he had brought St. Lucy: someone unexpected, even ugly perhaps, but someone divinely inspired. Someone who would spare him the shame of being shunned. But the Lion would never again come roaring in with light. This gray, solitary dawn might be the brightest one Little Brother would ever know.

Raphael turned away from his brooding as Father Alester entered his chamber. Without prelude, the chaplain announced, "Your High-ness, Pellain is besieged."

The prince closed his eyes. "And they will send to Camesbry for troops, so now we must find other men for the ball. Let us pray we can find our informant before the whole garrison deserts."

"Amen to that, Your Highness, but Lord Camesbry sent word he is still on his way."

Raphael wheeled around, nearly toppling out of his chair. "Why?"

"He gave no reason, but the men are coming. They will march tomorrow to the siege. Would you order them to turn back?"

Raphael gripped the arms of his chair, dark features distorted by every knot inside his lonely, livid soul. "No. Let them come. Tell the troubadours to be ready with their lyres. Whatever happens tonight, we shall have an epic tale for them to sing."

CHAPTER 23

$\mathcal{O}$n the morning of the ball, Allia awoke from a dream.

A prince, a dance, and midnight's toll—a mad dash into night—then the peddler, whose kiss plunged misery into a spell of cool, green rapture. Still, the serpents coiled until the faceless man freed her. "Faithfulness," he still promised her: nothing less and nothing more.

In the cold light of dawn, Allia laughed.

The sound roused three guards who shared her room in the packed roadside inn, all of them slumped into a heap on the far side of the communal mattress. Lady Demont had sent Sam and Garred under Sir Winters's command to keep her heiress safe, and the crush of maidens trekking toward the capitol had left propriety little room to lodge.

"Morning already?" Sam grumbled, kicking Johan as he rolled.

"Yes, such as it is," Allia answered. Fog lay thick across the valley where they had passed the night, so that the view from the window revealed only clouds. Allia half-expected to see the haze broken by the flutter of silver-bright wings, yet the cinder maid had already found a coach, an escort, and a gown. Lady Demont had left the fairy little magic to perform.

"I smell breakfast," Sam announced, rising and donning his sword. "Are you hungry, my lady? We can leave these two layabouts to their snooze."

"No, we'll come," Johan muttered as he stretched out on the straw. "Best to get an early start. We won't make good time in this fog."

With a sigh, Allia slipped her traveling dress over her shift and put on her shoes.

They descended to the common room and waded through a morass of maidens. They squashed themselves at last onto an over-crowded bench. Girls of every shape and disposition lined the tables, with merchants keen to profit from the bedlam sprinkled in between. Some sold the necessities of travel—cart wheels, horseshoes, water skins—but many more offered silks, bonnets, ribbons, flowers, or slippers, all the things these ball-bound girls might need to entice a royal partner. Allia kept her eyes open, wondering if Solomon Regis might be nearby, peddling her stepmother's potions. She ached to catch a glimpse of those inscrutable eyes, but she dared not hope he would come. The guards from Demont would arrest him on sight. There would be no serpents coiling with Sir Winters and his troop standing sentry.

The stout innkeeper and his stouter wife bumped and sidled amidst the commotion. They laid out a breakfast of hot sweet rolls drenched in butter, with roast partridge for those patrons who could spare an extra coin. Johan bought a whole skewer of birds for the foursome to share.

"So, my lady," said Sam, who always did his best to keep up a conversation at meals, "how long has it been since you last danced?"

"Nineteen years, I suppose, if capering in my mother's womb can be counted."

The guards dropped their knives and their jaws. After a moment, Garred stood and held out his hand. "Permit me to teach you, my lady."

"If you insist."

A young man near the fireplace produced a fiddle from under his cloak. Music touched the air like flint, and sparks of excitement ignited. Soon every maiden who could find a partner took the floor, while the rest of the company clapped and stomped, or drummed time on the tables. Garred led Allia in precise, mechanical circles, shielding her from the flurry as she stumbled along in time.

"Garred, you dance like a bloody mill wheel," Sam jeered.

"Perhaps you would like to teach the lady, then?"

"You know I never learned. But if I had, at least I'd know I had a woman in my arms, not a sack of grain."

One buxom maiden perked her ears. "Shall we try it, then, soldier? My feet are nimble enough for two." She held out her hand. Sam blushed like a radish as he took it.

"I might as well be a sack of grain." Allia spun gracelessly away from her partner to land on the bench beside Johan. "It doesn't matter, though. I doubt that anyone will ask me to dance."

"Then it will only be because they have fallen mute," Johan answered. "You will dazzle every man in the room, my lady."

Indeed, this past week, Allia had discovered that Lady Vivienne was not the only woman in the kingdom who brewed beauty in small bottles. Any number of brightly-colored concoctions had been lavished upon her hair, her mouth, her eyes, her skin, until the layers of gray labor gave way to silk and roses. Even Allia could not deny that her reflection was entrancing; she had stared at herself for long, lonely hours, seeing her mother in the glass.

"What men are going to be there besides the prince?" she wondered.

"It's the men from Anniton," the innkeeper's wife answered while she cleared away finished plates. "The soldiers from the battle, celebrating the victory, as it were."

Allia's stitched hands gripped the table while the roses drained from her cheeks.

"What is it, my lady?" Johan asked.

"My father," she whispered, too low for the other guests to hear. "He led the battle of Anniton. Every man at that ball will know me."

Johan's hand went instinctively to the hilt of his sword. "I will not allow him to drag you back into your slavery."

"How shall you stop him? By killing him?" She closed her eyes, but still the tears leaked out as she pictured the grieving man at her bedside in Demont, the strong, beautiful man forever broken by a lie. "He is my father. You will not harm him, Johan. Swear it by your knighthood."

"I swear, my lady. But what would you have me do?"

"I would have us all turn around and go back to Demont."

"You cannot snub the favor of both your great-aunt and the prince."

"Why does everyone speak as if the prince were eagerly awaiting only me? I have never met the man, and if he is aware that I exist at all, it is only as a name he has heard mentioned. He will not miss me."

"But Lady Demont?"

"She will not wish to see me horse-whipped in front of the whole kingdom. I promise you, my father will do it if I defy him, and he will leave me no choice."

Johan slid toward her to whisper in her ear. "My lady, the moment we arrive, you must plead your case to Prince Raphael. I will bear witness both to your innocence and to the fact that Lady Demont gave you a public acquittal and named you her heir. When you are under royal protection, your father will not dare harm you."

She stared into Johan's ardent eyes, and suddenly she was back in Camesbry, lying on her cold stone hearth, dreaming every night about the day when she would plead her case before Lennard the Lion. She had always believed he would see her innocence, though she dreamed the lying Rabignys spewed falsehoods at her side. She had thought her hopes of freedom died with her prince, but now the lies had died in their turn. With Johan to serve as an eye-witness, plus Sam and Garred to attest that Lady Demont had acquited her, even the senile king would be sure to grant Allia pardon—and maybe her father would, too.

She clasped Johan's hand. "You're right. Let us go."

All that foggy morning, Allia rode inside Lady Demont's coach while Garred drove; Johan and Sam rode horseback on either side. Secluded inside her box with only her racing thoughts for company,

Allia could not chase the shivers from her spine. Eight years, her father had shared her enslavement, the heart of a good and righteous man caged by anger and woe. As dearly as Allia longed for her own freedom, it would never be complete unless he shared it. She leaned on her upholstered seat and thought of the small twig of hazel planted by her father's hands that now had blossomed into a full, majestic tree. Had she alone been watching as the years turned it gold, then green, conquering winter frosts with increase and bounty? Or had her father sometimes turned his heavy-lidded eyes to see the legacy of life sprouting from the grave? Perhaps true love was really waiting past the threshold of an enchanted ball—the love Allia had been waiting eight long years to reclaim.

"Please," she breathed above the clatter of the wheels, the only word she knew how to pray.

The jam of traffic entering the city gates stretched back for miles. An hour past noon, the company was forced to halt. Sam rode ahead and learned that the people a mile down had already been waiting two hours.

"We must get through," Allia insisted. "Sir Winters, now is the time to prove the utility of having a sworn champion."

Johan bowed. Then he raised himself to his full height in the saddle and drew his sword. "Make way! Make way for the Heiress of Demont!" Sam rode abreast of his commander, and step by cautious, begrudged step, the crowds divided to let them pass. An hour still it took to reach the gates, where royal guards lowered lances across the only path.

"Halt! No passing. Go back and wait your turn."

Allia bounded down from the coach. "Sir, I am Lord Camesbry's daughter."

The captain furrowed his dark brow. "We're just about to clear out this queue to be sure he can get through. Go on. Take the east gate into the palace. There are rooms prepared for the noble ladies."

"God bless you, kind sir." With a curtsey, Allia remounted her carriage and listened to the clipping of the hooves that brought her closer to freedom. Onward they went through close-packed streets flooded by the filth of festival. Refuse piled in every alleyway, waste spilled unchecked down every slope, yet still the people twittered with smiling anticipation. The line of maidens waiting to enter the palace stretched unbroken from the city gates across the lowered draw-bridge, all the way into the sparkling quartz castle where the weary guards seemed to have given up and allowed the nearest guests a preview. Minstrels were already serenading would-be dancers, and servants moved through the line, offering sweet cakes and sips of cool water.

Grooms arrived to tend Allia's party and their horses. "It's only one escort per maiden allowed inside," one man informed them. "But I can welcome the other two to the servants' quarters, if you don't care to try your luck at the pubs."

Sam and Garred accepted the offer, and Allia and Johan wound their way through carriage yards and outbuildings toward the east gate. There, maidservants swooped down on Allia, whisking her into a suite full of rose-scented baths, dressing chambers, and feather beds, where a bevy of noblewomen were being transformed into goddesses. Johan blushed as he excused himself to stand guard at the door.

Allia found a quiet corner to unpack her gown and hung it by a window to air. Ruffles of pale pink silk fluttered in a breeze. She had chosen the gown from her mother's old wardrobe at Demont: a sweet dress, made for a maiden, its every tuck and pleat demure. It was no mystery that Lady Clara had left it behind when she married. Allia knew the dress did not suit her; the seamstress had had to let out the places where it pinched her muscled arms, and no pink ruffle could be made to match the gaudy seams of black across her hands. Still, the soft flutter of silk reminded her of the woman for whom it had been sewn. If memories of Lady Clara were all that remained, then let them be draped over her daughter's shoulders to dance once more.

When at last the church bells of the capitol tolled the festive hour, giggling servants led the noblewomen into the main hall. Allia slid on her slippers, as golden as her hope, took Johan's arm, and followed.

Ahead, she saw the bobbing curls of Lady Vivienne and Lilliane.

"What's wrong, my lady?" Johan whispered as Allia froze, but she dared not answer. She tugged him backward toward the dressing rooms until they were alone.

"My stepmother and stepsister nearly saw me. I shall never be able to speak to the prince before I am discovered."

"Then let me speak for you. We will wait here until the hallways are clearer. Then we will find a secluded place for you until I can beg His Highness for a word on your behalf."

Allia nodded and sank into a chair. She caught a whiff of some forgotten fragrance clinging to the wood, some note of musk and vigor faded into dust. She thought of the way her father's gouty legs leaned into his walking stick and of the purple bruises it had left across her back.

Without warning, she wept.

CHAPTER 24

A thousand slim, white candles filled the evening with its own fragmented sun. Crystal overflowed with luscious purple wine. Deft fingers tripped with reverence across impatient strings; the steady tap of drums lent a heartbeat to the night. Pan pipes called a marsh of milkmaids to rise as nymphs, reborn. Silk and wool, flax and linen swirled; rhythmic feet gamboled through patterns lithe and glad.

In the middle twirled the presumed prince—less graceful, perhaps, than some—bestowing the favor of his company upon a different maid with every song. His hollow eyes never rested, flitting with every flickered shadow toward new faces in the crowd. All remarked the haggard circles bulging gray beneath his eyes, and through the stained-glass windmill of gaiety, rumors whispered of war.

Father Alester listened, catching conversations like flies. Most were innocuous, or lecherous at worst, the soldiers of Camesbry trying to purge the title "maiden" from at least a few. Alester had no heart to lecture them about virtue, so shriveled was his own. Only duty led him now. The guiding light of righteousness had been snuffed out with George Couper.

Alester slinked through the edges of the gala until he found Lord

Camesbry. The general's eyes darted as restlessly as Tristan's. "I am in no mood for your intrigues, Father."

"I have no intrigues, my lord, only a question. Why have you come when, even now, the Darrivants may be burning through Morisse toward your home?"

"Do not presume to lecture me about war. Your domain is souls and secrets. Mine is swords."

"All the more reason why I am puzzled. I counseled His Highness to order you to march at once."

"So he does have the backbone to deny you now and then! Perhaps his father's blood is deeper in his veins than I had thought."

"He allowed you to come because he is more curious than I why you should march away from battle. Give me a reason I can bring him. If you wait for him to come to you, you may not like what he will say."

Lord Camesbry's eyes sought the dance floor, where Tristan wove a maid with chestnut braids through steps like knitting yarn. "Tell His Highness I am here to find what I have lost. That is enough."

Father Alester watched Lord Camesbry's eyes follow the rings of dancers. The old man's pudgy eyebrows twitched with the strain. The priest gave a curt bow to excuse himself; then he made his way toward a face he had not expected to see. Chancellor Narius's drooping mustache served to hide his scowl as he shifted in ill-fitting velvet breeches, sipping at a glass of wine. "Lord Chancellor," Alester greeted him with a bow. "I had not thought you one to take pleasure in a ball."

"There is no pleasure in seeing a lord march away from his duty. What did Camesbry tell you?"

"Only that he has come to find something he lost."

Chancellor Narius shook his head and turned downtrodden eyes toward the king. Simon the Unvanquished still cast a regal shadow, his stately spine unbowed as he led his daughter through dances his feet had not yet forgotten. "There he stands," said Narius, "content as only an old man can be, with his kingdom entrusted to the men who always served him best. And we are failing him."

Father Alester hung his head. "We are none of us his equal."

"Nor that reckless son of his, either. And yet, we muddle on."

Narius finished the last of his wine, set his glass on a table, and walked to conduct his own interview with Lord Camesbry.

Alester wound his way up the great wing-like staircase to the gallery, where Prince Raphael kept vigil over the proceedings below, sheltered by a white curtain. "What have you learned?" the prince asked. His knuckles strained against the armrests of his chair.

"Narius is merely worried about the war, as we are. Lord Camesbry would only tell me he is here to find something he lost."

"I know that look, Father. You have conjectured the rest."

Alester drummed his fingers on the gallery railing. "The soldiers are all his, so it cannot be a man. He arrived with only his wife and stepdaughter; that is to say, one maiden short. I presume his daughter must be missing."

"So the cinder maid tired of her servitude and endangered my whole kingdom by running away." Raphael ran both hands through his mop of black curls. "Is she here?"

"I do not know."

The prince nodded and turned to watch the dance. "Are you certain the informant will come?"

"Yes, Your Highness. I have dealt with her in good faith." Alester stared unblinking at the dance, seeing only the ghost of the jeweler as he stumbled, drooling and puking, toward his last breath. More than once since that day, Alester had longed to subject the woman in the woods—and himself—to the the same torment.

"She will not reveal her sources willingly, will she?" Raphael closed his eyes as if to shut out the informant's screams. Father Alester swallowed a sob of guilt because he felt no urge to do the same.

"No, Your Highness. I do not expect it will be a quiet night in our dungeons."

TRISTAN'S PALMS WERE SWEATING. Every lady he partnered seemed to slip like a fish from his grasp, though to be sure, they worked gallantly to hold on. Batted eyelashes, mute dropped jaws, demure flirtation, even offers to let him have his way in exchange for political favors; Tristan wanted to scurry into a hole and pull a blanket over his head.

"Your Royal Highness is an excellent dancer," his current partner chirped despite the evidence of her bruised toes.

"Thank you. Er, what was your name?"

"Melinda Withers, from Carnish-on-Levold. Have you ever been there, Your Royal Highness? It's a beautiful village. We make the best cheese in Armany."

Tristan blushed. "I have been there, and I do often long for a taste of your cheese." He dared not tell her he had grown up there; that the two of them had played together, ages ago, while their mothers joined forces to make a quilt to sell at the local fair. Tristan studied Melinda's sturdy peasant face, flat cheekbones with a wide smile, and realized she might well have been his wife but for Father Alester and Fate.

"I never realized the monks who raised you allowed you to travel," she said.

He coughed. "Not very often, of course. Just to visit their brothers in other monasteries."

"You remind me of someone. You may even know him. A young man from our village was apprenticed to a royal officer. He has a face like yours, though he always used to wear a beard."

Tristan felt his ears catch fire. "I, um, may have had the pleasure."

Mercifully, the song ended, and Tristan spun the girl away and fled into the crowds without so much as a goodbye. He should have thought to exclude Carnish-on-Levold from the invitation; another kernel of idiocy sown into his brilliant plan. He took a glass of wine from a waiter and downed it at one gulp. He turned his eyes toward the staircase, longing for escape—

And there she was.

She glided down while he stood rooted, her ebony curls piled high to reveal a neck as white and graceful as a swan's. Around it, a pendant of amethyst reflected the subtle violet undertones of her alabaster complexion. Those wide eyes smiled when they met his. She walked with her hand on an older woman's elbow. The sight of the older woman sent a shudder down Tristan's spine, but as the maiden drew near, he felt his heart clench with compassion. A cut had marred her rosy cheek, the bruise around it just beginning to bloom. "Mademoiselle," he said when at last she stood before him, "who has harmed you?"

Her dark eyes searched his, a glance so hopeful, so intimate, that Tristan felt a blush rise in his cheeks. "'Tis but a scratch," she said. "Your Royal Highness is kind to inquire."

He took her hand, her skin connecting against his with a sweetness almost too great to bear. "Will you dance with me, mademoiselle?"

"I would be honored." The heat of those shining eyes melted everything inside him. He was wet clay in her hands, but she was silk and eiderdown in his.

The older woman gave an oily smile.

Tristan closed his eyes to dispel the sight of her from his mind. But he opened them again, found Father Alester across the room, and nodded. He did not wait for any response, but took the maiden into his arms. A knight he had never seen before—out of place, in Demont livery—attempted to waylay him, begging for some garbled favor. Tristan cut him off and twirled the girl out onto the floor. "Ma'amselle," he pleaded as soon as they were insulated by the patterns of the dance, "what is your name?"

"Lilliane, Your Royal Highness." It touched his ears like the strum of a harp.

"Just Lilliane?"

She turned down those fawn-like eyes. "My surname does not tell my real position."

He dared to stroke one fallen curl away from her alabaster face. "Why not?"

"Because my father is dead, and my mother is remarried. My stepfather's house is far nobler than the one into which I was born."

Tristan's heart began to pound. Was it possible? Might she be a commoner, a girl of his own birth? "What was your father's trade?"

She twirled away and then back to his side. Tears pooled in the depths of those great eyes. "I should rather tell you that my stepfather is a lord. That I may very well become his heir, after his natural daughter is wed. He has no great love for her, but I…"

"Lilliane." The word tasted like ambrosia. "I am not asking about your dowry. Only please, tell me the name of the woman I love."

Her tears began to fall. "Is it true, then? Do you love me?"

"With every breath I breathe."

She twirled again and laid her head against his breast. "My name is Lilliane Delaine. My father was a wool merchant." She pulled back. "Does it matter?"

He clutched her tight and did not care that all the couples dancing near them stopped to watch. "Lilliane Delaine. A wool merchant's daughter." He burst out laughing. "I could cry." And cry he did, through peals of joyous laughter, while he twined her through the giddy steps of a dance he hardly knew. She cocked her head and seemed not altogether certain of his sanity, but she followed where he led. Across the hall, underneath the gallery, out toward a courtyard where the revelry had overflowed, he spun her through the shifting crowds until all thought of intrigue had been left behind. Only the two of them existed, clear and open as the starlit sky. "Lilliane Delaine," he whispered in her ear. He stopped their feet and held her fragile shoulders in his strong, broad hands. "I care for neither your father the merchant nor your stepfather the lord. But if my father were not the king…"

"I would love you," she declared. "In a palace or a pig sty. I swear it."

He clasped her body against his heart. "Lilliane…" How could he ask the most important question? If she were innocent, she would not understand. And if she were guilty…

"Your Royal Highness," she whispered into his chest, "I tried to write to you. After the funeral, to tell you who I was."

"Why did you not?" Oh, if only!

"My mother intercepted the letters. She burned them. She was right, it was very presumptuous of me. But you would have forgiven me, wouldn't you?"

"Forgiven you? I would have leaped for joy."

"I know. The moment I saw you, I knew." She reached up and touched his cheek. "I am yours, Your Royal Highness. I can never be anything else."

He leaned his cheek against that soft white palm. "I do not belong to myself. If you are mine, then you will always belong to the kingdom."

"I will serve it faithfully, Your Royal Highness."

It was the only affirmation of her innocence Tristan could bear to demand. He crushed her into a kiss, and her lips burned against him, branding him, stealing any joy he might ever know apart from this. "There are things I have to say to you," he gasped when they parted. "Things that will be difficult to understand. One week from today, in Carnish-on-Levold—" Surely, Prince Raphael would grant him leave — "at the ferryman's dock. I will meet you there to explain."

"Your Highness, I don't understand…"

"I know. But you will then. After you hear me out, if you will still have me, I will marry you that very day."

"Of course I will have you. I love you." She probed his eyes with hers, and Tristan wanted nothing more than to lay open his entire soul for her perusal. Instead, he kissed her again. She seemed dizzy when he let her go.

"One week," she whispered. "'Tis a lifetime."

How right she was, he did not think he could ever put into words. But he suddenly remembered the informant, who might even now be under arrest, and all he could think about was getting Lilliane out of the palace unscathed. "The woman who escorted you, was that your mother?"

"Yes. Lady Vivienne de Camesbry."

The name froze Tristan cold. "Your stepfather is Lord Camesbry?"

"Yes. Your Highness, what is wrong?"

He gripped her arm and fervently began to whisper in her ear.

LADY VIVIENNE RECOGNIZED the king's agent by his gait. They had only ever met on horseback with his face shrouded by a hood, but still she picked him out by the way he carried his lanky frame. His alb surprised her, but of course, on such a man, it did not mean he was really a priest.

"Good evening, Father."

"Good evening, madam. Permit me to introduce myself. I am Father Alester Warren, the palace chaplain."

She smiled. "If you like. You may call me Lady Camesbry."

Her name had the effect she intended; the man's shrewd blue eyes narrowed with something she thought might be fear. He recovered quickly, however, and clasped his hands behind his back. "Well, then, welcome, my lady. This is as much your ball as anyone's. Your husband has done the kingdom great service."

"Yes. He is well suited to the battlefield."

"It does, however, give me pause that his wife should have been the one to provide the location of the attack, since he was the one to propose its defense."

Vivienne only smiled and watched her daughter dancing in the prince's arms. The agent's eyes followed hers. "Is that your daughter," he inquired, "or Lord Camesbry's?"

"She is mine, though she was to be his heir. Did you know? My lord betrothed his own daughter to a common jeweler. Only, in the end, the jeweler refused to have her. He accused his own lord of trying to swindle him. If he had lived to bring the charge in court, he would have been hanged."

The agent gave no reply.

"I only mention it to set your mind at ease. What I asked of you was no crime. It was justice. But I had to know what kind of prince this Raphael is before I entrusted him with my child. There is a war going on, and a man like his brother, so fixated on ideals, could never win it. I will not let my daughter become a princess only to see her head mounted on a Darrivant pike."

"I understand you have the means to prevent that, my lady. If not for the desertions, the war would have been over months ago."

"Yes. Unfortunately, I did not learn the cause until more recently."

She untied the small purse at her waist and laid it in the agent's hand. "It saddens me to admit it, but the desertions have been caused by a member of my lord's own household."

The agent opened the bag and took out the vial of black liquid. "What is this?"

"A love potion. Do you recall that about a year ago there was a case of witchcraft in Demont? A peddler named Solomon Regis sold a concoction that was deemed accountable for any number of unwitting love affairs."

"As I recall, the man was never caught to stand trial." The agent passed the bottle from one hand to the other. "Is this one of his?"

"He did not brew it. He is only a buyer. I myself have been in business with him many years."

"Your cosmetics," the agent said. Vivienne was pleased that he kept abreast of such gossip, as a man in his position should.

"Regis was my peddler for six years, though of course I broke off ties when he became an outlaw. I presume he first encountered the person who made this by coming to my home to buy my wares."

"And how does a love potion steal men's loyalty in battle? I may be only a priest, my lady, but I do not think the soldiers from one side make a habit of drinking potions provided by the other."

"No, but they do make a habit of being struck by arrows. Tell me, has there been a single deserter who was not hit? Nor any evidence among the dead of poisoned wounds?"

The king's agent gritted his teeth. Then he reached into the purse and took out its other occupant, the scroll. "A bill of sale, I presume? Naming Regis and the potion's maker?"

"Regis himself did not sign it, but I doubt you could find him, anyway. He is likely behind enemy lines."

"So the only name I will find here is Allia de Camesbry."

Vivienne started.

"There are two explanations, of course. One is that the girl is guilty, as a child who murdered her own mother well might be. The other..." He took a step toward Vivienne; she would almost have said he slithered. "The other is that a woman who could not dispose of her stepdaughter through marriage has found a more expedient way to ensure that she herself inherits Camesbry."

A cold shiver slipped down Vivienne's spine, but she arched it nonetheless. "A quaint theory, Father, and I do not doubt you would spend the rest of the evening using the rack to convince me of its truth, if you could. But, alas…" She gestured toward the room, where every man except the palace staff wore the livery of Camesbry; toward the open door through which her daughter had disappeared, wrapped in the prince's arms; and toward her husband, sitting sour-faced at the edge of the proceedings, his beady eyes roaming through the dance.

The agent leaned to whisper in her ear. "Do not think they will stop me, my lady."

"I just saved your master's kingdom, Father. This is not the gratitude I had hoped for."

"My master's kingdom is not of this world." His voice was cold, forlorn, and for a moment Vivienne wondered if he might truly be a priest. But when she turned to face him, he was gone, and Lilliane was stumbling back inside with tears streaming down her cheeks.

"What happened, child? Did he hurt you?"

"Hurt me! Oh, no. He proposed."

Vivienne took her daughter's hand. "Then our business here is done." She looked toward her husband, brooding over his wine glass with violence in his eyes. She ducked away from his gaze and hurried Lilliane from the hall.

CHAPTER 25

For a quarter of an hour, Allia and Johan sat together after she dried her tears. She fidgeted with her sleeves while he fidgeted with his sword-belt. The music did not drift so far from the dance, but the sounds of passing feet, whispered giggles, and illicit love found their way through the dressing-room door. Strained smiles passed between the maiden and her knight, but, for minutes at a time, neither could find anything to say.

"Have you thought about how you will approach your father?" Johan asked at last.

"A thousand ways, all of them wrong. And the longer we sit here, the more I fear we shall not find the prince cooperative. He has come to dance, not to adjudicate eight-year-old injustices."

"Then we will discover what manner of prince he truly is."

"Do not judge him so harshly. Even a just man can be blinded by his own concerns." The eye of memory drifted back to her father holding court in his Great Hall. Hundreds of times, she had witnessed fair-minded rulings and wondered with her tears how such a man could condemn his own child.

The silence stretched once more. Finally, Allia stood. "Enough. We do not accomplish anything by sitting here except to fray my nerves."

Johan rose and went before her, peering around corners, creeping toward the ball. They approached the dance from the gallery above, and, for a moment, stood gazing dumbstruck over the rail. The green-and-silver soldiers whirled, a flurry of leaves caught in a breeze of lilting rhythm, some with a maiden on either hand, leaving none to lurk as flowers on the wall. Right in the middle, a cape of ermine fluttered from silver epaulets as the tall, proud figure of Prince Raphael spun a woman in his arms. Allia gripped the rail while her eyes absorbed his halting footwork: the evidence of miracles.

"I suppose I should wait until the song is ended to approach him," Johan said.

"Do you see my father?"

Both of them scanned the flurrying crowd, but Johan found him first. "There, against the far wall. Speaking with the priest."

Allia looked where Johan pointed. Both Lord Camesbry and his confidante appeared sour. Allia hoped that tonight, she might cure her father once and for all of that grim, mistrustful frown. Tonight, God willing, she might see her Papa smile.

The priest left Lord Camesbry, spoke briefly to another man, and then ascended the stairs at the far end of the gallery. Allia and Johan watched him secret himself behind a white curtain that seemed designed for no purpose but to hide. "You could wait there," Johan said, "after he comes out."

"There may be someone else behind it."

"But not your father."

Allia nodded. "All right."

"I will not fail you, my lady." The song ended. Prince Raphael spun away his partner, but instantly, another accosted him, and the musicians struck up another tune. Johan sighed. "It seems I shall have to wait downstairs and be quick. I will not return until he has heard me out." They both saw the priest depart from the curtain, and Johan nodded. "Go, my lady."

Allia squeezed her champion's hand. "God speed you, sir."

"He shall. My cause is just."

Allia moved toward the far end of the gallery while Johan

descended the stairs. She stopped before she reached the curtain to look again at her father. Lord Camesbry turned as if he had felt the weight of her eyes. Allia quickly ducked around the drape.

A young man sat behind it, his hands clutched tight around the arms of a chair affixed with wheels.

~

HER EYES REMINDED Raphael of hazelnuts.

She blinked repeatedly, startled speechless at the sight of him. When she spoke, she curtsied low. "Baron Immerville, I presume. I beg Your Lordship's pardon."

"Yes, of course," Raphael snapped, annoyed that anyone would disturb a curtain so obviously hung for the sake of seclusion. He returned his attention to the dance below. The curtain only hid him from the gallery; he could see the ball quite well through the railings. Tristan danced like a nervous grasshopper, making inelegant jumps that put as much space as possible between him and his partner. Father Alester still lurked on the edges of the crowd. Apparently, his quarry had not yet arrived.

The maiden moved to leave. Raphael could not explain why he stopped her. "Forgive my discourtesy, mademoiselle. Stay a moment. What is your name?"

She gave a tight smile. "I thought this curtain might prevent me from having to speak it—as perhaps you did, too."

"But you know my name."

"I do." Why should she speak those words so earnestly? And why should the sound of them make his heart add a beat? "Some names are dangerous, Your Lordship. Mine will not be safe until I have had an audience with the prince."

"What danger would you have His Highness save you from, mademoiselle?" Raphael turned again to watch Tristan, but he could not keep his gaze away from the maiden long. She studied him with a plaintive longing that so closely echoed his own.

"For a long time, I have lived under the shadow of a crime that was not mine. I have finally been acquitted by the court at Demont, but Lord Camesbry does not know that. I have brought with me both an eyewitness to the crime and two other men who can attest my acquittal. I must convince the prince of my innocence before Lord Camesbry can arrest me."

"Why would Lord Camesbry not listen to the same evidence?"

"I fear he can be rather blind where I am concerned. You see, the crime of which I was accused was murdering his wife."

Anger flashed with recognition, and Raphael felt himself scowl. "So you are here, after all. Did you know your father marched away from battle tonight in hopes of finding you?"

The color drained from her face. She had to work her tongue through her mouth several times to force her parched palate to speak. "Did he say what he would do when he found me?"

Such despair poured over him as Raphael had often felt but never seen reflected in another human soul. The anguish in her eyes drew back another curtain, one that hid a truth both beautiful and cruel. Her golden curls framed pallid cheeks drawn hollow by her fear; dainty ruffles pinched at brawny arms; her downcast eyes told stories of a spirit still sublime. Raphael's heart twisted brutally, picturing the life this caged bird had endured.

Her hands clutched nervously at her skirts, and Raphael caught a glimpse of reddened flesh and vulgar thread. Without waiting to ask her leave, he took her hands in his. The wounds were warm.

"Who did this to you, Lady Allia?"

Her eyes softened at the sound of her name. "They are the scars of my own hatred. But you have not answered my question."

"I do not know his plans, but if he gave you these wounds..."

"Not these. Other scars, perhaps, but these are mine alone." She took her hands away and then peered down toward the dancers, reminding Raphael where his duty lay. Tristan was with a different girl now, one whose company seemed to please him a great deal more than the last. A knight in Demont livery tried to cut in.

"Do you see that knight approaching the prince? That is my champion, Sir Johan Winters."

Raphael watched as Tristan waved the knight away and slid out onto the dance floor. "It seems your champion has been spurned, my lady. But I will arrange an audience for you tomorrow, if you will stay."

Raphael had never known a woman could look at him like that, with openness and gratitude, no trace of pity or scorn. His stomach fluttered in a way he had thought was only a story. "Will you be there?" she asked.

"If you wish it."

"And will you summon my father?"

"Alas, he must march to battle tomorrow. He is already too long delayed."

She moved the curtain just enough to fix her eyes on someone below. Raphael followed them toward Lord Camesbry.

"I have neglected to offer you my condolences, Your Lordship. I was unable to attend Prince Lennard's funeral."

"Thank you."

"I met him once, when we were children." She wiped a drip of salt from her cheek. "He will be sorely missed."

A sudden memory assaulted the prince, of his brother boasting about a sword fight with a little girl. Lennard had unsheathed Griffin's Claw and said, "I may be a lion, Little Brother, but she is an eagle." Perhaps it had been true then, but now Raphael would rather have called her a wren: small and crouched among the brambles, yet regal still.

The cheerful notes of wooden flutes wafted to his ears. "Lady Allia, it pains me that I cannot ask you to dance."

"Perhaps not as much as it would pain you to have me for a partner. I fear my feet are hardly more agile than yours."

The back of his neck prickled with ire. Only Lennard and Father Alester had ever dared to jest about his infirmity, but the offer of empathy in Lady Allia's eyes forced an unwilling smile to his lips. "My lady, I would cherish every bruise."

One hand rubbed as if by instinct at her shoulder before she turned again toward the dance. "I have lost sight of Sir Winters. Do you see him?"

Raphael looked down. He did not find Sir Winters—nor did he find Tristan. Father Alester was speaking in whispers with a woman. The informant! But...why was Father Alester leaving her? Why was she standing there, unshackled? Raphael wheeled forward, past the curtain, nearly bowling Lady Allia down. "Damn! Where is my valet? Charles, come!" The brash, red-headed carter had vanished into the dance. "Curse that traitor. Where is Father Alester?" But he could not catch sight of his chaplain now.

"What can I do to help you?"

"Find my valet! I must get downstairs!"

"I do not know your valet to look for him, but I can carry you."

"Nonsense. Your hands..." He pushed forward, but she blocked his path. "Lady Allia, I must insist you step aside."

Instead, she knelt. "If you command it. But these hands have borne greater loads than you... Your Royal Highness."

Raphael's breath caught in his chest.

Lady Allia bowed her head. "I told you that I know your name. Your brother swore me to secrecy, and I have kept it. I do not know who that man on the dance floor may be, but I came here to beg justice of the true and only prince. Please, Your Royal Highness. Let me plead my cause with service." She looked up, and the oath of friendship in her brown eyes burned upon his own. "With your leave, Your Highness." She bent toward him.

"Lady Allia..."

"Please. Your brother showed me kindness such as few people ever have. Let me repay him."

She slid one sturdy arm under his knees, the other around his back, and lifted. Her flushed cheek smoldered against his, igniting shame as bitter as the touch of her was sweet. "This way," he said. The ruffles of her gown fluttered as she obeyed. Down the staircase, right out toward the dance, she carried him. With every step, her panted breath whispered into the depths of his haunted silence. How desperately he wanted to disappear into some quiet nook and revel in the enchantment of her smile! But his kingdom could not wait. He prayed she could.

The moment they reached the dance floor, Lady Allia's champion approached them. "My lady?" he asked, nodding toward the man she carried.

She looked at Raphael, her eyes a question. With a heavy heart, he shook his head.

"I'm sorry," she said. "I cannot explain."

"Where is His Highness?" Raphael demanded.

"He went out into the courtyard with a girl," Sir Winters answered. "The girl returned a moment ago, but His Highness has not come back in. I am waiting to speak with him."

"Where is the girl?" Raphael could feel Lady Allia's arms underneath him sag, and the knowledge that he was hurting her fueled his anger.

"She left toward the carriage yard with another woman."

"Damn! Do you see the chaplain anywhere?" He twisted his body, and Lady Allia nearly lost her balance.

"My lady," said the knight, "let me relieve you..."

Raphael felt a protest sputter to his lips before he saw how pale Lady Allia had become. He wanted to trade places with her, to catch her in his arms and cradle her and never let her go. But just as she was about to pass him to Sir Winters, Father Alester appeared, dragging along a chair. "Here. Set him down. Is the wheeled one still upstairs?"

Lady Allia's arms left his body, and the air left Raphael's lungs. "Never mind my chair," he sputtered. "Where are they—the women?"

"Gone, but I will find them. Will you do me the honor of introducing your friends?" Father Alester toyed with a small blue purse. Raphael knew it must contain the secret of his army's desertion. He nearly snatched it from his chaplain's hands, but instead he turned back toward the girl with compassion brimming in her eyes.

"Father Alester Warren, may I present Lady Allia de Camesbry."

Father Alester's jaws twisted in gruesome mockery of a smile. "How fortuitous. She is just in time to keep her appointment with the gallows."

Lady Allia's eyes flew wide, launching white-hot shafts of accusation straight into Raphael's soul. In that moment, Raphael knew what his brother had felt when a wedge of fatal iron pierced his armor.

"My lady, no…"

She grabbed her champion's hand and slipped as if by magic through Father Alester's lunging arms. Quick as wings, the patter of her golden slippers vanished into the ball.

CHAPTER 26

"Stop!" the chaplain cried. "Halt in the name of the king!" Allia ignored him and dove headlong into the pirouetting sea. Dancers gasped, indignant, as she shoved them all aside. The musicians fell silent as the palace guards raced to answer the chaplain's cries. "Stop that woman!" echoed through the vaulted marble hall, but Allia and Johan swam forward, bumping, jostling, trampling toes, slicing through a net of snatching fingers with the blade of their resolve.

Sentries guarded the main entrance. Allia felt her cheeks grow pale as Johan reached for his sword. "No." She tugged him out another way, into hallways that loomed like ghosts, glossed with murals she had seen when once her prince had held her hand. Johan sputtered questions, but she only answered, "Run!" The halls wound on, she knew not where, while the hounds of persecution thudded closer in behind. An exit... any exit... Yes! The servants' door, a sluice of cool night air. A waiter dropped a tray of crystal, a boot-heel slammed down on her toes, claiming Allia's slipper as she wrenched them free. Onward still she flew, one shard of broken glass lodged deep within the soft flesh underfoot.

Past kitchens, privies, and barns they ran, to a smithy where a saddled horse stood tied. Johan sliced the tether, mounted, and then hauled his lady up behind. "Sam! Garred!" he shouted, but no answer came. He gave a vicious kick, and the gelding lumbered forward, twitching with blind fear. Allia clung to her champion's waist as they found a breach in the castle walls, the little iron northern gate. "Close it! In the name of Christ, close the gate!" rang out from behind, but Johan dug his heels into the dappled hide that carried them away.

Abrupt and sharp, the mountains swallowed them, bridle trails running off like rivulets through every crevice, crack, and vale. Johan snaked left, then right, then left again, until the sounds of the hunt faded into the cloudy night. Allia laid her head against his back and wept into his blue livery.

"We've lost them, my lady."

She nodded against him, lost to her tears.

"What happened back there? The gallows? Why?"

"I don't know. Some sort of trap... I thought..." But what she thought she had seen in Prince Raphael's eyes hurt too much to say.

Johan turned sideways on the horse to wrap an arm around Allia's shoulders. "My lady, who was that man you were carrying?"

"Oh, God, I wish I knew." Who was that man who wore a borrowed name to hide his royal birth, that prince with tenderness in careworn hands more hardened than her own? Was he just a hapless pawn, the echo of dead greatness, clinging like the soot of burnt-out candles to the walls of a darkened hall where lions used to roar? Or was he the kingdom's impresario, the unseen hand that pulled the royal puppets' strings? Had he been as shocked as she when the priest condemned her to the gallows, or had he baited her with friendship so his chaplain could spring the trap?

As painful as it was to think Prince Raphael had betrayed her, Allia found herself hoping it was true. Father Alester, whom she had never met, could have no reason of his own to condemn her. The malice he had spoken must have been reflected from some other source; and Father Alester was the same priest she had seen in conversation with her father. If Prince Raphael had not called for her death, then perhaps Lord Camesbry had.

Allia let out another sob as the horse bumped her foot against a tree.

"What ails you, my lady?"

"Glass in my foot." The real wound cut too deeply to explain. "Please, can we rest?"

"Of course, my lady." Johan nudged the horse forward, inching slowly through the darkness until he found a small copse of ash trees. Breezes tickled the leafy lyres, rustling an accompaniment to an owl's inquisitive song. *Who?* the night bird asked. Allia closed her eyes. She thought she knew the answer.

Johan secured their mount; then he helped Allia down and set her on a log. He tried to examine her foot. "My lady, I cannot see the wound. But this breeze may blow the clouds away from the moon. We will wait for the light."

"All right."

Allia leaned against the tree while Johan settled himself on the ground. The owl again cried, *Who?* She tried to stop her ears, but she could not stop her mind. Why would a man she had only met tonight —a prince with justice burning bright inside his eyes—plot to have her killed? It was her father who had nursed a toxic grudge through eight unrelenting years. Her father had marched away from battle to find her. Her father had been speaking in whispers with the chaplain just before he tried to have her hanged.

Her father wanted her to die.

Allia felt her tears drip down her face and unravel her soul. Why had her father finally fallen into the chasm of vengeance on whose edge he had teetered so long? Was it because the jeweler had refused her? Or because she ran away? Did it even matter why? Here, on the very night when she had hoped to free her Papa from the quicksand of lies, he had suffocated the last of his love. She felt an axe blade chopping at her heart and wondered if he had felled the hazel tree before he set out for the ball. In her mind, she watched its pale bark splinter, its broad green leaves tumble to the ground. So real to her was the imagined sound of fractured wood, she almost did not notice when an arrow zipped into the ash tree just inches from her ear.

"My lady! Get…" Johan's warning broke into a garbled cry. He toppled backward, a feathered shaft protruding from his left shoulder. He tried to draw his sword, but another arrow found his right arm. Allia drew the blade instead. Her stitched hands screamed against the hilt, but she only gripped it harder.

"Who goes there?" She wheeled in unsteady circles on her wounded foot. The frantic whinny of their tethered horse nearly drowned her words. She called into the darkness, "If you are come to arrest me, I surrender."

From behind her, laughter like a flash of lightning lit the midnight gloom. "Lady Allia," a warm voice crooned. "Again I find myself treating with you across a blade."

The moon peeked out from behind its cloudy curtain, illuminating a whole ring of assailants as they stepped out from the trees. "Solomon," Allia gasped as the peddler's inscrutable brown eyes met hers. They widened with respect.

"So you cared enough to learn my name." A pack of bowmen surrounded them. "You may keep the sword if you choose, my lady, but I am in command here. You have nothing to fear."

She glanced toward his companions: men with ice-blonde hair and arms marked with the ticklish fingers of spidery tattoos.

"Darrivants!" Allia gripped the sword with doubled strength. "Solomon, why…?"

The peddler came forward, his eyes unmasked. "The kingdom needs change, my lady. Your kingdom, where you were meant to be a queen, yet men like your father are allowed to oppress even their own children. Is it he whom you were fleeing?"

"I don't know." She tore her eyes away from her peddler to look at her champion. Johan lay sweating on the ground, his eyelids fluttering in and out of consciousness. "Johan…" She fell to his side and stroked his hair away from his drenched brow. "Johan, can you hear me?" He looked at her, but did not answer. Was it only a trick of the moonlight that made the blood around his wounds appear so thick and black?

Solomon peered forward. "Johan? Surely not… Rabigny?" His lip curled into an ugly snarl. He drew his sword, barking orders in a language Allia did not understand. His archers put away their bows to draw their blades. "Lady Allia," said Solomon, "is this the boy who nearly lured you to your death and then cursed you to enslavement by his cowardice?"

She stepped between her peddler and her champion, raising her own steel. "It is, and if you intend to harm him, you shall have to go through me."

Admiration deepened inside the peddler's dusky eyes. "So you have resurrected something worthy from this spineless worm?"

"No. That is what he did for me."

"Then it seems we have both been engaged in the business of rebirth." He sheathed his sword, said something in Darrivant, and his comrades did the same. "They will tend him," he said to Allia. "No harm shall come to him. I swear it."

Dubiously, Allia watched as one of the Darrivants came forward and poured something from a vial into Johan's mouth. Johan relaxed, his breathing growing steadier as he closed his eyes. "A poppy seed mixture, to help with the pain," Solomon explained.

The Darrivant carefully removed both needle-sharp arrows from Johan's arms. "Solomon, what is happening?"

"Invasion, of course. We are merely a scouting party, but the end of the war is not far behind."

Allia took a step toward him and cringed as the shard of glass sank further into her bare foot.

"You are wounded, my lady." Solomon eased his shoulder under her sword arm until it bore her weight. She hardly realized he was holding her until the tufts of his chestnut beard prickled her flushed cheek. She looked into his tawny, open eyes, and let Johan's sword fall to the ground.

The peddler set her on the same log she had vacated when the attack began. He took Allia's throbbing foot into the shelter of his hands. Under the touch of cunning fingers, the offending shard slid out. "Lady Allia, was it by chance you learned my name? Or dare I hope you have been searching for me?"

She exhaled the dizzying breath of her dying dream. "I did search for you. But now that I have found you scouting for the enemy, what more is there to say?"

"Enemy? No. Call me a spy, a traitor, a revolutionary, but until my dying day, I will always be your friend."

"Solomon, why?"

"Let me show you." He lingered there, holding her tiny ankle in the warmth of his strong hands. Then he stood to his full height and gave another command. The man tending Johan tied off his bandages, slung the unconscious knight over his back, and fell into marching order with his companions. Allia could find no words to wonder as the peddler untethered her horse, lifted her onto its saddle, and led them all away into the trees.

IN THE DOORWAY OF THE SERVANTS' entrance to the palace, Lord Eric de Camesbry stooped to pick up one tiny, trampled golden shoe.

CHAPTER 27

$\mathcal{B}$y the time Lady Vivienne summoned her coachman, the chaos had begun. Even from the carriage yard, she could hear the turmoil in the city. She felt the sweat on her coachman's clammy palms as he handed her into the carriage, but thankfully he was not the sort to question orders. As soon as she and Lilliane were settled, he whipped the matched pair of grays to motion.

A palace guard lowered a spear across the gate. "Best stay the night," he said. "The wenches figured out they won't all get in."

A crash accompanied by a scream of horses echoed through the streets, followed by shouts and the zing of steel. Lilliane's fingernails bit into her mother's arm. Vivienne called from the coach, "Your warning is noted, good sir, but we have had urgent word from home. James and the horses know their business, I assure you."

"As you will, then." He raised his spear to let them pass.

An overturned carriage less than a block from the palace accounted for the noise. Two city guardsmen kept the maddened hordes at bay while five men worked to free someone's unlucky horse that had been trapped beneath the wreck. As Vivienne's carriage passed the ruckus, two red-faced maidens broke into a brawl. They scratched and bit and tore each other's gowns while grown men tried without success to pry their feline claws apart.

Vivienne opened the window and called to the driver, "Take the back streets. Do not let the horses flag."

"Yes, my lady." The horses whinnied as the coachman turned, but his whip kept them at pace.

Lilliane stared across the coach with bitter, narrowed eyes. "Mother, what have you done?"

"I do not know what you mean, child."

"Prince Raphael told me to flee before his own guards should arrest you. He told me that I might be implicated in your schemes." She leaned forward, seething. "What have you done?"

The city guards were out in force, stationed in pairs on every block, though a hundred angry maidens and their escorts thronged the streets for every guard. A kingdom's worth of shrews invited to connive at winning a prince's hand; Prince Raphael had been cooped up in a monastery too long if he had not known a riot would result. Looking backward, Vivienne could see the palace battlements, where ruffle-clad invaders had begun to climb.

"I purchased his hand for you," Vivienne answered, "with a dowry no prince could refuse."

"I did not need a dowry! He loves me!"

"Indeed, but love is the one convenience a prince can never afford." Yet he was a strange creature, this Raphael, to propose before he ever laid eyes on the evidence that sealed their deal; to warn Lilliane that his own men were prepared to arrest her; to decree a ball that was certain to end in bedlam...

The coachman turned a corner, and in one hot, hellish breath, a street of flame and cinders opened wide, infernal jaws. The horses reared, the coachman swore, and Vivienne and Lilliane toppled to the floor. The wheels thumped hard beneath them and then jerked left, but there was no room. Vivienne scrambled to her seat and threw open the sash. A crush of people barred their path, mothers with babes in arms, racing men with buckets, sooty girls with half-burned braids. Tongues of fire lapped the heels of opportunists rushing past with livestock, furniture, or chandeliers. "Go!" Lady Vivienne screamed. The coachman cracked his whip. The horses flailed; hooves knocked aside whatever flesh stood in their way. More screams—a sound of crunching bone—a bloody man left lame. To their right, a howl like razors, where through the glass they glimpsed a grizzled man with breeches dropped, spilling virgin blood that would never be requited.

Lilliane shrieked and cowered, but Vivienne stared and watched. *This is all there is*, she would have told that ravished girl. *Ash and blood. This is our kingdom.* She had known that once, too well, back in the one-room house in Anniton where the burly, drunkard soldier kept his wife and child. She had known the ash when the fire grew cold because Papa went to war and sent no wages home. She had known the blood when that squalling, puny sister speared through Mama's womb only to asphyxiate in her cradle. Ash fell like deadly snow the year they burned the bodies when the cholera swept through. Then virgin blood—her own—had drenched her widowed Papa's grief. Ash and blood, the devil's dual currency; Vivienne had seen the wages he paid out with such largesse. Never again, she had sworn, and twice, she had conquered the demons. The first time, they had crept in like termites to eat her happiness from inside. Such a fool she had been, when the wool merchant wrapped her in his arms, to believe that love could last. When it ended, she had found a trade, and built her life on gold.

Gold was the only bedrock the devil could not break; power was the only fortress that held him at bay. There was power in the name of Camesbry, power in a general's sword, power in channeling a man's fury toward the daughter he could not bear to look at because love had failed him, too. Allia had been the cornerstone of their defense, but the fortress was crumbling now. Lady Camesbry looked at her daughter sobbing on the carriage floor, the cut her stepfather had left on her cheek limned in ghostly moonlit hues. The time had come to find a stronger citadel, and now they had: a prince, a palace, and a throne, gold the bedrock, power the walls. Yet here they sat, in exile, with the princess weeping as they fled through ash and blood.

"Lilliane," her mother ordered, "stop that moaning. Dry your tears."

"Sh... she..."

"I saw it, too. Rape, pillage, fire—this is your prince's city. We have chosen the wrong side."

The daughter raised her bloodshot eyes. "What do you mean?"

"I mean, when the Darrivants come, do these look like people who will rise to their kingdom's defense, or people who will offer their monarch's head as tribute to secure their own lives?"

"But he loves me..."

"Your father loved me, too. That did not save him. You have a choice, Lilliane: your husband or your life."

The girl shuddered. "What should we do?"

"What we should have done long ago. We join the victors and take the spoils."

~

FATHER ALESTER's lungs were burning. Running did not come as easily to him now as it once had. He leaned against a column in the dance hall, panting. The dancing had stopped while the musicians rumbled rumors right alongside the guests. Prince Raphael sat stranded in the chair where Lady Allia had placed him, still shouting for his vanished valet. The prince had not yet spied the chaplain across the room, for which Father Alester was grateful. He was not prepared to snuff out the light he had seen on his beloved Raphael's face when he introduced Lady Allia.

Tristan attempted to slink inside from the courtyard unnoticed, but sharp maiden eyes plucked him out from the crowd. Girls scurried toward him with gossip dribbling from their tongues. As always, Father Alester listened.

"Who were they, Your Highness?"

"She looked noble."

"He wore the Demont Coat of Arms."

Demont... Was that where Lady Allia had fled from her father?

196

Was that where she would flee again? Father Alester watched Tristan bolt down a glass of wine and shake the clinging harpies from his cape only to be accosted by an officer of the City Guards. The guardsman's livery was stained with soot. "Your Highness, the maidens that haven't gotten in are rioting," he whispered. "There is a fire in East Point..."

"Do whatever you have to," Tristan barked. "You have my leave."

The stunned guardsman gave a curt bow and went out while the word *fire* swept like a contagion through the hall. A few girls hurried out, screaming. "Blast it," Alester cursed. He marched toward the musicians, hoping a dance could prevent a stampede, but a shadow fell over his shoulder.

"They had best bring her in unharmed, Father, or the Darrivants will have one more deserter in their ranks."

Alester turned to see Lord Camesbry's fat face bloated red. "My lord, I would not make such threats if I were you. Your daughter stands accused of treason, and at the moment, so do you."

Lord Camesbry blanched. "You dare..." His fingers twisted at a shining object in his hands: a shoe.

"What is happening here, Father?" Chancellor Narius elbowed his way toward them. "Who were those people you were chasing?"

"One of them was my daughter," Camesbry grumbled.

"I shall explain in the council chamber," said Father Alester. "But first we must avoid bloodshed in this hall. Pardon me, gentlemen." He pushed his way toward Tristan. "Your Highness, I suggest you start dancing again before they riot."

Tristan's eyes seemed glazed, but he regained himself and looked around. The buzz of panic was growing louder, but it fell silent when Tristan clapped his hands. "Ladies and gentlemen," he cried in that booming, princely voice, "there is nothing to fear. There is a fire, but it is blocks away, and the guards have it contained."

Father Alester knew not whether to feel pride at the ease with which his student lied.

"Come, mademoiselle." Tristan offered his hand to the nearest girl. "Music, maestro!" The musicians jumped and dove headlong into a tune, its strains somehow gruesomely merry.

Alester sighed relief as the ball became a ball again. He turned his steps toward Prince Raphael, but the prince had found his derelict valet. The two of them were racing off in the direction of the chapel. No doubt, they were looking for Alester himself, but Raphael's livid face did not foretell a happy conversation.

Father Alester summoned the nearest server. "Put down your tray and run to catch up with Baron Immerville. Tell him to make his way to the solarium if he wants to hear the truth."

The server furrowed his brow, but did as he was told.

Alester exhaled and dragged his leaden feet across the floor. Most of the guests had begun dancing again, with determination now rather than delight. Midnight tolled from the chapel bells, and the Camesbry soldiers all seemed suddenly aware that tomorrow, they would march to battle. Clusters of them stood talking about where they might catch a few hours' sleep, ignoring the yawning girls who lingered without partners. Only Simon the Unvanquished still capered without care, spinning his exhausted daughter with childish glee. *Would that we were all as mad as he*, Alester thought bitterly. *The kingdom might be joyful then.*

Alester walked slowly, trying to give Prince Raphael time to become ensconced among the flowers, but he did not stop to speak to him. What had passed between Raphael and Lady Allia, Alester did not know, but he had seen its effects. For more than a decade, he had prayed that someday the child he loved would smile with the kind of joy that had lit his face tonight. That Raphael had found happiness in the company of a traitor was a message Father Alester could not bear to relay in person. He bypassed the solarium and went straight to the council chamber, where Camesbry and Narius were waiting.

Lord Camesbry stood with his hand on his sword hilt. "I suggest you tell me quickly why my daughter just fled this palace with soldiers on her heels."

"And I suggest you calm yourself, my lord. I will ask you to leave and speak only to the Lord Chancellor if you cannot contain your temper."

Camesbry's nostrils flared, but Narius gave a conciliatory shrug. "Please, Eric. Sit down."

Grudgingly, Lord Camesbry sat.

Father Alester took the small blue purse from the pocket of his alb. "I had an offer from an informant to tell me why our soldiers are deserting—the same informant who told me about Anniton. I asked her to bring the information here tonight, and she did. The evidence is in this purse."

"You do not expect me to believe that evidence implicates my daughter."

Father Alester withdrew the scroll and unrolled it. "Is this your daughter's signature, my lord?"

Lord Camesbry leaned forward, his fingers twisting at the golden shoe. "This is a bill of sale, but for what?"

"For this." Father Alester took out the vial. "I have not had time to test it, but the informant tells me it is a love potion, the same one that was outlawed in Demont last year. It seems the Darrivants are using it to tip their arrows—and, according to that bill of sale, it is your daughter who brews it."

Lord Camesbry closed his fist around the scroll. "Your informant is brewing lies. Arrows tipped with love potion... how much did you pay for that bit of battlefield wisdom?"

"It is a story that accounts for the blackened wounds you have seen yourself, my lord. But what I paid for the information should not concern you. What should, is the identity of the informant."

"Why do I care what conniving whore you keep in your employ?"

"Because, my lord, that conniving whore happens to be your wife."

Lord Camesbry froze.

"I would ask you to positively identify her, but she has already fled. If she had been anyone else, I would have detained her, but of course..."

"Vivienne," Camesbry whispered. "*Vivienne* told you about Anniton?"

"Yes, my lord."

"How in God's name...?"

"This changes matters," said Chancellor Narius gravely. "Your wife tells where the attack will come, and then you engineer its defense? Eric, if I had not known you thirty years..."

"Peter, you cannot think I had anything to do with this!"

"Your wife is extorting the crown with secrets, your daughter is colluding with the enemy," said Alester, "and this very day, you marched away from battle. Tell us, with this evidence before your court, my lord, what would be the verdict?"

Eric de Camesbry laid his head in his hands. When he raised it again, he spoke only to Chancellor Narius. "These are grave charges. I cannot answer for my wife, nor for my daughter. For myself, I can say only that I was ignorant of whatever they have done. I marched away from battle today to find my only child. She ran away some weeks ago, and with every maiden in the kingdom bidden here tonight, it was my last hope to find her. And I was right. She was here. If not for this rash spy of a priest..." He clenched his fists, but forced himself to release them. "Peter, your suspicions are understandable. However, if you detain me here long enough to investigate and hold a proper trial, Pellain will fall. If I do not march to battle tomorrow, my judges will be Darrivants, not Armans."

"I find it unlikely," said Alester, "that you endangered the entire kingdom for the sake of a runaway cinder maid unless you were also involved in her treason."

Chancellor Narius twirled his bushy moustache. "You have us in quite a spot here, Eric. It defies all logic to send an accused traitor out to battle."

"They are my men, Peter. Yes, my captains could lead them, but do you think they will be focused on the battle or on the fact that their lord, the guest of honor at a ball to celebrate his victory, has just been clapped in irons?" All the while he spoke, his fingers toyed at the unclaimed shoe.

"They are the only force within two days' ride of Pellain," Narius acknowledged. "If you do not march tomorrow, the garrison will certainly fall. But you can see, the fact that you did not march *today*..."

"You are right, Lord Camesbry," Father Alester butted in. "There is no hope unless you march and no time to make a complete investigation before morning. So I propose that, instead, you leave us a surety of your loyalty."

"Come, Alester," said Narius, "what are you thinking?"

"I am thinking about that shoe my lord has very nearly ruined."

Camesbry's red cheeks drained to white as he at last stopped twisting.

Father Alester put out his hand. "Give us the slipper, my lord. If Pellain falls, the girl who wears its mate shall meet the headsman's axe."

CHAPTER 28

$\mathcal{T}$he night seemed made of silence. Even the click of the palfrey's hooves on the mountain rock sounded soft as raindrops, as if noise might offend some starlit god. Allia watched the placid progress of the peddler's every step as he led her horse deeper into the unknown. His band of Darrivant soldiers followed, lethal ducklings on the march. They took turns carrying the unconscious Johan on their backs. Allia could have asked the thousand questions nearly bursting from her lips, but the sound, she knew, would somehow be profane. Her voice would shatter the vow of trust their silence sealed.

The summer night was cold this high up in the mountains. Allia had nothing but her ball gown to cover her as she shivered. A tension in the peddler's step, a tightening of his shoulders when her teeth chattered through the calm, told her that he knew her discomfort but carried nothing that could make her warm. She hunched as deep into the saddle as she could, near the heat of the horse's flesh, and watched the man she might have married stride undaunted through the perilous trails where one false step spelled doom. Every gentle tug of reins, every stalwart swing of his muscled arms, sent pangs of longing through Allia's goose-pimpled skin. Was this lust, this awful urge to let his bearded lips roam over hers, to feel the safety of his body sheltering her from pain? In her dream, a serpent had slithered through the peddler's thrilling touch, and Solomon Regis was a serpent: the worst kind, a betrayer. But could not a man who betrayed his country still be faithful to his wife? In her dream, faithfulness had saved her, but faithfulness to what? A crumbling regime where a lord had the power to hang his own child?

But the regime had not always been crumbling. It might have been one of those very archers marching just behind who launched the quarrel that killed her prince. It might have been the peddler who gave her his sword, his promise, and his hand, who also gave the order.

Now and then she dozed while the silent march crept onward. Every hour or so, they paused to let the men shift custody of their captive knight. At every exchange, Allia watched them check Johan's breathing and his bandages. Johan fluttered in and out of consciousness, but he never said a word; perhaps that was the work of the poppy seed medicine, which they gave him every few hours. Allia could hardly guess what prompted the Darrivants to treat their enemy so well, but she could not deny that Johan's breathing grew steadier as the night drew on. Whatever the Darrivants intended, it was clear they meant their prisoner no harm.

Dawn came at last in quiet hues of gold, and strains of distant birdsong filled the air. Allia unclenched her aching muscles, rubbing at her knotted neck as she forced herself to sit upright. Her stitched hands burned under fresh scabs.

"My lady," Solomon said, "there is a spring just off the path. Please, come drink." He lifted her from the saddle, careful not to set her weight on the injured foot that lacked a shoe. She stumbled as she took the first few steps, legs jellied from the ride. He caught her elbow and held her steady. His fingers seemed to sizzle through the pale silk of her sleeve.

They climbed a grassy slope that flattened toward a clear brook swollen with melted snow. Allia knelt and took a sip; a frigid burn of strength knifed through her chest. She splashed her face, washed her throbbing hands, and then looked up.

"You are not drinking," she said.

Obligingly, the peddler knelt beside her, dipped his hands, and took a draught. The water trickling from his beard left sun-kissed droplets on the bank. He turned impenetrable eyes upon her and brushed a matted curl from her forehead. "I would have ridden behind you, wrapped you tight in my arms, if you had been in danger of freezing. But we could not have gone far that way in the dark. The horse would have toppled over a cliff with no one to follow."

"'Tis of no consequence. I have survived more chilling cold than this."

"I know. I was there." His brown eyes stared into the brook, one icy mirror pondering another. "I was nibbling on a sweet roll. It was my idea of poetry, because I was on my way to an even sweeter roll with the girl who washed your great-aunt's clothes. I stopped to watch you skate." He smiled half a smile. "There were snowflakes in your hair."

Allia wrung her dampened curls. "Did you keep your assignation?"

He laughed. "No, my lady. You foiled it. The girl I was supposed to meet was the one who carried you inside."

"And you…?"

"I did nothing. A boy crashed through the ice to certain death, and I, a sergeant of the guards, stood rooted like a blasted tree and watched an eleven-year-old girl find the courage I could not."

"Eight years have passed since then. How many times have you visited my home during that time? Could you never have told my father what you saw?"

Solomon sighed. "I did. But no one saw me at the pond that day. I could provide no corroboration, and my word was not enough to melt as cold a heart as his." He laid his hand on hers. "God did not grant that my penance should be so easy as to testify. But if there can be a recompense for what you lost, then I have paid it."

"How can you buy back a vanished life?"

"By giving you a new one." The rising sun behind him burnished the mountainside with promise.

"I would accept it gladly. But..."

"But there is the small matter of those Darrivant archers down the way."

She nodded.

"You still hold out hope for this miserable kingdom, and I would not love you half as much if you did not. You will see, though. Hope for Armany does not lie in a system that judges a man's value by his birth and not his deeds. The Darrivants rise and fall by their own merits. That is what I mean to bring to Armany: a kingdom where tyrants can be crushed without war and justice done without a sword."

"Are arrows any better? They make men just as dead."

He traced his finger through the soil. "Do you mean your prince?"

"Yes."

"Did you love him?"

Allia sat dumb. Was it true to say she loved him, that golden ideal of a man she had wrapped so closely around her pain? All those years she had held his boyish smile in her mind, dreaming of the justice that would free her from the ashes—she had not dared, then, to think of him as more than just a prince. Now, however, when both the fairy and Queen Eleanor had named her as his bride... It would have been a political marriage. A prince could not afford to make any other kind. But politics could not change the fact that once a little girl had looked at herself through a prince's eyes and seen a woman who was more than decoration.

"Yes," she answered. "I loved him, and I would have loved him more, if God had given me that chance."

"So my tally of sins grows longer." Solomon shook his head. "But life is always bought with death, my lady. Then we rise." He squeezed her fingers. "There is more death ahead of us. It is always the way, when one clears out a choked and overgrown land to plant a fertile field. The flowers die alongside the thorns."

"What will you plant, after the land is cleared?"

"What every kingdom needs: justice, peace, and freedom."

His fingers twined like roots through hers, and Allia could feel his dream grafting itself onto the battered remnants of her own. "What will it look like, this justice? Who will decide it?"

"The people. There will be juries, not merely lords. The Emperor himself will be bound by their rulings."

"But the people do not make the laws. They do not choose the Emperor."

"No Emperor's son can take the throne without approval from his vassal kings, no king without approval from his lords, no lord without approval from his barons, and no baron without approval from his people. It is the people, ultimately, who reign."

"Who will be the vassal king in Armany?"

"It could have been your prince, if he had lived to bend the knee. If his brother is wise enough to love his people more than his power, he shall have the same opportunity."

Allia's spine tingled with relief, to think that joining her peddler need not implicate her in Prince Raphael's death. But she pressed her argument further. "Nothing really changes, then. All this bloodshed to clear the land, but the crops will be the same."

"Everything changes. You have not been to Darrivane. My lady, if I could only describe..." The sunlight glinted in his fathomless eyes. "Everything changes. And it begins on the day when you, a cinder maid, bring a charge against the Lord of Camesbry in a court where the people he used to rule shall decide his fate."

Allia could not help but feel conviction pulsing through Solomon's grasp, could not prevent her mind from wandering through halls where every bruise her father had ever given her cried out for atonement. She dared not ask what the sentence would be. She only listened to the imagined sound of the splintering hazel tree and tightened her fingers around his.

"My lady, this is your war I'm fighting, to bring you vindication."

"Why?"

"Because I should have been the one whose life was lost out on the ice. All these years, all those visits to your home to purchase your stepmother's wares but also to keep you in my sight, to make sure they could not crush you, that you would always be the girl who was willing to climb that tree after her friend..." He took her hand and kissed it, his lips unwilling to let go. "Allia, I have done it as a penance. But most of all, I have done it because I love you."

They were the words of magic—not of serpents but of seraphs, joyful words that poured a salve into her shattered soul. She did not try to stop her tears. Instead, she folded her body into the safety of his arms and let her happiness drip onto his hands.

"Allia, it's over now. You're free." He raised her to her feet and laid his lips on hers.

Allia's pulse raced as his arms curled around her, but peace flooded through her heart. For the first time since her mother died, she was not ashamed to be alive. If her tragedy could inspire this man to topple a kingdom, what could he build when inspired by her love?

Solomon finally pulled away and smiled. Allia could almost touch the kindness in his gaze. "Come, my lady. The men are waiting for our return before they take their drink from the stream." He took her hands, and where he led, she gladly followed.

Somewhere inside the whisper of the frosty mountain wind, Allia thought she heard a flutter of silver-bright wings.

CHAPTER 29

*T*he smoke from the capitol suffocated the sunrise.

At dawn, the Prince of Armany sat on a balcony, watching the steady work of the bucket brigade through his spyglass. They had contained the blaze to a neighborhood called East Point, a district filled mostly with homes, taverns, and the like. The flames had not touched the great storehouses that supplied the army, nor the merchant district where the kingdom's commerce thrived. That would be no consolation to the homeless, nor the injured or the dead.

Away from the flames, thousands of maidens and their escorts had spent the night in open streets. Those who had them slept in carriages, but many more lay huddled on cobblestone beds with no other cushion than the skirt of the next girl's dress. Stiff and dirty, the masses stretched as far as even the spyglass could see. From far and wide they had traveled to answer a royal decree and received for their efforts nothing but a royal snub. When they roused and the unburnt taverns ran short of breakfast before half of them were fed —what then?

Raphael swung his spyglass against the railing, shattering the lens. The thing was good for nothing but to magnify his sorrow.

"Your Lordship," came the voice of his valet, "I found the two men you wanted. They were in the servants' quarters. They say they are at your disposal."

Raphael choked down the lump in his throat. "And is it true…?"

"Aye, they confirm the story."

Beads of sweat broke out along the prince's brow. "Have them wait for me in the chapel, inside the confessional. Tell them to close the door, and I shall signal them when they are wanted. Then return to me."

The valet squinted. "Really?"

"Yes. Do not take no for an answer. After you have done that, give this to the steward." He handed the valet a scroll. "His Highness has ordered that the ball continue for two more nights, so that all the maidens may have their turns."

The valet could not read, but he peered suspiciously at the scroll nonetheless. "His Highness was dancing until the wee hours. He has not risen yet today."

Raphael crossed his arms across his chest. "Deliver it to the steward. Then return for me."

"All right. It's your head, not mine."

Raphael watched the valet depart and then sighed deeply. It had felt good to sign that scroll, *His Royal Highness, Raphael d'Armany*. Tristan would be livid at the prospect of two more nights of dancing, but the people must receive what they had been promised. *His* people.

Yet there was only one among them he truly wanted to call his own.

Raphael wheeled himself back inside the palace. The well-worn embrace of his wooden chair chafed him with its strangeness. All morning, he had twisted in his seat, unable to make it fit his body. His skin seemed fused into the shape of the girl whose arms had carried his heart into her exile.

Raphael had listened to the exchange between Father Alester, Lord Camesbry, and Chancellor Narius with a rage that bordered on apoplexy. He would have burst into the council chamber and possibly gotten himself run through on Lord Camesbry's sword if he had had his wheeled chair; but the valet had deposited him on an ordinary chair in the solarium, so Raphael had to sit and absorb the monstrous charges leveled against one of the kingdom's most powerful lords, his wife, and his daughter, without comment. Then, when Father Alester came to speak with him afterward... the result of that interview still left Raphael's insides burning. Never before had the chaplain openly defied him, and Raphael meant to see that it never happened again.

But Father Alester would have to wait. So would Tristan—who really was asleep—and whatever information he had gleaned from Lady Camesbry's daughter. One errand must come first, one that could not wait even another half an hour. Raphael fidgeted with the contents of his pockets and shored up his resolve with the memory of hazelnut eyes.

The valet returned at last. "All right, it's done, Your Lordship. You want to go down to the chapel?"

"First bring me to the lists. I would speak with Lord Camesbry."

The Camesbry soldiers were assembling in the space between the concentric palace walls, their green and silver kestrels now draped over plate and mail. Raphael found Lord Camesbry with his squire, just fastening on the last of his armor. "My lord," he called, "may I have a word? 'Tis about your daughter."

The general wiped his brow, his helmet in his hand. "Immerville? What the devil...?"

"She spoke to me last night. Before she ran."

Camesbry narrowed his beady blue eyes.

"In the chapel, if you don't mind, my lord. It's quiet there."

Lord Camesbry nodded and followed the valet through the bustle of soldiers. The sweat from Raphael's brow dripped onto his valet's shoulder. Inside the chapel, the air was cool, the stained-glass saints just rousing from their nighttime pallor into a dim palette of dawn. The valet set Prince Raphael down on a pew and then skulked away.

Lord Camesbry chose to stand. "I have to march." He toyed with the hinged visor on his helm.

"I shall be quick." Raphael withdrew from his pocket the pouch containing the vial of black liquid and the bill of sale. "You recognize these, of course, my lord."

As if of their own will, Lord Camesbry's fingers reached for the two small objects that spelled his family's doom. He turned the vial round and round in his hands. "They tell me Allia made this, but these are Vivienne's bottles. She buys them for her cosmetics."

"And is Lady Camesbry the sort of woman who would notice if they went missing?"

Lord Camesbry leveled his gaze at Raphael. "Yes."

"Would she be likely to lend them to Lady Allia for any reason? Or sell them, or give them away?"

Lord Camesbry set down the vial. "You are trying to prove my daughter is innocent."

"You will be pleased to know, Father Alester also admits the possibility, though he is not willing to wager much on its truth." Raphael forced himself to remain calm, though the very mention of the chaplain made the blood boil in his veins. "Would you take a look at the parchment again, my lord?"

Lord Camesbry pored closely over the slanting scrawl.

"Is that her signature?"

"I suppose so. We left Allia to make the transaction with my wife's peddler when we were called to His Highness's funeral."

Raphael's face fell. "So the signature is real?"

"I have no reason to think otherwise."

The prince's heart pounded an allegro against his ribs. "Did your daughter know what was in those bottles when she sold them?"

Camesbry sighed. "I cannot answer you for a certainty. My daughter is capable of unspeakable things…"

"You believe so, my lord, but I do not. Gentlemen," he raised his voice, praying the men he had sent to the confessional had not tired of their waiting. "Come out, please."

With aching slowness, the confessional door opened and a young, round face peered out. "Yes, come," Raphael repeated, and the man stepped slowly forward, followed by an older, dour figure. Raphael said a silent prayer of thanks that they both wore Demont livery.

Lord Camesbry's great brows drew taut. "What is this?"

"More evidence, my lord, though pertaining to a different crime.

212

Gentlemen, I am Baron Timothy d'Immerville, and this man before you is Lord Camesbry. Please, introduce yourselves."

"I… Sam Hemming, of the Demont guards," the young one managed.

"Sergeant Garred Shearer," the older one said, his eyes never leaving Lord Camesbry. "My lord, we escorted your daughter to the ball."

Every muscle in Lord Camesbry's face fell slack. "You… but…"

"She was acquitted, my lord," the one called Sam offered with a shy bow. "Of your wife's death, I mean. Lady Demont named Lady Allia her heir. I heard it with mine own ears."

"She… but what happened…?" Camesbry's tongue seemed to have thickened inside his mouth.

"The boy, Johan Rabigny, Sir Winters as he calls himself now, he admits he fell through the ice first. Your daughter went in trying to save him. He testified to it himself."

Lord Camesbry stood silent. Then he sank down on the pew next to Raphael. A gasp as deep as Noah's flood escaped the great man's bosom. He fell to his knees, eyes lifted toward the litany that lined the stained glass walls. Raphael followed his gaze to the nearest casement: St. Lucy, with her sapphire eyes outstretched upon a tray, luminous and clear.

"My lord, I will ask again. Did Lady Allia know what was in those vials when she sold them?"

"Of course not. Vivienne would never confide…" The sentence broke into another gasp.

Raphael turned toward the two guards. "Thank you, gentlemen. You may prepare to return to Demont. If you find Lady Allia there, please tell her what you have witnessed. Tell her she need fear no danger here. I give my word."

"*Your* word," Camesbry growled as he stood. "As if *your* word matters while that dastard priest still has that blasted shoe."

"As to that…" Raphael almost could not form his mouth around his words, so round and bitter was the memory of Father Alester refusing to relinquish either the slipper or his vow. *I shall not allow your infatua-*

tion to ruin the kingdom, Your Highness... Raphael raised blazing eyes toward Lord Camesbry. "Crush the Darrivants, my lord. In the name of Armany. Push them back from Pellain, and then follow them to the ends of the earth, if you must, until every last one of them lies dead. The kingdom will be safe, and so will she."

Camesbry stared curiously at Raphael. "I shall," he said, and then handed back the pouch of evidence. "She's enchanted you, hasn't she, Immerville?"

Raphael only answered with his blush.

"Of course she has. She looks like her mother. And the rub of it is, if you had not told me this, I would have said it served her right to marry half a man." Lord Camesbry extended his hand. "I thank you, Your Lordship."

Raphael did not meet Lord Camesbry's eyes as he shook his hand.

"Shall we ride with you, my lord?" called the younger guardsman.

"No, Mr. Hemming. Ride to Demont. If my daughter is there..." Lord Camesbry shoved his helmet roughly onto his head. "Tell her I am sorry. And then, for the love of God, bring every man in your company and make haste for Pellain."

"Yes, my lord," replied the guard as Lord Camesbry stormed past him out of the chapel.

"Many thanks, Your Lordship," said the older guard to Raphael. "It is good to know that Lady Allia has a friend in the palace. I daresay your word might mean more to her than it does to her father."

The prince knew not what to make of his expression. "Thank you, Sergeant Shearer, Mr. Hemming. The crown shall know of your service."

The two guards bowed and went out.

Raphael was left alone, listening to the clatter that preceded battle while he sat among the saints. He stared at St. Lucy's window, a more attractive likeness than the one Lennard had brought him, but no less damning. The mangled virgin martyr taunted him with light that broke over her tinted panes in colors bright and glad. "What more would you have of me?" he demanded. "What else could I have done?"

Her sapphire eyes only glowed more brightly on their tray.

If he could have run, or walked, or even dragged his worthless body like a snake across the ground, he would have punched her. He would have balled confusion, furor, and love into a fist and let it fly, to see if eyes so blessed could still turn black, to find out if she who so relentlessly bruised him with her stare could ever be bruised in her turn. But he could not reach the casement from his pew; so he snatched a candle from the nearest devotional and hurled it toward the glass.

With a tinkling like bells, St. Lucy's disembodied eyes fell out onto the lawn below.

The morning sun poured through, still mingled with the city's smoke, opening a hazy vista onto the white marble crypt that held the kings of Armany. Slim irises waved in beds around the base of the imposing tomb, their tired purple heads beginning to wilt. Someday, Raphael's bones would moulder in that box. Death showed no partiality to the Arman royals. Inside the palace walls, their mighty deeds still lived in art, but out there, they all lay equal, kings and queens and royal children, awaiting judgment together beneath the single monument that marked their single purpose: the blindfolded Lady of Justice with her scales and sharpened sword.

Through shattered eyes, Prince Raphael stared and thought, *What fools we Armans are.* Inside that tomb, his brother lay, at whose funeral Raphael had sent an imposter to spout the rhetoric of justice. A dream, he had called it, and that was all it was. As long as the eyes of the kingdom remained bound, its scales would swing unbalanced, its sword would slash without aim. If Lennard had taught him anything, it was that justice required vision.

Raphael looked up again at St. Lucy. "All right," he said, and bowed to her, or perhaps he only let his chin fall with fatigue. "You win."

CHAPTER 30

The stalks of oats beneath the horses' hooves gave way from green to ember-brown, the final line between Armany and Vivienne's Darrivant future. Her weary stallion whinnied in protest as she spurred him into the smoldering field. For all her prodding, the beast would go no faster than a languid trot. He had galloped across the countryside all night and into the morning. Now, as the sun neared its noontime zenith, he would not lift his hooves even when the remnants of flames licked at his feet.

"Slow down, Mother," Lilliane called from behind her.

With a sigh, Vivienne brought the stallion to a halt. She watched as Lilliane's mare meandered cautiously through the embers. Vivienne dismounted, shimmied out of her petticoats, and began carefully tearing at the stitching.

"Mother, this is madness. It makes no sense to flee from fire into more fire."

"It does if it means the difference between lighting it or being consumed." Vivienne pulled away the last seam that bound her most valuable possessions, two small parchment squares that would pay for her new life. She tucked one of them into her bosom, gave the other to Lilliane, dressed herself, and then remounted. The gold in her saddlebags jingled as she settled onto the saddle. Vivienne had made all haste toward the Darrivant lines at Pellain, but she had stopped in Camesbry long enough to collect her life's earnings.

"Mother," Lilliane said as she studied the parchment, "you cannot read these scratches any better than I. How do you know this will keep us safe?"

"It is a letter of safe conduct. It had to be written in Darrivant for the Darrivants to read it."

Lilliane winced every time her mother spoke the name of the enemy whom they meant to join. The girl had nearly fainted with rage when she heard the full confession of her mother's treason. There had been a great deal of tedious shouting, and Lilliane had threatened to turn her mother over to Prince Raphael. But Lilliane's conscience would never be strong enough to overwhelm her fear of making her own choices. After all these years, Vivienne was finally grateful she had given birth to a coward.

"Safe conduct," Lilliane scoffed. "You have only your peddler's word for that. These pages may tell the Darrivants to chop the head off of anyone who bears them."

Vivienne sat up straighter to hide her own misgivings. She had nursed the same qualm about the letters since the day Solomon Regis provided them, before she sold him the first batch of potion. A foxier creature than Regis she had never encountered, excepting herself. Yet the two of them had held each other's lives in their hands since the moment they first embarked on an enterprise of sedition. Vivienne knew that Regis would never betray himself.

She had been wary of the peddler since the day he first arrived at her doorstep, less than a year after she became mistress of Camesbry Castle. Her business was thriving, her buyers well-established, and any entrepreneur less daring than Vivienne would have sent Solomon Regis packing. What did a guardsman from Demont know about peddling cosmetics, much less about expanding the market into the foreign reaches of Darrivane? But Armany and Darrivane were then at peace, and Regis had arrived with gold in hand. Vivienne risked little by allowing him to try his scheme. When he returned six months later with a larger bag of gold to place an even larger order, she had to forego sales to her local buyers to fill it. Thus had a long and profitable partnership begun.

Vivienne always suspected there was more to Regis than met the eye. She began paying other merchants to observe him when they brought their own wares into Darrivane. They came back with stories about high-ranking officers of the Imperial Army who lingered long in conversation at Regis's stall. When the Darrivants began to harry the outskirts of Armany, testing the kingdom to discover if it might be ripe for picking, Regis continued to make his trips across the border unmolested. So, when Vivienne finally perfected her greatest creation, she called him into her private parlor and locked the door.

"I have a proposal for you, Mr. Regis, but I shall require both your honesty and your oath. Not a word of this conversation ever leaves this room, no matter its outcome. Is that agreed?"

Regis reclined in his silk-upholstered chair. "I can keep a secret better than most."

"I suspect you are keeping many, but there is only one I need." She set a bottle of her potion on the claw-foot table beside him. "I offer you an even trade. I will tell you what that liquid can do, if you will tell me the true nature of your dealings with the Darrivant Empire."

Regis never fidgeted when he pondered, only sat like a statue behind unreadable eyes. "How about, you tell me what manner of person could benefit from that concoction, and I will tell you if I have access to the appropriate market?"

Vivienne inclined her head. "We could sell it to ordinary folk and never want for gold again. But I believe it could be put to better use—for a military purpose."

"There might be someone I could speak to, if the price were right. What does it do, my lady?"

Selling the potion in Demont had been Regis's idea, a test to satisfy himself that the poison was truly capable of appropriating human will. The test had made Regis an outlaw, but he hardly cared; the new weapon had quickly elevated him to the top ranks of the Darrivant army, and he only returned to Armany now to procure new stores.

Vivienne envied him, that he could use her genius to establish his place in the society where she yearned to belong. But as long as Armany held the invaders at bay, she was still more secure as Lady Camesbry than she would be in Darrivane. If she defected, she might become nothing more than an exiled Arman noblewoman trapped in a foreign land.

That thought taunted Vivienne now, as she trekked through the devastated farmlands of Morisse near Pellain. The land seemed to erode beneath her horse's hooves, opening an unbridgeable chasm over which she could never return. She tried to console herself with memories of the taste of Darrivant rosewine. But when the abyss gaped too ominously behind her—when bright splashes of fear stained her vision, and even the jingle of gold in her saddlebags could not reassure her—it was the cut on Lilliane's white cheek that made Vivienne spur her horse onward.

"Lilliane, it is a gamble, to trust our fate to those letters. But if we stay in Armany, our fate is certain. We will die."

Lilliane narrowed her eyes. "If my prince's kingdom is dying, it was you who dealt the fatal blow. Do not think I shall ever forget that, Mother."

They pressed forward through the sultry afternoon, listening intently for any clamor of war. They had skirted Pellain, avoiding the main roads, taking bridle trails through the countryside to carve a berth around the fighting and meet the Darrivants in the rear. Both women rode with daggers bared, though both of them knew a dagger would be no match for an arrow. But it was not the zing of arrows that greeted them as they approached the Darrivant camp; screaming wafted toward them over the burnt fields, cold, unmitigated agony only the dying ever endured. Through the sweaty summer haze, they spied the wounded—bleeding, maimed, unconscious—stretched in queues outside a simple buckskin tent where men and women both worked to save them. One man who was missing a hand tried to bind the stump himself, using a dead man's tunic for a bandage. Another held his own entrails while flies swarmed to his wounds.

Lilliane's face curdled. "Mother, is this what you meant by the victor and his spoils?"

Vivienne had no time to reply as a watchman spotted them and raised an alarm. She raised herself in the saddle and waved a white handkerchief. "*Pax,*" she cried as two guards drew near. Both of them wore mail shirts and gilt-steel helmets, but only one could boast the six-eyed spider tattoo of an officer on his right arm. He approached with a spear in his hand and disbelief in his eyes. The other one wore a ravenous gaze that seemed to devour Lilliane.

"*Pax. Amicus,*" Vivienne greeted them. Latin was a common study for aristocrats in Darrivane, but these did not look like aristocrats. She pulled ahead of her daughter, placing herself as an obstacle to the one whose curled lip hungered.

The officer asked a question she did not understand. Vivienne shook her head. "*Pax. Amicus,*" she repeated, and took her letter from her breast. She handed it to him and withdrew.

The officer squinted over the writing. Vivienne's stomach sank as his brows drew together in confusion. Could he not read? Nine out of ten Arman soldiers could not spell their own names, but literacy was more prized in Darrivane. An officer would need to read his orders if they came to him by scroll. Surely, he must have learned...

He turned to her with a look as if, before his eyes, a dog had been transformed into a queen. "*Veritas?*" he said.

"*Veritas,*" she agreed.

He nodded toward Lilliane. "*Filiae?*"

"*Sic. Filiae.*" Lilliane handed forward her own letter.

The officer gave it a cursory glance and then waved for them to follow him. "*Pax. Amicus,*" he said.

The officer's declaration of friendship did nothing to abate the violence in the other soldier's eyes. Vivienne kept her horse between him and her daughter as they passed into the camp.

Beyond the makeshift infirmary with its menagerie of gore, the fields opened into rows of tents and half-extinguished cook fires. To the left, a paddock caged a hundred horses; to the right, a team of woodworkers transformed logs into a trebuchet. Boys of twelve or thirteen, a few already inked with their squire's markings, dug latrines or collected tinder for the fires. Of soldiers, there were few; battle was raging beyond the horizon. Vivienne ached to dig her heels into her mount and gallop toward the fray, to watch the arrows tipped in genius work a magic of her own making. But to act without the officer's leave seemed a sure way to find herself on the receiving end of that potion. She stayed her heels and held the course.

They stopped at a tent painted with a more elaborate six-eyed spider than the one on the officer's arm. He opened the flap to reveal a woman sleeping, draped in gossamer edged with gold. She, too, wore a spider on her forearm, which matched the one on the tent. Vivienne knew the marking named an officer's courtesan as his equal. Captains might have wives in their homeland, women who tended their children, whom the community respected. This woman, however, was a person the Darrivants obeyed.

The courtesan roused as the light entered through the open tent flap. She mumbled something, shielding her eyes, but when the tableau in front of her came into focus, she sat quite still and blinked. "You are Armans," she said. Her accent was only slight.

"Yes, I am Vivienne de Camesbry and this is my daughter, Lilliane."

The courtesan stood, her nightgown leaving little of her pale, firm body to the imagination, yet the men bowed in deference as she came outside. She spoke to the commander in Darrivant and then turned to the two Arman women. "He says you are most welcome. That you have given us service we cannot repay."

"Indeed, but I expect him to try. I have not come here to be sheltered, but to take what I have earned."

The courtesan relayed this and received a reply. "He asks you to name your terms."

"A territory of my own. Not in the conquered lands of Armany, but in Darrivane. It need not be large, but it must be fertile. And I will be no one's vassal. I will answer to no one but your emperor." Her body shivered at her own audacity.

The commander's eyes grew wide, but he bowed to Vivienne and muttered thickly, "Yes."

"Does he have the authority to grant that?"

"He has no authority to deny it. The empire has few allies as great as the one before us."

Vivienne took a deep breath, knowing that if the Darrivants lied, the moment she and Lilliane relinquished their horses would be their last. She met her daughter's eye and gave what she hoped was a reassuring smile. They had placed their wager. It was time to throw the dice.

"All right."

She slid her feet from the stirrups and threw one leg over, but before she could slide down, the brutal chill of screaming cut her to the bone. Inches from her horse's hooves, Lilliane lay pinned beneath the mass of the ravenous soldier. Vivienne fumbled for her dagger as the world blurred red. Another scream could not drown the sound of tearing fabric. Vivienne stumbled.

With a deeper scream, the man's body crushed itself onto Lilliane. Vivienne smelled the blood her hazy eyes could not see. Her stomach heaved. "No," she gurgled. "No..."

Gentle arms lifted her from the soil. "Shh..." A woman's voice: another courtesan, who whispered sweetly in Darrivant. Vivienne forced her breathing to steady, her eyes to see. Lilliane sat weeping in their translator's arms, but the blood on her skirts was not her own. The attacker lay prone where he had fallen, with a spear in his back.

The officer retrieved his weapon from his comrade's body. He looked at Vivienne as he wiped it clean. "*Pax. Amicus,*" he said.

"*Pax. Amicus.*" She shook as she replied.

CHAPTER 31

$\mathcal{T}$he moon had ascended once more into the heavens when Allia finally spied the smoke that marked their destination. All day, she had watched the mountains jut while Solomon led her horse northward through the twisting paths. When they passed through the Lagunde Tunnel—fifty yards of arched passageway hewn through solid rock, wide enough to fit a team of horses—Allia realized where they were, but she could make no sense of their route. Rumor had the Darrivant army encamped outside Pellain, west of the palace and fifty leagues from this wild place, yet Solomon insisted they were going to meet "the host that will restore Armany."

Restore. It seemed a strange word to use for establishing the reign of a foreign emperor in one's homeland, yet Allia found herself beginning to believe it. She spent the hours of their long journey basking in Solomon's joyful prophecies for the kingdom's future, her heart beating in time with the rhythm of his confidence. He held her hand as often as the narrow trail permitted it, and Allia clasped his tight with longing and disbelief. How could love come to her so easily, after such long years of pain? How could treason be so beautiful?

But no amount of beauty could soothe Allia's weary body. Her stitched hands burned without respite as they kept her grip on the saddle, and there was no food but what little the party could gather from the rocky soil. At dawn, the stringy roots of a plant she could not identify; at noon, a handful of unripe berries. One of the Darrivants took a rabbit with his bow, but they did not stop to clean and roast it. The man only slung it on his back for later.

Allia's eyes were drooping into a swoon when Solomon said at last, "Just around this crag, my lady."

They nearly stumbled on the sentry, his post so well concealed that a traveler passing yards away would never see him. Allia gasped as he raised his lance in salute. The man wore the kestrel of Camesbry.

"I have charge of the deserters," Solomon explained. "You see, my lady, it is truly Armany that brings its own restoration." The guard studied Allia's face as intently as she studied his, but neither spoke. A strange, inky bruise stretched up from the neck of the man's tunic onto his chin. Allia stared at it until Solomon led her horse around another crag, out into a clearing where his army lay in wait.

The soldiers were all sleeping except those few who had drawn a watch. As they passed the first few campfires, Allia saw that nearly all of the men still wore the livery of their Arman lords: Demont's blue and Camesbry's green, Falm's bright yellow, Tembria's amber, Abbleway's orange, and Morisse's deep red. The king's men wore the scales of justice on their purple coats. Two knights even bore Prince Lennard's lion on their chests. The gold embroidery of the king of beasts seemed to cower against their bodies, doomed to roar in silence.

Allia shivered. "Solomon, I'm cold."

"I know. We will take care of that."

He helped her down from the saddle, shook awake a squire, and gave the horse into the squire's care. The squire bowed to Solomon and led the palfrey away without a word.

The Darrivants who had accompanied their march spoke to Solomon in their own language. All but the one who carried Johan headed away into the camp. Johan had not roused all day, though Allia did not know if that was because of his injuries or because of the medicine the Darrivants fed him. She limped over and wiped her champion's hair away from his sweaty brow. He had no fever, and his breathing was not labored, although a bruise did seem to be blooming around the bandage on his arm. There was nothing Allia could do for him but say a prayer.

"I shall have Sir Winters placed in the tent nearest ours," Solomon promised. "He will be well tended."

The Darrivant inclined his head in acknowledgement. Allia dropped a curtsey to him as best she could. Solomon wrapped her tightly with one arm and led her through the maze of drowsing men. Despite the stanchion of his body, she had to favor her shoeless foot.

The sleeping host stretched farther than the moon and the firelight allowed Allia to see, but every glimmer revealed more Armans lying clustered around campfires in the open air. The only tents belonged to the Darrivants, leather cones that dotted the camp like wormholes through the trunk of a felled tree. Solomon's was the only one not marked with spidery paintings. As Allia limped inside the cozy buckskin world, fatigue reached out with deep, gray arms.

"Just here, my lady." The peddler handed her a pair of woolen breeches, a coarse tunic, and a cloak. "Forgive me that I have nothing suitable, but it will at least be warm."

"Thank you. I should also be grateful for food."

"I will see what I can find," he said. Allia leaned down to remove her one remaining shoe, and her curls brushed against his beard. Solomon cradled them to his face. "I have dreamed of this day, my lady."

"As have I. But I am too weary now for anything but more dreams."

"Then I pray they will be sweet." He let his fingers linger on her hair before he went out into the night.

She watched him go and then slowly untied the laces of her gown. The pink silk fell from her shoulders with a rustle soft as falling flowers. Her thighs quivered as she cased them in the strangeness of breeches, her body sliding into a world beyond the boundaries of both Lady Allia and the cinder maid. Were there any boundaries here? she wondered as she tugged on tunic, stockings, and cloak. She put her one remaining slipper into her pocket and then collapsed on a pile of blankets.

She fell asleep in an instant, but awakened much too soon when Solomon returned with her dinner. She devoured stringy bits of rabbit flesh and wild mushrooms until she realized she was licking the bowl. "Thank you," she said as she set it aside.

"I wish there were more to offer."

"But what you have, you give. Have you even paused to take your own food?"

"I have learned to make do without."

"There is no learning one's way out of starvation." She traced a finger through her empty bowl, willing it to fill itself again.

Solomon reached out and took her hand. He sniffed at the black stitches. "My lady, these must come out. Immediately."

She closed and opened her fingers, feeling the ache burn through her palm. Her wounds had finally formed a scab, but a yellowish ooze trickled out in the places where the thread poked through her skin. "All right," she sighed.

Solomon pulled his dagger from under his cloak. With practiced skill, he slid the blade through the first loop of thread. It popped as it gave way. Allia gritted her teeth against a cry.

"My lady, how did you receive these wounds?"

She attempted a smile. "I sliced them open with your sword."

"You held it as if you knew how to use it."

"Yes. I learned the grip from a very good teacher, but, alas, not very much else."

He held her hand more tightly, maneuvering his dagger with a surgeon's hand. Allia gasped as she watched her very flesh become unbound. "Solomon, how have you drawn so many Armans to your cause?"

He gave an enigmatic smile. "Justice wears a blindfold, my lady."

She cocked her head. "Commander Regis, you do not expect me to believe you are leading an army whose existence you cannot explain."

He raised his eyes to hers, and a taut ache stretched between them, fragile as a strand of hot spun glass. "You are right, of course.

But not all of my secrets are the stuff of dreams, and as you said, tonight you are too weary for anything more." He pulled the last stitch from her hand, closed her fingers, and held them tight to staunch the blood. "Morning will come, my love. There will be more to speak of then."

Allia stared into those fathomless eyes and felt like she was drowning, but she did not want to breathe. Solomon wrapped clean linen around her hands and kissed them. "Sleep now. Dream well. I will be here."

Allia lay down on the blankets, and Solomon wrapped her in his arms. When she slept, she dreamed that she wandered through a field where lions made of fire hid their faces in their paws. She reached out to stroke their manes, but the fires were extinguished at her touch.

She awoke at dawn to the sound of her own teeth chattering and angry voices raised outside. Allia groaned and pulled the blankets tighter. She could not understand the brittle Darrivant words, but she recognized Solomon's deep voice tinged with ire. A pair of small leather boots had been laid beside her head. She slid them on and stepped outside.

"Lady Allia, good morning." The sight of her brought a smile to Solomon's haggard face. His Darrivant companion bowed to her stiffly. "I am greeted with ill news this morning, my love. One of my officers is missing."

"Missing?" Allia looked around at the Arman soldiers beginning to rouse from their slumber. "Do you mean he deserted?"

"More likely, he only got lost when he went to look for food. He is a valuable man. I shall have to leave you to lead a search."

Allia trembled, looking at the men too numerous to count, with not a single other woman among them. "I can come with you."

"No, my lady. You need rest. Your wounds need to heal. No one in this camp will harm you." He tucked a curl behind her ear. "Sir Winters should be rousing soon. Stay with him, if it will make you feel secure. But I swear on my life, you will be safe here."

Allia swallowed bravely and tried to square her shoulders, but she melted when Solomon laid his lips on hers. "Wait a while, my love. I shall return before sunset." He and his companion walked briskly toward their horses.

Allia took a breath and stood up straighter. The men around her had begun to rise, stoking their fires that had gone cold during the night, or else making off in the direction of the latrines. She watched them go about their morning chores, amazed that none of them spoke to her. Among her father's men, the sudden appearance of a woman in a soldier's clothes would have sparked an outright mêlée of indecency. Many of these men darted perplexed glances her way, but none of them spoke a word. Solomon must be a gifted commander indeed, to inspire such discipline, but Allia had no wish to test its limits. She hurried off to find Johan.

As Solomon had promised, her champion had been placed in the tent next to his own. Johan's Darrivant nurse had apparently left on an errand, because Allia found him alone. His face was pale, his cheeks hollow and pinched, but he was sitting up, awake.

"Johan, praise God. How are you feeling?"

Johan turned at the sound of her voice. His green eyes registered recognition, but he said nothing.

"Johan?"

He took her hand and squeezed.

Allia inspected the bandages on his arms. Both of them were dry, although the bruises around them had grown larger and grayer than before. Even so, for a man who had taken two arrows through his flesh less than two days before, Johan seemed remarkably well. She kissed his clammy forehead in relief. "You cannot know how good it is to see you back in your senses. Has anyone told you where you are?"

Johan nodded while his eyes flashed with anger.

"I know. I do not know how you will ever accept this. I don't know if I have accepted it. But we must give Solomon a chance. He believes in justice…"

Johan squeezed her hand until she cried out in pain. She tried to pull away, but he only squeezed harder. "Johan! Johan, please…"

His eyes blazed with fury as he let go, but he spoke not a word.

"Johan?"

He only stared.

"Johan, can't you speak?"

He opened his mouth, and a gurgling, choking sound bubbled forth—a sound that Allia had heard before when her father hanged a murderer from the gallows.

"Johan..." Allia felt the blood drain from her cheeks. Her champion closed his mouth around the sound and gave a bitter, vengeful smile. Allia perked her ears to hear the howl of wind, the whinny of horses, the knock of hammers, the crackle of flames, but despite the noises of the camp, the mountain dawn suddenly seemed tainted by silence. Her heart pounded in her throat as she scrambled from the tent, back out among the host of Arman men. Just as before, they turned to stare at her, and as before, not a single one spoke—not even to each other. No laughter, no orders, no grumbling about breakfast, no jokes to stave off starvation. They only went about their tasks while their blank eyes stared with sorrow. Foul bruises just like Johan's seeped out from sleeves and necklines, creeping like rot over too many chins and hands. Then Johan's voice echoed through her mind, speaking in memory a word he could no longer utter in truth. Solomon had accounted for his treason, but never for his other crime.

Witchcraft.

CHAPTER 32

"*Y*our Lordship." The timid knock on Prince Raphael's door barely cracked his concentration. With a spoon the size of a robin's egg, he dripped three careful black drops into his alembic. Then he set the flask into a small furnace. The tools had been devised by alchemists, though Raphael expected no gold to be distilled from Lady Camesbry's sludge. But perhaps if he could determine what was in the poison, he could find a way to shield his army from its clutches.

"Your Lordship." The knock sounded more persistently this time. "Please, Your Lordship, it's urgent."

Raphael adjusted the coals in the furnace and sighed. There was nothing to do now but let the potion boil in the still. He rolled himself to open the chamber door and found the king's nurse standing on the threshold, her face the color of fog. "Please come. His eyes are rolling backward and his breathing is uncertain."

Raphael felt as though a hunk of solid lead fell into his gut. "Have you told the princess?"

"She is with him. I sent for the physician…"

"Un-send for him. Get Father Alester."

"But…"

"Madam, there is no physician in this kingdom half as learned as our chaplain. Now go." Raphael pushed himself past her and slung the door to his chamber closed. He could just make out the strains of the lyre in the great hall, where the third and final night of the ball danced on with the weary Tristan at its center. They would need to send for him if the situation were truly grave, but as Raphael pictured his proxy feigning grief at his father's bedside, the lead in his stomach began to boil.

He let himself into the king's chamber, where the first thing he saw was his sister's face drenched with sorrow. She threw her arms around him and collapsed onto his lap. Raphael stroked the soft locks of Briella's raven hair. The warmth of the small body weeping trust into his arms almost consoled him for the cold, rattled breathing of the one on the chaise.

Raphael wheeled toward the purple couch where their father lay, his head lolling on the down pillow. The king's closed eyes fluttered without rest, his dry lips gasping raggedly for air. He was draped with three sturdy blankets, but still he shivered, the fingers of his left hand fumbling at the wool.

"Has he spoken at all?"

"He calls for Lennard," Briella answered. "Not you or me. Only him."

"Shh. He loves you. So do I."

Briella pulled back to meet his eyes. "Are you planning to crown that whoreson ferryman when he dies?"

"Briella, a princess should not use such language."

"But are you? Because you can't. I'll tell the truth..."

Footsteps prevented an answer. Father Alester carried a lit candle as the nurse ushered him inside. The chaplain paused only to read the misery on the young royal faces before he knelt and examined the king. He took holy oil from the pocket of his alb and anointed His Majesty while he prayed.

As Latin incantations poured over the king's body, Raphael tried to lift up his own prayers. He tried to pray for his father's recovery, for strength to guide the kingdom, but the words would not come.

Instead, he watched his father's silver doublet rise with every labored breath and imagined that beneath it, an arrow wound festered with gray.

Father Alester made the sign of the cross over the king. "It will not be long. A day or two, perhaps. A week at the most."

Raphael swallowed, though his mouth seemed filled with ash. "What happened?"

Father Alester lifted the king's right hand. When he let it go, it flopped to the chaise without any attempt from its owner to control the fall. "Apoplexy. I have seen it before. There is no cure."

The nurse dabbed her eyes and found her voice. "We have to let the physicians try."

"Madam," Raphael snarled, "he is Simon the Unvanquished! Would you have him go to his grave draped in leeches, with holes punched through his skull?"

The nurse arched her spine. "I believe that is His Highness's decision to make."

"No!" Briella screamed. "Don't you dare bring him in here! Please... you can't..."

"Lennard," the king whimpered, "Lennard..."

Raphael gripped his hair with both hands and let out a roar. "Lennard is not here, Father! We are. Your other children. Briella and..." A sob choked away his name. He stared at the floor and bit his lip to keep the truth from strangling him.

Tiny fingers cupped his chin. Briella's eyes were wet with pleading as she lifted his face and nodded.

He leaned against her small, soft hand to let it hold his fear. "Raphael, Father. Briella and Raphael. We are here." Gently, he set his sister down from his lap. He brushed matted white hair away from a forehead wrinkled in pain. At the touch, the king closed his chapped and weary mouth. He took a deep, peaceful breath through his nose.

"Raphael," whispered the king.

"Yes, Father. Raphael and Briella."

"Br... Bri..." The king could not finish his daughter's name, but she grasped his left hand and squeezed it, and her father squeezed hers back.

Raphael stroked his father's hair once more, watching his forehead relax. "We are here, Father. Mama and Lennard will come for you soon."

With her mouth open wide, the nurse fell to her knees beside the wheeled chair. "Your Royal Highness..."

"Stand up, madam. I may be a prince, but I am neither royal nor high."

The nurse took his hardened hand in hers. "But you are kind," she said, and kissed it. "No kingdom can ever have too much of that."

Raphael could not stop his grief from flooding down his face. He laid one hand on the woman's auburn hair and blessed her. "Keep them dancing. No one but the four of us comes in here until it is done."

FATHER ALESTER'S candle guttered perilously as he closed the door to the king's chamber. He paused with his back against it, debating whether or not to wake Chancellor Narius. Duty decreed that the Lord Regent must be informed of the king's condition, but there would be no way to prevent him from intruding on the family's bedside vigil, nor from summoning Tristan. Alester shook his head and turned his steps toward the ball. Duty could wait until sunrise.

The lamps that lined the palace hallways had begun to smoke as the oil ran low. Many dancers had succumbed to cramping legs and blistered heels. They sat huddled in gossipy knots on the floor, unwilling to depart until the last enchanted stars surrendered to the dawn. Their smiles rasped against Alester like sackcloth and thorns. When had Armany become a place where maidens laughed while monarchs died?

The music, at least, had given up its merry pretense. Drowsy fiddlers determinedly scraped untuned strings as long as the prince kept dancing. Tristan held a pretty farm girl in his listless arms, nodding off between steps while she pursed her mouth in vexation. Alester rounded them without a backward glance. He skirted the edge of the dance floor until he found the guard he often used as a messenger. "Michel," he said, "any news?"

"This came for you, Father." The guard handed Alester a scroll, and Alester in turn passed him a coin. "The man who brought it would not speak. I am not certain he knows our tongue."

Alester's candle flickered with something like a glimmer of hope. "How long ago?"

"Only an hour."

"Has he departed?"

"Yes, though I would wager he is still in the city."

"Thank you, Michel." Alester added a second coin to the man's palm and slipped into a deserted hall where the torches had given up their smoky fight. His single flame illumined a mural where Eric de Camesbry and Simon the Unvanquished rode to battle side by side. He felt a sudden urge to punch the painted stone, but held his fist in check. Had there really been a time when governance was as simple as victory?

He tore the seal on the scroll and read. Then he looked out through a window to judge the time until dawn. Not long enough to travel to his closet in the tannery, yet if he met the man without disguise, he might never again be able to barter with the enemy. *What a blessed day that will be,* he thought, but then he thought of Raphael.

Alester shoved the scroll roughly into his pocket and marched to Tristan's rooms. He dug through Prince Lennard's wardrobe until he found an old doublet and breeches that might fit his thin frame. Alester did not let his fingers waver as he dressed, though every button he fastened opened a new wound in his memory. He transferred the contents of his pockets into his new attire, smoothed his hair and trimmed his beard, and then set off into the city.

The crowds that had packed the streets for the opening of the ball had thinned, though the refuse they left behind had not. Alester shooed scavenging dogs from his path and pondered how to clean the city before the king's funeral procession—not to mention that the route to the cathedral ran through the burnt district of East Point. He let his chin fall briefly to his chest, but then he raised it again. Regret could not rebuild a kingdom.

The scroll had directed him to the clothmaker's district, to a room above a wool dyer's shop. Alester found the door unlocked. Inside, a solitary figure sat in an upholstered chair, sharpening a sword by the light of a dying fire. He wore fine lambskin gloves and heavy brocade sleeves, too warm for the summer heat.

The man looked up. "You are here." His speech was heavy with the guttural tones of Darrivane.

"I am," said Alester, as he took another chair that seemed to have been placed for him. "However, I do not know if I have brought what you require. You failed to tell me your price."

The man shook his golden hair, a darker shade than the ice-blond common among his people. "The word you sent out was land. Rich Arman farmland." Despite his accent, he did not fumble for words. "But I do not want just any land. My mother came from Abbleway. Her father had a sheep farm there, and she was his only child. All I ask is my inheritance."

That explained things, then. Father Alester inclined his head. "It can be arranged."

"You have authority to reclaim it from whoever holds it now?"

"With the king's own seal." From under his doublet, Alester pulled out a chain he wore around his neck, from which hung a ring embossed with the royal sigil. "Now, what have you come here to sell?"

The man traced a finger over his glinting blade. "I know why the soldiers are deserting."

"Alas for you, my friend. So do I." Father Alester stood.

"You are famous on both sides of the lines, you know. You will not walk away from a prize like me." Slowly, the man rolled back one brocade sleeve. The spider tattoo on his forearm seemed to frolic in the shuddering light.

"I am not a military man," said Alester. "You are only a prize if you have information I do not."

"All right, you know why your men left you. But do you know where they are?"

Alester saw the glint in the man's eye and knew in an instant that the deserters were not at Pellain. He sat again. "You have my attention."

"What I have to say is worth more than a sheep farm," the Darrivant hedged.

"How much more?"

"I have served as a soldier thirteen years, as an officer for nine. I have killed dozens of your knights in battle. I am worthy to be called 'Sir.'"

"Only a knight or a lord can grant you knighthood."

"Are you not a lord?" The man raked his eyes over Alester's borrowed dress.

"Who I am does not matter. What matters is that you are a Darrivant officer in the Arman capitol. I am not inclined to arrest you. I would rather issue a pardon and a deed for your land, but I do not know any lords who will want you fighting in their ranks."

"Then your lords are all fools." The Darrivant gripped his sword with two hands, battle-poised. Alester wondered what it might feel like, to be tickled by that bright steel.

"If you have come here to kill the king's spy in the name of your people, then I beg you to get on with it. I am unarmed. But if you have truly come here for land, then tell me what you have come to say. I cannot promise you knighthood."

The man pondered the flicker of the firelight against his sword before he sheathed it. "The deserters are encamped in the mountains to the north, eighteen hours' ride along the road to Lagunde. Their commander is one of your own, a man called Solomon Regis."

Alester flinched with recognition.

The Darrivant smiled. "I only tell you his name because I have another to bargain with. A woman."

Alester did not make the mistake of reacting twice, though his heart began to race. He had heard from one of the Camesbry servants about Lady Camesbry's midnight flight through her own castle. To find her and tickle her with steel, he would knight every Darrivant in the Empire.

"Women are of no interest to me."

"This one is. An Arman noblewoman."

"A captive?"

"She was not bound. The commander carried her like a lover."

Alester could not picture Lady Camesbry allowing anyone to love her. He kept his silence, hoping the Darrivant would try to entice him further.

"She is quite beautiful," the Darrivant said. "Still wearing her gown from this ball your prince is having, though somewhere along the way, she had lost a shoe."

Father Alester's hand clenched tight around something in his pocket.

"Her name for a knighthood," the Darrivant said.

Despite the crushing weight in his lungs, Father Alester stood. "You have done me a great service, my friend. I shall have a deed for your land as soon as our scouts confirm your information. But if you choose to return to your post instead..." He took the object from his pocket and held it where the man could see. "Please inform Lady Allia that I have her other shoe."

CHAPTER 33

*L*ady Vivienne felt the heat of the rising sun before she saw its light. After so many years in a damp stone castle, she welcomed the sweltering buckskin tent as if it were the furnace that would forge her destiny.

"No!" A peevish voice polluted the morning air. "I will not parade myself like a harlot in such colors. Get out, leave me be..."

Vivienne rolled her eyes and sighed. She did not welcome Lilliane's whining.

She slipped on her shoes and stepped outside. Kathya, the Arman-speaking courtesan, departed Liliane's tent with another woman. Vivienne had requested to be housed away from her daughter, hoping to escape Lilliane's wretched moans, but from a distance of ten yards, she could still hear her daughter sobbing into the pillows at all hours of the night.

"Good morrow, Kathya," Vivienne greeted the willowy woman who carried herself like a soldier, and well she might. She was courtesan to the Lord Commander himself; in all matters except the execution of battle, this small woman's word carried the weight of law. "What mischief has my daughter wrought today?"

"Ilisaila went to take her measurements." Kathya gestured toward the other woman, who carried a bolt of splendid crimson silk. "We cannot allow such honored persons to go before the emperor in these plain clothes you have brought. I thought, too, that it might cheer her, to talk of silks and flounces. But... you heard what passed."

"Yes, I heard." Vivienne shook her head.

"Lady Vivienne, do you think she may be ill, to keep to her tent as she does?"

"If talk of silk and flounces could not cheer her, then she must be. Thank you, Kathya. I shall speak to her."

The two courtesans bowed and went their way. Vivienne lingered outside her daughter's tent, wishing that she need not go inside, but she pulled open the flap and stepped in.

Lilliane sat on her straw mattress with the blankets pulled up over her knees. Her bleary eyes stared vacantly at the leather walls. "Hello, Mother. Have you had my stepfather's head for breakfast today?"

"Tomorrow, perhaps." Lord Camesbry had arrived to make his stand at Pellain Castle, though it was still sure to fall. Vivienne wished the cut under Lilliane's eye had not healed quite so quickly. She could not point to it as evidence of Lord Camesbry's brutality anymore— evidence that Lilliane seemed quite determined to forget.

"And after you have murdered your husband, will it be onward to the capitol to behead the man I love?"

"Not for us. This time next month, you and I will be the guests of an emperor." The Lord Commander had promised them an escort into Darrivane just as soon as the siege was done.

Lilliane said nothing.

Vivienne sat down on a gold-embroidered pillow. "Lilliane, you may moan and sulk about your prince for as long as you wish, but someday, you will decide you have had enough of grief, and you will realize that I have built you a better life than any wool merchant's daughter ever had a right to dream of."

Lilliane turned her black eyes toward her mother. "And what of the wool merchant? What would Papa say, if he could see you now?"

Vivienne's heart seemed to freeze inside her chest, seeing the man she had loved peer out in anger from behind his child's eyes. "Lilliane, do not presume to think you are the only one who still honors your father's memory. Do you think he would fault me for raising his own child out of the gutter he left us in when he died?"

"He did not leave us in the gutter. It was that robber of a banker who refused to give us Papa's money that made us nearly starve."

Vivienne closed her eyes to keep out the memories of heartache, hunger, and shame. Never again had she entrusted a single coin of gold into another human being's care. Even here, she had chosen to bury her money under her tent instead of allowing the commander to place it in his trunk for safe keeping.

"Lilliane, this is all nonsense. We will live, and live well, in Darrivane. That is the only thing that matters."

Lilliane pulled her knees closer to her chest. "Go watch your battle, Mother. Brew your potions and kill your kingdom, only get out of my sight."

Vivienne stifled an urge to reach out and brush her daughter's limp black curls away from her pallid cheeks. "There was a time when you used to appreciate Darrivant silk. I hope you have not forgotten."

Lilliane made a scoffing noise deep in her throat, but gave no other reply.

Vivienne called for her horse and rode out toward the battle lines. She took her usual watch-post in the shade of an oak tree just beyond the range of both armies' arrows. The sun dazzled her eyes no matter how she shielded them, transforming the gray walls of Pellain Castle into a glittering gem that hung on the horizon like the fruit on Tantalus's tree. To know that her husband was just a few hundred yards away, starving and desperate, faced with imminent defeat... it took every ounce of Vivienne's fortitude not to storm the gates herself and laugh at his demise.

The carnage of the siege had ebbed as the Darrivants attempted to mine their way under the walls of Pellain Castle. Archers in siege towers stood positioned to guard the miners while they worked, but there was little guarding to do. Men who were underground made poor targets, and the mine entrances, where soldiers with baskets of earth scurried to and fro, lay out of range of Arman arrows. The two corps of archers traded volleys when they got too bored, but otherwise the battlefield might have been an ordinary quarry. Vivienne sat under her oak tree for an hour, watching, waiting, tasting the anticipation that filled the hot summer air, dreaming she could see the progress as the tunnels drilled below the algae-crusted moat. But at last she sighed, resigned that her time would be better spent elsewhere. "Soon, my lord," she whispered toward the horizon. Then she clicked her heels into her horse's sides.

Vivienne surrendered her mount to her groom and went in search of her new handmaid. She found the girl in the shade of a wild cherry tree, laughing coyly at some joke the sentry had just told. Vivienne cleared her throat and carefully wrapped her mouth around the Darrivant word for "Come."

The handmaid rolled her eyes, whispered something that made the guard laugh in his turn, and then dragged her feet in Vivienne's direction. The fifteen-year-old daughter of a captain and a courtesan had accompanied the invasion to learn her mother's trade and take her own place alongside an officer next year. To act as anyone's handmaid was beneath the station of this haughty, golden nymph, and Vivienne secretly admired her insolence. Nevertheless, she slapped the girl's cheek when she finally arrived.

The girl looked as if she meant to slap her in return, but instead she exacted her revenge by spewing out a rapid-fire sentence that Vivienne could not hope to catch. When the handmaid finished what sounded like a question, she grinned and waited for an answer.

Vivienne glared back, pointed to the tree, and carefully articulated, "*Bermit.*" The handmaid had taught her that word yesterday.

They spent a tedious afternoon trading nouns and phrases. The handmaid had no special gift for languages, and Vivienne hated to admit how tiring it was to catalogue these foreign sounds, to pair them up with pictures in her mind, to twist her tongue in odd directions and coax her throat to shape itself around new vowels. Even more, she hated to admit that the Darrivant language was guttural and coarse, not half as elegant as she had imagined it would be among a people so vibrant and cultured. But learn it she must, and quickly, because Kathya was the only person in the camp who spoke Arman, and she would not be joining Vivienne on the voyage into Darrivane.

Dusk came late on these summer days, so that the work of the siege often continued well past the time when the camp followers had eaten their meager supper and the soldiers who had drawn the duty of the night's watch took their posts. Vivienne took her meals with the courtesans. Tonight, for the first time, she caught a few snatches of their conversation. One spoke about her father; another said something about how she had prepared the deer for the stew. Vivienne would have allowed herself a smile except that Lilliane still had not deigned to join them.

"Shall I carry a dish to your daughter this evening?" Kathya offered.

"Thank you, but no. If she will not bestir herself to eat, let her starve. She needs to learn."

Kathya bowed and scooped out a bowl of stew to bring to the Lord Commander.

Vivienne made her way back toward her tent, debating within herself whether or not to confront Lilliane again. Her head ached already, and she knew her daughter's petulance could not be uprooted by reason. Lilliane's tent stood silent, for once. Vivienne decided to leave well enough alone. She stepped inside her own buckskin quarters—and fell into a gaping hole that had been dug in the earthen floor.

The gold. Someone had dug it up and not even bothered to cover the evidence of the crime.

Vivienne coughed as air turned to ash inside her chest. Her vision blurred with blood, and consciousness slithered through her grasp. "Kathya," she cried as she stumbled back outside, though she knew the courtesan would be near the front lines, giving the Lord Commander his supper. Her swelling ankle throbbed. She had not returned to her tent since she left it at sunrise. Might the thief already be long gone?

Vivienne fell to the ground. "Lilliane! Lilliane, we have been robbed."

She lay panting, watching the mottled world dance before her eyes, dimly aware that her daughter did not come. "Lilliane! I need you." Vivienne worked to take deep breaths, to suffocate panic with air. She raised herself enough to crawl. She pulled back the tanned buckskin flap of Lilliane's tent and blinked. As the shadows swirled away, the stab that pierced her pounding heart sent her weeping to the ground. The pillows had been neatly piled, the blankets folded and set aside. Otherwise, the tent was empty.

Lilliane was gone.

CHAPTER 34

*A*llia scaled the mountain peak as far as she could climb. Her bandaged hands gripped at limbs and brambles as she tugged her body free from the accursed camp, clawing toward the summit as fiercely as she had clawed toward air on that long-lost day when she had nearly drowned. But, just as on that fateful day, Johan snared her. Every time she gained a purchase on some higher rock, his silent eyes stared back from its bleak face. Every time the mountain wind whistled through her ears, she heard Johan's constricted throat still gurgling. The more she climbed, the more her heart pounded against the dull red X that forever marked her with the memory of watching him nearly die. When at last she reached a rushing stream, cold and deep with melted snow, Allia flung herself down on its jagged bank and cried.

She pursed her lips against the flowing water to drink. The cold draught washed through her with a freshness brisk and budding. So slight was the difference between being refreshed and being frozen, so narrow the distinction between drinking and being drowned. Allia stared into the racing water that weeks or even days ago had lain in silent snowbanks on the mountainside, unmoving. Now it surged, implacable, sprinting from obscurity down toward its destiny in rivers, lakes, and seas. All it had needed was the prodding of a few bright rays of sun.

Allia turned her face toward the golden daylight. "Mother," she whispered, "help me."

A gentle cooing touched her ears, and Allia turned to see a dove perched in the branches of a bush just yards away. It looked at her and cooed again before it flew away. Allia crept toward the bush and plucked a twig from its branches—a sprig of hazel, lush and green. She held it to her face, breathing in its earthy spice. In the shade of the hazel bush, she sat and watched the sun travel across the heavens.

All that afternoon, she thought and dreamed and prayed. She knew she must return to the deserters' camp. She must free Johan, but not only Johan. All those silent, stolen men must be delivered from whatever witchery bound them to the Darrivant cause. The fact that Allia had no inkling how to change them, no idea where to start, hardly mattered. No one else in all the world even knew their plight. She alone must find the answer.

But she was not alone.

Solomon would be there.

Thoughts of Solomon were agony, honey tinged with hemlock, deadly but still sweet. For the first time since she was a small child curled in her father's arms, Allia had passed the night sheltered by the warmth of a man who loved her. Even knowing the depth of wickedness to which Solomon had stooped in service to his cause, she did not doubt his love. It poured from his every word and touch, from the light in his eyes and the slant of his smile. If he had not been called away, she did not doubt that even now, he would be consoling her, gently explaining the reasons why he had become the commander of an army of thralls and how he would free them from the spell after Armany was free. Here in the seclusion of the mountaintop, Allia looked down over the past few days and knew that, if she allowed Solomon to make his excuses, she might accept them. He had tried to fill the cavernous void inside her heart; she thought that now to tear him out might kill her. But it would be worse to sit idly and watch Johan drown than it would be to die. Surely, Solomon—who had spent his whole life doing penance for that same sin—would understand.

An hour or two before sunset, Allia rose and picked her way back down the mountain. She had not been very mindful of her route during the ascent, and rather than become hopelessly lost, she decided to follow the stream. The soldiers could not have camped in such a deserted place without a source of water, nor would it be wise to try to find her way through this wilderness without one. Slowly, she negotiated her way through the brush, sliding down slick faces of rock while she whispered pleas for safety. Just as the bright orange sun began to sink beyond a far-off peak, Allia found a place where the mountain leveled, where two soldiers with buckets had come to quench their thirst. Their brows furrowed quizzically at the woman in breeches who dropped down from the sky.

They were the same royal knights she had seen sleeping when she first arrived, the only two who wore Prince Lennard's gold-embroidered lion on their breasts. Allia could not stop herself from reaching out toward the nearest one, to see if her cold touch would douse the shimmer of the thread.

The knight cocked his head at her and pressed her hand closer. Allia could feel the quickened beating of his heart that echoed hers. She heard the roar of blood rushing through her ears. She looked up into the man's dark eyes and, for an instant, saw the eyes of her prince smiling at her from the sunset.

She pulled back her hand and knelt at the two knights' feet. "Good sirs, I know you cannot answer me, but I beg you to listen. My name is Allia de Camesbry, daughter of Lord Eric de Camesbry and the Heiress of Demont. In my childhood, Queen Eleanor sought to betroth me to His Royal Highness, the man you used to serve. I know you cannot choose to follow me. You have been spellbound, or poisoned, or both. But if it is within your power, I beg..." Allia took a breath and searched their eyes that watched her with wonder. "I beg you would allow me to serve you." She bent forward and pressed her body prostrate to the ground. For a moment she lay there, afraid to raise her eyes and see hatred flaring from bewitched faces. But at last the silence so unnerved her that she lifted her head to look.

Both of them had fallen to their knees.

Slowly, Allia regained her feet and brushed the dirt from her cloak. She surveyed the two men and the buckets they had set down on the stream bank. They stood in the shade of a stout pine tree. Allia tapped the taller knight on his shoulder, a man who wore a thick red beard. "Sir, would it be possible for you to pull a limb down from that tree? The straightest one, there. It's just out of my reach."

The knight stood up, bowed, and jumped to catch hold of the limb. The sight of a gray bruise on his right hand made Allia shudder anew. He swung on the branch until it cracked from the tree; then he laid it at Allia's feet.

She stripped the small twigs from the limb until it was clean and straight. She filled the buckets from the stream, slung them on the ends of her pole, and carried it on her shoulders. "Which way is it back to the camp?"

Thus did she return to Solomon: at the head of an entourage of royal knights, hauling water like a cinder maid.

Solomon had set a patrol of men with torches to search the darkening mountain for any trace of the woman he loved. When he glimpsed her through the trees, he cried out, "Lady Allia!" and choked before he could say more. He crashed toward her through the brambles, but stopped when he saw the pole across her shoulders. "My lady...?"

"Yes, Commander Regis. I am here."

"Allia, I have not come to take you back if that is not your will. Only to be sure that you are safe and to offer you answers. I know the questions that must have plagued you all this day."

"I have only one question. How can these men be restored?"

"They can be. They will be. First Armany, then its citizens..."

Allia shook her head. "That is not the answer. I will stay with Sir Winters tonight. We will speak again tomorrow." She saw the pain that spilled across his eyes, but he stepped aside to let her pass. It took every fiber of Allia's courage not to look back.

She delivered the water to the part of the camp where the two knights had laid their blankets on the ground for beds. "I wish you could tell me your names," she said as they bowed to her in thanks.

The two knights looked curiously at each other. The one with dark eyes took a stick and began to trace it through the dirt. He stared at his own hand, as if unsure it would obey him, but soon enough his work was done. "Sir Dunstan," she read, and then curtsied. "It is my honor." Sir Dunstan nodded toward his red-bearded companion and turned again to his writing. "Sir Hamran." Allia curtsied to the taller man. "I am your servant." She laid her hands on each one's head in turn and said, "God bless you. I will see you on the morrow." Then she crossed once more through the eerie silence toward Johan's tent.

She paused when she reached Solomon's lodging, the cozy buckskin world where all was warmth and dreams. She could not hear him moving inside; he had not yet returned for the night. She reached out and stroked the leather, but then drove her feet onward toward her champion.

Johan clambered to his feet and hugged her.

She examined his wounds. Although he was alone again, his bandages had been changed since the morning. He was stronger now, able to sit up as much as he liked and even stand for short periods. The rings of darkness around his wounds had continued to grow, but they did not really look like bruises. Johan did not wince when she touched them, and the color was wrong. It was not the color of blood.

It was the color of death.

Allia kissed the stains on her champion's skin. She accepted a few mouthfuls of the boiled game someone had brought for him, and then, arm in arm, they fell asleep.

For the second night, she dreamed of lions. This time, they nuzzled her hands.

At dawn, she found Solomon sitting near her feet, his face lined with the fatigue of a restless night, his eyes haunted by sadness. "My lady, please, you must allow me to explain."

She sat up and folded her hands to keep herself from reaching out to comfort him. "There is no need. I understand. You believe so deeply in the justice you wish to bring that you will pay any price to bring it. But, Solomon, freedom cannot be built upon the backs of slaves."

Johan roused beside her. When he saw Solomon, his face clouded with hate. He wrapped an arm firmly around Allia to shield her, but Allia took it away. "Thank you, Johan, but this is my battle. I cannot send a champion to fight it for me."

Solomon raised his hands. "I have never fought you, my lady. You are the one who always holds a sword."

She stared into those eyes that even now made her want to throw herself across the tent into his dauntless arms. "There is only one blade between us. It is something you put on the arrows, is it not? Some vile poison that seeps into men's veins. I would wager that it is not even yours—that you purchased this wickedness from my step-mother. Solomon, you are better than this black-hearted sorcery. I am not asking you to abandon your quest and bend your knee to the king. Only set these men free from the evil that binds them, and I will go with you anywhere, to Darrivane, to the ends of the world. My justice is my freedom. Only grant it to them, too."

The tear that traced its way down Solomon's face burned like boiling oil as it fell into Allia's heart. "This is why I love you, my lady. If you allowed me to convince you of the necessity for what I have done, I would always feel that I had crushed one of the petals on the world's most beautiful rose. But it is necessary. You will see it some-day, when Armany is free."

They stared at each other across the sharpened edge of silence. Finally, Solomon stood. "Do you require an escort back to Camesbry?"

Allia laid her hand on Johan's shoulder. "My place is here."

"In a day or two, we will march to battle."

"Then I will tend the wounded and bury the dead. I will carry water and firewood and dig latrines. I will serve my kingdom." She squared her shoulders. "They are not your men. They belong to Armany."

"I know, my love. They always have." He wiped away his lonesome tear, gave a curt bow, and went out.

CHAPTER 35

*N*ight had passed to dawn and day to night twice over, but still King Simon lingered. Princess Briella never left his side, dozing in an armchair near his chaise when her young body betrayed her vigil, eating only the tiniest morsels of the food her governess tried to force on her. Raphael wished that he could be so constant. Three times now, he had left his father's bedside to continue his experiments with Lady Camesbry's poison. He was certain the potion contained iron, granite, nightshade, and traces of some creature's blood, but none of that information put him closer to understanding how it worked.

Twice, he had left to confer with Tristan. The first time, he had coached him about how to convince Chancellor Narius to let the family mourn in peace, how to describe the scene so that it seemed as if Tristan himself had been keeping vigil alongside the dying king. The second time, they had talked about Prince Raphael's impending coronation.

Raphael returned again to his father's bedside, relieved—as he was after each of his excursions—to find his father still breathing. Every harsh intake of air rattled through his lips more painfully than the last, but King Simon remained unvanquished. Raphael wheeled himself back to his usual place at the king's left hand. Briella had let it go as she drifted to sleep, so Raphael took the cold white palm in his. "I have returned, Father."

"Lennard…"

"He is coming. Soon."

Raphael had just leaned his head against the back of his chair and closed his eyes when the chamber door opened. For the first time since he had administered the king's Last Rites, Father Alester appeared. His face was almost as gray and wretched as that of the dying man. "What has happened, Father?" Raphael whispered, careful not to wake his sister.

"Nothing good, I fear. Come away from here so we do not disturb Her Highness."

Raphael sighed. "I have only just returned." He kissed his father's clammy hand and let it go. Father Alester held the door for him as he wheeled himself out of the chamber.

"Your own room is closest," Alester advised.

Raphael gave a weary nod and followed him down the hall.

Alester closed the door to Raphael's chamber tightly. "When I left your father's bedside, I went to meet with a Darrivant officer. My scouts have just returned from confirming his information. Your Highness, the Darrivants have formed a new legion from the deserters they stole from our forces. They are encamped on the road between here and Lagunde, and their object is to march on the capitol. I have already informed Chancellor Narius. He sent word to the captains of the royal guards and a messenger to intercept the troops from Demont now marching toward Pellain. We will almost certainly lose Pellain, and that leaves no one to defend Camesbry, but we ourselves will soon be under siege."

Raphael's head fell into his hands as if a millstone had been tied around his neck. "You are telling me we have lost half my kingdom. Without Camesbry, we are land-locked. If Lagunde is cut off, we have no source of weapons. We could retreat to Demont and hold there until we starve to death, but where is the route to victory?"

"Camesbry is not lost yet. If you wish to go to Anniton and flee over the sea, I will arrange it."

"To live out my life as an exile while my kingdom dies? No. We will fight and pray for a miracle, and if God does not grant it, I will die."

"What about your sister?"

Raphael gnashed his teeth. "Arrange for a ship. The King of Ritonia will not turn her away."

Father Alester rocked nervously on his feet, his hands stuffed deep in the pockets of his alb. "Your Highness... if we have any hope of victory, your father cannot die. You must not crown Tristan. And although you know how long I have advocated that you must tell the kingdom who you are, it cannot come in the midst of a siege on the capitol. There would be no more certain way to ensure our defeat."

"What are you saying? Is there some black magic that will keep him alive?"

"Nothing in the world can prevent God's will. I am only saying that no one must know. Even if we have to bury him in a pauper's grave in the dead of night, King Simon must not die—not until the Darrivants have been vanquished, if indeed they ever are."

Father Alester's words crashed against Raphael's mind as if they had been fired from a catapult. He saw immediately that the advice was sound; a kingdom in crisis required stability. The soldiers at the city walls would fight for Simon the Unvanquished, but who would be willing to defend the reign of a deceitful cripple? Yet to bury his father in the dead of night—to perpetrate yet another deception against his people—Raphael could not do.

"When my sister departs for Ritonia, so does any claim I ever had to throne. Having you and Tristan swear to my identity will not be enough. Briella is the one who matters. When she holds my hand and calls me brother, only then will the kingdom believe."

"Your Highness, surely you see..."

"Yes. I see that I am the one who has sunk the kingdom by my cowardice, and I see that I must be the one to raise it." He sat up straight, though he could still feel the weight of the millstone around his neck. He looked out the window to judge the time. "The night is already far advanced. Briella will need at least tomorrow to prepare for the journey, and neither the army at Pellain nor the one in the mountains will have time to conquer us before then. So, the day after tomorrow, invite the lords and barons, the guild masters, and as many of the merchants as can fit to the great hall. Make certain it is finished being cleaned from the ball. Tell them to come in the morning, so my sister will still have time to make her journey. And then, we will tell them. Let them kill me and crown my cousin Collin de Tembria, if they will, but we will own the truth." Raphael shivered. "And if my father is dead, we will own that, too."

Father Alester stiffened. "Your Highness, a month ago, I would have wept for joy to hear those words. But you must not sacrifice the kingdom to salve your conscience. You have a duty."

"My duty is to my people, Father. They will know that soon." He pushed himself toward his work table and began sifting through parchments in search of a quill. "Leave me now. I have speeches to compose."

Father Alester cleared his throat. "Your Highness, there is one more thing."

Raphael pushed his chair back against the wall, leaning on St. Lucy's tapestry. "There cannot possibly be one more thing."

"My Darrivant informant..." Father Alester took a breath and sighed. "There is no easy way to say this, Your Highness. The man commanding the army of deserters is the outlaw Solomon Regis, and Lady Allia is with him. My informant saw him carry her in his arms like a lover."

Raphael stiffened in every muscle as though a spear of ice had been thrust into his heart. He pictured that pair of hazelnut eyes shining up at a faceless stranger—a man who carried her, not one who needed to be carried. She had come to Raphael for justice, and he could not even save her from his own men. He could not blame her for running into the arms of the enemy. Perhaps she had seen the death of Armany written in its prince's weakness, and she had chosen to live.

"She duped you, Your Highness," Father Alester said. "Maybe she really was innocent of her mother's death, and maybe it was the injustice of her suffering that drove her toward treason. But she is a traitor."

"Father, where is her shoe?" Raphael's blood still boiled to remember Father Alester's oath to behead the girl who wore its mate. But now, Alester took the slipper from his pocket without a word and handed it to the prince.

Raphael ran his finger across the golden silk, remembering the softness of her golden curls. "Lady Allia did not betray the kingdom. It betrayed her. If we fall to the Darrivants, it is because Armany has become a kingdom that is not worth saving."

Raphael watched his chaplain's face tense with unspeakable sorrow. "You are right," Father Alester whispered. He stared at his pupil with haggard eyes; then he reached out and tussled Prince Raphael's curls. Raphael felt himself blush, but he also felt himself smile.

Alester's cheeks, too, were red as he retracted his hand. "The day after tomorrow, then. I shall have everything prepared."

Raphael nodded. "Good night, Father."

"Good night... my son."

Raphael followed Father Alester out and wheeled himself back toward the king's chamber. He tried to ignore the furious pounding of his heart against his breastbone, the tremor in his fingers as they held tight to Lady Allia's shoe. His body tried to coerce him with fear, to force him to turn back from the course he had set, to flee across the sea with his sister. But the die was cast. If he signed his own death warrant, at least he would sign it with his own name.

He opened the door to the king's chamber quietly. Briella still slept in the chair at the king's left hand, and Simon the Unvanquished breathed no more.

CHAPTER 36

*T*he mud under the log where Allia sat grew deeper with every renewed burst of the stifling clouds. She felt herself sinking as the long morning drew on. She reached out, scratched an O in the mire with a stick, and waited for Sir Dunstan to take his turn in their game. Sir Hamran next to him whittled the bark from a tree branch with his dagger. Both knights were drenched to the bone with no hope of shelter, their lion tunics squishing against their bodies every time they moved. Allia had chosen to sit with them in solidarity, but she was glad that a dry tent awaited her any time she chose to leave.

Sir Dunstan scratched an X on the ground and nodded for Allia to make her move. She drew her O and turned to him with a triumphant grin. "That's four in a row, Sir Dunstan. I think maybe it's time you surrender."

Both knights' faces fell suddenly slack, their expressions erased by an unseen hand. Sir Hamran dropped the stick he was whittling to curl both hands around the hilt of his dagger. Sir Dunstan stood and drew his sword from its scabbard. Both stood frozen at attention, as if awaiting orders.

For one brief instant, Allia's heart stood still. She stared up into their blank faces and saw in their tortured eyes the despair their faces could not show. She raised herself from her perch on the log, stepped around Sir Dunstan's sword-point, and put her hands on his shoulders. "Peace, my friend. This is no battle." She walked around to Sir Hamran and did the same. Both men slowly lowered their weapons.

Allia worked to steady her breathing while the mountain rain still fell. At last, she looked at her friends and said, "I must return to Sir Winters. I will come back to you tomorrow."

The two knights nodded in acknowledgment, but neither one could bring himself to meet her eye.

Allia's mind raced as she picked her way across the puddles that swamped the camp. Her eyes absorbed the misery of the men who sat in the downpour without shelter or occupation. She wanted to weep, but instead she decided on a plan.

"Johan," she said when she arrived back at his tent, "I want to try an experiment. To test the limits of the poison."

Johan stirred from his half-slumber and frowned. He was visibly stronger today, but to Allia, that only made it worse to watch him sit, confined.

"Stand up," she ordered.

Johan shrugged and stood.

"Go outside."

He rolled his eyes and stepped out into the rainstorm. Allia followed him.

"Hit me," she said.

Johan creased his brow in annoyance and did not obey.

"Good. So you do have some judgment left. Now, kneel before me as my champion. Lay your sword at my feet."

Johan unsheathed the sword at his side and held the hilt in both hands. He stood at attention, as unmoving as a statue.

A chill shuddered down Allia's spine. She opened her hands. "Sir Winters, give me your sword."

Johan lifted the blade as if to strike, but he only held it poised.

"If I continue to press you, will you kill me?"

Johan gave no answer, not a nod or a shake of the head, but a tear dripped down his stoic cheek. Allia wanted to catch it, to bring it as evidence before some court, but she could only lay her hands on his shoulders. "Peace, my friend. Put the blade away, if you can. Go back inside."

Johan exhaled and slowly obeyed. Allia took a deep breath of relief and followed him. They settled back onto the damp ground under the tent. Allia wrung out her wet hair and garments as best she could while Johan twiddled his thumbs.

They sat in silence for nearly an hour, until the rain stopped at last.

"We will need to go out and find food," said Allia.

Johan nodded, but neither of them moved.

A few more minutes passed before Allia noticed that the camp's sullen silence had cracked. She heard words: broken, accented Arman words, but words she could understand that were not spoken in Solomon's voice. She and Johan exchanged looks of wonder and then went outside. With her heart in her throat, Allia followed the sounds to find that the speakers were Darrivants. The tattooed men walked through the camp, barking single-word orders. "Ready," one said. Another added, "Tomorrow."

The soldiers nodded and began to collect their weapons from the ground.

Allia reached to take Johan's arm as the staggering realization washed over her that so few hours remained between these men and battle. But Johan had already turned and set his steps toward the tent that served as an armory. Allia did not know how Johan even knew the way; he had been confined by his injuries since the moment he arrived at the camp. He had never wandered out to explore. But he strode purposefully now, so swiftly that Allia almost had to run to follow him. A Darrivant stood at the armory's entrance. Johan could not speak to him, but he motioned to his chest, arms, and head.

Allia watched with tears in her eyes as the Darrivant fitted her champion with breastplate, helmet, pauldrons, gauntlets, and greaves. Johan's livery marked him as a knight, and the armorer made certain that Sir Winters was fully equipped. The mismatched pieces had been forged in varying grades of steel, some marked with the scrollwork spiders of the Darrivants, some of Arman design, but all of them had been brightly burnished. Allia watched her champion truly become a knight in shining armor, and she wanted to drive a lance through the armorer.

"Ready," the Darrivants still called as they made their way through the camp. "Tomorrow."

The line at the armory had grown, snaking back across the field of tents. Johan took Allia's hand to lead her away. Everywhere they looked, the silent soldiers had begun to prepare for battle: oiling their armor, sharpening their swords, tying feathers to the shafts of their arrows. Tomorrow, Armany's soldiers would begin the march to conquer their own capitol.

Allia did not sleep that night. She sat awake on the damp floor of Johan's tent, clutching his hand while he snored as if rest, too, were a part of his orders he could not disobey. All through that long, lonely night, she pictured boulders launched from catapults crashing through the walls of the dream-struck palace she had once thought was made of diamonds. Would Prince Raphael still be inside? Allia knew not what to think about the withered man in his wheeled chair, the man with kindness in his eyes whose flushed cheek had burned against her when she carried him. Had he found the courage yet to come out from behind his curtain? She wanted to believe in him, to believe his friendship had not been feigned. She wanted to believe that the justice she saw inside of him was real, not an illusion cast by her own desperation. She wanted to believe that a crippled lion could be a lion still. But she remembered the look of helplessness on his face at the moment she had fled. If he could not save one girl from injustice, how could he save his kingdom?

But Allia knew that even if Prince Raphael could rise up out of his chair to rally the kingdom—even if he could become as great a warrior as his father and brother before him—he still would not be able to turn back this army of living wraiths. If Prince Lennard had survived his arrow wound, he too would be sleeping on this mountainside, ready to march against his own reign.

Perhaps it was a mercy that the fairy had caught the wrong arrow.

The fairy flitted through Allia's thoughts, that strange, beautiful, enigmatic creature whom she had never quite forgiven for rending her world apart. If magic could not be perfect, then Allia would rather it did not exist at all. But if magic had stolen the soldiers' will, then she needed a magic weapon to break the spell.

"Godmother?" Allia whispered to the night.

Only the wind whispered back.

Long before the morning truly dawned, the soldiers began to rouse and pack away the camp. Allia served as Johan's squire, helping him to strap on his armor and fold up the tent. All around them, the soldiers began to move as if their steps had been rehearsed, assembling into regiments according to the Arman lords they had served. The Camesbry men gathered to the south, Falm to the east, Morisse to the west, Demont to the north, Tembria and Abbleway near the center. The royal knights formed the smallest group, eleven men with backs as straight as arrows whose purple livery defied the dirt to soil it. Nine of them wore the scales of justice on their breasts. Only Allia's two friends wore the lion. She nodded to them as she followed Johan toward the Demont regiment, but Johan did not pass. He stopped in the midst of the royal knights, inserting himself into the disciplined line of their ranks right between the two lions. The knights made way for him to join.

"Johan?" Allia asked, but of course he did not answer.

"Oh, blast it to hell."

Allia turned to find Solomon striding over in full armor, followed by the same Darrivant archers who had formed his scouting party. Solomon looked from Johan to Allia and back again. "I gave Demont the rear guard because I knew you would stay with Sir Winters. But he isn't sworn to Lady Demont, is he? He's sworn to you."

Allia trembled under the scrutiny of those fathomless eyes, more unreadable than ever as they peered out through the slit of his steel helmet. "Yes, but these are not my knights. They are Prince Lennard's."

Solomon bowed. "So you really were meant to be a queen."

Allia felt the last word as if it were a punch to the stomach. She looked at Johan in his Demont blue, standing in formation among the royal lions, living proof that the fairy's story had not been a lie. "Commander Regis," she said as resolutely as she could, "if I am a queen, then your cause to bring justice is already accomplished. I can learn from what you've told me about Darrivane. Our people can have the lives you want for them—only free these men. Please."

Gently, he lifted her chin with cold metal fingers. "My lady, if everyone in Armany had been granted the same vision as these knights, I would obey you. But the kingdom has no vision. Have you forgotten how I found you, fleeing the palace with royal guards on your heels?" He squeezed her hand, and turned to mount a horse that a squire had brought for him. "The royal knights are my vanguard, my lady. If you insist on marching with Sir Winters, I shall allow it only until we make camp on the night before the battle. When we ride to victory, you will stay behind, or I shall have you tied to a tree."

More horses were appearing, one for each of the archers and the knights. A boy led Allia's palfrey to her. She looked at him and ordered, "Bring me a sword."

The boy did not acknowledge her.

All through that weary day, Allia rode in procession behind Sir Winters while the army crept in single-file down the same brutal mountain trail she had ascended days ago. This time, she could not doze or daydream in the saddle. She could not ponder the colors of the sunrise or listen for the answers to her prayers whispered in the wind. She could not lose herself in watching the graceful swing of her peddler's arms. She could only stare at Johan's back and guide her horse's head. Her rear end burned with saddle sores, her stomach burned with hunger, but not until dusk made the road too perilous to continue did the procession halt. What would become of any common travelers who happened upon their camp, Allia did not like to wonder. She tethered her horse to the closest tree, leaned her back against the mountain, and tried to fall asleep. In the haze of the mountain twilight, she whispered, "Mother, guide me."

She woke up knowing what to do.

She only trembled for a moment while the gray fog of morning gave way before the dawning light. By the time she took a drink from her water-skin and foraged a breakfast of thistles, her hands had ceased to shake. Allia was not surprised that her mother called her to share in her own fate. The only hard part was the waiting.

She waited all through another silent day of riding. All through another lonely, half-starved night, she prayed. Then, just after dawn on the third day, the precipice that kept her bound in formation opened into wider land. She recognized the same copse of ash trees where Solomon and his archers had found her. Here, where Johan had been shot—here, he would be freed.

She kicked her heels into her palfrey to bring him to a gallop, passing up the line. She cut in front of Solomon, forcing him to halt. Behind him, the Darrivant archers and royal knights all reined in their steeds, sending a succession of whinnies through the throng.

"My lady," Solomon cried, "what's wrong?"

The archers rode forward, forming a half-circle around their commander. The knights, too, fanned out in formation, but Allia had eyes for Solomon alone. "You told me that life is always bought with death. I am here to buy their lives." She motioned to the army stretched behind them like a serpent, curled around the mountain far beyond any point the eye could see.

Solomon turned pale. "Allia..."

She pushed through the line of archers toward the royal knights. She dismounted and walked toward Johan, at the center of them all. She stared up into her champion's wondering eyes. "In the name of His Royal Majesty, Simon the Unvanquished, I command you to lay down your arms."

With a hesitation so palpable Allia could almost touch it, the knights all drew their swords.

"Allia, what are you doing?" Solomon flung himself down from his horse and ran toward her, but two of his archers dismounted and blocked his path. "Get out of my way!" he ordered, but the archers' blue eyes only narrowed. They did not obey.

Allia took a breath and raised her voice again. "In the name of His Royal Highness, Lennard the Lion, I order you to surrender."

As one body, the knights all raised their blades.

"Allia, they will kill you!"

"Not if you free them. Let them go, and I will live. I will owe my life to you."

Solomon lunged against the two archers' iron arms, but they did not give way. Behind him, the others nocked arrows to their bows. The arrowheads dripped with black poison. "Allia, if I try to free these men, the archers will shoot us both. Please, step away. Your death will accomplish nothing."

Allia watched her peddler's tears fall from those tawny eyes, and her heart broke inside her. Those stalwart arms that had felt like a fortress were as powerless as her own. She turned away as a sob broke in her throat, but she did not falter. She stepped toward Johan, who still sat on horseback with his broadsword poised to kill. She laid her hand on his knee, the only part of him she could reach. Then she looked back at Solomon and said, "My friend is drowning. I will always climb the tree and let him pull me in."

Solomon fell to his knees. "Allia, please..."

Allia looked up into Johan's glassy eyes and then closed her own. She tried to picture Prince Lennard's smile. She prayed to see him waiting on the other side of sacrifice with his hands outstretched to greet her. But a different pair of dark brown eyes gazed at her in her mind. From a throne with wheels, a different pair of callused hands reached out for hers...

People call me the lion, but I'd rather be able to fly.

The kingdom needed more than just the strength of a lion's claws. It needed the courage to soar.

Allia opened her eyes and looked at her champion. "In the name of His Royal Majesty, Raphael the Eagle, I order you to kneel."

Johan's broadsword thundered down—then crashed against a wall of light. The steel resounded like a cymbal, a strain of bells and bird-song that rippled outward in a silver tide. As it touched the men, they froze in place, until Allia alone could turn her head to gape with wonder at a puff of smoke the shape of a cocoon. It split open as if along a seam, torn asunder by a sword with a diamond-studded hilt whose brilliance dimmed against its steel.

The awe-struck maiden caught the sword and slashed it against the air. A roar of triumph and of longing echoed through her soul. From some realm she could not see beyond the blinding silver light, the thump of a wooden practice blade parried her stroke.

A flutter of wings beat against the light, and the silver bells rang out anew. "Allia," the creature sang, "rejoice with me. The Lion lives."

CHAPTER 37

$\mathcal{T}$he cloth-of-gold cape on Tristan's shoulders felt like it had been woven of lead. He stood behind the curtain Prince Raphael had hung in the gallery of the great hall to hide himself during the ball. Now, it blocked the view of the lower floor, where the kingdom's most important men had assembled at their prince's command. News of the impending invasion had already spread. The curtain could not block the sounds of worried grumbling.

Tristan wanted to wipe his sweaty palms, but he dared not soil the rich purple brocade of his tunic, nor the silver silk of his breeches. In just a little while, he would return his clothes to the custody of the crown. A few minutes from now, he would no longer be a prince. His horse already stood saddled to take him back to Carnish-on-Levold, where tomorrow—if she came—he would confess his identity to Lilliane and beg her to marry him. Gone were the constraints that she must hide in the palace as Princess Briella's lady-in-waiting while pretending not to be married to the man who was not a prince. Just moments from now, Tristan would trade places with Timothy d'Immerville. The baron would become a prince and the prince would become a baron. Tristan prayed that his new title would be enough to make the lord's stepdaughter accept him.

But first, he had to escape the palace with his life. In all his dreams about the day when Prince Raphael would free him from deception, Tristan had forgotten to imagine that the lords might hang him for treason.

"The lords are restless," Prince Raphael said as he wheeled himself toward his proxy. "It is not a good way to start."

Tristan had never before seen the prince so well dressed. Fox fur trimmed his green damask doublet, tiny pearls edged his breeches, and the boots that cased his worthless feet were laced up to the knees with golden cords. He wore no royal purple, but woven griffins perched on the tops of his epaulets. For the first time since Tristan had known him, Prince Raphael had tied his mass of raven curls with a ribbon at the nape of his neck. With his hair styled like his brother's, there was no mistaking the resemblance—except that Prince Lennard had never worn such a look of abject fear.

"Let them be restless," said Tristan. "It's you and I who must be calm. If you go out there trembling, we are lost."

A small voice answered, "We've been lost since Lennard died."

Both men turned to see Princess Briella walking toward them with her hand on Father Alester's arm. She wore no royal finery, only a sturdy blue traveling dress and leather boots. Yet the way she carried her slight frame made Tristan all too conscious of his own rough posture.

"If I were old enough to be queen, I could save us. But I will come back someday to take the throne back from the Darrivants."

"Your vote of confidence is heartening, sister." Prince Raphael rolled his eyes.

"It's not my fault you are a cripple."

"But it is your fault you treat him like one." Tristan stepped between the princess and her brother, aching as he always did to wash the cruelty out of her haughty black eyes, to free the child she ought to be from the constraints of the overbearing princess she was. "Life has not been kind to you, Your Highness, but that is all the more reason why you ought to bring more kindness into life."

The princess crossed her arms over her chest. "Like throwing balls that end up getting half the city burned? Is that what you mean by kindness?"

"Briella..."

"No, Your Highness. She is right." Tristan pondered the princess with her hand on Father Alester's arm, the chaplain whom the Church had sent to guide and teach her young soul. With a start, he realized that in all his hours studying priestly ministry at Father Alester's heels, never once had they sought her out—not to teach her the catechism, nor to console her after her brother's death, nor even while she sat at the king's bedside, watching him die. The crown had so consumed their energies, they had forgotten why priests were called "Father."

Tristan knelt, bringing his great frame down to meet the princess eye-to-eye. "I have sinned against you, Your Highness. It was my duty to teach you kindness, and I failed. But I will give you an opportunity to learn how to show mercy. Forgive me, Your Highness. Show yourself that you are more than just your bitterness. Show yourself that you are a true daughter of the True King."

Princess Briella stared back at him, her eyes as icy as they had ever been. But her lip began to quiver, and suddenly she flung herself on Tristan's neck. He wrapped her in his sturdy arms, cradling her shaking body against his heart.

When she stood, she wiped her eyes on her sleeve and slipped her small hand into Tristan's. The touch of it was peace.

"Come," she said to Prince Raphael.

The prince relaxed his white-knuckled grip on his chair. He wheeled himself forward and gently kissed his sister's cheek.

At last, she smiled.

THE BELLS of Pellain Castle tolled at full peal, sending an avalanche of sound clattering down on Lady Vivienne's aching head. For two days since her daughter disappeared, a migraine had kept her confined to her tent. Even the slightest whisper fell on her like an axe-blow to the skull. It did not matter. None of the whispers were happy. The Lord Commander had conducted an investigation into Lilliane's disappearance, but none of his own people were missing. The only conclusion to be drawn was that Lilliane had stolen the gold herself and fled of her own will. If the Lord Commander had suspected kidnapping, he might have given chase, but he was not willing to risk his men on a mission behind enemy lines to look for a girl who did not want to be found.

So Vivienne's head pounded on.

The noise of shouts and thudding feet joined the clamor of the bells. Next came a flurry of incomprehensible Darrivant words, horses' whinnies, and clanging armor. Vivienne gently raised her body from the ground and forced her lips to smile. The siege must have finally broken through. The only thing that might console her for the loss of her daughter—and her gold—was to watch her husband lose.

She lurched to her feet, and the ground wobbled as her brain reeled with its pain. She forced her lips to take a swallow from her wine-skin: not the prized rosewine of Darrivane, but a vintage strong enough to ease the agony even as it made the wobbling worse. Still the bells pealed triumph, while the sounds of feet and shouting receded toward the lines. Vivienne grabbed her spyglass and slinked outside. The daylight pounded down, every ray a nail driven through her tender eyes. She staggered on.

The paddock stood deserted but for her own horse. Her groom was an absentee, her handmaid nowhere to be found. Thank God she had been a commoner once. She could saddle her own steed. Her body cried in protest as she lifted the heavy leather seat, but her horse made no such fuss. She pulled the fastenings tight and swung herself onto her mount.

The stallion knew his way. His ears pricked up as he trotted toward their usual perch under the oak tree. The battle raged directly in front of them. The archers in the siege towers traded arrows with the Armans on the walls. The Darrivant footsoldiers lined up in formation just feet in front of Vivienne, waiting for the drawbridge to be opened by their comrades who were gaining access through the mines. The gears of the catapult groaned as its builders wound them taut. With a sudden *crack*, they let it fly. The boulder smashed the crenellations at the top of the castle wall, sending a shower of stones and bodies into the stagnant moat below. The noise sliced like knives into Vivienne's fragile consciousness, but the noise was also its own narcotic. The catapult wound for another volley, but an officer signaled it to halt. He shouted and pointed toward the walls.

Vivienne raised her spyglass and smiled. Among the green livery of Camesbry and the deep red of Morisse, the black spiders of Darrivane crawled from the stairwells like an infestation. A moment later, the drawbridge crashed down across the moat. The footsoldiers let out a victorious cry and ran forward, lances drawn.

Vivienne's stallion stamped and snorted, his flanks twitching as he swished his tail and bucked his head toward the fray. Vivienne wanted to let him run, but their moment had not yet come. She held the reins tight, knowing it would not be long.

Dying men shrieked, swords and lances clashed, and at last Vivienne could see wounded Armans locked in combat with their own men. Some of them still sported arrows lodged within their arms. So many hard hours of toil, so many sleepless nights spent dreaming—it had all been for this. Pride and exultation washed away her pain as Vivienne watched her own creation turn the tide of her own fate. Nothing could stop the Darrivants now. No one could keep her from becoming first among them, the greatest hero of the greatest empire the world had ever known. She sat up straighter in her saddle, her head reaching toward the clouds. Now that Armany was all but theirs, the Lord Commander could send men out to retrieve Lilliane. There was only one place Lilliane wanted to go. They would find her in Carnish-on-Levold and return her, and then the life Vivienne had toiled for so many years to build would finally be complete.

A cry went up from near the castle doors, and Vivienne shifted her spyglass. At the gates stood Lord Camesbry in blood-spattered armor, waving a white flag. Vivienne grinned and let her stallion run.

CHAPTER 38

*P*rince Raphael had never been as frightened as he was when Tristan pulled back the curtain. The rumble of worry in the hall crescendoed as the four conspirators made their way toward the center of the gallery. Chancellor Narius waited for them with the Cardinal, who wore his full regalia of miter and robes. Raphael prayed those jeweled hands would reach out to him in blessing, not condemnation.

"I have brought the crown, Your Highness," Chancellor Narius said to Tristan. "His Eminence is willing to perform the coronation now, before the fighting begins."

"Thank you, Your Eminence, Lord Chancellor. I pray the people will be as eager as I am to see that accomplished." Tristan looked at Raphael, took a breath, and turned to the assembly with his hands upraised.

Silence fell at his summons. "My fellow Armans, I..." He stopped and motioned toward Father Alester, Briella, and Raphael. "My fellow Armans, *we* have called you here today to give you grievous news. King Simon the Unvanquished has fallen at last. The heavens have received their most gallant son."

Murmurs rose to the gallery like smoke, layering new darkness over the already somber mood. But one sharp voice rose above the others, crying, "The king is dead! Long live the king!" Raphael peered through the railing and smiled to see Lady Demont raise her arm in salute. He sat up straighter as he laid his hand over the pocket where he carried Lady Allia's shoe.

"Long live the king!" the assembly echoed, though not as vigorously as Raphael might have hoped. Chancellor Narius fell to one knee before Tristan, and the crowd followed. Only the Cardinal, the princess, and Father Alester remained standing. Briella looked at her brother, her raven eyes wide with fear. He smiled as gently as he could and nodded.

"My fellow Armans," she said, but her tiny voice did not carry in the vastness of the hall. She cleared her throat and tried again. "My fellow Armans," she fairly shouted, and this time the assembly raised their eyes. "My father leaves behind a son, His Royal Highness, Raphael Ignatius Bartholomew d'Armany. He is my brother and a worthy king." Raphael felt his throat swell with pride. Briella coughed and lifted Tristan's hand. "But this man is not he."

Chancellor Narius's head popped up, one of the few people who heard her words clearly. "Princess, what are you doing...?"

Father Alester stepped to Briella's side and laid his hand on her shoulder. "Did you hear her, my lords? By my priesthood, by my sacred duty as the royal family's chaplain, I swear to you that she speaks truly. This man—" he swept his hand toward Tristan, who bowed to hide his shaking—"is not Prince Raphael."

Raphael clutched his wheels and pushed them forward, the longest cubit they had ever traveled. Briella took his hand.

Father Alester laid his hand on his shoulder. "This one is."

The crowd grumbled and shouted. Swords zinged against scabbards as their owners unsheathed them. The Chancellor's face turned purple with rage while the Cardinal's grew pale with disbelief. Father Alester raised his voice above the din and cried, "Long live His Royal Majesty, King Raphael!" He fell to his knees, along with Tristan and Briella. But Chancellor Narius stood up again. All the assembly rose from the obeisance they had paid to Tristan.

"My fellow Armans," Raphael shouted above the noise. The words he had penned by candlelight, the words he had studied and repeated all the long night before, tasted hollow now. The air was choked with anger, the kingdom ripe for war. His people needed more than words, but words were the only weapon a man in a chair could ever wield.

Lord Collin de Tembria charged up the stairs. "Treachery!" he cried as he raised his gleaming blade. "What say you, Your Eminence, Lord Chancellor? Shall Armany endure this perfidious charade? We need a king, not a cripple, and the princess is culpable, too." He pounded his chest with his sword-arm. "I am the next in line. Crown me."

Chancellor Narius's face puffed up, but he said nothing.

Lord Tembria shouted, "What say you all? What shall we do with this so-called prince who would play us all for fools?"

The crowd was not united in its answer, but a few of them cried, "Hang him!" Briella turned to Raphael with tears of terror in her eyes. *What would Lennard have done?* he asked himself, but just as quickly, he tossed the thought away. He could not become his brother. He could only become himself.

"My people," he cried above the sound of his cousin egging them toward murder. "My people, every word this man has spoken in my name," he gestured toward Tristan, "I have penned for him. Since the day my brother died, it is I who have been your prince." The grumbling began to quiet as his voice resounded through the hall. Raphael had never heard himself speak with such power, his voice echoing against the walls as if he were shouting through a horn. "I am the same man I was when you saw me wearing his figure. It was I who committed his follies, and I who steered you to the brink of destruction on which we stand. Yet despite my failures, you were ready to crown me, to let me lead you through this darkness into Armany's new dawn, as long as you believed I had legs. I ask you, what has changed? Is a man's height his only measure? Is a king's sword-arm his only strength?"

"Aye!" cried Collin de Tembria, but the word reverberated like a child's shout against the silence. A premonition seemed to fill the hall, the air as brittle as dry leaves waiting for a spark.

"My people." Raphael laid his hand on the kneeling Tristan's shoulder. "You once heard this man speak my words. I repeat them to you now. I am not a general, but I assure you that I am a prince. I am the son of a great man and a great dream. Justice is my birthright, as it is yours, my brothers. All true justice comes to us from the hands of the True King. That is why I will subject myself to it. Open your eyes to see not as man sees, but to look into the heart. I will abide by your ruling."

He bowed his head. His heart pounded, blood rushed through his ears, and he swayed slightly in his chair. Briella took both his hands in hers, but she could not calm his racing pulse. Raphael's people were not barbarians, but neither were they saints. One angry word would be enough to shatter the gossamer threads of hope, to ignite the kingdom in the blaze of chaos. But no anger touched its spark against the waiting fuel.

A sound of bells and birdsong pealed, a din of unbearable beauty that sent a gasp of terror shuddering through the crowd. Raphael blinked at a blinding flutter of silver, but his gaze came to rest on a smile that glowed out in mid-air beneath a pair of hazelnut eyes.

CHAPTER 39

 he mountain shimmered opalescent in the hazy light of
static time. Allia traced her finger across the steel of Griffin's Claw. "Is this mine?" she asked.

"Yes," the fairy answered. "The Lion bequeathed it to the Lion."

The maiden heaved away a sob and laid her cheek against the
blade, overcome with memories of the boy for whom this sword had
been forged—the boy who had vowed to build his kingdom on the
shoulders of a cripple and a girl. She had always dreamed that the
Lion would give her justice; she had not dreamed that he would ask
her to become it.

Allia took a breath and stood up straighter, knowing where her
future lay. "Has Prince Raphael revealed the truth?"

The fairy answered, "Yes."

"Has he been crowned?"

"No. The kingdom is still looking for its legs. It is too blind to see
its wings."

Allia turned to all the soldiers who stood motionless, suspended in
the light. Johan, with his sword half-way through its stroke. Solomon,
frozen in mid-lunge against the arms of the Darrivants who

restrained him. All the thousands of deserters snaked in silence along the mountain.

Tears sprang to Allia's eyes. "I cannot leave these men to go to him."

The fairy smiled. "That is why I'm here."

Then the creature sang.

SHE CAME to him clothed like a common soldier, the first woman Raphael had ever seen wearing breeches. She moved with feline grace, her feet soundless against the solid bridge of sunlight that supported her as she walked toward him through the air. She opened her mouth as if to speak, but closed it again and returned her soft, red lips into a smile. He reached out his hands.

He did not even notice the sword until she knelt and laid it before him. "My king."

He laid his hands on her bowed head, hardly daring to believe the touch of golden curls against his palms was real. He cupped her chin and raised her face toward his. His own joy, his own wonder stared back at him from the depths of those enchanting eyes. He knew not whether he was dreaming, but he did not care. "My queen," he said. "My love."

He laid his lips on hers.

ALLIA'S BODY BECAME WIND. The bridge of light supporting her turned to a wayward wisp of air, yet Prince Raphael's lips were all the anchor she needed to know where she belonged. The taste of him was sorrow as much as it was joy, but it was sorrow shared with understanding, the purging fire that coaxed open the stubborn seeds of solace to let them blossom into love. The boy who had been an orphan in his father's house twined his arms around the cinder maid, and together, they were home.

He reached down and picked up the sword. He gave it back to her, wrapping her fingers around the hilt and his hands around her fingers. "Use it well, Your Royal Majesty."

Again, a song resounded through the air, a canticle bright with bells that washed the lovers in its light.

Then Allia stood on the mountainside once more.

The men around her stared like deer caught in a hunter's snare. Freed from the spell of timelessness, they blinked in mute amazement at the fluttering fairy and the girl who held a royal sword.

Solomon fell to his knees. "Your Royal Majesty."

Johan dismounted and laid his blade at her feet. "Allia." He kissed her hands. She kissed his brow.

One by one, the royal knights all followed, their blades laid bare, their helmets doffed as they knelt in a ring of fealty around the maiden. "Hail to the Lioness," they cried. "Hail to the queen." Johan's armor covered his wounds, but the men whose faces and hands had been marred with gray stood whole and clean again. All along the mountainside, as far as Allia could see, men fell to their knees, laying down their arms in tribute.

Allia's tears splashed across her nose as she looked to the fairy. "You freed them."

"No. You did." The creature fluttered close and kissed her cheek. "I am a fallible creature, just like you. I offer what help I can give. But it is to your great love that these men owe their lives." The creature flitted its wings against the sword until the blade gave off its own bright sphere of light.

Allia looked around at her army and realized that even the Darrivants were kneeling. She pointed her sword toward them. "Where does your allegiance lie?"

The Darrivants looked at her quizzically, and Solomon quickly translated. "With you, Your Royal Majesty," he returned their answer.

"And you, Commander Regis?" Her heart caught in her throat.

He stood up and took three steps toward her, his tawny eyes awash with shame. "If ever there was a man who wronged a woman more than I have wronged you, I beg you would allow me to put him to the sword. Pronounce my sentence, and I shall carry it out myself."

She hefted her blade. "Kneel down."

He smiled sadly and fell before her. "As many times as you have faced me across a sword, that many times would I have gladly died by your hand. But please, let me do it. Leave your own hands unstained."

"I intend to." She laid her sword against his shoulder. "Do you repent of your crimes?"

"With every fiber of my soul."

"Then tell me what title you would have."

He stared at the ground, his face obscure. He did not look at her as he laid his hand on her arm—and Allia recognized the man from her dream, the faceless man who promised faithfulness, who freed her from the serpent. It was the serpent himself. "Do not grant me a title, Your Majesty. I will be nameless all my life if you only allow me to serve you."

She smiled. "Sir Summers, then—the one in whom the ice had to melt before you could be true. In the name of God, St. Michael, and St. George, I bind thee to their service. Rise."

He did, his eyes now wet with joy. Allia kissed his forehead. "Armany will profit from your vision. I swear it." She turned once more to the fairy. "Shall I lead them to the capitol?"

"No. To Pellain."

Allia's heart skipped a sudden, painful beat. "Papa."

The fairy nodded. "There is one more soldier you must save."

Allia's hands shook, and she lowered her sword.

"Don't be afraid," the creature whispered. "I am your godmother. Do you know who entrusted you to me?"

Allia swallowed. "My mother." The maiden squared her shoulders. "How do we get to Pellain?"

The creature only smiled. The birdsong swelled to a crescendo, and the doorway opened.

CHAPTER 40

*O*nder as thick as steam filled the air of the great hall. For long moments after the light was gone, hardly a soul dared to breathe. Collin de Tembria stood slack-jawed at one end of the gallery. Tristan, who had been on his knees when the light appeared, clung to the gallery railing as if he might fall. Chancellor Narius and the Cardinal merely looked like statues, while Princess Briella gazed toward where the light had been with a look that reminded Father Alester of the starry-eyed saints who lined his chapel walls. And Raphael... Alester stood as still as all the rest, mesmerized not by the magical vision, but by the joy he had never dared to dream he would see in Raphael's eyes. Alester had never seen a man so radiantly content yet filled with such pure determination.

Chancellor Narius was the first to find his voice. "Your Eminence," he said to the Cardinal, "we have a king to crown."

Raphael turned to them, and the miraculous light still shone out from his eyes. "Yes. That is the only way she can become a queen."

The others in the gallery exchanged confused looks. "*She*, Your Majesty?" Narius asked.

"Could you not see her?"

Princess Briella answered. "We saw Lennard's sword. A lion brought it, but it didn't have a mane."

"A lio*ness*," said Alester, though his palate grew suddenly dry.

"A lioness." Raphael smiled. "It suits her."

"Who is she, Your Majesty?" asked Narius.

"She is my bride. Allia d'Armany."

Alester could not suppress a whimper, but no one heard.

"Allia... de Camesbry?" asked the Chancellor. "The one who is accused of treason for creating that horrible potion?"

"The one who freed our men from its poison." Raphael turned toward the whole assembly and raised his impassioned voice. "My people, the deserters have been returned to our ranks. There will be no attack against the capitol. They are under the command of the Lion."

"Did she tell you this, Your Majesty?"

"Not with words."

No one dared to ask him more.

Father Alester watched in silence as the Cardinal led the coronation. He knelt when all the others knelt, gave the responses all the others gave, and cried, "Long live the king!" when all the others cried it. The hall resounded like a gong under the hammer of their voices. Alester watched the frayed ends of the kingdom he had served so long being woven back into a single cloth by the boy he loved more than anyone in the world, and his heart was full—but not with joy. He could barely draw breath, so suffocating was his shame. What had possessed him, to think that such a king as Raphael could build his reign on a foundation of intrigue and lies? What perfidy had blinded him, that he had tried to kill the girl who was fit to carry the Lion's sword, the girl who made the boy he loved glow with a love beyond any he could fathom?

What perfidy, indeed. Alester already knew that the chasm of his corruption had no bottom. He looked up from the depths of the pit that had replaced his soul, terrified by how close he had come to pulling Raphael down beside him. There was only one way to ensure that never happened—one way to ensure that Alester would never be tempted to forget his own shame.

The king wheeled toward his chaplain once the ritual was done, the golden circlet of his office glinting on his mop of unruly raven curls. "Father, will you not give me your blessing?"

Alester forced his lips into a weary replica of a smile. He extended both his hands over the king. "May the King of Kings always reign within you." He leaned down and, with his traitor's lips, laid a kiss on Raphael's brow. Then he turned and fled before his tears could fall.

The king would be busy for hours. The lords and barons would all take their turns kneeling to their new monarch, promising tributes, receiving blessings. His Majesty would be prevailed upon to give commands concerning his father's burial, to set a date for his wedding, and any number of other matters. Alester hoped it would be long enough for him to finish all the things that could not be left undone.

He went toward his chamber, passing through the chapel he could not avoid. He closed his eyes against the sight of St. Lucy's window that had been covered over with heavy cloth after Raphael sent a candle flying through it. The palace would never be free of such mementos, tiny details that assaulted Alester with the humanity of the boy who was now king. Was that why he had done so much to sabotage his reign—because he wanted to keep the boy for himself, instead of sharing him with the kingdom? Or was he plagued by the same short-sightedness he had always claimed to fight against? Had he ever really believed that a cripple could be a king?

In spite of himself, he stopped at St. Lucy's broken window. "Watch over him," he entreated. Then he mounted the stairs to his room.

A pile of parchments lay waiting: the deed to the land he had promised the Darrivant officer, a letter of credit for a petty thief in Tembria, a love poem to the widow in Lagunde who did not know her husband had died on his journey to the capitol two years before. Alester had taken up his pen in the husband's name, and in return received letters about the back-room dealings of the Lagunde sword-smiths' guild.

Father Alester sealed the Darrivant's deed and tossed the other parchments onto his fire. He wrote the widow a brief account of her husband's death and composed a few terse letters to other informants who were too valuable to be cut off without a word. He did not want his people to turn against the new king because of his own mistakes.

He finished his correspondence, rang a bell to summon a messenger, and sent the letters on their way. Then he sat and pondered the cords that bound his alb around his waist. They did not look strong enough to bind him forever to the fate of the betrayer. Instead, Alester opened the trunk where he kept his scrolls and took out a small apothecary's pouch full of dried leaves. They crackled venomously in his hand. He tucked the pouch into his pocket and once again descended the stairs to the chapel.

He stood at the foot of the crucifix. He did not allow himself to kneel. "I ask for no forgiveness," he told the face of mercy. "I deserve punishment and pain. Only grant that when I am in hell, I may see Vivienne de Camesbry writhing with me in the flames."

Father Alester took the pouch from his pocket and poured the hemlock onto his tongue.

VIVIENNE'S STALLION nearly threw her as she reined him to a halt, but she squeezed her knees against the saddle for dear life and held on. Her husband did not see her nearly fall. He was too busy kneeling to the Darrivant Commander, extending his arms to allow himself to be shackled. Vivienne wished he would shed a tear, but she knew him too well to expect it.

"Good morrow, my lord. Believe me when I say, the sight of you safely locked in chains gives me more joy than any victory."

Lord Camesbry turned his head, but hatred obscured any surprise he might have felt at finding his wife on the enemy lines. "No greater than my joy shall be when I see your head severed from your shoulders."

She dismounted and came toward him. One of the Darrivant officers put out an arm to stop her, but Lord Camesbry barked a few broken Darrivant words, and the man let her come. The only word Vivienne understood was "wife."

"Do you not wonder what I am doing here, Eric?"

"I do not wonder because I know. It was you who brewed the foul poison that has been stealing our soldiers and then blamed my daughter for it. What I do not understand is why you bothered to present your evidence to the crown if you were planning to defect."

Vivienne pursed her lips as her headache throbbed. "That was a matter of the heart. Did you know His Royal Highness is in love with Lilliane? Your stepdaughter would have been queen, if we had stayed. But it is better this way. She will marry in the court of an emperor, where we will both be lauded and adored."

"Then why has she not come out to gloat with you?"

Vivienne gritted her teeth as fresh needles of pain stabbed through her head. "That is neither here nor there. What matters is that I am here, and you are there, in chains."

Lord Camesbry rattled his manacles. "Exult, if that is what you have come for. Vaunt your triumph and be done."

"I am far from done, my lord." She traced a finger under his chin. "I saved a vial of my finest elixir just for you." She reached into her pocket and drew it out. The black liquid shimmered in the sun as she removed the wax stopper.

"What have I done to you? I gave you a title, a castle, a workshop for your craft. I gave myself to you as husband. I took you as my wife. Tell me, Lady Camesbry, what was my crime?"

She leaned in close to whisper in his ear. "Ask your daughter, my lord."

Lord Camesbry's face fell slack with grief.

"The only reason you never beat me was that you had her to be your whipping-post instead. The moment she was gone, you turned your hand against Lilliane. Do you think I do not know the blackness of your heart because you only vent it upon your own flesh and blood?"

He reached out his manacled hands and grabbed her wrist, trying to pry open the fingers that held the potion. "You dare to speak to me of Allia? After you tried to have her hanged for your treason?"

"Restrain him," Vivienne cried to the Darrivants, and they needed no one to translate her order. An officer with arms as thick as tree trunks pinned Lord Camesbry's arms while another man forcibly raised his chin. "Open wide, my love. I will do nothing to you that you have not done to your own flesh. You will make quite a spectacle as my cinder maid at my estate in Darrivane."

With all his might, Lord Camesbry pursed his lips and clenched his teeth, but Vivienne touched the ticklish spot under his chin that only she and Lady Clara had ever known existed. He laughed against his will, and she tilted the potion toward his tongue. He coughed to try to stop himself from swallowing, but the strong-armed Darrivant wedged his jaws apart while Vivienne kept pouring. She did not stop until his body fell limp, his eyes glassed over, and darkness like a bruise spread through his skin.

"Let him go." The Darrivants unshackled him. Lord Camesbry did not move.

But the sky behind him did.

A flash of blinding light scissored the horizon. The world split open to reveal a mountain hung like a mural, spilling armored horsemen from its rocky heights onto the plains. The victorious Darrivants froze as one body, gaping with open jaws at the apocalypse, until the first arrow fired from the vision struck down its first victim. Then they scrambled like ants back into formation and began to fight.

Vivienne hesitated, torn between saving her husband or her horse. She chose the horse. She threw herself into the saddle, dug her heels into the stallion's sides, and fled back toward the camp. Lord Camesbry rose and followed. He would shadow her like a puppy, she knew, though he could not keep pace with the stallion.

Behind her, she heard a woman's voice cry, "Papa!"

Vivienne drew her reins and turned. Cinder Allia rode a dappled palfrey, little better than a pack-horse. She wore a soldier's clothes, though no armor covered her tunic, no helmet protected the golden curls of her head. Her sword already dripped with red even while it enveloped her in a sphere of golden light.

Vivienne's stomach twisted like a wrung-out rag. She pointed her stallion's head toward Darrivane and kicked her heels with all the force her legs could muster.

CHAPTER 41

$\mathcal{T}$he Lioness raised her gleaming claw and brought it down through blood. The shock of striking armor and bone shuddered through her body even while her victim sprawled. Charging hooves carried her onward. She raised the sword again. Again, her aim was true. Steel as strong and sharp as diamond severed breath from body, channeling the pain the dead could no longer feel into the arms of the one who slayed them. Sweat like lava boiled down her skin. Bile bubbled in her contracting throat while she raised the blade again. But the more the weary work of war weighted down her arms, the more the memory of the man whose kiss gave her a kingdom raised them up to soar. His arms around her became armor; his smile soothed her strain. If she had fought for the kingdom, she would have faltered, but the Lioness fought for the king.

"My lady," Sir Winters cried at her right hand, "near the horizon. Look."

"Papa!" Allia saw him running, and her heart fell to her heels.

"Look past him, Your Majesty," Sir Summers called from her left.

Allia squinted in the sun. She could just make out the figure of a rider on a black stallion—the same horse she had fed and groomed and saddled for her stepmother more times than she could count. She ordered Sir Summers, "Catch her."

Solomon laid his body flat against his destrier and spurred it to full speed.

Allia trained her eyes on her father and kicked her palfrey to a gallop. She held her sword ready, but Sir Dunstan and Sir Hamran had maneuvered out ahead. The swathes of soldiers parted as the knights sliced through them like scythes through fields of grain. Allia burst through the Darrivant lines.

"Papa!"

He turned his blackened face to her but did not say a word.

She fell more than dismounted from her horse. "Papa." She stroked his sweaty hair out of his eyes. "Papa, no." She searched the air for the fairy, but the brutal spectacle of battle blotted out any vision of silver-bright wings.

Allia's stomach heaved as she looked at her sword.

Her father's disbelieving eyes bounced between her face and her bloodstained blade. His throat let loose a strangled gurgle. "No, Papa, don't try to speak. I understand." She scanned the field again, praying for someone to dissuade her, but her knights were all locked in combat. This battle belonged to her alone.

She kissed her father's cheek. "I did not kill my mother, Papa. She died to save me—as I shall do for you." Her voice broke on the words. It had seemed like nothing, to let herself be killed for the sake of all those stolen soldiers, but then she had had nothing else for which to live. Allia gazed into her father's face, trying to see past the image of disdain that had so long been burned upon her memory. What was the silent longing that stared back? Was it the yearning of a father for his child, or only the hunger of a dying man for life?

She looked down at her hands and felt the imprint of King Raphael's fingers where he had wrapped them around the sword. "*Use it well, Your Royal Majesty.*" Would he believe that she had listened, when he learned how she had died? She wanted to fling her weapon down, to run back to the far-off mountainside as it disappeared in a foggy haze. She reached out, wishing the fog would wrap her in enchantment, return her to the golden moment when her life had had meaning even while she was alive. But the fog vanished under scorching sunlight. The hour of magic was done.

Allia tightened her grip on the sword. Her scabbed palms burned with the wounds of hate while her heart drummed against the cross-shaped scar of love. No matter which she chose, it would leave her bleeding.

She laid a hand on her father's shoulder. "Papa, I know you wanted to take my life, but that is not why I give it. I give it because it is the only price that will buy your freedom." She handed him her sword. "I love you, Papa. Now, I order you to kneel."

Lord Camesbry's face contorted with unshed tears as his arms raised the blade to his chest.

"Swear your allegiance to His Royal Majesty, King Raphael."

His tears fell.

Allia's strength deserted her. She sank to her knees. "I forgive you, Papa. For everything." Her voice leaked out in whispers. "Now... claim me as your queen."

Allia counted her own heartbeats, waiting for them to end. Her father's desolate eyes met hers. A sound as of an earthquake rumbled from his throat. Lord Camesbry heaved his arms above his head like Atlas hoisting heaven on his shoulders.

Then he turned the sword and drove it through his own belly.

"Papa, no!" Allia leaped up and helped to ease his massive body toward the ground.

"Allia." Even as his blood poured out, the inky curse receded from her father's skin. Allia sank her sobbing head against his shoulder. He wrapped her weakly with one arm. "Daughter." He stroked one curl back from her face and whispered, "Live."

VIVIENNE HEARD hoof-beats pounding behind her and plastered her body flat against her stallion's back. At such a speed, she could hardly see to maneuver her way through the wilderness of buckskin tents, but her sure-footed mount leaped over the ones he could not dodge. Vivienne's stomach turned like a cart wheel, but she held on until a tent pole sprang out across her path.

The stallion gave an anguished whinny as he crashed, hurling Vivienne headlong from the saddle. Instinctively, she thrust out her arms to break the fall. She heard the crunch of bones as her left wrist bent impossibly backward and her body connected with the ground.

"I do not know whether to call you a traitor or a failure."

Pain blazed through Vivienne's consciousness while she listened to the wail of her injured stallion, but she opened her eyes. Kathya stood over her, still holding the tent pole she had thrust out to bring Vivienne down. "Either way, I hope the demons will devour your flesh in the carrion heap of hell." The willowy woman raised the pole to strike.

Vivienne closed her eyes, but the blow never fell. The hoof beats that had been chasing her arrived.

"Kathya," said a voice that Vivienne could scarce believe was real. "Do not harm her."

Kathya spat, and Vivienne felt it splatter near her ear. "You dare to give me orders? Why should I not dispatch you, too, Commander? You have failed the Empire as much as she."

Vivienne worked to steady her breathing, to force her mind to comprehend that Solomon Regis was sitting on a horse just yards away from her, already acquainted with the Lord Commander's courtesan. He brandished his sword. "If you wish to dispatch me, I dare you to try. As for this harridan, she is stepmother to the woman who just conquered your army. It is Her Majesty's right to pronounce sentence."

Vivienne turned her head enough to see Kathya narrow her eyes, but she only half-listened to the response. Her mind had snagged against the words *Her Majesty*. Cinder Allia could only have acquired that title one way. Vivienne pictured a dock on the Levold River where her daughter would sit—for how long?—waiting for a prince who never came. Her swimming consciousness flooded with red, but she forced herself to rise.

"Take me to her. But do not deceive yourself, Commander. She will not allow you to use me to purchase your own pardon."

Regis slashed his sword to end the screaming stallion's misery and then turned to face Vivienne. "Her Majesty has already pardoned me. More than that, she has knighted me. You shall need to try her mercy for yourself. Kathya, if the Lord Commander is still living, it is your duty to be with him even when he bends the knee."

The courtesan spewed a string of Darrivant invectives so sinister that Vivienne wanted no translation, but they did not crack Regis's determined mask. "I did betray the Empire," he answered. "I bowed to someone stronger than the Emperor, and before the day is over, I daresay you will, too."

Kathya only spat again in answer.

At sword-point, the two women trudged across the camp. Some of the courtesans and camp followers had fled in the same direction Vivienne had tried to go, but many more remained, setting fires, destroying anything an enemy might find useful, turning Vivienne's dreams to ash. She stumbled often as she cradled her broken wrist against her body, but that did not stop her right hand from searching out the dagger hidden in her skirts.

They approached the oak tree where Vivienne had sat such a short time ago, gleefully watching a Darrivant victory. Now the field between it and Pellain Castle lay covered in kneeling Darrivant soldiers. By the hundreds, they knelt with hands upraised, patiently abiding while Arman knights walked through the ranks, collecting their weapons. The Lord Commander himself wore cords around his wrists, watched over by a guard of... Darrivant archers? Yet so it was. The tattooed men stood at attention, their bodies ringed around him like a prison.

"They have been struck with the poison," Kathya murmured.

"No," Regis answered, "they have been struck with the truth."

Kathya went and stood outside the ring of archers, conversing with the Lord Commander. She returned to Regis a moment later and announced, "He wishes me to meet this woman who leads you."

Vivienne scanned the field, searching for the woman with the sword of light, but instead she saw a mass of blonde curls on the ground. Allia was alone except for a single knight in Demont livery, who knelt with his hands on her shoulders. She lay with her head on a suit of armor with a dead body inside.

Vivienne tried to smile, but even the sight of her husband's body hot with blood could not console her when Regis called Allia, "Your Majesty."

Allia raised her tear-stained face. The knight beside her offered his hand to lift her to her feet. She did not take it. She pulled out the sword that protruded from her father's belly and carefully cleaned it on the grass. It did not seem to cast a glow around her now, but Vivienne still noted the gleam of diamonds in Lagunde steel.

Allia stood and nodded toward Lord Camesbry's body. "Stepmother, this is your work."

"That was not my sword in his stomach."

"But it was your poison in his veins, and in the veins of my champion, and every Arman man on this field. Death is too kind a punishment for what you have done."

"Do what you will with me. I will not beg a cinder maid for mercy."

Allia's brown eyes tightened with disgust. "Nor is there any mercy you deserve." She held her sword in her right hand and laid the blade across her left, weighing it, as if her hands were scales. "But I will not be mastered by hate. If you do not wish to die..." Her voice caught on the word. "You may come to the palace to work as a maid. You will not be crushed the way you crushed me. You will receive fair wages. You may work with dignity—and, by the grace of God, you may learn the dignity of being humble. But the moment you try to run away, or experiment with potions, or do an unkind deed toward anyone, your life will be forfeit. Do you accept?"

Vivienne stared into her stepdaughter's bright young eyes, and they tortured her with sincerity. How had it happened that this naïve zealot of a girl, this cinder maid who had no more gumption than to agree to marry a witless jeweler, had come to stand in judgment over the woman who had built an empire on her own cunning? How could the walls of power crumble before an onslaught of innocence?

"I will serve you on the day the devil bows before God's throne."

"So be it." Allia nodded toward the courtesan, who had stood silently watching the exchange. "Sir Summers, who is your guest?"

"Her name is Kathya, Your Majesty, the Darrivant Lord Commander's courtesan. Her position among her people is equal to his."

Allia inclined her head. "Please tell her she is welcome."

"I speak your language, Your Majesty," Kathya answered. Her shrewd eyes absorbed the queenly soldier while hatred and respect warred to shape her features. "I thank you for your welcome. But I do not know your name."

Allia gazed toward the horizon and then looked down at her sword. When she spoke, she seemed to savor the words, as if tasting them for the first time. "I am Allia d'Armany. King Raphael's bride."

Hearing confirmation of her daughter's heartbreak shattered the last of Vivienne's pride. She pulled the dagger from her skirt and lunged.

With a cry, Allia raised the sword that she still held across her hands. The dagger hit the royal steel and bent into a worthless metal wave. Allia leaped backward while Vivienne fell to the ground. The knight in Demont livery pinned her under his weight. "Give me the word, Your Majesty."

"Bind her," Allia ordered.

The cords cut into Vivienne's broken wrist as the knight lashed her firmly to her ruin. She bit her tongue until it bled, but even that could not stop her from screaming.

Allia d'Armany ignored the cries. She turned to the enemy courtesan. "Your people have done our kingdom great injustice, but I do not delight in blood. Please tell the Lord Commander that both of you are invited to the capitol as my guests, to meet with the king in order to arrange the terms of our peace. Your men shall remain here, under guard but safe, until we have a treaty."

The courtesan bent at the waist in a bow. "We accept your hospitality, Your Majesty."

Allia extended her hand. "I hope in time, you will accept my friendship, too."

The courtesan shook hands with the queen, and respect won the war over her face.

"Sir Winters," Allia called to the knight, "send Lady Camesbry to the palace dungeons. Let her rot there until the day God sees fit to dispose of her. Stepmother, farewell. I leave you in His hands."

Allia tucked her sword into the cords at her waist and walked away into the fields. Vivienne wept while she tasted blood and her world turned to ashes.

CHAPTER 42

$\mathcal{T}$he Levold River babbled welcome as Tristan rounded the mountain pass toward its familiar bank. Its gushing was the music that had accompanied Tristan's childhood. He reined in his horse as he neared the rocky shore, breathing in the scents of pine and water and open air. A flat-bottomed barge floated slowly by, propelled by a man with a pole and a wide-brimmed felt hat. Tristan raised his hand in greeting. The man smiled and waved back. To Tristan, even the sight of this stranger told him he had come home.

He let his horse meander lazily through the last mile of their journey, partly to allow himself the pleasure of soaking up familiar sights, partly to try to calm the fearful pounding of his heart. It had only been a week since he held Lilliane in his arms at the ball, but that week had seen a lifetime's worth of change. Anything could have happened to prevent her from coming, or to make her change her mind. Even if she was standing on the ferryman's dock, right where he dreamed she would be, she still thought she had come here to marry a prince. Tristan fingered the royal deed in his breast pocket that granted him a barony. King Raphael had signed a new one to make its validity undeniable. This was his own land Tristan rode through now: his forest, his farms, his river, his people. But the more of his own things he saw, the more it seemed the one thing he truly wanted would never be his.

The Oar and Lantern Inn marked his entry into the town of Carnish. The wooden building, painted red, had always reminded him of a barn. Gray smoke curled from its chimney, and the happy noise of a fiddler in its tavern floated to his ears. Tristan paused. This inn marked the root of all his sorrow and all his hope of joy, the place where he had first met Father Alester. He stopped in the inn yard only long enough to shake his head.

The road through town followed the bank of the river. Craftsmen's workshops and an open-air market lined the landward side, but only an occasional tree obscured the view of the swollen Levold. The town of Vareth, on the other side, looked like a land of doll houses from here. Tristan had a sudden urge to dive into the river, to feel the icy water race across his body, to submerge himself in what had been the life-blood of his existence since he was born. He went so far as to remove his hat, but the weight of the royal deed in his coat pocket stopped him. Baron Carnish ought not to be introduced to his people naked.

He passed through the market, surprised that no one recognized him. Old Tom still sat there with his three good teeth and his row of butchered chickens, fending off stray cats from his stall, exactly as he had for as long as Tristan could remember. Caroline must have gotten married while he was away; she had a toddler at her feet and a belly great with child, but her lace-work appeared as fine as ever. He waved to his old friends as he passed. They waved back kindly, but as if to a stranger. Tristan rubbed his hand over his cheek, where his inky black beard had only just begun to grow back in. Had he become so good at disguise, he could not take it off even when he tried?

But of course, Tristan Ferryman had never ridden through town on a sleek bay mare from the king's own stables. He had never worn a silk coat and fine linen breeches. This was not the merchants' old friend who rode through the market; it was their new liege.

Tristan shuddered.

The ferryman's dock lay to the far north of town, past everything except Tristan's family home. But Carnish-on-Levold was not large, and all too quickly, Tristan saw the old, familiar wooden dock pilings rising from the water. His heart drifted upward into his throat. His father sat on the pier, repairing a coil of rope—and talking to Lilliane.

Tristan dismounted and quietly led his horse behind the rock formation on the bank where he always used to hide when he wanted to avoid his chores.

"I can't say His Highness has ever been here before," he heard his father say. "There were royal officers who came through a few years back to take care of the bandits. That was how my son got his job at the palace. He's studying with the royal chaplain to become a priest." His father's voice flushed with pride. Tristan had to swallow back a tear.

"His Highness will come." Lilliane's words fell hard and flat, like the slap of a paddle. All the lilting music in her voice had disappeared. Tristan peeked around the rock. Her great dark eyes stared hollowly across the water as if looking across the chasm of lost time.

"Well, His Highness is most welcome, and so are you," Tristan's father said, "but I really can't fathom why he asked you to meet him here."

"I have braved the Darrivant Army to find him. He will come."

Tristan could bear no more. He stepped out from behind the rocks and walked toward them on the shore. "Mademoiselle Delaine, I am here."

Both people on the pier turned to him, their eyes wide with surprise. Lilliane fell to her knees, weeping as she cried, "Your Royal Highness."

The ferryman murmured, "Tristan?"

"Yes, Father." He removed his hat and stepped up onto the pier while Lilliane's jaw dropped with disbelief. Tristan paused to press his father's hand and then went to his knees beside the woman he had dreamed about for so long. "Lilliane." He traced the tracks of her tears with his thumb. "I am not a prince. I was his stand-in. The real Raphael d'Armany revealed himself two days ago, after his father's death. He is now our king. I am only a..." He was about to say "baron," but he stopped himself. Sitting here, on this dock where he had learned his trade, he was no such thing. "I am only a ferryman. My name is Tristan. This good man is my father, Alphonse, and this is my home."

He gazed into the stunned, silent face of the woman he loved. In just a week, the cut on her cheek had healed, but her cheeks themselves had grown hollow. Her graceful, swan-like neck had slumped, her ebony curls had fallen lank around her shoulders, and her skin like silk and eiderdown had burned red in the sun. Tristan wanted to cradle her in his arms and nurse whatever wounds she had endured.

"A ferryman," she said breathlessly.

The royal deed of his barony hung heavy in his pocket. He answered, "Yes."

"But… do you love me?"

All the words he wanted to say caught against the dam of his lips. He only repeated, "Yes."

She fell against his chest, weeping.

Tristan raised his eyes to his father in a question. His father answered with a shrug. Tristan held Lilliane while she cried, confident as he had never been before that here were the place and the person to whom he would always belong. But she had not said, "I love you, too."

At last, Lilliane quieted her sobs and dried her face on her dirty sleeve. "Do you still work for the prince? I mean, the king? Will you return to the palace?"

"No. I have come home to stay."

"So from this day, you will always be a ferryman. Nothing more?"

His heart thumped against the parchment in his coat. He did not know why he could not bring himself to show it. "Yes. I am a ferryman—nothing more."

Lilliane heaved a sigh. "Thank God. I have seen the results of my mother's ambition. I am a wool merchant's daughter. I will be content to be a ferryman's wife."

Tristan stared into her haunted eyes. They had grown up too much to remind him of a spring fawn anymore. She was no longer a dream, but a woman, errant and broken—and Tristan loved her more. He laid his lips on hers; the shape of them still fit perfectly against his own.

He stood up and helped her to her feet. "Father, this is Lilliane Delaine. My bride."

Alphonse Ferryman clasped her in his arms. "Welcome, Daughter."

"It's good to be here, Father."

Tristan slipped the deed from his pocket and dropped it into the river. The Levold washed the parchment clean as it carried it away.

CHAPTER 43

"*In paradisum deducant te Angeli,*" the line of monks chanted as they processed through the streets of the capitol behind the body of the king. *May the angels lead you into paradise.* King Raphael knew the words and the melody, but as he sat with his sister in the coach that carried their father's coffin, he prayed them for a different Father. The capitol was playing host to two very different burials today: one in the white marble tomb in the palace churchyard, and one in the unhallowed cemetery kept for prostitutes, atheists, and suicides.

What would the kingdom think if they knew King Raphael's tears flowed more for the unshriven chaplain than for the unvanquished king?

Raphael swatted at his leaking eyes and sat up straighter on the carriage-box. His fingers curled around Lady Allia's shoe in his pocket and the scroll that had joined it there this morning. *I am coming to you victorious,* she had written, *but first I must bury my father.* Every king's reign began with a father's burial, but three seemed too exorbitant to bear.

Princess Briella leaned her small, dark head against his shoulder. Raphael laid his cheek against her hair, inhaling the fragrance of the white orchids she carried to place before the tomb. He found it strange how much he had clung to Briella the past few days, stealing away from courtly business whenever he could to be with her in the solarium, where she stayed for hours, patiently tending the flowers. To Raphael, the solarium would always be filled with memories of the night he had sat there all alone, listening impotently through the horn while his kingdom unraveled and his new-found love was accused of treason. But for Briella, the solarium was the place where solace bloomed. Briella was the only person in the palace who had known Raphael as himself for more than seventy-two hours. To be with her, even in that room where he had cultivated lies, felt like coming home.

"They are calling for the angels," she whispered, "but I never see them come. Do you think Father Alester was tired of waiting for them?"

Raphael closed his eyes. "I think he was afraid of the angels. I think some people become so used to the darkness, even the thought of light makes them blind."

Briella shivered and snuggled more closely against him.

The white marble tomb in the palace churchyard stood open, ready to receive yet one more royal corpse. Inside, Prince Lennard's casket still shone with polish, though Queen Eleanor's had faded and begun to splinter. Neither the flowers strewn across the doorway nor the swinging incense could mask the vile stench; nor could Raphael stifle his sobs. Helplessly, he watched the royal pall bearers heft his father's remains into the crypt. The monks continued singing as the marble doors swung shut.

"Charles," King Raphael said to his valet, "arrange for the carriage to come at nightfall."

"Yes, Your Majesty. Where are you going?"

He stared at the closed crypt door. "I'm going to bring the angels into the darkness."

THE WIND in the hazel boughs moaned as Allia could not. Gentle rain dripped onto the mound of freshly-turned earth, shedding the tears that Allia could not find. She leaned her cheek against the trunk of the hazel tree to reassure herself that it still stood. So vivid had her imagination been the night she thought she heard it splintered and chopped down, she had fallen to her knees the moment she saw it still living. But that was yesterday. Now her father's funeral was done, the requiem sung, the mourners all gone from the grave except the maiden who had spent the night on a blanket listening to the rustle of leaves and the cooing of doves. Sir Winters stood at a distance, just visible through the hazy dawn. He had kept guard all night, though Allia told him there was no danger. In the shadow of the hazel tree, nothing but grief would ever harm her—though grief left more enduring scars than any sword. But the rain that dribbled down her cheeks would sustain the grass and the doves and the flowers for ages yet to come. In the shadow of the hazel tree, Allia knew that grief had been given to her to nourish her joy.

She stared at the palms of her hands, where the cinder maid's calluses still reigned over the scabs that had finally begun to flake away from new pink skin. She laid one hand on the fresh earth above her father, the other on the grass that had long since grown over her mother. "Show me how to use them," she prayed to them both.

"My lady." She looked up to find Johan walking toward her. "We should go, if you want to make the capitol by nightfall."

"He cannot give me away at my wedding," she murmured toward the grave.

Johan touched the tree. "He will still be there."

She stood and took her champion's hands. "Will you? Give me away, I mean?"

"Only if I can still keep you, too."

She kissed his cheek. "Always." She brushed her hand one last time against the tree's green leaves. The doves did not stir from their perches. "Come. I owe a kiss to someone else before we go."

Johan started. "My lady...?"

"His name is Alfred. He's one of the castle guards." Johan looked at her askance. Allia raised her hands, showing off her scars. "Someone had to teach me how to wield a sword poorly enough not to kill you. What sort of queen would I be if I left that debt unpaid?"

Johan shook his head. "I do not think you will be any sort of queen Armany has ever seen before."

Allia smiled. "At least, I think it's safe to say that I shall have the ugliest hands."

~

KING RAPHAEL SAT upon the damp earth, rich with the smells of rot and renewal. A half moon glowed in the heavens. The graveyard seemed suspended somewhere between this world and another, as if its wooden gates opened directly into Limbo. Someone had planted a rose bush on one of the many unmarked graves, but no one had pruned it. The thorny limbs snaked across the grass and twined upward around a young sapling, but they bore only a single white flower. Its petals hung over the forsaken land like the beacon of a lighthouse.

Raphael cut the flowering branch from the vine and planted it on the newest grave. "I will not be bullied by your selfishness, Father. You will not leave this world unmourned." He had spent the afternoon in the chaplain's quarters, ferreting through ecclesial scrolls until he found the proper blessing. He took it from his pocket and unfurled it. The cramped Latin script danced before his eyes, but Raphael had already committed the words to memory. "I may not be a priest," he told the clods of earth, "but you are. Surely, that must count for something." He took a deep breath and began. *"In nomine Patris, et Filii, et Spiritus Sancti. Amen.* Look upon him, O Lord, and let all the darkness of his soul vanish before the beams of thy brightness. Fill him with holy love, and open to him the treasures of thy wisdom. He sought thy face; turn thy face unto him and show him thy glory. Then shall his longing be satisfied, and his peace shall be perfect."

"Amen."

He turned at the sound of a voice like an angel's lyre, but he knew to whom it belonged. He smiled to see her still wearing soldier's breeches, still carrying the sword at her waist. "Allia. How did you find me here?"

She came and sat beside him on the ground. "Your sister told me."

He laced his fingers through hers. "I'm sorry. I should have been at the palace to greet you."

"No. You are a king. You are doing the work of the Kingdom." She moved her free hand to touch his face, but stopped. "May I, Your Majesty?"

"Allia, if you think I shall be in the habit of telling you 'no,' you will spend your life sorely disappointed."

She smiled and tucked a stray curl behind his ear, but then blushed and laid her hand on the hilt of Griffin's Claw. "Your Majesty..."

"Raphael," he corrected.

"Raphael." The warmth of her voice sent shivers down his spine. "There is something you should know. Your mother wrote a letter to my mother shortly before they both died. She wanted me to succeed her as queen."

"She wanted you to marry my brother."

Allia looked at the ground.

"Are you sorry that I am not he?"

Her eyes met his. "No, Your Maj... Raphael. But it was not the fairy who gave me this sword."

He squeezed her hand. "The Lion chose his successor well. But I have something for you, too." He reached into his pocket and pulled out the golden slipper.

Allia laughed. "Of course."

"Your father found it. Allia... I found your witnesses and presented them to him. I want you to know that he believed them. He forgave you."

The tears Allia could not find that morning sprang to her eyes now. She looked up toward the moon and saw the shadow of a kestrel soaring across its light.

"Allia, I cannot promise there will be no more sorrow. But I do promise that we will rise up from these graves." Raphael leaned over, unlaced her clumsy leather boot, and slid the slipper over her toes.

She reached into her pocket and took out the other shoe. "A Lion that wears silk slippers."

"And an Eagle with wheels for wings."

They shared a smile; then Raphael gently unlaced her other boot. When both her feet were clad in gold, he pulled her face toward his. In the light of half a moon, their lips united, and the night glowed with hope.

CITATIONS

"My dwelling, like a shepherd's tent, is struck down and borne away from me; you have folded up my life, like a weaver who severs the last thread."- Isaiah 38:12, New American translation, used by permission of the United States Council of Catholic Bishops under the blanket exemption for all excerpts less than 5,000 words

"Look upon him, O Lord, and let all the darkness of his soul vanish before the beams of thy brightness. Fill him with holy love, and open to him the treasures of thy wisdom. He sought thy face; turn thy face unto him and show him thy glory. Then shall his longing be satisfied, and his peace shall be perfect." - adapted from a prayer attributed to St. Augustine of Hippo (354-430)

ACKNOWLEDGMENTS

To thank everyone who helped bring this book into being would run very long, and I would likely forget someone who very much deserves to be thanked. To all of you who helped me develop it, thank you. Thank you also to my editor, Katy Carl; my cover designer, Fiona Jayde Media; to S.M. Schmitz, who formatted the text for printing; and to all of you for reading it.